A Crack in the Union

by rickshaw

Printed in the United States

Hardcover ISBN: 978-0984650286
Paperback ISBN: 978-0692296066

A Crack in the Union

Acknowledgements

To my lovely wife Kathleen for her daily support

To my sister Karen for her tireless computer skills

To my children Steven, Beverly, Marilyn, Lori and grandchildren Tim, Eric, Emily, Abby and Casey.

And last but not least

To my writing partner who required thousands of chin scratches and belly rubs while laying on my paper while I'm trying to write. My cat "Annie".

I have been blessed by many things in my life, and I'm so very grateful to the man upstairs.

rickshaw

CONTENTS

INTRODUCTION

The western states of California, Arizona, New Mexico and Texas have informed the state governors, President Obama and Congress that they are seceding from the fifty-state union as of today, July first.

They broke this earth shattering news at the annual Governors conference held in Washington, D.C. The four western states want to break away from President Obama's socialistic government and form a new nation with a conservative government where the voices of the people are heard loud and clear.

Since the Obama administration won't stop the flow of illegals from crossing their border, the four states will defend their southern borders with Mexico using their considerable military forces to stop the flow of illegal aliens, drug cartel members and Mexican military from crossing the border and entering their four states.

Mexican Present Edwardo Longo was also informed that the entire two thousand mile border with Mexico will be closed immediately.

United States of America

Main characters

President	Barack Hussein Obama
V.P.	Charles Goodwin
Secretary of State	Maggie Wilson
Secretary of Defense	Jon Marshal
President's Secretary	Mrs. Winfred (Winnie) Oaks
Chairman of the Joint Chiefs	General Phillip Wolford
Commanding General Z	I.Lt. Gen Charles Wittingham
Commanding Gen. 101st	Maj. Gen. Mark Alexander
Commanding Gen. 82nd	Maj. Gen. Joshua Simons
Air Force Commanding Gen.	Gen. Jefferson Taylor
Commanding Gen. Marine Corps	Lt. Gen. Robert Allen
President's Marine Corps aide	Col. Brian Peterson
National Security Advisor	Malcolm J. Jennings
Governor of California	Eric Richardson
Governor of Arizona	Sara Williamson
Governor of New Mexico	Richard Paul Anderson
Governor of Texas	Marilyn LaCrosse
Chief of Staff	Robert Mott
Mexican President	Edwardo Longo
Chinese Premier	Choi Sin Woo

Western States of America   4 States

Seceding States Main characters

President	Sara Williamson
V. P.	Eric Richardson
Secretary of State	Paula Catherine Anderson
Secretary of Defense	Ralph Waterman
Secretary of the Treasury	William J. O'Neil
Chief of Staff	Michael McCarney (Buck)

Secretary to the President	Mrs. Ruth Bakker
Assistant to the President	Beverly Wolcott
Communication Director	Marian Wilcox
Commanding General California	Lt. Gen.Charles Wittingham
Commanding Gen. Texas forces	Lt. Gen.Carter T. Wadsworth
Commanding Gen. Arizona forces	Maj. Gen. H.G. Miles
Commanding New Mexico forces	Colonel Marcus Wheeler
Special Ops Officer (Mexico)	Colonel Michael Montgomery
California Governor	(Eric Richardson) ConradSchiller
Arizona Governor	(Sara Williamson) Margo Lane
New Mexico Governor	Richard Paul Anderson
Texas Governor	Marilyn LaCrosse
President of Mexico	Edward Longo
V.P. of Mexico	Pedro Lazzara
Chinese Premier	Choi Sin Woo
Mexico's Commanding General	General Rōjas
Russian President	Alexander Petrovich

Western States of America   5 States

Additional States Wanting to Secede

Main Characters

Wyoming Governor	Brian Adams
Alaska Governor	Berry Torcello
Washington Governor	Pauline Winslow
Oregon Governor	Lila McPherson
Hawaii Governor	Honokao Millerson

Chapter 1

SECEDING FROM THE UNION

During the annual Governors' conference in the Nation's capital, the Governors of California, Arizona, New Mexico and Texas stepped up to the podium and jointly announced that their four states were seceding from the union as of today, July first.

With this crushing announcement, a deadly silence settled over the entire gathering as the words reverberated through the great hall. The four Governors continued, they said that formal notification to the President and members of congress was being delivered as they spoke.

The silence in the hall was broken when a Governor shouted "My god this will be the second "civil war" that this country has endured since eighteen sixty-one."

Sara Williamson, Governor of Arizona continued. "We have invoked martial law in our four states and also activated all our National Guard and Reserve forces which total over two hundred thousand armed forces. As for Arizona, we have positioned a fully equipped division of armed troops along the border with Mexico from Gadsden to the west and just beyond Douglas to the east.

California, New Mexico and Texas have done the same by sending troops to their respective borders with Mexico to stop, once and for all, the incursions by Mexican nationals, drug cartel members and Mexican military personnel. Along with this border action, our state and local law enforcement agencies will be profiling Mexican nationals at airports, train and bus stations, sport events, etc. We will be purge our states of all illegal aliens no matter what their nationality.

"Remember, it's the right of every state to secede from the union when the Federal Government doesn't protect its states citizens from foreign incursion that murders, kidnaps and poisons untold millions of Americans while costing our states billions of dollars without any action by our Federal Government to stop this human invasion."

Texas Governor Marilyn LaCrosse said "Our Texas border with Mexico is the longest of the four secession states and will be manned by National Guard and Reserve units from California as well as our Texas military units. These combined land and air forces will stop any Mexican incursions into our border states with deadly

force. Any illegals trying to cross the border and enter our four states will be subjected to deadly force. Remember, deadly force will be the order of the day starting tomorrow morning.

"The Mexican Government was also informed of our intentions to stop all illegals with extreme force since our U.S. Government has elected to do nothing about this problem."

New Mexico Governor Anderson said "Let's take a quick look at the total military forces that are stationed within our four states and compare them to our National Guard and Reserve units:

New Mexico:

Army	420
Navy/Marine	252
Air Force	10,970
active duty personnel	11,642
*State National Guard and Reserve personnel	= 8,935
Texas:	
Army	60,945
Navy/Marine	6,909
Air Force	40,981
Coast Guard	1,409
active duty personnel	108,835
Arizona:	
Army	5,388
Navy/Marine	4,559
Air Force	11,323
active duty personnel	21,240
*State National Guard and Reserve personnel	= 18,737
California:	

Army	7,697
Navy/Marine	80,572
Air Force	21,428
Coast Guard	<u>4,811</u>
active duty personnel	109,697
*State National Guard and Reserve personnel	= 98,292

Total major Federal military installations	
New Mexico	4
Texas	23
Arizona	6
California	<u>41</u>
Total number of major government	74

bases within the four seceding states

Governor Richardson of California said "Our four states are assuming the Federal Government will send combat troops to stop our runaway states from seceding and forming a new nation. We are going to defend our state rights as well as defend our borders from foreign incursion and a Federal Government that has turned a blind eye to its citizens that are being invaded by illegals coming from every country in the world.

"All the resources that our four states can muster will be directed towards defending our borders with Mexico while purging our states of all illegal aliens and fighting the Federal Government for states' rights and self-preservation. We have learned earlier today that many Army and Air Force base commanders stationed within our four states will side with us to defend our individual state rights while protecting our border and fighting the Central Government. These active duty Air Force, Coast Guard, Navy, Marine and Army personnel will join our states National Guard and Reserve forces to form a very

substantial fighting force against the Federal Government and possibly Mexico.

"The call went out today to the rest of the nation to come and join us in our defense and secession from the Union. Come and join us and strike a blow for freedom from a government that has done nothing to prevent massive incursions from Mexico. We don't want this to turn into the "Second Civil War", but we will fight for our God given right to secede from the Union and form our own government and a new nation. This current Obama administration kowtows to criminals and many nations that want to bury this nation, while not enforcing the existing laws that are supposed to protect all American citizens from illegals that cross our two thousand miles of border with Mexico without impunity. Our Central Government houses numerous Congressional leaders that should be jailed and tried for high treason. Their numerous un-American activities while siding with foreign leaders who outwardly champion the demise of this great nation will no longer be tolerated.

"Our four states just want to start over, form our own government and create a new nation with solid conservative values. We need leaders from all parties who have conservative ideas and will represent the people and vote the wishes of their constituents. Members who believe in limited small government and use common sense in spending the American public's hard earned money.

"We don't need roads to nowhere and bridges to islands with no houses. Responsible leaders in our new country will shape a new government and a new start for millions of Western Americans."

Governor Williamson continued, "We do not want another three and a half years of President Obama and his socialistic ideas and policies. As our President, he has continued to lie to the American people over and over again. He just can't be trusted. He hates America and what it stands for. He believes that America has gained world power and status by stealing resources from other countries and screwing the American public through big business and capitalism. President Obama wants more people to rely on bigger government with all its social programs that hold a class of Americans in the clutches of his big brother socialist government. In the coming years he will continue to destroy the middle class and create an even bigger group of Americans and non-Americans that are totally dependent on big government. Obama has robbed the federal treasury by giving billions of dollars to his union buddies and liberal friends.

"Now that Obama has been given another four years as your President by the millions of ignorant and uninformed Americans who were fearful the living and eating at the government trough might come to an end if Obama lost the Presidential election. President Obama has promised everything and has not come through with anything. Instead of a workhorse President that works 24/7 to solve our domestic and foreign problems, he is a horse's ass who solves absolutely nothing.

"If you Governors and the rest of the nation agree with his social philosophy then you'll probably love the coming years under his tutelage.

"Mark my word. During his remaining term in office he will make millions of illegal aliens American citizens and make restitution to all black with billions of your hard earned dollars. Remember that money is yours. The government has none.

"I and the other three Governors are returning to our respective states to start forming a new nation with conservative ideas and where a truly democratic government will hear the voices of the people loud and clear."

With that parting statement the four Governors quickly exited the stage and headed for a pre-selected private airport just outside Washington.

President Obama received the crushing news and immediately called his military leaders to attend an emergency meeting in the Whitehouse war room at 11:30 sharp.

The President's emergency meeting started on time and he again stated the news of the day to his military and civilian staff. Upon hearing this, the room fell silent for a full minute before General Taylor broke the long silence by saying, "Some of our military will surely join the four states in their effort to secede from the union."

Lt. General Charles Wittingham from California stood up and announced in a loud voice that he was leaving the U.S. Military as of today, and joining the four state cause for independence, self-rule and to start forming a new government and nation.

 rickshaw

President Obama and his military staff were shocked and beyond belief that one of their own staff would give up his long military career to join the four runaway states defying the united fifty-state union.

General Wittingham stood up, straightened his uniform and said, Excuse me gentlemen, I have a new nation and government to form." With that parting statement he exited the Whitehouse war room and headed for home.

The President was speechless until the three-star General left the room. "That is not a good sign," he said in a low voice to the remaining staff. "Not a good sign at all. If this is what we can expect from our top military leaders, many of the lower ranks may flood to the defense of these four runaway states." The President continued, "Gentlemen, we must act quickly to put down this state rebellion before it becomes a cry for independence and freedom against the Federal Government."

General Taylor said "I agree, Mr. President, we must act quickly, but we had better be careful on how we use government forces against these states. If we're not extremely careful, this could turn into the "second civil war". That would certainly tear this country to shreds and set us back a hundred years or more."

Major General Alexander said "We must send a strong and heavily armed force to those four state capitols and a stronger military force to the entire length of the Mexican border.

"If we capture these state capitols and shut down their state governments, the state military machine will die on the vine when confronted with a much superior force. The quicker we do this the loss of American lives can be held to a minimum. Of course, the unknown factor is how many Americans in the remaining 46 states will side with the runaways and flock to their defense. It could be millions joining them," he added as he sat down.

"How about the military bases within these states?" Lt. General Robert Allen asked the group. "They could help swing the balance for a quick put down and victory for our government forces." But he added, "If they side with California, Arizona, New Mexico and Texas, we could have one hell of a battle on our hands with huge numbers killed on both sides. The sad part is all of the dead would be Americans and that's not acceptable to me or the nation."

Chapter 1 - Seceeding from the Union

"I agree, General," the President quickly added, "but what other course of action could we take?" He added, "We should storm these states and put down this rebellion before it spreads nationwide."

Air Force General Jefferson Taylor said "Gentlemen, remember some of these states have access to numerous nuclear weapons. The bases must be neutralized first and the launch code kept secure and out of reach. They also have nuclear tipped artillery shells as well as thousands of S.T.A. (surface-to-air) missiles and large quantities of hand held shoulder fired S.T.A. missile launchers that can knock down low flying aircraft. All these things must be considered before we blindly strike out against these runaway states," he added.

Marine Corps Commanding General Robert Allen added, "Ordering Americans to fire on Americans should not be our first option. We must negotiate with these four Governors at all cost to prevent the massive slaughter of thousands upon thousands of American citizens." He continued, "If we strike out with massive military force against these four states, what will our military units overseas think about our Federal Government attacking our neighbors? Will these units support the Central Government like good solders or rebel against their commanders and head for the Z.I. to join their home state cause to secede?" He added, "Mr. President, your guess is as good as mine on what they'll do."

President Obama picked up the secure phone and called directly to the Secretary of State Margaret Wilson who was about to board a government plane for a planned trip to Warsaw, Poland. He asked her to contact the group of four governors and schedule an emergency meeting somewhere of their choosing. "I will meet them anywhere," the President added quickly. He replaced the phone and said, "I agree with General Taylor, we must talk first before any military action is played out. When the meeting is set I want you Phil, General Wolford and the Secretary of State to accompany me to the site when we meet the four Governors."

"Do we raise the alert level?" General Allen asked the group.

"No. Not until we talk to the Governors," the President said. "I must go on national T.V. this evening and inform the American public of what has transpired this morning and what their government is going to do about this turn of events. In the meantime get your staffs working on a plan of attack if our talks fail to resolve this national issue. I want several detailed plans if all attempts fall through within the next day of two. Also, we need intel from the Mexican border right away," he added. "I'll call President Longo from the oval office to alert him, but I'm sure he already knows what's going on. I'll try and calm his fears when a large military force suddenly appears knocking at his doorstep."

"Let's get busy gentlemen." The war room cleared quickly and the Commander-in-Chief headed straight for the oval office. President Obama entered the oval office and sat down slowly as he was thinking of the upcoming telecast. He reached for the intercom and said, "Winnie, please get me the Mexican President as quickly as possible."

"Yes, sir," she answered. "Right away."

She is the real boss in this Whitehouse, he thought as he leaned back in his thirty year old black leather chair. *This old beat up chair looks out of place in the oval office, but I don't care.*

The light started blinking on the switchboard line and the President pushed the button and said, "Obama here."

"Mr. President, the Mexican President is on line #3," the switchboard operator said quickly.

"Thank you. Put him through please."

He picked up line #3 and said, "Good afternoon, Edwardo, this is President Obama. Thank you for returning my call so quickly," he added before the Mexican President could even answer. He continued, "Mr. President I have some very disturbing news I must share with you."

Edwardo said, "Mr. President, I have already been informed that your four border states on our border are leaving the union. Is my information correct?" he asked.

"Yes, it is," the American President sadly admitted. "The four border states informed my office this morning of their plans to secede from our union. The reason I'm calling you, Edwardo, is to alert you that these seceding states are sending a large military force to the border area. That includes the entire two thousand miles of your border, sir." The President continued, "Please do not take any military action and do not cross our border for any reason," the U.S. President warned his counterpart.

Chapter 1 – Seceeding from the Union

"The U.S. Government will handle this crisis as a national problem, and we don't want any outside interference into our country's affairs. I'm sure their military units will not cross the Rio Grande and enter your Mexican territory," he assured the Mexican President. If necessary, I will send Federal troops to the border and disarm the state forces within the next few days, if need be. Please make sure your military leaders know the real facts and caution them to do nothing to provoke the forces gathering at your border."

"Mr. President, as Mexico's President I will do whatever it takes to defend our border from any invasion from the north. If one of your soldiers crosses our border the Mexican Government would consider it an act of aggression, Mr. President."

"I understand, Edwardo, but I must again warn you that such action on your part would lead to disastrous results for Mexico. Please refain from taking any military action," the President strongly suggested.

"Thank you for your warning," the Mexican President said as he abruptly hung up the phone.

"Well," President Obama said out loud, "that's the first time that someone has hung-up on the President of the United States. That's not a good sign," he added.

At 15:00 hours sharp, the cameraman pointed to the chief executive and said, "10-9-8-7-- you're on Mr. President."

"Good afternoon, ladies and gentlemen. I'm sure by now most Americans have heard the very disturbing news that the border states of California, Arizona, New Mexico and Texas have informed the Whitehouse and Congress that they intend to secede from the union effective today July first. This is an illegal act and this administration will not tolerate this action by those states. This action could easily develop into the second "civil war". As you know the first civil war between eighteen sixty one and sixty five caused over six hundred thousand military lives as well as thousands of civilian lives. It took twenty five years to get over the devastation caused by that "civil war", and even today that memory of the war is not over for millions of Americans." The President continued, "A second civil war would surely cost millions of lives and they would be all Americans. We cannot allow this to happen.

"I have requested an emergency meeting with the four Governors to see if we can resolve this act of treason against the United States before it spins out of control.

"As Commander-in-Chief, I will not order Federal military forces to fire upon the National Guard and Reserve units of the four states in question at this time. But if we can't find a suitable and permanent solution to this crisis, military action be this administration may be our only option. Remember, this great country had had fifty states since nineteen fifty-nine and as long as I'm your President, the total number will remain at fifty states. I will continue to keep you abreast of any changes pertaining to this runaway group of states. In the meantime, please remain calm and be responsible law abiding citizens. We will solve this national problem like we have many other great problems and issues that have plagued this great nation. That's all I have for now, but I'll keep you informed up to the minute on the secession attempt by those four states.

"Good afternoon, ladies and gentlemen."

The President sat back in his chair as the cameras went blank and the T.V. crew gathered up their gear and quickly exited the oval office.

Before he could gather this thoughts, the secure phone lit up and he answered, "Yes."

"Mr. President, the Governors of California, Arizona, New Mexico and Texas are on your secure line number two."

"Thank you, operator, put them through, please."

"Mr. President, the Secretary-of-State asked us to contact you," the Arizona Governor said.

"Thank you, Sara, for responding immediately," the President said.

"I would like to meet with you and the other three Governors at a location of your choice as quickly as possible," the President asked.

"We're not sure we should have this meeting," Sara Williams told President Obama, "We have collectively made up our minds as a group and will not change our minds. We will secede from the union as of today. You are well aware of just why we took this action, Mr. President. You and your administration have done nothing to stop the influx of illegal aliens from invading our two thousand miles of border each and every week, Mr. President, and you don't give a damn what happens to our states and our poor citizens who live in fear from this foreign invasion and our loss of sovereignty." She continued, "Our states are broke because of these illegals and your Federal laws and mandates that allow those people to become eligible for medical care, food stamps, housing allowance and every other giveaway program as well as allowing their newborns to automatically be given American citizenship and entitlement to everything.

"Mr. President, as Governor of Arizona I cannot stand by and watch my state's inhabitants be violated by these illegal aliens, drug runners and Mexican military when your administration allows them to continue to flood into our desert areas without lifting a finger to turn back this human tide by force of arms. We're not waiting any longer, Mr. President, we're sending our own state military to solve this problem and we don't need or want your help in stopping this human invasion of unwanted guests."

"Governor, you must stop all military action immediately," the President said in a loud voice. "I will not allow your four states to leave the union. I'll send troops to crush this rebellion and put the four of you under arrest and trial for treason where the penalty is death."

"Mr. President, as Governor of California your threats of jail or death are falling on deaf ears and if you send armed Federal troops to our states we'll fight with all our combined resources. If you insist on a fight, this country will see a blood bath that will make to civil war of 1861 seem like a minor skirmish. People throughout this land will flock to our defense and possible rally large numbers of the remaining fort-six states to our cause."

With that last statement the phone went dead. The President slowly replaced the phone in the cradle and sat motionless for a long period. He was struck by the fact that the four Governors actually hung up on the President of the United States. When he regained his thoughts he asked his secretary to contact the Secretary-of-Defense and the Chairman or the Joint Chiefs and ask them to come to the Oval Office as soon as possible.

Within forty-five minutes the two men were in the doorway of the Oval Office and the President motioned them to be seated without saying any salutations. "Gentlemen, I was talking by phone to the four Governors and the conversation started to get a little hot and then suddenly they hung up. It's okay to hang-up on Barack Obama, but not the President of the United States." He continued, "That's the second time today someone has hung-up on me," he told his two guests. "That's not a good sign, gentlemen, not a good sign at all. I haven't had a cigarette in over thirty years, but I might start. They're not going to meet and talk over this crisis, so the ball is in our court," the President said in a low voice. "What do we do now?" he asked.

"Mr. President, me must strike quickly and overpower them before this gains more momentum and millions join their breakaway cause," the Defense Secretary said quickly as he stood up and paced back and forth. He added, "We don't need another "civil war" to set this country back two hundred years or more. I'd like to suggest, Mr. President, that we send troops to each state capitol and arrest the state leaders to take away their authority and ability to issue orders to the state National Guard and the Reserve units at the Mexican border and throughout key areas of their states the Secretary suggested."

"If we do this, what military unit do we send?" the President asked the four star chairman.

"I would use the 101st and 82nd airborne for starters, Mr. President. They should be dropped at mid-morning to insure capture of state leaders and the complete takeover of the capitol with a minimum loss of life," the chairman advised. "They should have orders to return fire when fired upon. They're not going to fight with dozens of rules of engagement restrictions either," he added. "You can't fight with one arm behind your back and expect to win this type of limited war. Believe me Mr. President it will be all out war. The terrible part is Americans will be killing Americans on American soil." he added, shaking his head.

"Will the two airborne divisions be enough to settle the issue?" the President asked.

"No, sir. It will require much more than the two divisions. They are very lightly armed and will need some armor support to take and hold each capitol. I would have the 4th armor division and the 10th Mountain Division added to the mix Mr. President. They are at full strength and that would bring the total manpower to around sixty-two thousand men including service units. We must not only strike at each of the four state capitols, but the bulk of their units are at the Mexican border, and that, Mr. President, is a real nightmare of a problem. Not only do they have boots on the ground but Air Reserve units in the sky patrolling the border."

"Do we shoot down their planes the Secretary asked? My God, the Mexican government will have a ring side seat to this national disaster if all out fighting erupts along the border. I'm sure Mexico will not set on the sideline and do nothing while all out fighting continues along the entire border with Mexico. Of course the real question, Mr. President, is what will China and Russia do while we're embroiled in a civil war? If they didn't strike at the U.S. directly, they could invade Europe for the third time in less than one hundred years or occupy a foothold in South America as a springboard."

"Gentlemen there is also another solution to this problem," the President said, starring out the Oval Office bay window, "and that's give in to these four states and let them breakaway and form a new country."

"Would you really stand for that defiance, Mr. President?" the Defense Secretary asked. "What about the American people, would they overwhelmingly be in favor of stopping these runaway states from forming a new nation, or would they side with them because this administration has done almost nothing to stop the flow of illegal aliens from entering their border states?"

"I really don't know. Your guess is as good as mine," the President said in a subdued voice. "But, gentlemen, we had better find out in the next day or so."

"Mr. President, we're currently at DEFCON #2, I would suggest we should elevate the alert status to DEFCON #3 which is yellow," the four star General suggested.

"I agree with General Wolford." the Secretary added.

"Okay, issue the order, Mr. Secretary."

"Yes, sir, Mr. President." The Secretary picked up the phone and ordered the Pentagon to raise the national alert status to DEFCON #3.

"Gentleman get with staff and your commanders and prepare various scenarios that we have discusses. Also have your sections get a feel for the troop sentiment on the matter. I'm sure there will be many defectors among our military units. I don't think they'll like the idea of fighting brothers in arms within their own state."

Both men headed for the Pentagon and marathon meetings with their staffs and corps commanders.

 rickshaw

President Obama pressed the intercom and said, "Winnie, please ask Colonel Peterson to come in."

"Yes, sir."

Marine Corps aide Colonel Brian Peterson quickly entered the oval office and stood at attention.

"Yes, sir, Mr. President."

"Good afternoon, Colonel, please schedule a war room meeting in the Pentagon for 18:00 hours today with all civilian and military staff present."

"Right away, sir." The full bird Colonel headed for his small desk outside the oval office to set in motion the war room meeting.

Arizona Governor Williamson was in her large mobile trailer somewhere in the desert close to the Mexican border along with two Major Generals and her civilian staff looking over a huge map of the border area between Arizona and Mexico which also pinpointed the position of each military unit and their current strength. Sara was well qualified to be Commander-in-Chief of all Arizona state forces because she was a Brigadier General in her state National Guard as well as Governor.

Her military service had spanned more than thirty-five years and she had come up through the enlisted ranks, then became an officer and rose quickly to General status. She attended the war college in Washington and knew how to position a military fighting force. She was well aware that trouble can come from both sides of the border.

"Gentlemen, as you know we have a total of four of these mobile trainers that can direct our forces along our borders and throughout the entire state. If the Federal government finds one or more trailers, the remaining mobile units can continue to issue orders to our state forces. We must dig in and be prepared to fight any federal forces that are sent to neutralize our forces. General Miles and General Winslow, I want you to head for the border and take command of your respective divisions and get ready for an all American dog fight if it materializes."

California Governor Richardson and Texas Governor LaCrosse were in their mobile trailers near Eagle Pass Texas within a stone's throw of the border.

Governor Richardson had sent a full division of National Guard troops to Texas to join their forces. California's border is short in distance and the Texas border with Mexico is huge and will require additional forces to patrol and defend the two thousand miles of border. Governor LaCrosse had positioned her forces at key points along the entire border. The state of Texas knew all the points of entry used by the illegal aliens and drug runners and would defend their state's rights to stop this flow of unwanted guests entering in the border states. Some five divisions of army and air force units were scattered through the border and had dug in and were ready to defend their borders and the right to secede from the union. With the additional division from California helping patrol the border, the flow of illegal entry into Texas would slow to a trickle.

Texas had six mobile trailers positioned throughout the border area with each unit capable of directing all forces throughout the state.

Lt. General Carter J. Wadsworth was the commanding General of all forces defending Texas. He was a General officer with forty-two years of military service which includes combat action. The General would not let Texas down, he would fight whomever comes to derail the state's right to defend their border and secede from the union. The Texas Governor was happy to have such a fine career officer defending their right of survival.

New Mexico's Governor Anderson said that they had only about one hundred and seventy-five miles of border with Mexico, but had positioned his eight thousand National Guard and Reserve personnel to defend and stop the flow of unwanted aliens from crossing into New Mexico. This also included two Air Force fighter groups that would fly sorties over the border 24/7. Anderson had two fully equipped mobile trailers close to the border near Hachita and just south of Deming. Each trainer was well camouflaged and wouldn't be found by Federal forces.

Both units had the capacity of scrambling their broadcasting from being captured by outside sources. The Governor had put Colonel Marcus Wheeler in command of all New Mexico forces along the border. Colonel Wheeler had twenty-three years of service and had attended the war college in California for special officers with emphasis on strategic troop deployment. He would position his troops along the border to acquire the maximum efficiency with the limited number of personnel at his disposal.

China and Russia, upon hearing the news that four states were seceding from the union, started planning joint meetings to explore the possibility of gaining a foothold in North America.

Chinese Premier Cho Sin Woo told his military leaders to formulate the necessary plans to invade the United States directly or indirectly. He reminded his huge military staff that this could be their golden opportunity to finish off their old enemy once and for all with a swift thrust through their black heart.

The Chinese leader continued, "We must, in conjunction with our Russian friends, plan a swift and deadly end to the United States or maybe I should say 'not so united.'" With that remark his military leaders gave him a standing ovation that lasted almost three minutes. He added that Chinese and Russian military leaders would meet in Peking next week to formulate a future plan of attack to wipe the U.S. from the face of the earth. "While the U.S. is engaged in civil war we'll strike a series of military attacks that will eliminate them as a world super power. Do not rule out limited nuclear war." he added.

President Obama headed for the west lawn with Colonel Peterson in tow as they boarded Marine-One helicopter for the quick trip to the Pentagon and the emergency war room meeting with his entire military and civilian staff. The large war room was packed as the Commander-in-Chief entered the underground nuclear bomb proof room and took his position at the head of the huge table.

"Please be seated everyone.

"As you're aware, we have a national crisis on our hands and we must solve and settle this issue as quickly as possible." The President continued, "This attempt to secede from the union by these four border states has many ramifications as you can imagine. Here are some of the options as I see it.

#1. Do we send Federal troops to stop this exodus?

#2. Will Mexico react to the fighting between state and government forces along the borders?

#3. What will China and or Russia do if we engage in another civil war?

#4. Do we let California, Arizona, New Mexico and Texas leave the union?

#5. How will our military react to our force of arms against these states?

#6. How many Americans will flock to their cause and rebel against the Federal Government?

"These are just some of the questions that must be answered and I want them answered very quickly," the President said as he sat back down.

"Mr. President, we cannot allow these four states to abandon this union and have the potential to cause the downfall of these United States," the Secretary-of-Defense called out.

"I agree with the Secretary, Mr. President, as Chairman of the Joint Chiefs I believe we must stop this act of treason before it affects the entire nation and plunges our country into the abyss of despair and destruction. He continued, "While we're struggling with this issue, both China and Russia will be planning the demise of this country. You can bet on it. I certainly would if I was a Russian Marshal or a Chinese General, Mr. President."

"Thank you, General Wolford. Who's next?" the President asked.

Vice President Goodwin stood up and said, "We just can't attack the state forces along the Mexican border without it becoming an all-out war between the Federal government and state forces along with the Mexican military mixed into the fray. The American public will not tolerate this action where Americans are killing Americans when the Federal government has done absolutely nothing to prevent the influx of illegal aliens along the entire two thousand mile border with Mexico. As Vice President I'm partly responsible for the lack of protection that should have prevented this influx of unwanted peoples from all corners of the world to slip across our border without impunity. I am guilty as many others in this room are for this crisis we're addressing here today. As Vice President I have failed the American people and I should be held accountable for my lack of action to prevent this massive invasion of unwanted human beings."

"Thank you, Charles." the President said motioning him to set down.

"I'm sure there is enough blame to go around, but what can we do to solve this matter right now?"

25

Maggie Wilson, Secretary-of-State stood up and said "Gentlemen, we should replace the state military forces at the border with federal troops and secure the entire length of the border and prevent this overwhelming tide of illegals from entering our country. Mr. President, I agree with the Vice President, we should have secured our border years ago. Instead of putting up a flimsy wire fence in some places that wouldn't stop anything, we should have installed a barrier that would stop all illegal traffic once and for all. I am also guilty of neglect and complacency to the American public for not insisting that our borders be sealed tight." With that outburst the Secretary-of-State slowly sat down.

The entire war room erupted in loud clapping and cheering at what they just heard by the Vice President and Secretary-of-State.

President Obama stood up and motioned everyone to be seated.

"I do agree with the last two speakers. We, or I should say "I," did almost nothing to stop the flow of unwanted aliens. I take full responsibility for the failure of this administration to act responsibility in this matter. But this is here and now, and now we face a critical period in this country's history."

"How do we neutralize this very serious problem that effects every single American?" the President asked the group.

"We must somehow talk to the four Governors, Mr. President. Unless we communicate with these states, whatever we do will be wrong," the Defense Secretary stated.

"Okay, Jon, send your special forces to find and persuade these four Governors to contact me as soon as possible," the President ordered.

"Yes, sir. General Wolford, please make it happen," the Defense Secretary told his top general.

General Wolford picked up the phone and gave the order to find and detain the Governors of California, Texas, Arizona and New Mexico.

Four detachments of Special Forces were assembled and given standing orders to find and detain the four Governors with a minimal of awareness by the public. All units headed for their assigned state capitols and anticipated a quick grab of the Governors and Lt. Governors.

Chapter 1 – Seceeding from the Union

The first unit reached Sacramento on Wednesday just before noon to find the state capitol building almost empty. Only small groups of secretaries, social workers and a scattering of staff members were present. The same void was found at the Governor's residence. The Colonel in charge of the operation felt like a damn fool when they stormed the state capitol with his armed troopers to find no Governor but were booed by frightened women. He gathered up his force and exited the huge building. After reporting his findings to his commanding officer, they were ordered back to Fort Ord.

Unit #2 stormed the Texas state capitol at Austin and found the same thing, a few groups of secretaries and staff workers but no Governor or her second in command. The Special Forces officer was told, "We knew you were coming long before you arrived," a staff secretary said with a smile. The Lt. Colonel contacted command headquarters at Fort Hood and was promptly ordered back to base as soon as possible.

Unit #3 lead by a major stormed the state capitol at Phoenix and the residences of the Governor and Lt. Governor and came up a fat zero. There was not fifty people in the whole state building when the armed troops searched through two hundred rooms looking for Governor Williamson. The major and his force were ordered back to Fort Huachuca for another assignment.

Unit #4 was commanded by a Lt. Colonel and his force of thirty-five Special Forces, they found absolutely nothing when they searched the entire state capitol building in Santa Fe. When they headed towards the main entrance to start their Governor search, the large doors were opened by staff members who ushered them in. "Some surprise raid," his men joked. After turning up nothing and not knowing the whereabouts of Governor Anderson, there were ordered to return to Camp Cody immediately. They bordered their helicopters and headed for their base camp.

None of the four military groups got any clues on the whereabouts of the four Governors or their second in command. Upon hearing the results from the infamous raids, the Defense Secretary and President Obama were furious. The Governors had given them the slip, they anticipated the government's move and went into hiding.

"Well, gentlemen, we must find them and find them quickly," the President urged. "Let's put out all the stops and use all our resources to find them. Use ground search units, satellites, triangulation and every other possible way to find these people." He continued, "If by some chance we can't locate them in the next day or two we'll have to revert to another plan of military action."

"Let's adjourn for now but stay in touch with Winnie or Colonel Peterson on your whereabouts in case we must meet again quickly," the President urged the packed war room. The famous Pentagon room emptied quickly and the President and his aide headed for the oval office.

The Mexican government positioned about ten thousand regular army troops along their side of the Mexican-American border to counter the massive deployment of state forces. The Arizona state forces could see and hear the artillery pieces being positioned along with mortars and other assorted weapons.

Major General Miles contacted Governor Williamson and alerted her of the latest development with the Mexican military massing across the border with Arizona.

Sara wasn't surprised by the action of Mexican President Longo and his military staff. She reminded the General that they had been looking for an excuse to confront the U.S. and have cause to enter our country and cause havoc. "Put your forces on high alert, but don't engage the Mexican military unless fired upon. If they fire on our forces, eliminate the problem, but do not enter Mexican territory. Between our artillery and Air Force there should be no reason to cross the border into Mexico."

The Secretary-of-Defense authorized the formation of one hundred squads of federal troops to search the four states for the Governor and Lt. Governor. They would be questioning hundreds of state workers to acquire any leads to the whereabouts of their state leaders.

Some squads searching the Arizona desert got too close to the border and were captured by state military forces without firing a single shot. They were transported to the nearest state prison for safe keeping.

After three days of twenty-four hour searching the four states for their leaders, the President called off the massive search. He admitted that the deserts of Arizona, New Mexico and Texas could hide many divisions, let alone a small group.

Chapter 1 – Seceeding from the Union

With this setback, President Obama again called for a meeting with his entire civilian and military staff for 08:00 hours the next morning. He sat back in his old leather chair thinking of this potentially disastrous situation, he knew that every day the Federal government did nothing, the four states were getting stronger and stronger. He was told that thousands of supporters from all over the nation were heading for their state of preference to join the secessionists in their revolt. Earlier in the day the Defense Secretary had informed him that thousands of regular military personnel were packing up and heading for the seceding states. He thought it may be too late to squelch this uprising with Federal troops that surely would cost many thousands of American lives.

Along the Texas border just south of Del Rio, some Mexican forces crossed the Rio Grande and entered U.S. soil. This incursion by some one hundred Mexican military troops quickly turned into a fire fight that ended in death to all forces who crossed into American territory.

Governor LaCrosse, upon hearing of this invasion called the Mexican President and told him to stop immediately. "Mr. President, tell your military leaders that the state of Texas will not tolerate this incursion by your military. If you don't stop and withdraw any and all forces that have crossed the Rio Grande, we will declare war on Mexico. Between Texas and the other three states the war won't last many days." She continued, "This is the only call and warning I'm going to give you, sir." Without waiting for the Mexican President to answer she abruptly hung-up by slamming the phone down. "That's all we need is a mini-war with Mexico," she said pounding the table in the mobile trailer. "Excuse me, gentlemen, but President Longo is such a stupid man. He shouldn't be in charge of a garbage truck let alone an entire country," she said shaking her head.

Sara picked up the phone and called Lt. General Wittingham who was Commanding General for all forces along the entire two thousand miles of border with Mexico.

"Yes, ma'am," he answered.

"Good work, General. Your border forces did well when confronted by Mexican forces today. Tell you commanders that we're very proud of their action against the Mexican incursion."

 rickshaw

"Thank you Governor, I will certainly pass on your comments to all our military personnel along the border," he assured the next President of their unnamed nation.

"Keep a sharp lookout, both north and south," she advised her top General.

"Yes, ma'am, we will."

Governor LaCrosse called Sara and said that she was so mad and unnerved at the actions of the Mexican government. She told Sara that she had called the Mexican leader and threatened him with war if he didn't stop. "I agree with you." Sara told her Governor in Arms. "I hope your call did the trick," she added. "This action by Mexico could easily escalate into a full blown military action if President Longo doesn't heed our warning." Sara told her aide to contact the other two Governors and fill them in on the military incursion by Mexican forces.

California Governor Richardson had all but closed the border between Mexico and California allowing only a trickle of foot traffic to cross. Even though the border is only about one hundred and fifty miles long with Mexico, it was by far the busiest. The traffic on the Mexican side was backed up for more than fifty miles on all roads leading to the California border. Thousands of eighteen wheelers that pass into California every day were now parked bumper to bumper. Many truckers had left their rigs and headed for their homes. When possible, the trucks had backed up to each other end to end to prevent looting.

The truck traffic that normally crosses the many bridges into Texas had also been halted. These vehicles were backed up for almost one hundred miles clogging every main and secondary roads leading to the Rio Grande. Trucks loaded with perishable goods were left on the road to rot in the sun. Similar back-ups occurred along the entire two thousand miles of border with Mexico. The overall Mexican economy was quickly grinding to a halt and would be at a standstill within a week or less. Basically, all traffic, foot and vehicle, had been stopped from entering the U.S. through the four border states. Fruits and vegetables for Mexico, Guatemala, Honduras, Belize and Yucatan Peninsula had stopped delivering their goods by road or rail into the remaining forty-six states. The monetary loss in just a few days could reach into the billions of dollars and pesos. The perishable good growing industry throughout Mexico was basically ruined in just forty-eight hours. Without huge refrigerated warehouses, the vegetables were left in the field to rot under the relentless Mexico sun. Growers picked their vegetable crops, but with no transportation available due to the huge backup from the border south past Monterrey, the produce was piled high on the farms only to spoil within a couple of days. Not only were the crops lost but thousands of farm workers had to be laid off and sent home.

Mexican President Longo called President Obama and demanded that the entire length of the border be reopened immediately. President Obama told the Mexican leader that he had been unable to contact the four governors, but he was going to appeal to them with an address on T.V. and radio shortly. President Longo said "The economy of Mexico is at stake unless something can be done quickly. Goods, services and workers sent north from Mexico is the life blood for our nation, and without access to the U.S. our country might not survive," he added.

"Yes, I realize that," President Obama told the desperate leader. "But before I speak on radio and T.V. you must pull your military away from the border. We don't need added problems to this already complicated and critical issue." With that statement he hung-up abruptly. He reached for the intercom and asked Winnie to please contact his communication chief and have her schedule time on T.V. and radio that should only last about fifteen minutes. "Remind her that's time on all stations throughout the country. I'm not asking for time. I'm demanding the air time. Have her make sure the network executives understand that," he added.

"Yes, Mr. President, I will," she answered.

"Oh! Winnie, I forgot about the time. Let's make it at 17:00 hours this afternoon."

Chapter 2
SEALING THE BORDERS

At 17:00 hours the camera man said, "You're on, Mr. President."

"Good evening America, I'm addressing all Americans today but especially the Governors of California, Arizona, New Mexico and Texas. It is imperative that these four state Governors contact their President as soon as humanly possible. We have been attempting to locate the four state leaders but with no success. I will confer with them on the phone or face to face anywhere of their choosing, but for national security reasons and the well-being of our neighbors to the south I need them to contact me without delay.

"As most Americans know, by sealing off the two thousand miles of border with Mexico, the Mexican economy in a matter of days has ground to a halt. Thousands upon thousands of trucks are setting idle because the bridges and roads are closed and their goods cannot be delivered to the U.S. This situation cannot continue, the shipment of goods from Mexico and other countries south of Mexico must be allowed to enter the United States and eventually even Canada. But before my administration takes action to untie this can of worms, I would prefer to discuss this matter with the four Governors. But if after a day or two they don't contact the Whitehouse I will authorize military action to free up the entire border for international trade. I'll keep you the American public informed on all national and foreign issues that threaten the freedom of international trade and the free flow of goods.

"Thank you, ladies and gentlemen, and good evening."

Governor Williamson of Arizona was listening to President Obama's brief cry for help and when he finished she immediately contacted the other three Governors who had also heard his speech. The four breakaway state leaders agreed that they should contact the Whitehouse, but only by phone. Sara told the group, "If we meet the President face to face we'll be arrested, jailed and have no chance of seeing daylight again."

A call to the Whitehouse was placed and the President quickly answered.

 rickshaw

Governor Richardson of California said, "Mr. President, sll four of us are on this line awaiting your comments."

"Thank you for coming forward quickly," the President answered. "What can I do to convince the four of you to drop this un-American idea of seceding from the union?"

Richard Paul Anderson, Governor of New Mexico said, "Mr. President, we don't believe there is anything you can say or do to change our minds. It's too late, Mr. President. You had over four years to secure our border with Mexico and have basically done nothing but install a few miles of wire fence. Our state residents have been murdered, kidnapped, raped, shot and held prisoner in their homes. Once the sun goes down ranchers close to the border hide in their homes under arms to protect their families. Mr. President, while our people live in constant fear, you're traveling worldwide living high on the hog and not caring a tinkers damn about the plight of our border residents. Since you don't seem to care what happens to American citizens living in America, we four state Governors have decided to stand up and take over the job of protecting all our citizens along the entire length of our border with Mexico. Our state forces have closed the border with only a trickle of foot traffic allowed to enter the U.S. In just over forty-eight hours the illegal alien traffic entering our four states has all but stopped. Instead of a thousand illegals entering our soil every day, only a few get through."

Anderson continued, "Millions of Mexicans and other nationals have been allowed to slip through because of your total neglect for the laws that should be protecting American citizens from this invasion. Now that we have stopped the human tide from sliding unopposed into this country you want us to stop and withdraw our troops and allow this silent invasion that is costing the American citizens hundreds of billions of dollars per year. You must be loco, Mr. President. We're not going to withdraw a single soldier form the border because your administration has total disregard for its citizens' safety and security."

Governor LaCrosse said, "Mr. President, there is another invasion taking place as we speak. Thousands upon thousands of Americans throughout this country are starting to flock towards our four states to join the ever increasing cry for freedom from you, Mr. President, and your liberal ideas that have within a few years have reduced this once great and powerful nation to its present third world status. You have trashed this country and made it a laughing stock worldwide and laid it open for attacks from any two-bit terrorists with a box cutter or a bottle of acid while airports are frisking old ladies, nuns and children. Instead you should be profiling, clear and simple. Who are the terrorists, certainly not old ladies and children? They're Muslims, Muslims and Muslims. Good god, Mr. President, what the hell is wrong with you, wake up and see what you're doing wrong. Profiling is the only answer. Stop being a puppet for the Muslim world and start being an American President with a pair of all American balls.

"Unless you have some profound reason for us to withdraw from the border, just leave us alone to solve our own problems."Without your help we will form a new government and a new nation that will address these issues and solve them like Americans have done in the past. President Obama, these talks are over as far as the Governors of California, Arizona, New Mexico and Texas are concerned. Goodbye, sir." With that the phone went dead.

President Obama couldn't believe it, for the third time in less than a week someone had hung-up on the President of the United States. As he replaced the phone he said, "Well that cuts it. We now know the path the Governors are embarking on don't we?"

"Mr. President, what the hell do we do now?" the Defense Secretary asked, setting down with a thud. "Good god, what do we do?" he muttered quietly.

"We must strike a fatal blow to the border troops," the Chairman of the Joint Chiefs urged his boss and the Commander-in-Chief.

"General, if we attack the state forces on the border what will Mexico do? Will they stand-by while state and federal troops fight each other and spill over to the Mexican side of the border, without getting involved? It would be a huge blood bath if they stand and fight our government troops. I'm sure many of our Federal troops would not fight state National Guard and Reserve members. We could have massive desertion if we're not careful," the President said.

While the President and his entire staff was pondering just what to do next, the seceding states were preparing for the fight that was surely coming. Almost a year earlier the states of

California, and Texas started building huge quantities of cement k-rails for the sole purpose of blocking major highways, secondary roads, bridges and airfields form being entered from other states. These k-rails were delivered throughout the year to the four states and stacked new each state line to await to go ahead signal to put them in place and block off all traffic.

In just a few days the four seceding states were being swamped by well over one hundred thousand Americans that had left their homes in the other forty-six states to join the cause and were willing to fight for the right to leave the union and form a new nation. Millions of Americans were tired and fed up with this current administration and their do nothing attitude towards protecting all American citizens. Tent cities were springing up throughout the four states. Even sports facilities were being used to house the new arrivals before being assigned to a military unit. Others were bringing their families and buying homes and settling in the seceding states to be a part of the new government and fledgling nation.

While the number of new comers to each state was swelling by the thousands, the four Governors had issued the order to start blocking off all major roads and bridges and access from adjoining states. The k-rails would be piled high to prevent any unauthorized vehicles from entering the four states.

Thousands of law enforcement and military personnel had been assigned to road block service.

Radio and T.V. stations had been informing their seceding state residents that if they chose to leave California, Arizona, New Mexico or Texas, they were free to do so. The message also said that if you decide to leave the four states before war breaks out between the Federal Government and the breakaway for, you must do so quickly. To expedite your chosen departure, the individual states would purchase your home or property at fair market value.

Once the k-rails were in place and the immigration booths were built and manned, the traffic entering and leaving would slow drastically. Overall business between the four states and the remaining forty-six would continue, but state lines will be similar to the border between Canada and the U.S. Passage of American citizens between the seceding four states would be quick and easy. Non-Americans would be scrutinized very carefully before being allowed to enter their state. Profiling would be the order of the day. Airports, bus and rail stations as well as all ports were to be staffed with state officials and military personnel to weed out illegal non-Americans who do not possess the required visa documentation. Violators would be deported without fanfare, delay or due process. These breakaway states would be free of illegal aliens and the former government's rules and regulations that provided basic services and entitlements to all aliens from every country once they showed up inside the U.S. Citizenship to this new country will be granted to very few non-Americans. American citizens from the remaining forty-six states would also be scrutinized because a wide variety of foreign immigrants had been given citizenship and were now American terrorists. Not all, but most have been Muslims. The old open door, 'come one and come all' policy was now over. This new country would be very, very selective on who becomes their new citizens. The new and pure democratic form of government is when the populate vote elects the policies or individuals. The republic form of government with its electoral college is not what most Americans want. Whom ever gets the most voters wins.

The new capitol would be Flagstaff within the state of Arizona. The capital district would extend ten miles in all directions of downtown Flagstaff. The city of Flagstaff was to be be transformed into the new capitol of this unnamed country. The first President of the new country would be Sara Williamson, who was currently the Governor of Arizona. She was asked to serve by the other three Governors and their selection committee. Sara's base of operation would remain in Phoenix until the new capitol building could be built along with other government buildings. All government agencies including military headquarters (similar to the Pentagon) would be within the one hundred square miles of the capital district.

President Obama started the emergency meeting at the Pentagon war room by stating that all suggestions and ideas he received over the past four days leaned towards attacking the state forces at the border with Mexico and capturing each state capital.

"Well ladies and gentlemen, I'm not going to order an attack on our American brothers and watch tens of thousands of Americans on both sided lose their lives and plunge this country into a civil war that will return the nation to the sixteenth century. As President I cannot wage war upon all Americans because of personal ideology and self-serving satisfaction that 'I'm the President' and rule over the country and I cannot allow this breakaway to happen. After many sleepless nights I have decided that if California, Arizona, New Mexico and Texas want to leave this union, let them go. As President I cannot plunge this great nation into a civil war that will eventually allow certain foreign governments to attack our country during this tragic dispute.

"I pray that this breakaway will be done in an orderly and safe transfer. If the four states fail to achieve a new country status, they are welcome to rejoin the union and become the "United" States again."

When the President finished his speech you could hear a pin drop. The large war room was dead quiet, and the entire group was speechless after his remarks. After almost two minutes of silence, the Secretary of Defense broke the deafening silence by saying, "Mr. President, are you really going to let those states throw mud on the constitution and defying the Federal government?"

"Yes, Mr. Secretary, I am."

"Maggie, please contact the four Governors and set up a meeting and inform them of my decision to allow them to secede from the union without any reprisals of any kind form this administration."

"Yes, sir, Mr. President, right away." she answered.

The Secretary of State finally contacted the four Governors and explained the President's position and decision. When the Governors heard the news that President Obama has agreed to allow all four states to leave the union without any action or reprisals, they were very surprised and very dubious.

Sara said, "No matter what the President has said I know he would never allow such a breakaway to take place without a fight. The President is a weasel and always will be. He can't be trusted and would say anything to buy time before striking out against his enemies. He now wants a get together," Sara said sarcastically.

Governor LaCrosse of Texas told her patriots in arms that President Obama gave in too easy. "We should be doubly vigilant and very wary of his decision. He just gave in too damn easy for me," she said echoing the others.

New Mexico's Governor said, "Now do we meet with him or not?"

"Yes, we should," Sara answered quickly. "I agree with Marilyn, I don't trust that man as far as I can throw him. And since he is tall that wouldn't be very far," she said with a smile. She continued, "If we meet with him, he must come without an entourage or any armed personnel. He won't like it but he'll agree in the end. If it's alright with the rest of you, lets have General Miles contact the Whitehouse and make the arrangement to meet the weasel."

"That's fine," the other Governors said, "but where do we hold this meeting?"

"How about Albuquerque?" the New Mexico Governor offered to the group.

"That's fine with me," Marilyn said, and both Sara and Eric agreed to meet the President in Albuquerque as soon as possible. General Miles immediately contacted the Obama Whitehouse and made the arrangements to meet with him in Albuquerque on Wednesday the 13th at 13:00 hours. The General also insisted that the President come with an aide and one cabinet member.

President Obama quickly agreed with the arrangements and the date of the meetings.

The four Governors, their aides and a general staff officer arrived in Albuquerque on the 12th to insure that the safety of the Commander-in-Chief was in place and to their liking. The meeting was to be held in a two hundred year old sprawling Spanish hacienda that covered a full acre and was surrounded by some thousand acres of cactus filled desert and sprawling hills and canyons. It was a breath taking setting for this historic meeting between the President and the representatives of the four states that were seceding from the union. This meeting could well determine the future of the United States and the outcome would be somewhere between peace and a devastating second civil war.

The President arrived in Albuquerque with three other people at 10:00 am mountain standard time and immediately was directed to the meeting location that was one hour away by car.

The meeting started at 13:00 hours sharp with all four Governors, their military aides, the President, his military aide

and the Secretary-of-State plus her aide were present. The six participating members were seated around a huge round table made of cactus wood with thousands of small holes throughout. This unique and striking table was over one hundred and fifty years old.

Once seated, the Governor of Arizona started by saying, "We are thankful, Mr. President, that you agreed to attend this important meeting here in Albuquerque."

President Obama stood up and said, "I agreed to this meeting for one reason, and that's to try and convince the four of you and your seventy million Americans not to secede from this united nation." With that opening statement he sat back down.

"Well then, we've assembled her for the wrong reasons," the Governor of Texas told the assembled group. "We did not come here to be kowtowed into changing our minds and returning to your fold, Mr. President. We're seceding from the union because of you, sir, and your liberal administration that has done absolutely nothing to protect our citizens from foreign intervention," she continued, "you have had more than four years to protect the citizens of our four border states and that's long enough for us Mr. President. Since you won't, we will stop most of the illegal aliens from entering our four sates and raising havoc in benefits and entitlements and giveaways that should be only for American citizens. We have also warned the Mexican government that we'll do whatever it takes to stop the flow of illegals, drug lords and Mexican military from entering our united border states. And that, Mr. President, includes war with Mexico if necessary," she added.

President Obama sat speechless for a full minute before answering. As he recovered from the Governors comments and threat of war with Mexico, he said in a loud voice "If you engage in war with Mexico I will order our military to attack your state forces and eventually force your runaway states to rejoin the union with great loss of American lives, mostly yours," he said with a threatening gesture. His face was red as a beet, and his blood pressure had to be sky high.

Sara stood up and said, "Well, Mr. President, I guess this meeting is over," and with that the other three Governors stood up and motioned to their aides that they were leaving.

Before leaving the room Governor Anderson said, "We were under the assumption, Mr. President, that you realized our four states were going to depart the union no matter what you said or did. We agreed to this meeting so we might iron out various details such as military bases, intersection highways, airports, seaports and immigration concerns for the remaining forty-six states as well as the Mexican problem. But I guess we were remiss in thinking that a peaceful and equitable solution to our decision to exit your union was without wanting for the President to answer," the Governors and their aides left the meeting room and immediately exited the grand old Spanish hacienda. They drove without delay to another pre-arranged location not far from Albuquerque to discuss the very short and unproductive meeting with President Obama.

"Well that was a real bust," Governor LaCrosse said, taking off her shoes and flopping down on a well-padded sofa. "The meeting was so short the Secretary-of-State never said a single word. We should have known the weasel wouldn't offer any suggestions or solutions to anything, but I was hopeful," she said, shaking her head. "Remember, we must be careful when we leave here, the President would really like to know where our home base is located when we return to our home state. I know we each have plans to slip any federal tails in case they are watching, but we still should be extremely careful. As an example when I reach a certain point within my state, my car will be met by six or eight cars exactly like mine with the same license plate number and then disperse in different directions. That should really confuse them if they're watching from a satellite."

After having something to eat and an adult beverage, they relaxed for an hour before settling down to the business at hand. "We must settle the border issue with Mexico and get prepared for the onslaught that is surely coming from the Federal government. We certainly don't want to fight on two fronts with our forces caught between two armies even if the Mexican army is only a third world military force."

Sara asked the group, "Don't you think our forces should be on high alert after our disastrous meeting with President Obama?" The other Governors nodded their heads and Sara instructed he aide to contact Lt. General Wittingham and ask him to elevate that alert status to color orange. Sara's aide left the room to make the alert elevation call to military headquarters near the Mexican border. Sara continued, "I believe combat between Federal troops and our State forces will commence

within a week at the latest. That's why we have only a week or less to end the tension with our Mexican neighbors. We must insist they dispense their national forces and not just move them back from the border area."

Governor LaCrosse said, "Since you're going to be our first President don't you think you should call President Longo and insist his military back off?"

"You're right, I should make the call." Sara asked her military aide to place the call to the Mexican President. Within thirty minutes President Longo was on the phone.

"Mr. President, this is Sara Williamson, Governor of Arizona."

"Yes, Governor, I know who you are," he answered in perfect English. "Just what do you want?"

"Mr. President, as you know our state and the other three border states are seceding from the union. Our President had done nothing to stop your countrymen from illegally entering this country. Well we are doing something about it, we have shut down the two-thousand mile border with our country and it will stay closed until your administration takes whatever action is necessary to stop the flood of Mexican nationals from illegally entering our states. Your national economy is grinding to a halt and it will even get worse Mr. President. We can see trucks backed up on all roads leading to the border for more them fifty miles. Your perishable goods are rotting in the trucks and thousands of drivers have abandoned their loads and are heading for home.

"If we don't reopen the border your third world country will slip back a hundred years and total anarchy will rein throughout your country," Sara told the Mexican President. "Pull back your military at least ten miles from the border, and stop the flow of your countrymen from attempting to enter our states. Until you do this our borders are closed to Mexico."

"For your information, Governor, I have asked your President Obama to force you and the other states to reopen the border. He assured me that the borders will be open again very soon. Your state forces will be crushed by your own Federal government," the Mexican President said with a voice of confidence.

"No matter what our President told you, the border will be closed tighter then a drum for quite a while," Sara told the arrogant Mexican President. "And when we see you making progress on both these issues, only then will we reopen the border. Even then there will be various restrictions," she added.

"Goodbye, Mr. President."

Sara hung-up the phone before the Mexican President could even answer.

"That will give him something to think about," Governor Anderson told the listening group.

"We're not going to wait very long for President Longo to react," Sara informed the other Governors. "We'll keep the border locked up tight for as long as it takes and I wouldn't care if the border was locked down for good," she added. "Also, we must consider ordering our state forces to surround the Federal bases and demand their immediate surrender and evacuation. We can't have this large government force stationed within our block of states. Each base must decide whether to leave, fight or join our seceding states."

"You should issue the orders," Governor LaCrosse told their next President of the union of four. The other Governors of California and New Mexico agreed.

"Before we issue any orders, let's have a pow wow first with our military staff," Sara suggested.

"Okay, but let's have all our meetings from now on in the future Capitol," Governor Anderson offered.

"Good idea, Richard, so be it. From now own we'll have all meetings within the new government's land mass in greater Flagstaff." Sara called their communication director Marian Wilcox and asked her to call the military staff and make arrangements to meet in Flagstaff the next morning at 11:00 am.

The four Governors, their aides and the military General staff from all four states were present for this nation changing important staff meeting. The actual meeting place was in the city of Belle Mont just west of Flagstaff.

The meeting started at 10:50 am and Sara opened the meeting by saying that she was proud of the progress made to date in dealing with Mexico and the large influx of new state citizens who have left their home states to join our defiance of our Federal government. "We're assembled here today to discuss how we're going to deal with the Federal bases within our four states. I would like to send our state forces to surround the largest of these bases and demand their immediate surrender.

Once their bases are covered, their forces can either leave, fight or join our secession from the union. I'd like to throw that general idea out for discussion gentleman." With that Sara sat back down.

Without saying a word, Lt. General Wittingham stood up and went to the large map of the Western United States. He put pins where the largest bases are located within the four states. He turned to the assembled group and said, "California and Texas are the greatest problems. They have a combined force of over two hundred and eighteen thousand active duty personnel. The Air Force personnel total approximately sixty-two thousand members with a wide variety of aircraft. Some seven thousand five hundred first line fighters, almost eight thousand helicopter, five hundred tankers and cargo planes. Not counting seventy-two hundred bombers with includes a little over six thousand in mothballs scattered throughout the deserts of California, Arizona, New Mexico and Texas. California alone has forty-one major installations and Texas has some twenty-three. That's a lot of military bases to cover all at once with our very limited number of service personnel," the Commanding General said shaking his head. "I don't think we can cover them all Governor." With that quick answer he turned and returned to his seat.

"Well, that's some challenge you've described, General."

"Governor, it's almost impossible," the forty year career officer said in a loud voice. "One more thing, once the Air Force gets the word to scramble, they'll launch all their aircraft for bases outside our four states. They will take most or all of the nuclear weapons with them. Whatever they leave behind they'll deactivate and make useless."

"I would like to add something else," General Wittingham said standing to address the group. "California and Texas have some large and very formable group of Army, Marine and Air Force bases. Let me just list a few:

California:	
Travis AFB	Camp Pendleton
Edwards AFB	Twenty Nine Palms
Vandenberg AFB	Fort Irwin
Beale AFB	Fort Hunter Liggett
Los Angles AFB	

Texas:	
Randolph AFB	Fort Bliss
Lackland AFB	Fort Hood
Laughlin AFB	Sheppard AFB
Dyess AFB	Goodfellow AFB
Arizona:	
Luke AFB	Davis-Monthan AFB
Gila Bend AFB	

The General continues, "If we decide to fight, and I mean "if" we fight, there are certain bases we should neutralize first. The Air Force bases are the real problem. If we can prevent these aircraft from leaving the major bases it will deprive the Federal government of thousands of first line aircraft. We could accomplish this by destroying their tarmac and preventing most aircraft from taking off. This should be our first priority if we elect to fight."

"General, what do you mean 'if we elect to fight,'" Sara asked the Commanding General of all their forces.

"Well, ladies and gentlemen, in my estimation and with over forty years of military service, we cannot win an all-out fight with the Federal government. There are too many bases and too many troops to win a quick victory without costing us huge losses of American lives on both sides."

"Governor, if you elect to fight the Federal government I'm very certain we will be defeated and that's the assessment of my staff as well," he admitted. "One more thing, we should remind ourselves that we could be fighting on a two front battlefield if we're not careful. Remember Mexico has about 200,000 active military personnel with another 300,000 in reserve. Their General staff officers have been attending various segments of our war colleges throughout the U.S. for the past ten years or more. They have many very capable senior officers, I know because I've worked with many of them. Also their equipment has been upgraded in recent years with new attack helicopters and front line fighters.

"On the U.S. side, they have 1,385,122 active and another 1,458,500 in the reserves for a total of 2.85 million troops available for duty. With our meager forces sandwiched between

almost 3.4 million U.S. and Mexican forces it makes our ability to wage war almost impossible the three star General admitted."

"My God, General, it sounds like we can't win and shouldn't secede from the union," Governor LaCrosse asked the General.

"No, Governor, I know it sounds bad, but we do have a number of good options," the General answered. "We knew in the beginning that all-out war was really not an option. We couldn't win in the end. What we should do is allow the Federal government to maintain these bases and pay a royalty to us the same as they do in any foreign country and agreeable way out of this dilemma."

Sara said, "General, I like your idea, both parties are somewhat winners in this matter. What does everyone else think about General Wittingham's idea?" she asked.

Governor Anderson said, "For me I like the idea of not killing Americans."

"We also agree," the other two Governors chimed in.

"Okay but once we have successfully seceded from the union and some time has passed, we'll request some of the bases be closed and turned over to our new country," the future President suggested.

"Sounds good to me," Lt. General Wittingham said with a big wide smile. "Now we've got to sell this foreign idea to President Obama and his group of hungry Generals, which won't be easy if I know his senior military staff. I believe Chairman-of-the Joint Chiefs, General Phillip Wolford might be our biggest no vote. Now who is going to propose this wonderful idea to the President?" he added.

Eric said, "Sara I think this is also within your duties as our first President."

"Yes, you're right, I'll contact the Whitehouse and set the stage for another meeting, but this time in the Whitehouse."

Sara called the Whitehouse and got the President immediately. After the usual pleasantries, she told President Obama that she may have a solution that would prevent any American bloodshed.

The President said, "Fine. Come to the Whitehouse tomorrow at 13:00 hours if that's okay with you?" he asked.

"Yes, that's fine, Mr. President. See ya tomorrow."

"Boy, that was almost too easy," she thought, replacing the phone. "Tomorrow at 13:00 hours in the Whitehouse," she informed the waiting group. "Almost too easy," she said shaking her head. "Just too easy," she muttered to herself.

"Who will accompany you on this trip?" General Miles asked.

"I want General Wittingham and yourself to accompany me to Washington, but I want both of you in civilian clothes," she ordered. Sara called her communications chief and asked Marian to make the arrangements for their tip tomorrow to the big house.

Once President Obama hung-up the phone he sat thinking, "What do they have up their sleeves?" He immediately called Winnie and asked her to call an emergency staff meeting for 18:00 hours today in the Whitehouse war room. "Winnie I want no exceptions, all parties there today."

"Yes, sir," she answered.

Sara and her party of two arrived at the Whitehouse at 12:45 and were ushered into the Oval Office waiting room. After only five minutes the President opened the adjoining door and invited them into the Oval Office.

"Does anyone want a drink, or anything?" the Chief Executive offered the group.

"No, thank you," they answered.

"How are you, General?" the President asked looking at his old friend with a cool smile that could freeze a full glass of water.

"Fine, Mr. President."

"Sorry, Sara, I forgot my manners. I hope you're well, Governor."

"Thank you, Mr. President."

"Okay, let's head down to the basement war room and hear your idea that will solve all our problems." President Obama led the way and everyone stood at attention upon entering the dimly lit war room.

"Please be seated, everyone." The President went to the head of the huge table as usual and slowly sat down. "Governor and General Wittingham, I know you know everyone here so let's get started."

 rickshaw

"Mr. President, I would like General Wittingham to present our position and propose a solution to our immediate problems."

"That's fine," the President said quietly.

General Wittingham arose from the table and slowly walked to the huge map of the United States. He pointed to the border with Mexico and said:

#1. The states of California, Arizona, New Mexico and Texas have seceded from the union.

#2. We have deployed our military forces along the entire length of the border with Mexico to stop the flow or illegal aliens.

#3. If the Federal government tries to stop us from becoming a new nation, we will fight for our rights to leave this union.

#4. The Mexican government has ground to stand still and will continue to get worse with every passing hour. We have talked with Mexican President Longo and informed him that if he doesn't stop the illegal entry of his citizens onto American soil our blockade of all entry into our four states will continue and even get tighter.
Mexico must stop the flow of illegal entry into the U.S. through our four states or we'll take even more drastic steps like permanently block off the bridges or as a last resort we'll blow the bridges and stop all traffic form flowing into the U.S. and Canada.

#5. Mr. President, last but not least we would like to suggest in some cases and insist on others.

"As for the Federal bases within our four states, we propose that you, the government continue to maintain these military installations and pay each seceding state a yearly royalty payment the same as you currently do with all foreign countries. This agreement would prevent any military action by either side. Even though you have a superior military force the loss of life on both sides would be great. No just military but civilian casualties as well.

"Any conflict of this magnitude would certainly destroy the country as we know it today. We know a "second civil war" would set this country back a hundred and fifty years or more.

"Another point that our border states will insist upon is to continue to guard and defend our state borders with Mexico. If we can stop this massive exodus from Mexico into the United States with the help of Longo's government as well as our states, the entire border would be reopened and free trade access would continue. But, no matter what, security would remain very tight and profiling would be the order of the day.

"All illegal Mexicans will be returned and our combined states will finally be free of unwanted squatters and the saving of billions of dollars in government programs and medical benefits. Undocumented Mexican mothers who have children while illegally in this country will be deported along with their offspring. Their children who were granted U.S. citizenship by your liberal government will forfeit their citizenship and be returned to Mexico along with their mothers and any other illegal family members."

After presenting the five points to the President and his entire staff, General Wittingham slowly returned to his seat. The war room was deadly quiet until the President finally said, "Well, that's one hell of a list General."

"I will consult with my staff on your suggestions and demands, Governor. We'll contact you in a day or two with our answers," the President told the Arizona Governor and her aides. "One thing we must solve immediately," President Obama said to the parting group. "The border must be reopened and trade with Mexico returned to normal."

The Governor stopped and listened to President Obama's remarks, but left the Whitehouse war room without answering his last remark. Sara and her staff departed Washington and headed for Arizona to confer with the other Governors.

Within the war room General Wolford said, "Mr. President, I'd say no dice to all five of their points. They're well aware we can crush their forces and force the seceding states back into the union."

Jon Marshal, the newly appointed Secretary-of-Defense stood up and addressed the group. "Gentlemen, we must consider the total ramifications if we don't agree to their suggestions and even some demands. The destruction of this country could well be total if we're not careful, Mr. President. Let's not forget, the constitution allows the individual states to rebel if the Federal government does not provide the protection and security entitled to them."

General Taylor Air Force Commanding General spoke up and said, "Mr. President, I'm in agreement with Secretary Marshal. To stop the possible carnage that would tear apart this great nation and put millions upon millions of Americans against each other the same way the first civil war pitted Americans against Americans. We must prevent this from happening no matter what it takes.

"The Federal government should back down and give in to the five suggestions offered by the four states. I'm sure certain foreign governments would use this internal dispute to attack our country. We must end this standoff right now and defuse this national issue and return this country to normalcy." With those comments the Air Force General sat back down.

Secretary-of-State Wilson added her two cents by saying that she was in agreement with the Secretary-of-Defense and General Taylor. She added, "We must end this now before World War III erupts and the United States no longer exists."

"Well, we certainly have a wide variety of opinions within my civilian and military staff," the President said shaking his head. "Mr. Jennings, I'd like to hear from you as my National Security Advisor."

"Mr. Jennings as a child had polio and had been confined to a wheelchair for most of his sixty-four years. But it didn't prevent him from obtaining two PhDs and authoring seven books on governments of the world. His expertise on national security is well known throughout the world."

"Thank you, Mr. President."

Malcolm wheeled his chair to the map of the U.S. and pointed to the Mexican border and said in a loud and clear voice, "This border problem is bigger and more important than the four states seceding from our established union. The Mexican problem is two-fold, Mr. President.

First: We must stop the flow of illegal aliens from entering this country. We as your administration, Mr. President, have done almost nothing to stop this flow of unwanted Mexican nationals from sliding into our country. In fact, Mr. President, we have encouraged the Mexican population to break the law, enter this country and receive all our government benefits and giveaways. These huge giveaways are costing the U.S. taxpayers over 460 billion dollars a year and that's a modest and low dollar figure.

We have also issued thousands of visas to foreign nationals with very questionable backgrounds. Once the visas are issued, these individuals just disappeared off the radar and out about their subversive activities until they surface into illegal activities. We must immediately stop visas' helter-skelter and clamp down by only issuing very few. Thousands of individuals are roaming our towns and cities without our knowledge, whereabouts or activities. This open policy to the world must stop, pretty soon more non-citizens than Americans will be roaming our streets. Rome found out the hard way and eventually paid the price with the total collapse of the Italian society. If we're not careful the demise of this country will follow like the 'fall of the Roman empire,'"

With Mr. Jennings' last statement, a few members of the administration stood up and clapped loudly and yelled, "Yea-yea, it's about time the truth came out!"

After that outburst the National Security Advisor wheeled back to his space at the table and looked at the President.

President Obama stood up slowly and said, "Thank you, Mr. Jennings, your point is well taken. I admit that we, or I should say "I," have not done much to stem the flow of illegal aliens from entering these United States. I know many of you have championed the effort for me as your President to do something about this issue, but I ignored the efforts to stop the flow of Mexican nationals and other illegals." The President continued, "Now we have bared our souls and admitted our true feelings on this subject, but the original problem still exists. Do we give in to all their demands as presented or do we fight with all our government power?"

After being briefed by Sara, the three Governors immediately held civilian and military staff meetings. They knew beforehand that President Obama would never agree to the five points presented to him and his staff. The Governors agreed that they must continue to prepare and upgrade their military positions at the border as well as throughout their four states.

Mexican President Longo contacted Arizona Governor Williamson and demanded the border be reopened immediately. He reminded Sara that he had contacted President Obama and asked for his military intervention in the border dispute.

After a short pause, Governor Williamson said, "With respect, Mr. President, you don't ever demand anything from my state or any other border state. Our border with Mexico will remain closed until you show proof that you're stopping the flow of Mexican nationals from sneaking into our country. If you continue to do nothing about immigration, your country's economy will slide even further into the toilet. There will be anarchy throughout your country and your citizens will most likely march on your government buildings and demand your resignation or even your death, Mr. President. You stop the flow into our new country and we'll consider re-opening the entire border,"

Sara told the Mexican President again. "We will even consider investing large sums of money into joint ventures with your government and private business if you stop this influx of illegal persons."

Sara continued, "Mr. President, you have very little time left to decide whether you want total anarchy and the destruction of your country. Your population of one hundred twelve million will be without hope and certainly take their revenge out on you and your do nothing administration. You must act quickly, we're already hearing rumors that lawless acts of looting, murder and roving gangs are forming to confiscate the necessary goods to survive. The lawless groups are armed to the teeth and will kill to obtain food and other supplies. Again, Mr. President, you must act quickly to avert this potential disaster that well spread throughout your country quicker than any wild fire.

"The other Governors and I will be watching for any signs of stopping your nationals from entering our space." With that last statement Sara Williamson replaced the phone before the Mexican President could answer.

Sara contacted the other Governors and related her conversation with President Longo. They all agreed to watch for any positive signs of the Mexican authorities preventing their countrymen form entering the border states. The border states ground forces are on alert level #3 (yellow) and their Air Force were flying numerous sorties along the border photographing any Mexican military movement in preparation of military action if necessary.

Vice President Goodwin stood up and said, "Mr. President, if we attack these four states, the economy of this country will collapse like a balloon. Most of the large ports on the west coast would be shut down to all foreign and domestic trade going to and coming from Far East counties as well as significant trade coming from South America."

The V.P continues, "This country cannot afford the loss that military action would cost our country. The loss in American lives would be huge, Mr. President. The destruction of roads, bridges, power stations, communications and etc. would certainly push us back a hundred years or more. Also consider the foreign elements that would take this opportunity to strike a blow to end the freedom that this country represents. I beg of you, Mr. President, to allow these four runaway states to secede from our union." With that appeal the Vice President sat down.

More than half of the members in the war room stood up and clapped and cheered at the V.P's statements. After a full two minutes of showing their support, the group sat down and waited for President Obama's response.

"Well, ladies and gentlemen, I guess our course of action is now quite clear," the President said in a very subdued voice. "Mr. Marshal, please call the Pentagon and reduce the alert level back to a normal blue color. We're not going to stand in the way of California, Arizona, New Mexico and Texas from leaving the union. Now that this is settled, how about the border problems with Mexico?" he asked the group.

Before anyone could answer, the special phone at the President's side started flashing, which startled the President. He quickly picked up the green phone and said, "Obama here." After four or five minutes of listening, the President said, "Thank you,Governor, for the latest update on the border blockade. Sara, before you hang up I'd like to inform you and the other three Governors that I have decided not to interfere with you seceding from the union of the United States."

"Well, that's good news, Mr. President, the residents of our four states will be very happy with your decision. With that decision you have saved thousands upon thousands of American lives on both sides."

"Now that you have demanded action by Mexican President Longo, how long will you wait before you take any further action?" the President asked.

"Not long, Mr. President, if Longo does nothing, we will close the border even to all foot traffic. Even the oil deliveries to the U.S. will mostly dry up. A lot of refineries are in Texas, Mr. President."

"I'm asking you, Mr. President, to contact President Longo and put pressure on him and his so called government to stop the flow of illegals into the U.S. instead of encouraging his citizenry to become law breakers and cross the border. If he doesn't act quickly, his government will collapse and total anarchy will rein throughout the entire country. Remind him that the drug traffic cartels will overrun what's left of his country and return Mexico to a lawless state like it was in the eighteen hundreds. It's bad enough now, but two hundred years ago it was even worse, Mr. President.

"You alone can solve this Mexican problem by insisting that Longo start showing some balls and start acting like the government leader he is supposed to represent. Mr. President, you know he doesn't really have a choice. He must prevent the Mexican population from exiting the homeland for all the U.S. freebees given by you, Mr. President. You're certainly part of this overall problem with Mexico, Mr. President, and you know it.

"You must also show the strength of your office and force Mexico to stop this exodus once and for all. You can start, Mr. President, by supporting our border position with talking to Longo."

"Governor Williamson, what the hell do you want from me?" , the President asked in anger.

"I want you to be the President and stand for something that benefits all Americans and stop kowtowing to foreign leaders and special liberal groups. Be forceful and threaten the Mexican President when necessary to get him to act."

"Thank you, Governor, I'll take your ideas and suggestions under advisement and I'll get back to you soon."

"Thank you, Mr. President." Both parties hung up.

The President asked that the entire conversation with Governor Williamson be played back for the war room group to hear.

Chapter 2 – Sealing the Borders

After the lengthy conversation ended, the President said, "Okay people what do you think? Is Sara Williamson right or not?" he asked the entire group.

"Well, she doesn't mince words." the Secretary-of-State said quickly. "She wants you to solve the border situation by forcing President Longo to stop the flow of unwanted Mexicans from ending up wards of the U.S. If you accomplish that, she will reopen the border and the Mexican economy will spring back to life. I personally like the idea, Mr. President," the Secretary said, returning to her seat.

"Okay, okay. I'll call President Longo today and apply whatever pressure I can muster to force him to act as quickly as possible," the President conceded. "Get President Longo on the phone quickly," he ordered the Secretary-of-State.

"Yes, sir" she answered.

Within fifteen minutes the Mexican President was on the phone with President Obama.

"Mr. President, what do you want? I'm extremely busy with our current crisis created by your southwestern states," the Mexican President said in a curt voice.

"Yes, President Longo, I understand your present problems, but I'm going to add to your problems the President admitted.

"Number #1. You must stop the flow of your countrymen from illegally entering our country or the border blockade will continue.

"Number #2. Your government is close to collapse and your population will riot in the streets if your economy continues to deteriorate. To prevent anarchy you should put your military on the border and stop the exodus.

"Number #3. The entire border will open when you actually stop the flow of illegal entry into the U.S. Your time is running out, you must act quickly, Mr. President. One more thing, your oil shipments to the U.S. will be curtailed somewhat due to many refineries located in Texas."

"Mr. President, you do as you see fit but don't ask for any help when the total collapse of your country takes place."

 rickshaw

With that last statement the Mexican President slammed the phone down in anger.

"Well, let's see what happens now," the President said replacing the phone and rubbing his ear. "It's totally up to President Longo now. Maggie please call Governor Williamson and relay my conversation with our Mexican friend."

"I'll call right away, Mr. President."

Chapter 3
OBAMA'S THREATS

After receiving the call from the Secretary-of-State and hearing the President's remarks to Longo, Sara thanked Maggie for her quick response. Sara immediately called the other three and related the President's remarks to the Mexican President. She added that the Mexican military might return to the border to prevent any Mexican nationals from attempting to enter the U.S. "Please alert your commanders to be aware and watchful of the activity on the Mexican side. I for one still don't trust the Mexican President no matter what he says. Let's be on alert, you never know," she added.

Sara hung up the phone and leaned back in her not so soft chair. She wondered, "When will all the unpleasantness be over so we can concentrate on our new country and write our constitution and get established in the world as a leader with conservative values and fairness to all our citizens? I guess we will have to wait a little longer," she thought as she tried to concentrate on both the problems at hand and possible future ones.

California Governor Richardson was alerted by General William Barker that Mexican troops were massing at the border with California. The General said that his border troops were on high alert and ready for anything the Mexican military might try.

"Keep me informed on any changes, General," the Governor asked his favorite General.

"Will do, sir," the General answered.

Along the Arizona, New Mexico and Texas border the same massing of Mexican troops was taking place. They were concentrated on the usual avenues the illegals took to enter the United States. The coyotes had holes in the fences, specially marked water paths across the Rio Grande and marked trails across the desert areas of Arizona, New Mexico and Texas. These numerous avenues of escaping across the Rio Grande and entering the U.S. were now being watched and guarded by both the U.S. military as well as the Mexican military troops.

Governor Anderson said, "This action by the Mexican government is all well and good, but how many illegals are being

turned back and arrested by Mexican authorities? And what are they doing with those hundreds of arrested nationals? This could be an exercise in futility if they are catching these illegals as they attempt to cross the Rio Grande, slapping their hands and then turn them loose to try to escape again and again. We must know where these people are being held and how many arrests are being made."

The New Mexico Governor called Sara and told her, "We need a liaison officer who goes back and forth to Mexico and monitors these activities, arrests and holding centers for these Mexicans attempting to smuggle into the U.S."

"I agree, Richard, but let's have a liaison officer for each of our four states," she replied. "One person could simply not cover the two thousand miles of border and deal with the various military units."

"I'll contact the other Governors and propose your ideas," she offered.

"Thank you, Sara."

Sara contacted the Governors of California and Texas. They agreed to the idea and agreed to pick the best officer to represent their states. "Now all we have to do is persuade President Longo to allow our liaison people to interact with his military and have free access to roam the Mexican countryside and monitor their activities to ensure we're not being hoodwinked in the matter. Good god, I can't believe I wanted to be the first President of our new country. I'm not in office yet and I'm swamped already," she thought. Sara called Marian Wilcox and instructed her to contact Mexican President Longo and set up an emergency meeting somewhere in Mexico.

President Longo returned the call quickly and agreed to meet Sara in the Mexican city of Nuevo Laredo on the border with Texas.

Sara arrived in Nuevo Laredo's airport at 10:15am and was taken to an all-girls school just three miles from the border. The beautiful school was built in 1836 by Spanish architects. The school was painted all white and was surrounded by a beautiful, ornate wrought iron fence, and even has a bell tower that can be seen from downtown Laredo, Texas. This school was selected by President Longo for this meeting with Governor Williamson.

The Governor came alone to the meeting, and Edwardo only had an aide with him.

"Thank you, Mr. President, for not having a large group at this meeting. I prefer only you and I to discuss this proposal."

"Yes, Governor, but please get to the point of this hurry up meeting," the President urged his lovely guest.

"Certainly, Mr. President. Now that you have positioned your military at the border to prevent your nationals from slipping into our country we have no way to monitor your progress in your attempt to stop this exodus. We must know how many persons you're stopping, how many are under arrest and where are they being detained once arrested. I'd like to propose that we appoint four liaison officers, one from each state to monitor your activity in this military exercise. We don't want to repeat offenders as before, Mr. President. We captured and returned some Mexican nationals a dozen times over the years. Unless they are incarcerated, there is no sense to the exercise, Mr. President."

"You're demanding a lot," the Mexican President said, leaving the table and pacing back and forth while puffing hard on his large cigar. The blue smoke almost hid his face as he pulled on his expensive Cuban cigar.

"If you agree, Mr. President, our men must have your assurance that their safety is top priority with your military."

After pacing for another few minutes he said in a loud voice, "I will agree to your request, but I insist that your liaison officers be accompanied by an English speaking Mexican officer at all times while inside Mexico."

"That's fine, Mr. President, I think that's a good idea. Along with that, the U.S. will furnish four helicopters for our liaison personnel and your accompanying officers. The aircraft will also be under the command of your officer while visiting the various military units along the border if you agree, sir."

"Yes, that's okay," the Mexican President said quickly.

"Mr. President, once we're satisfied that your actions are producing visible gains in the reduction of illegal aliens crossing the Rio Grande and attempting to enter our country, I'll start opening our border to your country, but not before," she added. "I'll inform your office on our choices of liaison personnel and set

up a meeting with your military leaders on actual locations and an overall itinerary for monitoring your progress."

With that the meeting ended. The Mexican President shook Sara's hand and departed without saying a single word. Sara was driven to the airport and returned to Arizona to confer with her staff and consult with the other three Governors on her meeting with Edwardo Longo.

President Longo returned to Mexico City and held a staff meeting with many of his top military leaders. He discussed his meeting with Governor Williamson at great length and after the meeting he called his general in charge of all forces along the border. He instructed General Rōjas to start arresting and detaining all persons entering the Rio Grande and attempting to enter the United States illegally. "Use whatever force necessary to prevent any Mexican nationals from entering the U.S.," the President ordered.

General Rōjas answered, "Mr. President, once these people are arrested what do I do with them?"

"Send all arrested persons to Monterrey and we'll house them in the old military compound and jail until we can decide what to do with them."

"That's all good and well, Mr. President, but there will be thousands of our countrymen sent to Monterrey every month," the General complained.

"I know, General Rōjas, but we must somehow impress upon our people that long prison terms are in order if they attempt to enter the United States. I'm planning a nationwide T.V. address to alert and warn our people that attempts to illegally enter the United States will result in long prison sentences or even death. If we don't stop this exodus our border will the U.S. will continue to be closed and our national economy will drop into the pit of despair and anarchy will rein throughout. We have enough lawlessness in our country as it is. If we don't stop this illegal entry and get the border reopened very shortly the roving gangs and drug lords will rule the entire country like the bandits did two hundred years ago.

"We must show the Arizona Governor that we're doing something to stop our people and other persons from around the world from gaining access to the United States coming from

Mexico. Just order your commanders to start the roundup right away General and I mean right away."

In the meeting with the other three Governors, Sara covered the meeting with President Longo and felt he would actually start doing something to stop the influx of Mexican nationals.

Governor Anderson said that he had his doubts that President Longo would actually arrest his own people.

"Well, we will see very shortly," Sara answered quickly.

"General Wittingham, would you please pick four of our officers, one from each state to become our liaison officers with the Mexican military. Of course, they must speak perfect Spanish and willing to fly back and forth across the border while visiting dozens or even a hundred Mexican military encampments along the border. These four officers must set up reporting procedures with the Mexican military and be allowed to visit the location where these arrested Mexican nationals are being held. We don't want them arrested then to be released for another try and a larger head count. Once arrested they must be held in jail for the crime of attempting to enter a foreign country without a proper visa. Please pick these liaison officers quickly, General," she urged the top military officer in their fledging government.

"Yes, ma'am, right away."

Once the meeting ended, General Wittingham contacted the top military commander in each of the four states. After explaining the previous meeting in brief, he asked them to submit the names to fill these liaison positions within twenty-four hours. They all agreed.

From the Laredo, Texas side of the Rio Grande the stationed troops could see and hear the new activity across the border and in the water of the Rio Grande. Mexican troops were in the water stopping Mexican nationals from wading across and attempting to enter the United States. Some distance away they could hear gun fire, either coming from the Mexican military or cartel members trying to cross the Rio Grande. Running gun battles along the Mexican side will surely escalate as the clamp down continues.

General Rōjas was flying up and down the border to see first-hand how his troops are responding to his orders to capture and arrest anyone attempting to cross the Rio Grande and enter

the U.S. illegally. His orders also stated that anyone not stopping would be shot.

General Wittingham received the short list of possible liaison officers he requested. The list only contained four names. Two Lt. Colonels and two Majors.

"Well, that eliminates choosing from a list," the General thought.

The chosen men were Lt. Colonel Josh McBride and John Holcomb, and Majors Wilson Hernandez and Karl Jorgensen. These four men were already on their way to meet with General Wittingham and Governor Williamson to receive their very special instructions on how to gather and report the necessary intel required to determine the effectiveness of President Longo's commitment to stopping the illegal traffic from crossing the border and slipping into the U.S.

The meeting with Governor Williamson, General Wittingham and the four appointed liaison officers convened almost immediately upon their arrival at the undisclosed location somewhere in the Arizona desert. The men were briefed on the conversation between Sara and President Edwardo Longo just forth-eight hours ago. They were given instructions on how to gather the reports provided by the Mexican military on the numbers and locations of all arrests of persons attempting to leave Mexico and enter the U.S. Also they must inspect first hand all detention centers and jails used to house the arrested Mexican nationals and other arrested persons. They must work hand in glove with their Mexican counterparts while flying from military instillations and the various small camps and detachments along the entire length of the border. Once these people were arrested they must be photographed and fingerprinted for future identification. The American helicopters have Mexican authorization to fly within a hundred mile distance of the border to inspect all holding areas for arrested persons.

General Wittingham and the four liaison officers met with General Rōjas and his staff at Nogales, Mexico to iron out the specific details of their mission and any restrictions the Mexican government might insist upon. The four American officers met their counterparts and their dialog began in Spanish then reverted to English. Once the meetings and fencing was over, each group was assigned a specific area to patrol and they were supplied with locations of all military units scattered along the Mexican border within their assigned areas.

They would start their assignments at first light the next morning. The Mexican government insisted that the four American officers not be allowed to carry any weapons while inside Mexico and the four gunships must not be armed. Each gunship was required to have special markings and Spanish lettering so the Mexican military could distinguish them from all other American aircraft.

Each helicopter would have a pilot, co-pilot, American liaison officer and their Mexican counterpart. While in Mexico the Mexican officer had control of the aircraft and its destination. All four aircraft were to be in contact with General Rōjas and American General Wittingham at all times.

President Longo contacted President Obama informed him of the agreement with Governor Williamson and General Wittingham. He also told the President that his indecision about the border problems had led to the lowest relationship with Mexico. "You can't even hold on to your runaway states let alone control a whole nation. Your government is finished, Mr. President."

Before President Obama could answer, the Mexican President Longo hung up abruptly leaving the American President holding the phone and wondering, "Not again. Good god, now the Mexican government is dealing with a Governor and not the American Federal Government and me." He slowly replaced the phone and immediately called his National Security Advisor, Mr. Jennings, and asked him to set up a meeting in the Pentagon war room with all is military leaders and civilian staff.

The NSA said he'd get back as soon as possible with the time of the meeting.

Within thirty minutes, Mr. Jennings called the President and informed him that the meeting was on for 13:00 hours the next day if he approved.

"Tomorrow at 13:00 hundred is fine," the President answered.

At 05:00 hundred all four helicopters left their American bases and crossed the Rio Grande along the Texas border and the desert border between west of El Paso and east of San Diego.

 **rickshaw**

After picking up their Mexican liaison officers they headed for the first Mexican outpost along the border.

As the copter assigned to Arizona was flying over the desert border they could see dozens and dozens of Mexican nationals attempting and obtaining entry into Arizona without being challenged by military or state authorities. Even with more than four divisions of state forces scattered along the entire length of the border, there are huge holes along the border where the illegals could walk through with no difficulty what-so-ever.

The Mexican military positioned their small outposts about twenty miles apart with about fifty or so troops at each station. Some outposts had helicopters but most do not. They used high speed military vehicles but had few boats for use on the Rio Grande.

The four American aircraft assigned to border duty were only on duty for a few hours before they realized that four aircraft to cover the two thousand miles of border was a futile effort. Lt. Colonel McBride assigned to monitor the Mexican side of the Arizona border called General Wittingham and explained the hopeless situation of the four assigned aircraft. General Wittingham immediately called the commanding officer of each state and asked for more help. He instructed the California military to add one more liaison officer and aircraft, Arizona to add three more officers and Texas to add three more officers and New Mexico to add only one more. With a total of twelve liaison officers and added gunships, the monitoring of captured Mexican nationals and alerting both Mexican military and American authorities would be easier and quicker.

The eight new liaison officers, plus their crews met in the desert of Arizona with General Wittingham and his staff. The new officers consisted of five Warrant Officers, Two Majors and one Lt. Colonel. Once briefed they were assigned specific fly zones that divided the border into sections instead of flying helter-skelter from Mexican outpost to outpost. Once the new choppers are properly marked, the new group of liaison officers would head out to their assigned areas.

General Wittingham called Mexican General Rōjas and informed him of the increase in monitoring personnel and aircraft. General Rōjas wasn't happy with the increase in choppers flying about his command and snooping around his various military encampments along the border. Rōjas immediately called his President and complained to high heaven about the increase of monitoring gunships and crews. He added now he must find another eight officers he can trust to fly with the Americans.

"I agree, General, I'll get back with my answer in an hour or so," the Mexican President told his top General.

"Yes, sir," Rōjas answered.

President Longo called Governor Williamson and complained vehemently about the increase in traffic along the Mexican side of the border.

"Mr. President, if you want to border reopened any time soon, you better stop complaining and get the job done of stopping illegals from crossing our border."

President Longo said "fine," and abruptly hung up. He then called General Rōjas and told him to "get cracking so the Americans will open the damn border."

General Rōjas contacted General Wittingham and said that he could supply the additional eight Mexican liaison officers in a day or so.

'That's fine," the American General told his Mexican counterpart. "We'll have the added choppers and our crews ready by then. If it's okay with you, let's assemble again in the Arizona desert as before."

"The desert compound is fine with me," Rōjas answered.

The President, his National Security Advisor and his entire military and civilian staff was present for the 13:00 hour meeting in the Pentagon War Room. As usual, the President started off by relating the conversation he'd had with Mexican President Longo and his dealing with Arizona Governor Williamson. "Now Mexico is in bed with the border states and have apparently rejected the American Federal Government and especially its President, me. Now ladies and gentlemen with this latest turn of events with Mexico and our four border states, what the hell do we do now he asked? In the past couple of weeks we have sat here and virtually done nothing, absolutely nothing. I'll shoulder the lion share of the blame for being wishy-washy on the seceding states and not taking a hard stand and preventing them from leaving the union. Now their acting like a separate country and they're controlling our whole two thousand mile

border with our neighbor Mexico. Sara and her herd are holding the border for ransom and forcing the Mexican government to stop the flow of Mexican nationals from entering our country or the border will remain closed."

"Mr. President, with respect sir, we should have done what the Arizona Governor is currently doing," the Secretary-of-State told the entire group as she stood up and addressed the President's men.

A total silence fell over the war room, you could hear the heavy breathing of many of the President's Generals as they sat in wonderment while digesting the anti-government, less than liberal words coming from their Secretary-of-State, Maggie Wilson.

Maggie continued, "We could have stopped this influx of unwanted persons years ago, but for a hundred reasons we elected to ignore the issue turn a blind eye." She continued, "Our liberal philosophy had basically bit us in the ass and now we're paying for our many mistakes." With that the Secretary-of-State slowly sat down.

General Wolford broke the long silence and said, "Mr. President, I believe we have a conservative in liberal sheepskin."

"General, you can call me whatever you want, but you know damn well I'm right," Maggie shot back at the Chairman of the Joint Chiefs. "We must get our heads out of the sand and actually help the four border states instead of planning their demise," she said in a very loud voice.

"Ladies and gentlemen, let's be civil to each other," the President told the group. "We're her to solve these problems and not create more problems."

Maggie stood up again and said, "Why don't we contact the group of four and offer our assistance in any way they consider it helpful. We can't stand by and let these seceding states make all the decisions that affect the rest of the country. We shouldn't go to war over their seceding, but we should step in and help solve these problems that we've ignored for so long." Maggie turned around and said, "Gentlemen, how many of you actually agree with me and support my ideas on this critical issue?"

She waited, and out of thirty-five persons attending the war room meeting, only five members supported her ideas and suggestions. Not surprisingly to her, all five were civilian members of his staff. "Thank you," she said as the Secretary finally sat back down.

"My, my people we certainly have a difference of opinion among my staff members," the President said with a hint of annoyance in his voice. "Well, I'm not sure we shouldn't just attack the four runaway states and force them to rejoin the union of fifty. But with Mexico thrown into the mix that's not an option anymore. Maggie, since you're our point man on this issue, I'd like you to contact Sara Williamson and set up a meeting between myself, you, Malcom and Sara's group. Let them pick the time and place," he insisted.

"Thank you, Mr. President. This is a great first step," the Secretary shouted.

"Mr. President, are you sure you want us to join the rebellious four or at least help them?" the Secretary-of-Defense asked.

"Yes, I'm sure, Mr. Secretary," the President said quickly and curtly.

Maggie finally got in contact with Governor Williamson and she agreed to the meeting but insisted that the get together be held in the future capitol of the fledgling country.

Sara called the other Governors and asked them to attend the meeting with the President and his group scheduled for the next day. Two of the three Governors said they would attend, except Governor Richardson who was with General Baker in the town of Calexico across the border from Mexicali, Mexico where trouble was brewing.

The meeting in Flagstaff started at 14:00 sharp with everyone present except California's Governor. Sara opened the meeting by saying, "I hope we're not here to cover the same ground we attempted to plow weeks ago."

"On the contrary, Governor," the President quickly inserted. "I'm here to offer our help in any way you deem helpful."

A deadly silence fell over the room. Governor Williamson and her group hooked at each other in complete wonderment. "What the hell is going on?" she thought as she sat there speechless. She recovered quickly and said, "Mr. President, I don't understand your offer to help."

 rickshaw

"As President I have decided not to fight you and the other three states that are seceding from the union. This country cannot afford a second full blown "civil war" that would certainly rip this country apart and lay it open for foreign attack and plunder. We just can't allow that to happen, Americans fighting Americans is a lose, lose situation at best," the President admitted. "Now I must tell you frankly, Sara, there was a large group of my military leaders that want the Federal Government to attack your state forces along the Mexican border and throughout your four states. Now, you and I both know the Federal Government would eventually win that battle, but admittedly with considerable loss of American lives on both sides."

"Yes, Mr. President, we knew in the beginning that we couldn't win in such a fight but we certainly could fight balls to the wall on all fronts for the right to leave the union," she added.

"Now, Governor, let's cut to the chase, where can we help you?" the Secretary-of-State asked.

"Well, we have locked the border down tight and stopped all vehicle traffic from entering our border states. This has backed up truck traffic for more than one hundred miles along all roads leading to the border and basically shutdown the Mexican economy. President Longo has agreed to start intercepting and arresting their nationals attempting to enter the border states. Whether they try to cross the Rio Grande or the desert of Arizona and New Mexico, the Mexican authorities must stop them.

"Our military forces alone have captured thousands of Mexican nationals in just a few weeks. This invasion by Mexicans must and will stop one way or another," she insisted. "If necessary, Mr. President, we'd declare war on Mexico to stop this influx of unwanted persons. Something had to be done, you and your administration didn't lift a finger to defend our border with Mexico or either admit there was a national problem, and your liberal social programs allowed these illegal persons to live in our states and receive every entitlement an American citizen was entitled to. Those policies are wrong, Mr. President, and you and your party know it. You were only concerned with the number of new voters they would generate."

"Yes, Governor, you have told me that many times before, so let's put that behind us now and look to the future for admirable solutions," the President asked.

"Oh! It's now okay for you to pass on all the states problems we've had to deal with for the past four plus years and the cost of billions to our strapped state residents!" she quickly added in disgust.

Marilyn LaCrosse, Governor of Texas, said, "Mr. President, how far will you go to help us in our struggle with Mexico and our independence from your government and control?"

"People, I'm willing to do almost anything to help solve the Mexican border problem and help in your transition into forming a new government and nation. Along with this I'm willing to pay your states for the stationing and occupancy of our federal troops at our bases inside your states or territory. Basically the same arrangement as any other foreign country. Will this arrangement be acceptable to you and your group?" the President asked.

Governor Anderson asked the President, "Sir, just what do you want in return for these offers to help our new nation?"

"Well, Richard, I want the Mexican stalemate resolved and the entire border reopened quickly and the flow of goods to the U.S. allowed to pass. If the Mexican economy continues to slip into the abyss of despair and all out anarchy reins, a civil war inside Mexico will certainly spill over into the United States. The many drug cartels are already gaining strength within Mexico as we speak. A power struggle between the cartels and the Mexican government will result in the Mexican government losing big time. The cartels' vast wealth will win over the government's lack of funds in a very short period of time," the President added in a low voice. "Remember, if Mexico should fall, foreign interventions from China would surely take place quickly I'm sure. We must at all cost not allow this to happen."

"Okay, then the first thing you can do, Mr. President, is to apply pressure to President Longo to set up his round-up of Rio Grande waders and desert lizards that want free passage to the promised land. When we see hundreds and hundreds of arrested nationals being held along the entire length of our border, then we'll reopen the border with certain restrictions. We will continue to profile Mexicans within our states to purge any undocumented illegal Alien and return them to the Mexican authorities for incarceration. Another thing, Mr. President, no Mexican trucks will be allowed past the truck terminal for unloading their goods to an American trucking company. Their trucks are uninsured, unsafe and their drivers don't read or speak English for the most part. Dozens of Americans have been killed and paralyzed for life due to these unsafe factors."

"Well, that's quite a start, Governor," the President said, getting up from the table and walking over to the large window. He stared out the window onto the beautiful Arizona desert with its twenty foot chimney cactus and beautiful flowering scrub brush. "I'll agree to your requests so far, now what's next?" he asked.

National Security Advisor, Malcom Jennings stiffened in his wheelchair and said, "Mr. President, I don't agree. We cannot allow these states to profile suspected illegal Mexican nationals. That's against all our current policies and the other remaining forty-six states will want the same latitude."

"Please calm down, Mr. Jennings, we must change some of our ways to get certain things done in an expeditious manner," the President answered with a look of dissatisfaction.

His top advisor slowly calmed down and pushed his wheelchair away from the table in disgust.

"What else, Governor?" the President asked returning to his seat.

"Mr. President, we're currently in the process of building various government buildings here in Flagstaff. Be we only have one completed and a couple others are halfway finished. We need help in creating passports and visas for entry into our new country. We would appreciate your help if you could loan us someone from your passport office to guide us through the paper maze."

"Certainly we can help in the creating the necessary forms and security to insure smooth entry into your unnamed country," the President answered with a bit of sarcastic humor.

"Thank you, Mr. President, I think," Sara said with a smile. She continues, "Another thing, all main roads leading into our four states from the remaining forty-six are now manned with border personnel and are ready to stop and check traffic when we're officially a country and have provided the necessary entry paperwork and I.D. badges. Your military personnel stationed within our territory will not require a passport or visa. Their military I.D. will be sufficient to travel in and out of our new nation. Civilians working for your military will be required to have special paperwork and different I.D. badges.

"Mr. President between your office putting pressure on Mexican President Longo and our state forces monitoring his progress on stopping the illegal entry of his nationals, we should be able to determine his effectiveness within a day or two. Remember, if he fails to halt and reduce these trespassers to a trickle the border will remain tightly closed. We will fight to stop this invasion Mr. President. It's been going on for too long," Sara reminded the group, "but it will stop now."

"Okay, I have agreed to many things this afternoon," President Obama told the gathering, "but now I want something, Governor. No matter what, I want that border reopened within the next forty-eight hours at the latest. I want the free flow of goods to continue without any delays or any kind," he insisted.

"It depends on President Longo, Mr. President, totally on the Mexican President."

"If President Longo fails to meet your expectations on stopping his people from attempting to enter your border states, I still, no matter what, want that border reopened," the President stated. "If the border is not reopened within the next forty-eight hours as I said, I will order the military to attack your state forces along the border and reopen the entire two thousand miles with deadly force."

Governor Williamson sprang from her seat jarring the table and spilling the glass of water. Once she recovered, Sara calmly said, "Mr. President, if you attack our state forces, Americans by the tens of thousands and eventually millions will die. Not only military combatants will die but innocent civilians will also pay the ultimate price. Please reconsider your last statement and allow the Mexican government time to solve this immigration problem," she pleaded. "All-out war is not the answer," Sara answered as she gathered her briefcase and assorted papers and motioned to her group the meeting was over. The three governors left the meeting and headed for the only government building completed in the capitol of Flagstaff.

 **rickshaw**

President Obama, Secretaries of State and Defense, along with the President's National Security Advisor headed for the airport and waiting Air Force One for the flight back to Washington and a meeting with his entire military and civilian staff.

Once inside the new federal building in Flagstaff, the three Governors sat down and admitted that the border situation could have turned for the worse with the President's statement and time deadline. "We better contact General Wittingham and have him alert our forces that the Federal Government might attack our troops within the next few days."

"I'll contact the General," Marilyn offered as she left the room to call the Commanding General and authorize him to up the alert status to all troops along the border. "The possibility of combat between Federal troops and State troops is getting greater by the day."

Sara told the group that she was going to contact President Longo and tell him that the states were growing short of patience and wanted to see more activity by his Mexican military along the border. He was running out of time. Between his immigration problems and the various drug cartels trying to take over the entire country, his administration was going to be short lived. "If he isn't assassinated during all this, I'll be very much surprised," she admitted, shaking her head. Sara called Mexico City and for once got the Mexican President within minutes.

"Mr. President, we need more action by your military in rounding up your nationals trying to enter our border states. You are running out of time, sir."

"Governor, I don't like the tone of your voice, it sounds to me like a threat," the Mexican President answered quickly.

"You can call it what you want, sir, but our border will remain closed, and I mean closed tight, if you don't stop your nationals from crossing the Rio Grande and the desert areas and entering our states. If you don't stop this unlawful act, our border troops will start shooting your people as they attempt to enter American soil. Once they set foot on U.S. soil they are fair game," the Arizona Governor said in anger. She continued, "The various drug lords are planning to overthrow your administration and government, Mr. President. We have many field agents inside these cartel organizations and the word is you're through as President of Mexico. Before this takes place, stop your people from crossing our border or we'll do it for you with deadly force." With that, Sara hung-up the phone without waiting for President Longo's answer.

"That son-of-a-bitch still doesn't get it," she said, pounding the table in anger and disgust. "Please contact General Wittingham again, I want to get his military opinion on shooting these lawbreakers trying to enter our country."

The Commanding General was on the phone within fifteen minutes and voiced his opposition against shooting unarmed Mexican nationals. But indicated that armed intruders would be shot on sight.

Sara thanked the General for his opinion and asked if our border state forces were ready for an attack by federal forces.

"Yes, Governor, they are ready and fully equipped to meet the federal forces," the General said with confidence. "But, as you know, and we have all known from the onset that state forces could never win an all-out battle with the federal government and with its collective military power. Every week more than fifteen hundred new recruits join our military to fight against the central government and specifically President Obama and his do nothing administration towards saving this country from outside forces." The General continued, "I still have the feeling that other states will secede from the union within the next few months. The number of states could eventually total some twelve states seeking independence from our federal government. We must not give in, our leadership in the endeavor must be solid in unity and states' rights must be upheld. Is there anything else?" Governor the General asked.

"No, General, that's all, and thank you for your comments."

"Governor, it's Lt. Col. McBride on your secure line."

"Thank you, Marian."

"What's up, Colonel?" Sara asked.

"Governor, our twelve teams of liaison officers visited more than sixty-five military camps along the Mexican border and we have repeatedly seen the Mexican military capture a few nationals crossing the Rio Grande or trucking across the desert while allowing many more to escape and enter the border states.

 rickshaw

We're wasting our time Governor, while they're catching a few they're allowing many to slip through and enter the states. I have spoken to General Rōjas but my complaints have fallen on deaf ears."

"Thank you, Colonel, I'll get back to you shortly," Sara told her lead liaison officer.

Both parties hung-up.

Governor Williamson called the other three Governors and related the call form Lt, Col. McBride. She continued, "Our friend General Rōjas is not doing the job he promised to do. His troops are only doing a token service in rounding up these people trying to enter our country. I'm going to call President Longo and tell him the plan to stop all illegals from crossing our border isn't working."

"Good morning, Mr. President. Thank you for returning my call right away," Sara said in a calm voice.

"Thank you, Governor, what do you want?" he said in a voice with a hint of annoyance.

"Sir, our arrangement between us is not working. General Rōjas and his men are not stopping the bulk of Mexican nationals from leaving your country and entering ours. Unless this changes immediately we will take charge of this problem and stop all traffic trying to enter our four states. And, Mr. President, when I say stop, I mean stop for good. No capture and no return, most probably death, Mr. President."

"You're telling me, Governor, that you're going to kill my fellow Mexican citizens?"

"My god, Mr. President, you finally got it. Yes, we're going to shoot your citizens upon entering our country by crossing the Rio Grande or the desert area of New Mexico, Arizona and Texas. We're done screwing around with you and your government Mr. President. The only thing you understand is action and action you will get. You have just twenty-four hours to make significant changes and much needed results or we'll take over and solve this hundred year old problem. No more talk, Mr. President, just action on our part if you don't stop this exodus." With that Sara slammed the phone down in anger. "Damn him," she said throwing her note pad across the room. She thought, "Dealing with these third world leaders is like trying to talk sense to a three year old."

Sara called General Wittingham and informed him that the next twenty-four hours will determine the outcome for the twelve liaison groups covering the two thousand miles of Mexican-American border. She told her Commanding General that she had informed the Mexican President that they would start shooting all illegals that attempt to enter our four states. Before the General could respond, Sara said, "You know, sir, we will not shoot unarmed civilians, but Longo doesn't know that."

"You're right, Governor, we will not shoot any unarmed civilians, but we will shoot anyone carrying a weapon. But, we're not going to return these illegals to Mexico so they can try again and again to enter our country. Once captured I would recommend that they be sent offshore to a secure island and held for an undetermined length of time."

"Yes, General, I agree, now let's see what happens during the next 24 hours. If President Longo does nothing, we'll recall our liaison people and take over the duties of stopping these people."

President Longo called General Rōjas and ordered him to stop capturing and holding Mexican nationals from leaving Mexico and attempting to enter the states.

The General was happy to get that order, he disagreed with the orders of stopping all nationals from attempting to upgrade their lives in America. Rōjas called his border command center and ordered them to stop arresting all nationals, but be prepared for anything the Americans might try or do.

Twenty-four hours passed and no word from President Longo or General Rōjas was received in Governor Williamson's headquarters. Sara was about to contact Lt. Col. McBride when she was informed that the Colonel was on the phone.

"Good morning, Colonel, I was just about to call you. You first Colonel."

"Governor, the Mexican military has pulled back their people that were stopping the nationals form crossing the border. It's back to open season for all illegals to flood across the border as before. What the hell is going on with our Mexican friends? I thought they wanted the border reopened so their economy can restart," the Colonel added.

"So did I, Colonel," Sara said, shaking her head. "That son-of-a-bitch," she muttered to herself. "Please contact the

Mexican President," she asked her communications director, Marian Wilcox.

"Yes, ma'am."

After an hour wait, the Mexican President returned Governor Williamson's urgent call. "What is it now?" the President asked in broken English and a very sarcastic and nasty sounding voice.

"Well, sir, I just heard that you pulled all your troops away from their prime duty of stopping all illegal traffic from entering the U.S. What the hell is wrong with you, Mr. President, you have obviously lost your small mind. I guess you don't give a rat's ass about your own people and what's going to happen to your country as a whole.

"I'm putting you on notice, Mr. President, that you're now responsible for all deaths occurred at the border by not stopping the border crashers. Since you failed to uphold your bargain with me, I have ordered the two-thousand miles of border with Mexico closed to all traffic. That means all vehicle and foot traffic, Mr. President. Your trucks filled with cargo have backed up for more than one hundred miles will remain nose to tail until they turn to dust as far as I'm concerned. I've been told, and our spy in the sky satellites have seen, that your stalled trucks are being broken into and their merchandise stolen.

Mr. President, you will not survive the economy shutdown and the total anarchy that will certainly rein throughout Mexico. It's going to be dog eat dog. The drug cartel will now be in charge of the Mexican government and all the people of Mexico. Bands of bandits will roam throughout your country, Mr. President, robbing, killing and plundering everything worth having. Your country will revert back to the early 18th century and all its lawless factions. Goodbye, Mr. President, I shan't call you again," the Arizona Governor told the Mexican President. With that Sara carefully replaced the phone and sat back in her chair thinking of the disaster that is about to happen.

"Well that cuts it," she said out loud. "Get me General Wittingham A.S.A.P."

"The General is on line #2."

"Yes, Governor, I know, Colonel McBride has just called me and I have recalled all twelve liaison officers and their helicopter crews. Before leaving Mexico they dropped off their liaison Mexican counterparts and all twelve groups have safely returned to their home bases Governor."

"Thank you, General, for taking fast action and protecting our men in harm's way. Make sure your individual commanders along the border are aware of the latest pull back by the Mexican military. I'm sure most are already aware of the changes," she added. "I want the border closed even tighter than ever, no one allowed from Mexico to enter our four states along its entire length. Please make this happen, General."

"Will do, Governor, a Mexican mouse won't be able to slip through, I promise you."

"Great, General Wittingham. Please keep me informed 24/7," she asked.

"Will do, ma'am."

"Marian, call Governors Richardson, LaCrosse and Anderson. Let them know the latest turn of events and if necessary have them call me."

President Obama received an urgent call from Mexican President Longo complaining that the border was still closed. The Mexican Chief Executive said, "I will order an attack on the border states forces if the border isn't reopened in the next few hours."

"You better not start a war, Mr. President, you can't win that type of conflict, sir. Your Mexican forces will be crushed in short order and your country will suffer huge military and civilian deaths once the smoke clears. Your country will turn into lawless mobs and your government rule will end quickly."

"Your Governor Williamson has basically told me the same thing," the Mexican President revealed.

"Well, Mr. President, I agree with Sara, and you better think twice about attacking our state forces, General Wittingham and his military forces will turn your country into a fifth class country in a matter of days. You have plenty of critical problems to deal with, Mr. President. Currently the drug cartels are licking their chops in anticipation of your stupid move to attack our border forces. You better start acting like the President of all Mexican citizens and stop the illegal traffic on both fronts. First, stop your citizens from crossing our border; and second, stop the illegal traffic in drugs.

"Let me be frank, Mr. President, your administration is completely rattled with corrupt government officials, judges and every level of city, town and village officials. Local law enforcement are in bed with the drug cartels and receive payoffs to look the other way.

"I understand the fear of being murdered and their families harmed if they do their jobs. Not only are your government officials being bought off, but your military is in cahoots with the drug lords and allowing their poison to flow into the United States. Not only do they turn a blind eye, but they help them cross the border in the form of protection from our border guards.

"You have done nothing to stop this escalating drug problem that well completely engulf your country within the next six months or less. You better get your act together my friend or your country will slip back into the lawless land of centuries ago.

"Let me give you a little advice and warning President Longo. If you attack the state forces along the border, I will order my federal troops to assist the state forces in their fight against your forces. I will not standby and allow your peasant country to rein its terror throughout our mutual border. Maybe it would be to our advantage if we overran your country and shot all members of these drug cartels along with your officials that are on the payroll of the drug lords. But if we did that, your administration wouldn't have anyone left, Mr. President. You better change and act immediately or you and your government are finished."

Without another word the Mexican President slammed the phone down and ended the one way conversation with President Obama.

President Obama asked National Security Advisor Jennings to contact the Chairman of the Joint Chiefs and arrange an emergency meeting in the Pentagon war room as soon as possible.

Prior to the war room meeting President Obama called the Arizona Governor and related his lengthy conversation with Mexican President Longo. "I know, Governor, that we're at odds on many fronts, but not when it comes to the safety of your four states and the balance of the United States. If that idiot in charge of Mexico attacks your border forces I'm offering our military to

78

assist in your defense. I know I'm late, but better late than never."

"Thank you, Mr. President, I'll keep you informed minute by minute if necessary," she added.

"One more thing, Sara, I know I'm largely to blame for this Mexican immigration problem. I should have stopped this illegal invasion years ago but I ignored the threat for millions of illegal votes and I was wrong. The safety and security of all U.S. citizens along the border should have come first. For this I regret my previous inaction."

"Thank you, Mr. President, for your candid remarks and I'll keep in touch, sir."

Both parties hung-up and Sara thought, "My god he finally admits his shortcomings after all this time, but it's never too late to come clean."

Chapter 4
MEXICO'S NEW LEADERSHIP

Sara called the other three Governors and brought them up to specks on all conversations with both Presidents. She warned them to be on high alert do to the unpredictability of Mexican President Longo. "Since our Mexican friends aren't stopping the illegals, let's gather them up and start housing them in the camp south of Gila Bend. This facility will hold about two thousand inmates but can be expanded quickly to house more than five thousand. There are a few buildings and many long rows of squad tents to house our guests. This camp is very secure the outside perimeter consists of two fifteen foot high barbed wire fences operated by a ten foot guard path. This will be a good holding facility until we can determine just what to do with these illegals. I don't think that transportation will be a problem, but if it is we can use school buses along with our military vehicles. Does that solution sound okay with you guys?" she asked her fellow Governors.

"Yes, Sara, that sounds good to me. A desert facility sounds better than a city holding pen," Marilyn LaCrosse added.

"We also agree," Eric and Paul chimed in.

"Good. If you experience any problems let me know quickly," Sara told the group.

"Yes, ma'am," they answered.

As Sara replaced the phone she wondered, "What the hell will transpire in the next day or so. Will there be war between Mexico and our four states, will there be war between us and the Federal government? Will the country of Mexico slip into the lawless abyss and be governed by the drug cartels? If that happens, the United States will be largely effected with the input of thousands of pounds of cocaine, heroin and pot. The U.S. will become the prime buyer of all the poison they can smuggle across the border. Good god, the world is getting crazier by the day," she said with a sigh.

President Longo was leaving his Presidential residence in Mexico City and about to enter his armored car when a car drove up and three masked gun men jumped out and spayed the President, his two body guards and driver with automatic gun

fire from their AK-47s. The President and his bodyguards were killed instantly. The driver tried to close the car door but one of the gun men stuck his gun through the open window and shot the President's driver dead. The masked gun slingers made sure President Longo was dead before speeding away.

The Mexican nation was shocked at the death of their long time President. The Chino drug cartel sent a note to the local T.V. station claiming responsibility for the shooting death of President Longo.

Vice President Pedro Lazzara was in the coastal city of Mazatlán when he heard the news of the assassination of his long time friend and president. His Chief-of-Staff immediately requested an additional security force for the next President of Mexico. Once the shock was over Lazzara proceeded by air to Mexico City and the President's residence to comfort Edwardo's wife and children.

The new President went on national T.V. and denounced the wanton murder of the President. He assured the country that the killers of his friend would be brought to justice and punished to the fullest extent of the law. He also told the nation and the numerous drug cartels. "Beware, this country will not stand for this open violence and be assured this administration will not tolerate the drug cartels and this country will not be overrun by these monsters. Enough is enough, this must stop now. God bless our country, and I'll keep you informed on our progress in solving the President's death. Good bye for now my friends."

When his national address was finished, he called for a meeting with all his top military and civilian leaders. The following day at 10:00 am he had his first meeting with his staff. "Gentlemen, as you new President I'm going to issue this warning just once. Anyone that is caught taking bribes in cash, goods and favors from any drug lord or cartel will receive a jail term of life in prison. That covers everyone from this staff to the local judges and the cops that are charged with protecting small villages. We must stop these huge drug consortiums from bribing their way into poisoning and destroying our fine country. If anyone fears for their lives, and cannot do their jobs under these burdens, I want your resignation here and now. This group is going to be squeaky-clean or in jail. We're going to start right now, gentlemen, let's start cleaning up our cities, towns and streets of these less than human beings. Now let's bury our President and get on with the business of saving this country from ourselves."

President Longo was buried next to his parents in a small cemetery north of Mexico City in the town of Texcoco. Many foreign representatives were present at the funeral including the Vice President of the United States, Charles Goodwin.

Two days after the funeral, President Lazzara called a meeting with his Commanding General Rōjas and his staff. "Gentlemen, the first thing I want is your understanding that I will not tolerate any activity that degrades the office and command you hold. And that includes all ranks under your command as well. You're an officer and a gentleman and I expect nothing less form all of you. Do you understand my meaning?"

"Yes, sir, we do," they said in unison.

"Good.

"Now the second thing. I want a full company of two hundred and fifty men for a very special and dangerous assignment.

#1. These men must be single
#2. These men must be bi-lingual (English)
#3. These men must be paratroopers
#4. These men must wear special uniforms
#5. These men must not want for any special equipment necessary to complete their assignment
#6. These men must be crossed trained in everything from radio operator to helicopter pilot
#7. These men must be smart and not just trigger happy
#8. These men must be of the highest caliber
#9. These men will receive special pay three times their rank.

"Search your units and assemble these men for this special and deadly assignment. I need these men within the next two weeks, gentlemen."

"If we know, can we tell them what the dangerous assignment is, Mr. President?" a General asked.

"No. I will explain their duties when they are assembled. Good men won't ask," he added.

"Now let's get busy and find these special individuals so I can put them to work." The meeting was over and the room cleared quickly. "I think they probably can guess why I want this special group of men and women, but I won't tell them," he thought.

President Lazzara asked his aide to contact Arizona Governor Williamson as quickly as possible.

Within an hour Sara Williamson was on the phone with the new Mexican President.

"Congratulations, Mr. President, even though it's under very disturbing circumstances."

"Thank you, Governor, for your comments and understanding," the Mexican President said in flawless English. "May I call you Sara?" he asked.

"Yes, sir, you certainly may," she answered.

"Very good," he said.

"Why I'm calling, Sara, I need an American Officer of high rank with long service and with combat experience but not a politician. He needs to be a soldier first and have a great common sense. He must be single, fearless and speak fluent Spanish. He must also realize that this assignment is dangerous and could cost him his life. You're wondering why do I need an American to lead instead of a Mexican officer.

"I'm forming a special company of two hundred and fifty men who speak English and are comparable to your special forces. Once this unit is formed and ready for their assignment their prime duty will be to locate, arrest and stamp out drug activity and capture every member of the many drug cartels as well as any member of my government that are accepting bribes of any kind. I want an American officer to share command with General Rōjas and lead this special unit.They will report to me and me alone."

"My god, Mr. President, you lay a lot on a girl during our first telephone call." Both laughed.

"I'll get back to you within a day or so," she told the new head of state.

"That will be fine," he answered.

Both parties hung-up without another word.

"Boy that's some request coming from Mexico's new President," she thought. Sara asked Marian to contact the other governors and schedule a meeting somewhere of their choice. After contacting the governors, they settled on the city of Sacramento at noon the next day.

Sara started off the noon meeting by saying, "You're not going to believe this, but here goes." She related her telephone conversation with Mexico's new President in great detail and when she finished there was dead silence. "Well, what do you think?" she said standing up.

Eric broke the silence, "I think this is a golden opportunity to upgrade our relationship with Mexico since we now have a new and progressive President at the helm. I like his plan to attack the drug problem head on and balls to the wall type of action."

"I agree with Eric," Marilyn said looking at the large map of Mexico. "If he can make a dent in the drug traffic with his Special Forces unit, we should consider giving him additional special equipment in support of his unit."

"I like that idea also," Paul told the group. "When we decide on the American leader and he has addressed the issue and reviewed what equipment is available in Mexico, I'm sure he will have additional requirements and ideas."

"Alright, let's start the search," Sara told her cohorts. "Please call General Wittingham and get his staff searching for this Major or Lt. Colonel who better be a superman and a warrior first class. Tell the General the whole story and remind him we need this unique individual as soon as possible."

Within two days General Miles called Governor Williamson and said Wittingham's staff had called and indicated they believe they had found their man. They gave the following description of this unique individual:

He is 54, and shortly will be 55.
He is a Lt. Colonel, soon to be a full bird.
He is single.
His service is 31 years (9 years in the Army).
He is 6'4" and 235 lbs.
He speaks fluent Spanish and French.
He served two tours in Iraq and two in
Afghanistan.

He participated in the Grenada landing.
He has his airborne wings (can fly fixed wing and helicopters)
He is willing to take on this very special assignment in Mexico.
He is a top notch Army officer and first class warrior.
His name is Lt. Col. Michael Montgomery.

"Ma'am I can't wait to meet this very special officer," General Miles told his boss.

"With that description, General, I believe he could be our man," Sara indicated looking over her glasses. "Call Wittingham's staff and ask them when I can meet with Colonel Montgomery."

"Right away, ma'am," the General said, picking up the phone and calling General Wittingham's command headquarters.

Within ten minutes Sara had her answer, Lt. Colonel Montgomery would arrive in Flagstaff tomorrow morning.

Chapter 5
DRUG CARTELS

Colonel Montgomery arrive at the capitol building in Flagstaff and General Miles guided him to Governor Williamson's office. The General introduced the light colonel to the next and first President of their new nation, and after a handshake they quickly sat down for this unusual interview for an Army officer.

"Thank you Colonel for offering to take this very special and unusual assignment. The only reason I requested this get together was due to the great importance of this operation to our new country and our Mexican neighbors. If the border is going to be reopened soon, the Mexican government must stop all nationals from attempting to enter our border states and beyond. The new Mexican President seems like he wants to change his country by stopping the drug cartels from spreading their poison and also stopping the illegal entry into the border states and the rest of United States."

Sara continued, "You will have one hell of a job in finding, capturing and bringing to justice and even killing the cartel members when required. You'll be in command of a company of the best Mexican military personnel they have. Your group will be dropped into the Mexican jungle or the center of a larger city in search of drug cartel members. Colonel, your 'officer and a gentlemen' status will not work in Mexico. Your fair play and high moral values will have to be left behind once you cross into Mexican territory. In some respects you'll become a military killer, stamping out the scum of mankind that brings poisons to our children and adults in our country." Sara said, "It's a shitty job at best and no American officer should be required to accept this almost no win assignment. With all this, Colonel, are you sure you want to take on this terrible assignment? You know it most probably will cost you your life."

"Yes, Governor, I'm well aware of the risk involved in this endeavor with the Mexican government. I'll do whatever it takes to complete this very unusual assignment."

"You might be required to shoot first and ask questions later," she added.

 rickshaw

"Yes, Ma'am, you're probably right, some circumstances may require just that," the Colonel added. "I'm dealing with cartel members, restraint is not an option, Governor. They only understand death and death is the only answer I'm afraid."

"Okay, Colonel, when can you meet with the Mexican President and start this critical action against the many drug cartels?" the Governor asked.

"Right away," he answered.

"Thank you very much, Colonel, you're one hell of an officer," she added.

The next morning Colonel Montgomery flew to Mexico City to meet with Mexican President Lazzara. General Rōjas met the American Colonel at the airport and they headed for the President's residence and their first meeting. Once the introductions were over and President Lazzara read the Colonel's jacket, they got down to the assignment and its particular and unique requirements. After only fifteen minutes the Mexican President was convinced this American officer was the right man to share command of his Mexican Special Forces unit. Most of the meeting was conducted in Spanish with some English terms slipped into the mix. After the meeting, General Rōjas accompanied Colonel Montgomery to Army Headquarters outside the city of Queretaro which was two hours by plane from Mexico City.

General Rōjas assembled the special unit and had Lt. Colonel Montgomery address the elite group.

He spoke in Spanish and laid out the general plan as he knew it. They were to locate, capture, arrest and kill if need be to break up the cartel and all its members. The captured cartel members would be held in a maximum security prison under extremely heavy guard and electronic monitoring to insure non escape or outside attempts to free the cartel members.

When Colonel Montgomery finished he asked the group if they had any questions or concerns about their primary assignment. He also reminded them that a certain number of them would surely be killed during the many raids and encounters with the heavily armed cartel members, and if any man wanted out of this unit he should step forward now. With that one member of the company stepped out of line and approached the Colonel and said, "I'm not going to resign, sir, but you should know I'm a woman and I can fight and kill when required as good as any man in this outfit. My name is Anna," she informed her Colonel. With that she returned to her position in the company.

"Well, Anna, I'm very glad to know you and from now on your name is Butch as far as I'm concerned," the Colonel added. With the comment the whole company broke into laughter and started calling her Butch.

"Thank you, gentlemen and Butch, we'll be receiving our first assignment tomorrow morning, and at the time we'll cover the usual where, when, how and who details."

"Company, attention."

"Officers, release your men until formation tomorrow morning at 06:00 hundred." When the company had dispersed, the Colonel returned to their headquarters building to confer with General Rōjas and his staff.

General Rōjas informed Colonel Montgomery that throughout Mexico they had identified some five separate drug cartels. "Four of which are very large and control most of Mexico. While these cartels generally work in their own territory, from time to time war breaks out between them and blood flows like water while many members die."

Rōjas continued, "The Mexican government has pinpointed the headquarters and location of three large cartels. The General's Chief of Staff placed all the location maps on the table for Colonel Montgomery to review.

"Gentlemen, before we commit our forces I want some satellite photos of these areas before we attempt to engage these cartel members. We need to know the following, General:

- What is the terrain
- How many buildings
- Approx. how many cartel members are present
- What type of weapons do they have
- Where will we land
- How will we escape
- What are their communications
- What is their route of escape
- Do they have any aircraft
- What is the nearest town
- Can we land helicopters
  And so on.

rickshaw

   "I'll have some Tasker birds reassigned and realigned to fly over this area so we can have the latest intel and clear pictures of the jungle sites," Col. Montgomery added.

   The Colonel immediately placed a call to General Wittingham and requested the re-alignment to a Tasker bird to cover the areas in question. Wittingham said he would call the Chairman of the Joint Chiefs and have him authorize a bird reassignment to cover the Mexican locations under review.

   "How long before we'll have these photos?" Colonel Montgomery asked.

   "Unless these is a problem, I would guess within four hours or less," the General answered.

   "That's fine, sir." Both parties hung-up.

   "General, is that okay?" the American Colonel asked.

   "Well done, Colonel," the Mexican Commanding General said in amazement that the Tasker birds could be changed so easily.

   "Now we just have to wait for the photos before we can plan our attack, General."

   "Let's have a quick bite to eat while we're waiting," the General suggested.

   "Good, sir, I'm starved," the Colonel answered.

   Within hours the Tasker birds were realigned and the photos started coming in. They were crystal clear and showed every little detail on the ground. Without these photos any attempt to storm the cartel compound would have ended in complete disaster. Gun towers were seen in the photos as well as underground entrances. Even Ford 150 pickup trucks were seen in the photos with machine guns installed in the beds.

   President Lazzara called General Rōjas and asked how the roundup of our nationals was progressing along the border.

   "Well, Mr. President, the order has gone out to step up the apprehension of all persons attempting to cross the border and enter the United States. We have also contacted the American military guarding the border to start up their liaison flights again. They can again verify our current efforts and upon seeing our progress will shortly reopen the entire Mexican/American border."

   "Very good, General, but operation round-up must show immediate results so the damn border can be reopened before our economy grinds to a complete halt," the Mexican President said with annoyance in his voice.

"Yes, sir, I understand, and I'm confident when the Americans see our progress, the entire length of the border will reopen within the next day or two."

"I hope you're right General, we must get the border opened without further delay," the President pressed his top General.

Sara was informed by General Wittingham, "The Mexican government has restarted operation <u>round-up</u> and have asked that we start monitoring their program again with our liaison officers and twelve helicopter gunships. We're assembling the crews and ships today and we'll start the flights and monitoring the round-up as early as tomorrow."

"That's great news, General, let's hope they mean it this time so we can reopen the entire two thousand mile border and have goods and services restarted in Mexico so their economy can leap forward. Their economy has ground to a complete halt and anarchy was gaining momentum until President Longo was assassinated and the likable Vice President Pedro Lazzara was elevated to the Presidency. General, would you have Lt. Colonel McBride call me daily on the Mexican round-up progress?" Sara added.

"Yes, Ma'am," the General answered.

Both parties hung-up.

Sara contacted the three other Governors and related the latest effort by the new Mexican President to stop the illegal entry by their nationals. "In the matter of days he has restarted operation round-up and operation special ops is about to become a real force in attacking the drug cartels on their own home turf. Remember, he also asked for an American officer to command his special ops group. He seems to have the where for all to get things done in short order," Sara related.

Colonel Montgomery and General Rōjas received the Satellite photos of the three known areas where the drug cartels are operating their billion dollar enterprising endeavors. The Colonel and the four Mexican officers of the Special Ops Company poured over the photos for hours to understand all the possible things that could go wrong when their attack starts.

The first area of intent was outside the small town of Santa Maria, in the providence of Chihuahua. The cartel was located in a chunk of no man's land almost sixty sq. miles of thick brush and scrub trees that could hide a division let alone a cartel with some one hundred members. It was located just west of Route #45 and north of the San Pedro River. Entrance into this area was only by a single dirt road which was easy to defend. The area was truly wild and wooly. The cartel within the area are known as the "Digno" Cartel. This group of ruthless killers would waste anyone regardless of stature or position to continue their work of spreading their poison.

The second area was inside Durango Providence just west of the town of San Louis del Cordero, between Route #45 and the river Nazas. The area was approximately twenty sq. miles of low rolling hills covered with thick underbrush and cactus, with only one dirt road in or out. Their handle was the Chavez" cartel, and the home base of about two hundred members scattered throughout the fifteen buildings that made up the entire complex. Also there was a small runway that could accommodate any type of two engine aircraft. The usual trucks, jeeps and assorted weapons were also visible in the overhead photograph.

The third area of interest was the town of Matamoros in the providence of Hidalgo in an area east of Route #190 and west of Route #150. The area was some thirty sq. miles of very thick jungle where travel is very difficult. The satellite photos showed very little of the large compound that was rumored to be under the jungle canopy. Only a small section of a roof could be seen in all the photos provided. But the infrared heat sensors showed some one hundred and forty cartel members within the sprawling compound. The photos even showed workers inside a large building in an assembly line configuration. This lack of overall intel could really be a problem in mounting an offense in this cartel stronghold. This cartel stronghold was known as the Santiago cartel. They controlled most of the lower half of Mexico and were by far the largest and most deadly of the five known cartels.

Now the Mexican military and Colonel Montgomery needed to decide on how and when to strike at these three known cartel strongholds.

Lt. Colonel McBride called Governor Williamson and reported, "After only one day, they have seen the Mexican military and local law enforcement personnel intercepting hundreds of Mexican nationals along the entire length of the border. Along the Rio Grande the military is actually in the water to stop everyone from entering the border states."

"That's great news, Colonel," the Governor said, pounding her desk. "This new President is keeping his word to me. If this continues for the next day or two I'll consider lifting the blockade on the border and allowing Mexican trucking to again reenter the border states and proceed throughout the remaining states. Colonel, are all the helicopter gunships seeing the same round-up?" Sara asked.

"Yes, Ma'am. They are. All twelve ships are seeing the same gathering."

"Thank you, Colonel."

Both parties hung-up.

President Lazzara called General Rōjas and asked when the first attack was scheduled on the drug cartels.

"Sir, I want you to talk to Colonel Montgomery."

"Put him on, General."

"Colonel Montgomery, Mr. President."

"When is your first attack on the drug cartel scheduled?" the Mexican President asked the American Colonel.

"Well, sir, I'd prefer not to say over the phone. When we decide on the time only General Rōjas and I will have that information. Our troops will only know the exact location minutes before we land. Remember our chances of a complete surprise attack is almost nil, Mr. President, because of cell phones and the payoffs for protection throughout your government, sir."

"Very good, Colonel, keep your plans are close to your chest for security reasons. Call me after your raid is over and fill me in on all the details," the President asked.

"Yes, sir, will do," the American Colonel answered.

"General, I think we should attack the Dingo and Chavez cartels at the same time. We'll split our forces and send one hundred twenty-five men into each area. You command one group and I'll fly the lead helicopter and command the second group. There will be less chance of one cartel alerting the other about a pending attack. The Santiago cartel will certainly require our whole force and much more intel," the Colonel advised. "We'll need a minimum of ten choppers to transport our forces and their equipment to each site, General. Once the compound is overpowered and rendered secure, the captured cartel members and their equipment, product and various supplies will be transported by land vehicles to our secure location in the Province of Zacatecas, outside the town of Caritas. The old prison facility is perfect for housing these cartel members, it's out of the way and can be defended very easily.

"General you should pick these men who will guard these cartel guests. Men above reproach who can be trusted one hundred percent. I've been told we can house approximately five hundred inmates at that facility. Do you agree General?"

"Yes, I do, Colonel. I will personally pick these guards and I'll vouch for them myself. They'll be at the location within 24 hrs."

"Good enough, General."

After days of monitoring the Mexican operation round-up, Lt. Colonel McBride and his fellow liaison officers agreed that the Mexican authorities were getting a real handle on the operation to stop the flow of illegal entry into the border states. Even the State military guarding the border had only captured a few Mexican nationals in those few days. They also agreed the Mexican operation is working.

Lt. Colonel McBride contacted General Wittingham and informed him, "As far as I'm concerned, the Mexican government is fulfilling their promise to stop the influx of illegals." He has also talked to General Miles, Barker, Wadsworth and Colonel Wheeler. They agreed with the overall consensus that the flow of nationals trying to enter the U.S. was drying up.

"Thank you, Colonel. I'll contact Governor Williamson and suggest to her that we reopen the entire border as soon as possible. Please contact the rest of your liaison groups and have them drop off their Mexican officers and return their helicopters to our bases in the various states."

"Yes, sir, I'll inform all groups right away," the Colonel answered.

"Governor, General Wittingham is on line #3," her aide said, passing her the secure phone.

"What's up, General," Sara asked.

The General related his conversation with Colonel McBride and the other commanders. "As the result, Ma'am, I would suggest we open the border as quickly as possible."

"Well, sir, I agree. Please give the order to your border commanders to reopen all bridges and highways leading into the U.S."

"Please give me fifteen minutes while I contact President Lazzara and tell him we're reopening the border immediately," Sara asked.

"Call me when the Mexican President has been informed," the General asked.

"Certainly," Sara answered.

Within ten minutes, Mexican President Lazzara was on the phone and was pleased to hear the words, "We're reopening the entire border immediately. Mr. President, you kept your word to me and I'm keeping mine to you, sir."

"Thank you, Governor, I'll get the word out to all our trucking companies that the border has been reopened and the word is go. I'm sure it will take a day or two to get things moving again. I know some trucks have been robbed and some disabled, but once they're cleared away some fifty thousand plus trucks will be rolling towards the border. One more thing, Governor, we're about to launch operation "Special Ops". After the initial attack and capture I'll call with the details. Both General Rōjas and your Colonel Montgomery have done a great job getting their forces ready for the coming mission. With the help of your country, the satellite photos have provided much needed intel on the exact location of these drug cartels. One more thing, we currently have sufficient number of helicopters to complete the missions but we don't have any spare aircraft. If we have mechanical trouble or they're shot down, we don't have any replacements. Can you help?"

"Certainly, Mr. President. The twelve copters used to monitor your round-up effort will be available for your use, sir. Let me know when and where you want these helicopters delivered. They are armed with the latest weaponry available, Mr. President," she added.

"General Rōjas or Colonel Montgomery will contact you shortly with the information. Thank you again, Governor, or can I call you Sara?" the President asked in his usual perfect English.

"You certainly may," she answered.

Both parties said "Goodbye," and disconnected.

Sara contacted General Wittingham and asked him to prepare the twelve helicopters for shipment to Mexico. The

 rickshaw

Mexican President said, "General Rōjas or Colonel Montgomery will contact us with the when and where to deliver these choppers. Right now this is only a loan," she added.

"The choppers will be ready within a few hours," the top General assured is boss.

"Thank you, Charles."

Both parties hung up without another word.

Governor Richardson called and said, "All the signs are up at each major road and bridge entering into California. These immigration check points are up and ready but not staffed until the rest of the three states are up and ready. One thing we left off the signs is the name of our new country."

"That's great, Eric, I'll contact the others and see when they'll be ready to open their checkpoints. As far as Arizona goes, we should be ready in a couple of days I've been told by our highway superintendent."

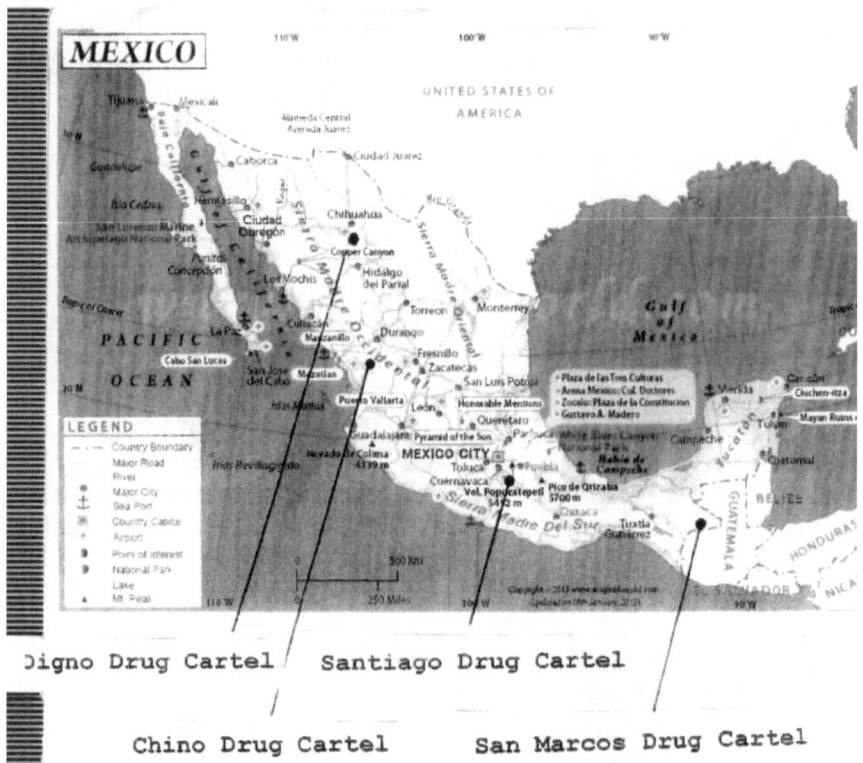

Digno Drug Cartel   Santiago Drug Cartel

Chino Drug Cartel   San Marcos Drug Cartel

Chapter 5 – Drug Cartels

"Now about the name, I've been thinking about our future name for months the same as you. What do you think of asking all our people to come up with a name? Let's have a prize for the winning name submitted by a resident of the four states. We can start off the contest with the following names:

The New American West	Western States of America
New America	America South
America West	Americona
West America	Union of Western America
United Western States	Western Union of American States
Western American Union	United Western America

"I think that's a good idea Sara, but let's have the four of us Governors be the judges and have the final say to our future name."

"Okay, but contact the others and get their input," she suggested.

"Will do," he answered.

At 02:30 half of the Special Ops Company under the command of Colonel Montgomery were assembled and ready to hear the destination and cartel name they were going to hit.

Colonel Montgomery stepped up on the platform and said: "Attention."

The company snapped to attention and waited for their leader to finally divulge their target.

"At ease," the Colonel yelled.

"Our night goggles and special gear have been loaded in our choppers, and we'll be boarding our ten helicopters within fifteen minutes. I'll pilot the first chopper and lead the way into the Digno cartel new the town of Santa Maria in Chihuahua providence. All our cell phones and radio communications will be turned off until we reach the destination area. Communications will resume when the green light appears on your radios.

"Remember, leave the safeties on your weapons until you hit the ground. We don't want any eager beaver to squeeze off a round early and warn our cartel friends. I know they'll hear choppers while we're still about a mile away. But once they hear our approach we'll be on the ground within thirty seconds. I'm sure some cartel members will be awake and ready to welcome our arrival.

"Okay, gentlemen and Butch, you know your job, now let's strike a blow against the drug cartel and hasten its elimination."

"Attention: Board your assigned choppers the Colonel yelled at his Special Ops group."

With that command they scattered and boarded their choppers for the forty minute flight to ground zero.

General Rōjas and his group were on their way to San Luis del Cardero in Durango providence and will spring their attack at the same time as Colonel Montgomery's group in the north.

As Colonel Montgomery's group was landing, their helicopters were being hit by ground fire. All ten choppers landed safely, but four of them were damaged but still air worthy. The Special Ops team quickly killed the guards and rounded up the cartel members that surrendered. They were gathered in the clearing and forced to lay face down while their hands were tied. A large amount of weapons and equipment was collected.

As the Mexican military entered the underground rooms they were amazed at what they saw. The underground cavern was almost one hundred yards long and some sixteen yards wide with thousands of gallons of various processing chemicals and assembly lines that employed about two hundred workers that come from surrounding towns and villages. Huge stainless tanks and open vats were filled with cocaine and its byproducts at various stages of manufacturing. The whole process was a manufacturing marvel. From the receiving dock to the drying room to the final weighing and packaging the whole process was smooth and highly efficient. In the final storage area the kilos of coke were stacked to the ceiling awaiting transportation. There was a helo pad and a dirt road that doubles as an air strip for removing their very expensive end product.

The whole operation and fire fight only lasted about eighteen minutes once the government forces landed and secured the entire compound. The operation did have its cost in human lives, the drug cartel lost fifteen members killed and ten wounded, while capturing thirty-five. Colonel Montgomery's group unfortunately lost seven troopers with twelve wounded, of which only one was critical.

Of the almost two hundred civilian workers inside the underground facility, there were twenty-two killed and more than thirty-eight wounded or injured during the attack. The cartel members inside the processing area sprayed machine gun fire throughout the building in an attempt to escape government forces. Only a few did escape.

Colonel Montgomery and his men quickly gathered up their dead and wounded and transported them by chopper to the nearest hospital. He also contacted President Lazzara in Mexico City and related all pertinent info pertaining to their very successful raid.

President Lazzara was saddened by the loss of so many good soldiers.

"Mr. President, has General Rōjas reported in yet?"

"No, Colonel, he has not. I hope that doesn't mean anything went wrong," President Lazzara said quickly.

"His objective is probably not fully secure yet, Mr. President."

"Let's hope you're right, Colonel. After you have looked after your dead and wounded, please come to Mexico City and see me," the President ordered.

"Yes, sir, I will," the American Colonel answered.

Both parties hung up without another word.

The Colonel listed the total casualties as follows in his final report.

Dead	**Wounded**
7 Gov. Troops	12 Gov. Troops
15 Cartel members	10 Cartel members
<u>22 Civilian workers</u>	<u>38 Civilian workers</u>

44 Dead	**60 Total Wounded**

General Rōjas and his men landed outside San Luis del Cordero and were immediately fired upon with automatic weapons and heavy machine gun fire. Two government helicopters were blasted from the sky by shoulder fired S.T.A. (surface-to-air) missals. All twenty-four combat troops and the four pilots were killed instantly on impact.

The cartel was warned of the government attack and were just waiting in ambush seemingly unafraid. The Chavez cartel was finally secured after an hour of intensive fighting and heavy loss of life on both sides. Government forces lost forty-four dead and twenty-six wounded with four listed in critical condition. Cartel members killed totaled fifty-two with forty-six wounded and eleven listed as critical. Civilians working in the various buildings throughout the compound had twenty-two killed and twenty-one wounded or injured. None of the wounded were listed as critical.

General Rōjas was wounded slightly, he was shot in the left arm but would recover the use of his arm shortly. Once his medical team bandaged his wound, he immediately called his President and reported the action at the Chavez compound.

President Lazzara was shocked at the heavy loss of lives on all sides. He ordered his top General to report to him as soon as possible.

"Yes, Mr. President," the General answered.

Both groups headed for Army Headquarters outside the small city of Queretaro after the government's groomed forces arrived at both locations to transport the remainder of the cartel members to jail, and start destroying the whole compound.

President Lazzara called Governor Williamson and related the government's action against the two drug cartels and the very disturbing cost of human lives on both sides.

Sara reminded the Mexican President that the evil drug cartels only know violence and death. And only violence and death can be used to stop those people. "You must overpower them, but realize that causalities on the government side will be high as well. When dealing with fire you're most likely to get burnt," she said.

"I guess you're right, Sara, but I don't like the cost of doing business with these devils," he answered.

"Just keep after them, Mr. President, don't give them any space or wiggle room. You and your forces must eliminate them from your Mexican society once and for all," Sara insisted.

"Yes, you're correct, Sara, in what you're saying," the President admitted finally.

"Thank you, again," and the Mexican President replaced the phone without saying another word.

Sara thought, "I should have asked how Colonel Montgomery was. I hope he survived his raid on the cartel compound. I'm sure he would have mentioned if our Colonel had been injured."

In Washington, President Obama heard about the two government's attacks on the large drug cartels headed by Lt. Colonel Montgomery and General Rōjas. He thought, "It's about time Mexico took the lead in trying to stop the drug lords from spreading their white poison throughout the States and the world. Sara is getting results from Mexico that my administration couldn't achieve over the past seven and a half years," he thought. "Maybe we deserve these defections by the four states since we did absolutely nothing to stop both the illegal entry by Mexican nationals and their drug traffic," he said in a low voice. "We should have acted."

General Rōjas and Col. Montgomery arrived in Mexico City early in the morning and were quickly driven to the President's residence. His private home was located high on a hill overlooking the sprawling city with its twenty-two million inhabitants. From his front door you could see the early morning smog that embraced the entire city while getting thicker as the day unfolded. Only church spires in the distance were visible above the gray death.

Both officers were ushered into a waiting room and were told that President was in an early meeting and would be available shortly.

The Colonel asked his Mexican friend how his arm was, and the General said, "It hurts like hell." But he added, "It could have been a lot worse."

President Lazzara and his aide-de-camp entered the large waiting room and both officers jumped to attention and saluted their military boss.

"Gentlemen, please be seated, you must be very tired from your fighting two days ago. How is your arm, General?" the Commander-in-Chief asked his favorite officer.

"Fine, sir, just fine."

"That's good," the President said as he settled into a large leather high back chair.

"I've heard and read your reports on the two engagements with the drug cartels and I'm very concerned about the large number of deaths all around." Before either officer could answer the President related his conversation with Governor Williamson while mentioning her comment, "'When dealing with violence and death, you yourself must be violent and willing to kill if necessary.' While I agree with her, I'm still concerned about the number of deaths. I worry about all the deaths but specifically the number of civilians that were killed. Gentlemen, is there anything we can do to lessen the number of civilian causalities during these drug raids?"

"Yes, sir, there is," Colonel Montgomery answered quickly. "By not alerting the cartels that we're coming, Mr. President. Without question someone had alerted the "Chavez" drug cartel that General Rōjas and his men were coming and that's a fact, sir. Rōjas was a setting duck before he even touched down on his LZ. They were just waiting, sir, fully armed and ready for a fight. The only thing to our advantage was the strength and number of our force. When we questioned some of the members they indicated they knew we were coming sometime that day. Mr. President, you have a major leak within your organization either in the military or your civilian staff. We must plug this leak quickly before we hit the "Santiago" cartel in their jungle hideout. If they're alerted somehow it will be a disaster for our Special Ops outfit sir. Our men and woman are too precious a resource to squander away, Mr. President. Please find this piece of shit so I can put a bullet in his brain," the Colonel offered.

"I know how you feel, Colonel. And believe me we'll find this bastard P.D.Q. I promise you both," the Mexican President said.

"We must uncover this prick before we attack the Santiago cartel."

"We'll be on hold until he is arrested and shot," the Colonel added quickly. "We must return to our post, Mr. President, we have many dead to bury and wounded men to tend to."

"By all means, gentlemen, please keep me posted on your injured men," the President asked.

"Will do, sir."

Both officers stood up saluted the President and quickly left is residence.

Governor Williamson called a meeting with the other Governors to start addressing some of the pending problems that are critical to the new nation. The four chief executives of their states gathered in Flagstaff at the new government building that was completed this month.

Sara started the meeting off by saying, "Now that the Mexican President is doing something about the illegal entry problem, we can start concentrating on the numerous problems pertaining to our seceding from the union. I've been told the new passports and visas are printed and ready for distribution but without on official name for our country. Now, I know we agreed to have a nationwide name contest, but for now why don't we just pick a name so the new documentation can be completed for now. Any objections?" Sara asked.

Everyone shook their heads no.

"Okay, let's start with the name, 'United Western States'" she said.

"Sounds good," they answered in unison.

General Richards asked the group if they could talk about state and federal taxes. He continued, "Our state and federal taxes should now be a flat or user tax now that the I.R.S. no longer exists. A rate of 15-18% is somewhere in the ballpark, I believe. That flat rate would pertain to most purchases with the exception of food. No tax on any food should be considered. State and federal taxes could be combined under this flat tax plan. Not only would this give relief to our overburdened tax payers but it would also make filing their federal taxes much easier. Are we going to continue to call our new government the Federal government or something else?" he asked.

"For now, leave the word 'Federal' to mean our government," Sara quickly answered. "I'm sure we agree that other taxes that have weaseled their way into our society throughout the years should be eliminated. This includes taxes on phone bills, electric bills, and numerous other hidden taxes that has crippled our society but had given our politicians huge sums of our money to squander away on their pet projects to advance their political existence. This type of taxation must stop if our new nation is going to survive this breakaway."

The Governor of Texas stood up and said, "Before the four of us continue on the huge number of topics addressing our nation, shouldn't you, Sara, address our four states covering the many subjects that must be addressed?"

"Yes, I agree, Marilyn. Let's halt this meeting and schedule an immediate radio and T.V. address to our state residents." Sara

asked her Communications Chief Marian Wilcox to make arrangements for her to address the new nation as soon as possible.

Within twenty-four hours, the local radio and T.V. stations throughout the four states agreed to a 18:00 hour speech by their first President elect, Sara Williamson.

Sara decided to address the new nation from the capitol building in Flagstaff, Arizona. She sat behind a large and uncluttered desk in an unfinished room within the new capitol building. The T.V. producer said the usual, "5-4-3-2-1 and you're live, ma'am."

"Good evening to all residents of our new fledgling nation. We thought with so many things that have happened in recent weeks that an update and explanation would be in order. Let me start off on a light note. We currently don't have an official name of our new country. I'd like to have a nation-wide name contest to come up with a proper and befitting name for this great and unique country. All name suggestions should be sent to your state capitols. Please put the words 'name that country' on the outside of the envelope to make it easier to sort. And of course, send your e-mails to the capitol web sites as well. Your local stations will have the proper address and e-mail. A grand prize will be determined at a later date.

"Now to move on to more serious issues. As most of you already know the new Mexican President Lazzara has started to stop his nationals from attempting to illegally enter our border states. Before his cracking down, our state military units assigned to protect our border were intercepting over one thousand Mexican nationals every day along the entire two thousand mile border. Now that the Mexican military has clamped down, only a few dozen are getting through and most are being apprehended by our border units. If President Lazzara keeps his word and continues to keep his people in Mexico instead of illegally crossing the Rio Grande or desert areas some of our financial problems will ease a little. Along with Lazzara's action, we're going to purge our four states of all illegal aliens. If a Mexican national has illegally lived within our border states for at least five years and has a clean record while holding a steady job, he or she will be given citizenship to our country. But all other illegal Mexican nationals will be arrested, held and then deported.

"We cannot afford to have illegals from any country residing in our states and have free access to our medical facilities as well as welfare and a host of other social giveaways that should only be available to American citizens. Once we have purged our border states of unwanted squatters, we'll start removing people from the welfare rolls. Our final goal is to eliminate welfare altogether within the next year or so. We cannot continue to spend billions of our hard earned dollars to give it away on non-producers who watch the Days of Our Lives, drink beer and wait each month for that free money provided by hard working citizens. No more giveaways. I'll cover this welfare and food stamp problem and giveaway at a later date, but the current people on welfare should be ready when the monthly check stops coming. Between purging the unwanted and stopping the terrible welfare and food stamp systems, we might have a chance to run our country with a budget in the black for a change. We need a country of seventy million persons who have good paying jobs and contribute to the overall success and well-being of our nation. Other issues are as follows:

- Military bases within our border states
- State and government representatives
- Foreign access thru California and Texas
- Interaction with Mexico (illegals & drugs)
- Interaction with President Obama & his administration
- Power grids, in and out of our country
- Influx of thousands of new residents
- Passports & visas
- Access to our country thru airports, roads & seaways

And hundreds of other items we must address in the coming weeks and months. As your next, and first, President of this newly formed nation, I will keep you well informed and up to date on all pertinent issues. Thank god our seceding from the original union was completed without the loss of a single American life. I'm also thankful that President Obama and his military staff had cool heads and the wherefore to show great restraint during these very difficult and trying times in this country and around the entire globe.

"Good evening, ladies and gentlemen, I will talk to you again very soon."

With that the T.V. producer said, "That's a rap, ma'am, were clear." After the radio and T.V. crews exited the room the other governors and their staff entered the media room and all started talking at once. Sara started to laugh, she said, "My god what a circus we have created." With the comment the room became quiet.

Colonel Montgomery and General Rōjas arrived at Army Headquarters outside Querétaro and participated in the military burial ceremony of their fallen soldiers in arms. A total of fifty-one graves were dug and honored at Army Headquarters. After the ceremony, the Mexican General and the American Colonel gathered their complete staff and tried to piece together the disaster that cost their Special Ops Company over thirty-one percent dead and wounded troopers. The Colonel stated by saying, "We know someone or somebody alerted the two drug cartels that our units were about to attack their compounds. This person or persons will be charged with fifty-one deaths of our own soldiers and I want to be the bastard who shoots this piece of shit," the Colonel said.

General Rōjas added, "We must come up with a plan that hits their compound fast and furious before they can react with deadly force."

Montgomery jumped in by saying, "Now we must start planning for our attack on the Santiago cartel buried deep in the jungle of Hidalgo Providence." The Colonel continued, "Gentlemen, the jungle in that area is thicker than a mulligan stew and doesn't have any sizable LZ for our helicopters to land. There isn't any sizable clearing within twenty miles of the compound. Now with that scenario, how are we going to get in there?" the American Colonel asked the group.

Butch stood up and said, "Colonel, I know how we should gain access to the compound."

"Spill it, Butch."

"What does 'spill it' mean?" she asked in broken English.

"It means 'go ahead and tell us,'" the Colonel said with a big smile.

"Oh!" She said, a little embarrassed. "I would fly cargo planes at high altitude and parachute our forces into the jungle wearing night goggles."

Chapter 5 – Drug Cartels

Colonel Montgomery walked over to Ms. Butch and gave her a big hug and a broad smile. "Butch, you came very close, but rather than parachute from a great height, we're going to parachute from only three hundred feet above the jungle canopy. We want to be on the ground quickly and not be scattered for miles. Now jumping below three hundred feet is tough enough, but added darkness, stormy weather and a jungle canopy that can reach sixty feet and some would say that could cause some problems.

"But we're all experienced night jumpers and have parachuted into jungle settings before. If we get hung up in the tall canopy, we'll cut ourselves loose and descend to the ground by rope.

"That's why we'll carry a one hundred foot coil of rope so we can repel to the ground when stuck in the tree tops. Once we hit the tree tops it will take the better part of an hour to reach the ground and assemble into a fighting force. Now, during the next week we're going to parachute at night into a patch of heavy jungle and practice repelling to the ground." With that statement the small staff gave out a loud groan. "Don't kid yourself, gentlemen and Butch, we will have a few causalities during this parachute jump. But if we don't take at least one dry run jump before the actual attack, we will certainly lose a significant number of our forces during the real thing. Remember practice makes perfect. Oh! One more thing. When I parachute in I'll be carrying a location beacon that will send out a signal so your location unit will guide you towards our assembly point."

During the next week, two practice jumps were done in heavy jungle in preparation for the real attack. The rehearsals were not without causalities. Five troopers sustained broken legs and ten were entangled in the tree canopy and couldn't get free. But overall the practice jumps were successful and a good learning experience for all Special Ops personnel. The equipment recently supplied by the U.S. President worked fine and allowed Colonel Montgomery's people to see at night in perfect detail. These new night goggles were first line and encompassed all the latest bells and whistles for night probing.

General Rōjas and his American Colonel were in agreement. They were as ready as they could be. Now the critical part was to pick a date for the attack. A very dark and black night is preferred by both officers for maximum effectiveness. The calendar, weather and the moon will now determine the exact date of the attack.

President Obama and his staff are receiving numerous complaints about the loss of revenue from the four states and their seventy million inhabitants. The Treasury Secretary said, "The losses from California and Texas alone could reach eighty to one hundred billion dollars' worth of various federal taxes. This amount of financial loss in these times are huge amounts to be removed from our Federal coffers," the Secretary added.

"I understand, Mr. Secretary, but do you want to start the second civil war over the loss of revenue?" the President asked.

"No, Sir, I don't. I'm just bringing to the table the amount of lost dollars by leaving the union, Mr. President."

"Mr. President, we still haven't settled the problem pertaining to our military bases within the four states in questions. As you know we have enough personnel, equipment and arms to overpower all the state forces. Most of their troops are starched thin alone the entire length of the Mexican border," the Chairman of the Joint Chiefs stated.

"General, I've already told Governor Williamson that we'll pay for the use of these bases the same way we have paid for the use of our foreign bases for the past sixty years. And, gentlemen, I'm going to say this one more time, we are not going to attack these runaway states and force the country into another civil war that will certainly bring this country to its knees. Let's not forget, these four Governors have done something that we couldn't do. They worked with the Mexican President and his government to stop the flow of illegals from crossing our border and melting into the American society. We didn't even try, my friends, we just turned a blind eye and let the border stand in name only. Our border patrol units were not even allowed to shoot when confronted by armed drug cartel members, illegal nationals and government military units. It's no wonder the American public didn't come to Washington and demand the resignation of all government officials. We're not going to let the American public down again," the President told his staff.

After a brief phone call to the other state leaders, Sara asked her communication chief to please contact Mexican President Lazzara as soon as possible. "I've got a couple of ideas to run past the new President."

Within an hour the Mexican President was on the phone with the Arizona Governor.

"Thank you, Mr. President, for returning my call. As you're well aware, we're going to profile Mexicans and all illegals will be arrested, detained and deported back to your country. We cannot afford to support all your illegal aliens that are currently on public assistance. Billions of our hard earned dollars are spent every year on your illegal squatters and that Mr. President will stop shortly. Now with that said, I'd like of offer some possible solutions to the problem."

"I'm listening," President Lazzara said in a very low and cool sounding voice.

Sara continued, "Our new country would like to join with Mexico in a variety of joint-ventures. We'll provide start-up monies for building the facilities and acquiring the necessary equipment to produce a quality product."

There was a complete silence when Sara stopped talking. After a full minute Sara said, "Mr. President, are you still there?'

"Yes, I am," the President finally said. "I was just pondering various things," he admitted.

"Sir, the billions spent on your illegals can now be used to benefit all the residents of your country. Along with that money we'll add significantly more funds to start and finish the many projects."

"What projects do you have in mind?" the Mexican President asked.

"Well, sir, let's start with desalination plants along your thousands of miles of coast line to provide clean and salt free fresh water. Other projects would involve providing a strong infrastructure of quality roads and people movers such as monorails. Also with the improved water quality, the manufacturing of electrical components of all kinds would be possible she offered. Even chemical plants and other petro-chem facilities are possible," she added.

"Well, Governor, that sounds great, but when and how do we start this grand project of yours?"

"You don't sound very h-appy and enthusiastic, Mr. President. I'm offering you the availability of billions of our dollars to get your country out of the 18th century," she reminded the new President. "Now you asked when can we start these many projects. Well, that's very simple sir, when we have purged our border states of your illegal squatters we will start talking about the many joint-ventures I've been proposing, but not before, Mr. President. Somewhere about twelve million of your countrymen are illegally in our four states alone, sir, and it will take a gargantuan effort on our part to purge our new nation of all your unwanted countrymen.

Sara continued, "You, Mr. President, can help in our cause by telling your illegal countrymen to return home and help start making your country a good place to work and help bring Mexico into the twenty-first century. Your country could be a paradise, Mr. President. Between your great weather, the beautiful mountains and breathtaking deserts along with thousands of miles of beautiful beaches, coves and inlets on both the Gulf and Pacific Ocean. You must concentrate on two major issues. First is the drug cartel problem that is overrunning your country as we speak. And second is the purge and return of millions of your countrymen.

"While we are purging our unwanted guests, you should be pulling out all stops and eliminating every drug lord and cartel member within your country. That includes all elected officials and government employees that are on the take. No half measures, a full court press is required, Mr. President. I know you have started addressing the drug problem by hiring our Colonel Montgomery, but that's only the start, sir. You must press these poison pill pushers and press them hard."

"Well, Sara, I like the overall idea, but controlling the drug problem is a huge undertaking when they control a huge portion of our society," he answered. "It's not enough in dealing with all the drug members, but purging my government of people on the cartel payroll is another thing. We must first find these people and them put them away for life. They are as guilty as the people pushing their life destroying product as far as I'm concerned," he added.

"That's great, Mr. President, you concentrate on the drug problem and we'll start rounding up your countrymen. Please alert your military and border personnel that we're going to start returning illegal Mexican nationals shortly.

"I'm sure you understand, Mr. President, that these returning nationals will certainly put some strain on your economy," she added.

"On second thought, Mr. President, how about we make a slight change in our joint-venture agreement, sir. How about once we have returned about one million illegal persons, we'll free up large amounts of money to start some of our ventures. In the mean time you should get your staff together and make a wish list of projects that will benefit all Mexicans as well as our border states. I will do the same, sir.

"Goodbye, Mr. President."

Both parties hung-up without another word.

Sara related her conversation with President Lazzara to the other governors and also asked them to consider various joint-ventures that would benefit both nations. She also said, "We must come up with a quick plan on how to round-up and deport these unwanted visitors. All Mexicans within our border states will know our new policy within the next day or two at the outside," she added.

"According to the national weather bureau of Mexico, the perfect weather for a night incursion will be on the night of Saturday the nineteenth. There will be complete cloud cover, no moon and rain overnight to cover their landing and attack on the Santiago cartel."

General Rōjas entered the room and was asked by the American Colonel whether he had read the weather report received early today.

"Yes, I saw the report," he answered. "It's made to order, as you Americans say."

"Good. Let's start making the necessary arrangements but not divulge the day of the operation. Remember, we still have a mole, or I should say a rat, in the barn. If possible, we must find this bastard before he causes many more deaths."

"Let's gather our staff officers and start checking our very sophisticated gear and see if we've missed anything," the Mexican General ordered.

"Sounds good to me, General. I'll call a meeting," Montgomery answered.

When the eighteenth came, the Special Ops Company was ready but not given any word on when the attack date was scheduled. With two practice jumps under their belt and a host of new communication and night equipment supplied by the United States and the four border states, they were charged and ready for a fight. At 20:00 hours the call went out for assemble the Mexican General was standing on the platform ready to address the elite group of hand-picked men and woman. Colonel Montgomery was standing on the ground next to the platform awaiting the General's command.

"Attention!" - he yelled in a booming voice.

The company snapped to attention and waited for their commanding officer's remarks.

"At ease," he shouted.

"Good evening."

"Tonight, or I should say very early tomorrow morning, we'll leave for the town of Matamoros which is approximately one hundred and sixty-five miles from here. Our C-130 flight time is about one hour and fifteen minutes give or take due to the stormy weather around or tree top LZ. Once we have stormed the compound and secured the area, we'll signal the land forces to come in and cart these bastards away."

The General continued, "As planned, we'll land in two separate areas in the jungle and converge upon the compound from two different directions. That means one group commanded by Colonel Montgomery will come in at the nine o'clock position. This should prevent each group from firing upon each other. Our glow in the dark strips on our uniforms should do the trick.

"Remember, only remove the protective covers off the glow strips after you hit the ground and not before. Anyone without a glow in the dark uniform is your prime target. Don't take any chances, 'shoot first and ask questions later' is the rule of the day. Let's not be overtly trigger happy, but shoot first or you'll pay the penalty of death. As you can tell by my instructions, we're not going to screw around this time. We lost far too many good men during the last attack on both cartel compounds."

The General continued, "We'll board the two C-130 transports at 22:00 hrs. and lift off at 22:30 hours. We should arrive at 23:45 hours and be on the ground and at our assembly area by 00:45 if everything goes according to plan. Then we have about a one mile hike through thick jungle before entering the compound. Once more thing, we must steer clear of all known trails because most likely they'll be booby trapped or have some kind of sensor device to alert their guards.

"That's all I have, but good luck and may god protect us in this operation. Try and get some sleep or at least relax if you can," he said.

"Colonel, do you have anything to add?" the Mexican General asked turning and looking down at his co-commander.

"No, sir. I think you have about covered everything," the American Colonel answered.

"Attention: troops dismissed," the General bellowed.

Governor Williamson, in a meeting with the other three Governors and their staff members reminded them that President Barak Hussein Obama won a second term under some very dubious election returns from various cities like Philadelphia where in many precincts he won every single vote. "Not a single vote against him was recorded. Something smelled fishy after the November election but no matter what, he was elected for another four years to take this nation down the path of high unemployment, despair and higher taxes for all Americans. This was why we elected to secede from his union. President Obama started his drive during his fist four years and now has a clear an unobstructed path to drive this country into bankruptcy and possibly total anarchy. Riots and roving mobs could run wild in the big cities when the federal government programs can no longer be funded and passed out like candy. I believe by the time his next term is up, he could run their national debt to twenty-two trillion and even as much as twenty-four trillion dollars.

"Remember, his policies and federal mandates that hamstrung our states, cost our state residents billions of dollars to support these illegal aliens. Obama did absolutely nothing to stop the massive flow of illegal aliens crossing our borders. His hands on policies kept the border patrol officers from doing their job and protecting the American people. If they shot an illegal or coyote they were prosecuted and thrown in jail to rot for doing their job.

"We must continue to keep our four state residents informed on just why we elected to secede from the Obama union and form our own government and nation. I could go on reporting the lies, cover-ups, character assassinations, guns to cartels, Obama care and dozens of other costly mistakes during the past four and a half years that put the United States into a steep slide towards self-destruction, but I won't. He is the forty-fifth President and that's it."

One last thing Sara said. "Obama's forty-six states are in deep trouble tax increases for all Americans. His middle class will slide into a lower class that is burdened with supporting the millions of government trough feeders."

"That's all I have for now," Governor Williamson said, returning to her seat.

Governor LaCrosse asked Sara if they could step up the "name the country" contest and pick a grand winner. "We have received over a million suggestions so far and I'm sure they have run the gamut of possible names," she said.

"Sure, Marilyn, let's collect all the entries, have them separated by computer and get a final list of acceptable names we can pick from. Let's finish this before the end of this month," Sara suggested. "Is that okay with the rest of you?" she asked.

"Certainly," Marilyn answered, "I've talked to both Eric and Richard and they both agree, let's get this done. Without an official country name it's holding up many projects and legal aspects that must be addressed quickly," Marilyn told her President elect.

"Okay, let me know when the data has been collected and the final list is compiled," Sara asked.

"Will do," the Texas Governor answered.

"Let's rap up this meeting, we have a million things to do within each of our states," Sara told the three state Governors. "Please watch the borders with a keen eye," she said in parting.

At exactly 22:30 hours the two prop C-130 transports were given the green light for takeoff. Their flight time to Matamoras was approximately one hour and fifteen minutes. The attacking force was counting on the thunderstorm and heavy rain in the drop area to muffle the plane's engines and give much needed cover for their low level jumps. Three hundred feet over standard ground was plenty, but over jungle is pretty dicey at best, but necessary.

The two planes loaded with Mexican military elite and one American Colonel were surprisingly relaxed but ready for anything once they hit the jungle floor.

With the tasker birds directing their jungle excursion to their destination with pinpoint accuracy, their chances of getting lost or misdirected was nil.

Chapter 5 - Drug Cartels

As the two transports approached the drop zone, the standup order was given and a final check of equipment was done, then the hookup of all static lines was ordered. The C-130 door was opened and the jump master stood in the doorway waiting for the red light to change to green.

The jungle canopy was a blur as the planes flew less than three hundred feet above the tree tops.

The light changed to green and the men, along with Butch, in both planes started their silent but very brief decent to the jungle floor. As predicted, the weather was stormy with heavy rain, and the continuous claps of thunder drowned out any noise from either aircraft.

In less than eight minutes the whole force was on the ground with only ten or twelve men caught in the jungle canopy. Once the men were cut free the two separate groups headed for their final position prior to the main attack.

The jungle was thick and the men in front took turns in cutting away the vines and underbrush. The progress of Colonel Montgomery's team was slowed when they ran into a patch of cobwebs that housed a hundred or more huge black hairy spiders the size of pie plates. Being in almost total darkness with sticky cobwebs and monstrous spiders the elite group was unnerved at least.

General Rōjas and his men arrived at their final position at just after 01:00 hrs. and Col. Montgomery's group arrived at 01:15 hrs. Both groups would check their equipment and rest for thirty minutes before starting the attack on the cartel compound.

Colonel Montgomery thought, "We still haven't found our mole, let's hope his alert to the cartel isn't accurate. If they are warned there will be a massacre. We'll find out shortly," he mused.

At 01:45 both groups started their assault. Very slowly and quietly, the guards were taken out. A total of five cartel gunmen were silenced without alerting the sleeping cartel members. This was accomplished with American Special Forces' crossbows that are deadly accurate at one hundred yards. The arrow (not bolt) tips are specially made to explode quietly after entering the victim's body. This eliminates any outcry from the target. The crossbow has one hundred fifty pound pull and propels it's arrows at three hundred and eighty feet per second. Silent and deadly efficient in capable hands.

rickshaw

The two attacking groups quietly entered the various buildings before an unseen guard sounded the general alarm. At that instant all hell broke loose. The sleeping cartel members came from everywhere firing their AK-47's at any shadow or form. The assault troops were ready and returned fire with deadly accuracy. Their night vision goggles made spotting their targets very easy in the close quarters in and around the many buildings. The fire fight lasted only fifteen minutes and when the last shot was fired, some forty-seven drug cartel members were dead.

General Rōjas lost four men and Col. Montgomery lost three killed and six wounded. Sixty-four cartel members were captured and turned over to the ground forces when they arrived by truck.

Tons of coke in various stages of refinement were collected then destroyed, and cash and gold that totaled over one billion dollars was stacked neatly in metal racks wrapped in plastic. No Mexican Pesos were found, only American $100.00 dollar bills in ten thousand dollars to a bundle.

Once everything was photographed and filmed and the wounded cared for, the explosive charges were set among the many buildings.

The two groups assembled some distance away to see the explosions and fireworks that followed. The order was given to detonate some five hundred pounds of C-4 and assorted captured explosive devices. With that the whole compound above and below ground erupted in one gigantic explosion that shook the ground and jungle for over a mile. The explosion could be heard in a small town some thirty-five miles away.

After the smoke had cleared, a final check of the destroyed compound was conducted to insure nothing was overlooked.

Once satisfied, the elite forces boarded Army duce and a halves and headed for the nearest airport for their return trip.

Only one cartel big wig was absent from the compound when the raid occurred. He would be hunted down and most likely killed.

General Rōjas was in contact with the new Mexican President and filled him in on all the details of the raid. He also informed the President that a truck load of files was saved, and hundreds of names of persons on the take were listed.

President Lazzara asked that the General and Col. Montgomery meet with him as soon as possible and bring that important list of people being paid by the cartel. "It certainly will make very interesting reading," the General answered.

"See you both in Mexico City tomorrow," the President said as he hung up the phone.

"Colonel, wait until he reads the names of the cartel money recipients. I believe his brother's name is on the list. If it's him, the President will surely have him shot. Our meeting with President Lazzara will certainly be interesting at the least," the General said, shaking his head. "I'll say one thing for our new President, he's not afraid of the many drug cartels and the possibility of himself being gunned down," the General added.

"I agree, General, but let's hope he survives long enough to clean-up this drug mess and return Mexico to its people," the American Colonel quickly added.

General Rōjas and Lt. Col. Montgomery arrived in Mexico City in late afternoon and quickly drove to the new President's place and compound. They were seated in the outer waiting room and were only there a few minutes before the Mexican President entered the large room. He was accompanied by his younger brother.

General Rōjas quickly glanced at Col. Montgomery as they stood up and saluted the new Mexican President. "I'm glad you both came through the raid without any serious injury," the President said as he shook both men's hands. "Gentlemen, do you know my brother, Ricardo?" he asked both men.

"No, sir, we don't," the American Colonel answered.

The President introduced his younger brother and the four men quickly settled down around a small table. "Your jungle raid was a complete success," the new President told his top military team. "The loss of life was much less this time," he added.

"Yes, sir. We were very lucky this time," the General told his Commander-in-Chief.

"Now, gentlemen, you have in your possession a list of persons who are receiving payoffs from the drug cartel."

"Yes, Mr. President, we do have that list in question. It is fifty-one pages long and contains almost fifteen hundred names."

"May I have that list?" the President asked.

"Certainly, Mr. President." The General handed the President the folder which contained the long list of traitors.

"Maybe you should read the list in private, Mr. President," Colonel Montgomery suggested.

"Yes, I will," the President answered as he continued to scan the first page. His eyes came upon a name that was underlined in red and he slowly closed the folder.

"Gentlemen, please excuse my brother and myself, but please remain," he asked his guests. With that, the President and his younger brother exited the large waiting room.

General Rōjas said, "Colonel, all hell is about to break loose in this palace."

Within five minutes the Mexican President returned and slowly sat down at the small table. In a low voice he said, "As you know, my brother's name was on that terrible list. He has been arrested and will most likely face a firing squad for his crime against his country. His despicable action that caused the death of many military and civilian personnel is only punishable by death under Mexican law.

We have a small detention center with a dozen or so cells in the sub-basement of this palace where he will be held in solitary confinement until I can talk to our elderly mother who never thought he could do any wrong even as a child.

I want these fifteen hundred traitors tracked down and put away for life or shot for treason. City, town, village and government officials will be shot as far as I'm concerned gentlemen. We must purge this country of these despicable, worthless human beings. Please start this nationwide roundup as soon as possible the President ordered. Whatever resources you need, just ask and it's at your disposal. One other thing, no one on that list is exempt and that includes my family, gentlemen."

"Yes, Mr. President, we understand," his top General answered.

It took almost two weeks for the Mexican government to clear more than fifty thousand eighteen wheelers that had clogged every road leading to the two thousand mile long border with the U.S.

Most trucks were damaged one way or the other, missing tires, wheels, engines, doors, trailers and most cargo. The military and civilian police could not guard the vast array of vehicles that blocked every road. Those vehicles had to be towed away and stored awaiting repairs by the company owners. The perishable goods that spoiled inside the trucks were painfully removed and taken to dozens of temporary dumps.

The ultimate cost to the government and the hundreds of companies topped more than one billion American dollars. It would take months to regain the daily flow of goods shipped north to the States.

The Mexican farms that had laid off most of their workers had to replant their crops and wait for the next harvest to appear. Tens of thousands of Mexican farm workers, truckers and general laborers were without work or income for many weeks and even months to come before the general economy throughout Mexico could return to prior border shutdown status.

In the meantime, the roads and bridges into the four border states were open for foot and vehicle traffic. But all Mexicans that tried to enter the border states were scrutinized very closely. All needed the proper paperwork and I.D. before being allowed to cross into the four seceding states. Only one out of four trying to cross the border was allowed in. Mexican border police were on the American side of the border helping the American officials sort out I.D. problems.

The four state capitols reported that over twelve million potential country names had been submitted by their residents. The computers sorted out six hundred and eighty different names among the twelve million names submitted.

Sara contacted the other governors and said, "Now we have the list of names, let's quickly pick one and get on with other matters."

They all agreed.

Two of the Governors liked that name "Western States of America". One Governor didn't care what name was chosen, but asked Sara to pick the name.

"Okay," she answered, "I vote that the name of our new country shall be called "Western States of America" or WSA."

"Good," they said. "So be it then."

"Now, how many people sent in the specific name?" she asked

"Some eight hundred thousand people sent in that name," was the answer.

"Well, we'll put all their names in a barrel and have someone pick out a single name. Of course, it should be done in front of a T.V. audience nationwide," she added.

"Okay, Sara, now what is the grand prize?" Governor Richardson asked.

"How about a prize of fifty thousand in cash and a new car? Both tax free of course. Let's set up the drawing for this coming Saturday if the T.V. networks agree. I'll contact Marian and have her set up the national coverage. Do all of you agree?" she asked.

"Sounds good to us," was the reply.

General Rōjas and his Security Chief had poured over the fifteen hundred names looking for high government officials that were on the take. There were hundreds of officials that made the list. Members of the united congress, mayors, police chiefs, border officials and lesser positions within the Mexican government.

The names were matched with home addresses and business addresses to prepare for the massive seizure and roundup of these turncoats. A hundred towns housed these payoff recipients. Local police would have to purge their own ranks before the roundup could start.

A force of one thousand selected government and local officials armed with local names started the massive gathering of these national traitors.

"This large force will be armed to the teeth and will not hesitate to shoot anyone who resists being apprehended. Small town and villages will send their arrested individuals to the nearest large city for detention until transferred to the main holding area near Mexico City. Trials for these people will be quick and most likely final," the General commented.

"I'll be in constant communications with the top officers in charge of this huge gathering and roundup of Mexican nationals who have disgraced this nation. The cartels poison money has filtered down to the Mexican people who have no idea of illegal activity vs. common sense and the right and wrong of their upbringing. It may take a while, but we'll stamp out these large cartels and kill the top leaders if I have anything to do with it."

"General, I couldn't have said it any better," the newly promoted Full Bird Colonel told his military partner and friend.

"What do you think President Lazzara will do with his brother," he asked?

"Well, Colonel, I would guess he will order his brother's death without delay the General guessed. We'll know in a day of so, I'm sure," he added.

Colonel Montgomery placed a call to Sara Williamson and filled her in on the raid and the captured list of cartel payoff persons. He assured his next President of the "Western States of America" that the new Mexican President Lazzara was doing a good job and had a great start to wiping out the cartels' strangle hold on the Mexican people and its poison they spread throughout the Americas and the world.

"That's good, Colonel, but please keep me informed on the overall progress of your Mexican roundup and President Lazzara's fight against the many drug cartels."

"Will do, ma'am," the Colonel answered.

As the American Colonel replaced the phone, General Rōjas entered the room and slowly sat down at the table across from Colonel Montgomery. "I have some good news, and I have some bad news," the Mexican top General told his American soldier in arms and friend.

"The good news is our mole, or rat in the barn, has been found. The bad news is that the traitor is the President's younger brother Ricardo. Under very intensive interrogation, which means torture I'm sure, he admitted he passed critical military info he learned from President Longo and his military staff for some years. He received payoffs from at least four major drug cartels. One other thing, he has a Swiss bank account with assets over 1.3 million dollars. Ricardo worked in the Longo administration for years in various roles that bridged the military and civilian sides of government. He attended all the high level meetings on both sides and was privy to all plans and actions against the drug cartels."

"Good god, General, how come no one suspected this first class rat?"

"Most likely because his brother was President Longo's Vice President," the General surmised. "Above suspicion, you might say."

"Now what will happen to this piece of crap?" the Colonel asked.

"Under our current laws, he most likely will be shot within a few days at most. No lengthy trial. A federal judge will make the call and it will be very quick, I assure you.

"You see in Mexico we don't screw around with dogs like this. You Americans wouldn't put him to death for years, or most probably never. Slick lawyers would claim his mother didn't hug him enough or his father treated him poorly so he had to rebel against society and his government," the General concluded with a slight smile.

"You're one smart bastard," the American Full Bird told his Mexican counterpart. "You've got our justice system pegged just about right, I might add. We waste a lot of time and money housing certain criminals when we should get rid of them quickly like other countries," he added.

"I'm hungry, General, let's get some chow. I wonder if your mess hall has S.O.S. on the breakfast menu," he joked.

"Not likely," he assured his American friend.

The television national drawing was scheduled for nine o'clock Saturday evening to determine the winner of the name the country. Some sixteen million entries were submitted from the four breakaway states. The T.V. producer said, "5-4-3-2-1 and you're on."

Sara said, "Good evening ladies and gentlemen. We have progressed from a no name country to a country with a fine name. And that name is 'Western States of America' or just WSA for short. Some eight hundred thousand people picked that name and now one lucky person will win the grand prize, tax free I might add."

"Without any further delay, I'll be blindfolded and reach into this huge barrel with all your names and withdraw a single winner." Sara's aide tied a black blindfold around Sara's eyes the turned her around three times and guided her hand into the opening and down into the almost million cards. She scattered the cards inside the huge barrel then pulled her arm from the barrel and a single card in her hand. "Please read the name," she asked her aide.

"Ladies and gentlemen of the 'Western States of America' the grand prize winner is Miss Maggie Johnston of Bakersfield, California. She wins a cash prize of fifty thousand dollars and a new Chevy S.U.V., and they're both tax free. Congratulations to Maggie and the millions of other people who took the time to enter this name our country contest. Thank you, everyone, and good evening."

The cameras went dark and the T.V. crew gathered their equipment and quickly left the unfinished room in the new capitol building in Flagstaff.

"Thank goodness that's over and done with," Sara told her trusted and long-time aide Beverly Wellington. "Now we can start putting our new name on all our official documents, money and everything else," she quickly added.

"Just think, Sara, our new name and country will now be added to the list of nations worldwide," her aide reminded the next and first President of the new country.

"Yes, Beverly, that has a great sound and ring to it, nations of the world."

President Lazzara called General Rōjas and Colonel Montgomery to the President's Palace in Mexico City. Both military officers were patiently awaiting the Mexican President. Finally after a full hour of waiting the President entered the large foyer and quickly apologized for the delay. "I know you both have more important things to do than wait for me. I'm sorry for the delay, gentlemen."

"I've asked you to come today so I can assure you that the mole or leak in our organization has been plugged. Federal Judge Perez of the 9th district in Mexico City has ruled that Ricardo Lazzara must be put to death within the next twenty-four hours. It saddens me and my family, and especially my mother, that the traitor was a family member. Now, I would like you both to witness the execution tomorrow at first light. Since my brother caused the death of so many Mexican nationals and countless Americans across the border I want you both to have closure to this treasonous act. He will be shot in the Palace Square Garden at dawn tomorrow with only a few people looking on. You two will be my eyes, I will not witness the execution of my brother. Is that arrangement acceptable to the both of you?" the President asked in a low and subdued voice.

"As you wish, Mr. President, we'll be there at first light," the Mexican General answered. The American Colonel nodded affirmative.

"Thank you, gentlemen. I understand this is an unpleasant task but it must have closure, you understand."

"Yes, sir, we do."

"Please excuse me, gentlemen," the Mexican President said as he got up from the table and exited the room.

Both men stood up, snapped to attention and saluted the Mexican President and their boss.

When the President left the room, Colonel Montgomery said, "The trial didn't take long."

"One man judge, jury and executioner," the General answered.

The first rays of the rising sun streamed across the Palace courtyard and at 04:57 General Rōjas and American Colonel Montgomery were ushered into the very large and beautiful center courtyard of the President's Palace. There was a small army detachment of twelve riflemen, an army Captain and a military Chaplin and a civilian doctor. Beside General Rōjas and Colonel Montgomery only four other men in civilian clothes were present.

"Do you know the four other men in civilian clothes?" Colonel Montgomery asked.

"No, Colonel, I don't know any of them," the General answered quietly.

A large ornate wooden door opened to the courtyard and Ricardo Lazzara was lead into the large area wearing handcuffs and leg irons by two military M.P.'s and headed straight to the high wall where many executions had taken place through the years. The President's brother stood at attention between both M.P.s facing the twelve member firing squad.

A small door opened on the second level surrounding the large courtyard and a small man dressed in a judge's black robe came down the stairs and walked straight to the condemned man. In Spanish he read the long list of charges and passed judgment by saying guilty on all charges. This judgment was passed by a military court. "Before sentence is carried out, do you have anything to say?" he asked Ricardo.

"Yes, I do," he answered.

"Proceed," the judge told him.

"I want to apologize to my mother and to my brother for doing these despicable acts against my country and my family for only money. I want my Swiss bank account to be distributed among the military and civilian people killed in the three raids on the drug cartels. I'm guilty on all counts and should pay the price by firing squad. May God have mercy on my soul, I'm sure the Good Lord will find some terrible job for me to do."

"Are you finished?" the judge asked.

"Yes."

The judge turned to the Army Captain and ordered him to carry out the sentence.

The Captain said, "Attention. Prepare to fire. Fire."

The twelve rifles fired in unison and Ricardo Lazzara fell dead to the ground.

The doctor rushed over and knelt beside Ricardo. "He is dead," he said in a quiet voice.

Two men carrying a canvas stretcher appeared and carried Ricardo's body out of the courtyard.

General Rōjas and Colonel Montgomery were about to leave the Palace courtyard when a young Lieutenant came rushing up, saluted and said, "President Lazzara would like to see you both as soon as possible."

"Thank you, Lieutenant."

"Do you know the way to the President's office?" the young Lieutenant asked.

"Yes, we know the route to the President's waiting room," the General answered a bit annoyed.

"Yes, sir."

The Lieutenant saluted again and departed quickly.

Both men arrived at the large waiting room and sat at the small round table next to the wall. Within fifteen minutes President Lazzara entered the vast room and approached the two officers.

The General and Colonel jumped to attention and saluted the Mexican President.

President Lazzara returned the salute and said, "My good friends, please be seated."

As everyone sat down the President said in a low voice, "Justice has been served. I hope my brother is going to a better place. As you can expect my very religious mother is devastated at Ricardo's deeds and his death by firing squad. I guess I'm off her list of good sons," the President added. "But someone had to pay for that crime that took an untold number of lives."

"Gentlemen, we're still investigating the possibility of more conspirators involved with my brother and his activities with many drug cartels and many officials in government and private companies. Enough of this," the President said. "I appreciate both of you coming to this very unpleasant but very necessary military firing squad to rid our country of scum like Ricardo. I hope God will forgive me for saying that against my own brother."

The President shook both officers' hand and said, "I'm sure you have more important things to attend to. Please keep me informed on stamping out the remaining drug cartels."

"Yes, Sir, we will," Colonel Montgomery answered.

President Lazzara quickly stood up an exited the large room before the two officers could standup and salute.

Both officers left the Palace and headed for Army Headquarters outside Querétaro to concentrate on the remaining drug cartels and the shipping of their poison north to the United States. Additional smaller drug cartels had been located and military interventions would be planned and attacked shortly.

General Rōjas had ordered additional troops to guard the U.S. Mexican border. These additional military personnel had a two-fold mission. Number one was to stop all Mexican nationals from entering the U.S. illegally. Number two was to stop the drug traffic from shipping their hundreds of tons of white poison north. Rōjas had replaced over thirty high ranking military officers who had done nothing to stop or report drug traffic activity and had turned a blind eye to various illegal activities that their troops were engaged in. Most of these officers were on the drug cartel's pay roll. Only five of these officers escaped long jail terms. The purge of all branches of the Mexican military would continue until most of the personnel on the various cartel's payroll were exposed and prosecuted and sent to jail for many years.

President Lazzara called Arizona Governor Sara Williams and explained his current policy in dealing with the terrible drug problem and the war on all cartels. "We have made a significant dent in the drug production and distribution by attacking the major drug cartel manufacturing sites. Their main plants have been destroyed and all captured drugs burned. I didn't want these many tons of white poison stored in some warehouse and then mysteriously disappear back into the drug stream again. All captured powder will be destroyed on the spot, never to reach the market again."

The President continued. "While I'm on the subject of drugs I'd like to thank for sending us that fine army officer, Colonel Montgomery. He's been a great asset to General Rōjas and myself. He is fearless and has trained and developed our Spl. Ops people with professionalism and great enthusiasm. We have learned a great deal from this fine American officer and I'd like to retain him a little longer, if that's okay with you, Sara."

"Thank you, Mr. President, for your kind words pertaining to Colonel Montgomery. And, sir, I have no problem if the Colonel stays in Mexico and works on the Mexican and American drug problem."

"Good," the Mexican President answered. "I'll keep you informed on our progress," he assured the first President of the new country.

Both parties hung up.

After talking to the Mexican President, Arizona Governor Williamson asked her Communication Chief Marian Wilcox to schedule T.V. time for 20:00 hours on Saturday.

From government building #1 in Flagstaff, the T.V. producer said the usual 5-4-3-2-1 and he pointed to the first President elect of the fledgling country.

"Good evening, citizens of 'Western States of America', I want to update all our citizens on the latest turn of events with our Mexican neighbors, their new President and our old federal government in Washington.

"Mexico's new President Pedro Lazzara has started to clamp down on the drug cartels by attacking and stamping out their manufacturing facilities and arresting the drug cartel leaders and cartel members. They will be held at secret locations off shore so there will be no chance of being broken out by other cartel members. That facility will be a maximum secure facility guarded by military Special Forces. President Lazzara has pledged to stamp out the whole drug industry and return Mexico to its citizens. The drug cartels have made Mexico a country governed by fear and terrorism. Full of pay offs, kidnappings, thousands of murders that is approaching anarchy. When President Longo was assassinated, Vice President Lazzara stepped up and set the example and the path that Mexico is going to take.

"Not only is he aggressively attacking the many drug cartels and the grower of the white poison, but his military and civilian authorities have started to stop all Mexican nationals and others from crossing the border and entering the four border states.

"Our military units stationed along the entire border with Mexico have seen first-hand that the action taken by the Mexican military is stopping all persons trying to cross into our new country. Out of the thousands who attempt to cross our borders every day, only a small number actually get through. Thousands of Mexico's military are participating in this national clamp down on the illegal entry attempt by its citizens. Some illegals that have slipped by the Mexican military have been picked up by our military personnel.

"Let me make one thing 'crystal clear' as they say, we want our border with Mexico sealed tight. No illegal entry will be tolerated by any nationality.

"Another thing that President Lazzara has agreed to, as you know we have started to profile Mexican nationals and Muslims to insure they are legally in our country.

"President Lazzara has agreed to repatriate any Mexican national that have illegally entered our four states. This is a huge break-through in our Mexican/American relations. If this new trend continues, the relationship between our two countries will grow to new heights. As an example, Mexico and Western States of America could enter into numerous joint ventures that would benefit both countries. By building new dams, roads, power grids, desalination plants and hundreds of manufacturing facilities throughout Mexico, the living index of Mexico will rise sharply and put millions to work at good paying jobs. With good working wages the Mexican nationals will want to stay in their own country and participate in the reconstruction and revitalization of their nation.

"With the President's new policy of stopping drug trafficking the fear of the drug cartels and their death squads has diminished and a feeling of some relief has been noted by the general population throughout Mexico.

"Another breakthrough President Lazzara mentioned in our discussion was he would now allow American citizens to work and live in his 'New' Mexico. With the many joint ventures we're proposing, that alone will help jump start the various projects by allowing U.S. citizens to stay and work in Mexico.

"We will work with Mexico to bring their standard of living throughout their country to a level where Mexicans will want to live and work in their own country while feeling safe and secure.

"One last thing on Mexico, our new country, in its short existence has done more to stop the illegal entry of foreign nationals than President Obama has done in almost five years. Our new relationship with President Lazzara and his new administration is the turning point in Mexican/American policy and direction.

"Now for some Western States of America updates. The Treasury building in Flagstaff is now starting to print our new money. The denominations will be $1.00, 5.00, 10.00, 20.00, 50.00, 100.00, 500.00 and 1,000.00 bills. The pictures on the new bills will be of many icons and some famous scenes like the Golden Gate Bridge. This new money will be sent to our central bank and then be distributed to all our banks in short order. The general public should start seeing these colorful bills within a month.

"On a more serious note. The roundup of all illegal aliens currently in our country is going in high gear. Thousands of undocumented illegals have been stopped, arrested and deported back to Mexico. So far only a handful of illegals have entered our states coming through Canada.

"One last note," Sara added, "as of November 1st all roads, highways and waterways leading into our new country will be blocked and maintained by our federal border guards. American passports will be honored throughout all our entry points. No resident of the other forty-six states will gain entry into our country without a valid passport. The only exception will be children under the age of twelve. Our country will be free of illegal aliens as much as humanly possible.

"All airports will have immigration stations while trains and buses will be stopped at our border to insure all persons entering our country have proper I.D. Without the required I.D. all persons will be denied entry into the Western States of America.

"One thing I'll promise all our residents of W.S.A. Your government will stay as much as possible out of your lives. As your first President, I want less government, less regulations and more freedom to start new business and create thousands of new

 **rickshaw**

jobs throughout our country. It also includes less all around taxes that burden our former fifty states. There are hundreds of other items and projects we must address now and in the coming months. As you know starting up a new country is a huge task, let alone the problems with our former government as well as border problems.

"As your President I will continue to have many of these up to date meetings to insure all citizens of Western States of America knows what your new government is doing and planning to do. Backdoor or backroom politics and after dark decisions are not a part of this administration.

"Thank you, ladies and gentlemen, and good evening."

The hot lights and T.V. cameras went dark and the T.V. director said, "Ma'am, that's a rap." Sara pushed back from her desk with a sigh of relief.

"Well, that's a start," she told her Communications Director.

Chapter 6
FIRST WOMAN PRESIDENT

Once the network crew cleared the office and closed the door, Sara said, "Marian, I need to pick a Chief of Staff. I've held off long enough, I need a top notch person to help me run my organization and keep things straight while I attack the various problems and issues."

"I agree, Sara."

"Do you have anybody in mind?" she asked her boss.

"Yes, I do," Sara answered. "I like Michael McCarney, Congressman from San Francisco. He's a good organizer and has tons of energy which we'll surly need."

"Not only is he a good organizer," Marian added, "but he is a very handsome man and single besides," she added with a smile.

"Yes, I know. He is fifty-two, never married and has devoted his entire life to conservative values and electing Republicans to public office. Let's find out, Marian, get in touch will Congressman McCarney and arrange a meeting with him. Please ask him to come to Flagstaff if he will entertain the overall idea. Oh! Marian, please call Eric first as a courtesy so he knows what I'm proposing."

"Yes, ma'am. I'll get right on it." Marian disappeared quickly to make the call.

Within fifteen minutes Sara's phone rang and it was California Governor Eric Richardson.

Eric started by saying, "I liked your first update and chat to our folks in Western States of America."

"Thank you, Eric."

"Now, I got a call from Marian explaining your possible choice for Chief-of-Staff in your Flagstaff Whitehouse. I think your choice is a good one," he told the President elect. "He's a perfect gentleman, very conservative and a real smart politician. He has great common sense and speaks his mind. He doesn't mince words, if you're wrong or full of shit he will tell you directly. If Mike takes the job, he will do a great job."

"Do you want me to talk to him first?" Eric asked.

"No, please don't," Sara asked.

"Okay, I won't."

"Thank you, Eric."

Both parties hung up without saying another word.

Before Sara could gather her thoughts the phone rang and slowly she picked up the receiver. "Yes," she answered.

"Sara, I forgot to ask you something," Eric said quickly.

"Shoot," she answered.

"I think you should take the oath of office as quickly as possible. The other Governors agree. We shouldn't wait any longer. You should be seated before the President elect of the other forty-six states is seated in Washington on January 21th. Remember, Sara, before being re-elected he made a lot of comments about what he would do if re-elected. Before Obama actually takes office to start his second term, you should take the office as our President."

"I agree, Eric, but I don't want a large spectacle that costs millions of dollars. I want a semi-private ceremony that can be viewed on T.V. without a lot of hullabaloo. A quick ceremony so we can get down to the business at hand and put this new country on the straight and narrow path. Remember, we represent over seventy million citizens of the 'Western States of America' and our population is growing daily. We can't be wasting money on an elaborate spectacle that does not benefit our citizens other than establishing a head of our new nation.

"I agree," Eric said quickly. "But now the question is when do we swear you in?"

"I'd like to take the oath of office within the next two weeks," she added.

"That's pretty quick Sara, but we can do it. I'll set up a group to get things started immediately."

"Before you start the ball rolling there are a few things I'd like to suggest if I may."

"Certainly, you're the Chief," he answered.

Sara began:

"First: I'd like to be sworn in at our new capitol building in Flagstaff.

"Second: I'd like the ceremony to last only about one hour.

"Third: I'd like Kathleen Wilson our Chief Justice of our Supreme Court to give the oath of office.

"Forth: Make sure every citizen in our country knows that my term of office is for only two years. After my term of office is over, we'll have general elections and appoint a new President for a full term of four years.

"The rest of the general details for this ceremony is up to your appointed group and you three Governors."

"Yes, ma'am, I'll get right on it."

Congressman Michael McCarney arrived in Flagstaff and was quickly driven to the new capitol building. He was ushered into the future President's office and awaited her arrival. Within a few minutes, Sara entered her office and walked directly over to Congressman McCarney. He hardly had time to jump to his feet before she stood in front of him.

Sara extended her hand and warmly greeted her guest. She noted he was taller than she remembered, slightly gray and very handsome to boot. "Please be seated," she quickly told her first official guest in her new office.

"Thank you," he answered.

"Do you have any idea why you're here?" she asked

"Not a clue," he answered. "But I'm sure it has something to do youth your new government."

"Yes, it does," she said quickly. "Michael, I'd like you to take the position of Chief-of-Staff within my new administration and government."

That request hit him like a ton of bricks. He sat there speechless for a full minute before recovering and asking, "Are you sure I'm the right person for this very important position in your new government?" he asked,

"Yes, Michael, I believe you're the right person to fill this very important position. Your organization skills and direct approach to all problems and issues are just what we need to cut though all the bull shit of political dancing and the old Washington two step. Direct approach with common sense to all issues is your strength," she added. "I know this request comes a shock to you Michael, but I'd like your answer shortly. I need a strong Chief-of-Staff before I'm sworn in within two weeks."

"Please think about this Michael and consider this opportunity for you to serve within the Flagstaff capitol and becoming my Rock of Gibraltar. You'll be the strength behind the President taking daily care of thousands of problems while keeping all parties on the straight and narrow."

"As you know ma'am, I'm not married and I don't need to consult with anyone before making my decision. So with great pride I accept your offer to serve as your Chief-of-Staff." With that Michael stood up, came around the desk, bent over and planted a kiss on Sara's cheek.

Sara was surprised but recovered quickly and said, "That's great, when can you start?"

"I'll return to San Francisco to tie up a few loose ends as quickly as possible," he answered. "How about if I report to this office in one week, if that's okay with you?"

"Certainly. That will be just fine," Sara told her first Chief-of-Staff.

Both parties stood up, shook hands and Michael quickly left the office and headed home to California.

Sara sat back down and smiled to herself. She was happy she filled for most important position in her upcoming administration.

The next two weeks passed quickly without any major problems or setbacks. The new Mexican President Pedro Lazzara was keeping his word by preventing his countryman from illegally entering the four border states. Very few illegals slipped through his ring of containment across the entire two thousand miles of border.

Finally January first arrived and some one hundred thousand people from just about everywhere flooded into Flagstaff to get a glimpse of the formal seating of their first President of the 'Western States of America.'

Hundreds of large T.V. screens were placed throughout Flagstaff to insure everyone could see the swearing in of their first President. The oath of office will be given to Sara on the steps of the new capitol building. Only about twenty-five hundred people would be allowed within the confines of the capitol building and the official seat of the fledgling country.

The Chief Justice of the California Supreme Court and a Catholic priest were waiting at the glass podium for Sara Williamson to appear. As the President elect came into view a roar from the crowd became deafening. She waved to the crowd and proceeded to the podium.

She wore a light green business suit that fitted her figure like a glove. Being very tall, very leggy with an above average bust she was a beautiful sight to behold. The men everywhere knew that their first President was a good looking, well-built dish.

Chapter 6 – First Woman President

Once Sara arrived before the Chief Justice and placed her right hand on her family bible, Justice Wilson started to administer the newly worded oath of office to the first President of the 'Western States of America.' Usually a Vice President is given the oath of office at the same time, but a Vice President had not been chosen yet. Sara promised to pick a second in command within a month.

When Sara repeated the oath of office, the Chief Justice shook the new President's hand and twenty-five hundred people attending went ballistic. Thousands of colored balloons were released, all church bells started ringing and every device that could make noise was turned on.

Thousands of pictures were snapped to preserve the moment and the historical event of the first appointed (not elected) President of their new country 'Western States of America'. Not only their first President, but the first woman President to boot.

Throughout the evening of January first dozens of parties and hundreds of mini gatherings were celebrating the main event of their newly formed country and now government.

President Williamson attended a few gatherings throughout the evening, but quickly slipped away shortly after midnight. She retired to her almost complete office in the new capitol building with Marian Wilcox and the four Governors from California, Arizona, New Mexico and Texas. Lt. Governor of Arizona was sworn in during the afternoon as Governor of Arizona.

"Where is Michael?" Sara asked her Communications Director.

"He said he might be a little late," Marian told the new President.

"May I propose a toast, Madam President?"

"You certainly may, Governor Richardson."

As everyone started to lift their glasses, a knock on the door stopped that toast.

"Come in," Sara said in a strong voice. The door opened and the new Chief-of-Staff entered the room and before he could say a word, he was handed a full glass of champagne.

"Okay. We're all set," the Governor of California said. "Let's toast to the first President of our country and a great person, Sara Williamson."

The group emptied their glasses and threw the empties into the oversized fireplace to complete the toasting ritual.

"Thank you, my most trusted friends, we have just started to form our new nation. We have many appointments and positions to fill in the coming weeks as well as establishing federal and state agencies to fill the gaps that the old United States maintained before we seceded from the Union.

At least we have a capitol building and a treasury building that's almost complete, and we're starting to construct the military headquarters complex similar to the old Pentagon in Washington. It will be small compared to the size of the Pentagon, but adequate for our military and civilian purposes I've been told. Our government structure and building facilities must be able to handle the requirement of our population of seventy million plus. And we should be ready and prepared for any additional Western States that might want to join our new country," Sara said with a smile.

With that statement she received a loud clapping from the entire group.

"Well said," Marilyn told the new President. "Oh! There is one question I would like to ask you."

"Shoot." "Will you retain your active General rank now that you're our President?"

"No. I will resign my commission as of Monday morning," she replied. This is a civilian government and should not be run by a leader who is still in military service. I hope you all agree?" she asked.

Everyone in the room agreed with the exception of Michael McCarney the new Chief-of-Staff. He said he wasn't one hundred percent sure but that he would advise Ma'am President to hold off on that decision for a little while.

"Okay, Michael. I'm surprised you feel that way, but I'll put that on the backburner for now, but we must address this issue shortly."

"The first thing tomorrow morning, please contact Colonel Montgomery," she asked her Chief-of-Staff. "We haven't received any new info for almost a week," she added.

"I'll contact the Colonel first thing," he assured his boss.

"Good," Sara said covering her mouth to hide the yawn that indicated just how tired and spent she actually was after the most grueling day of her life. "Let's call it a day," she said removing her jacket. "Oh! This is the start of a new day," she quickly added. "Whatever it is, good evening and good morning," she told the small group. Everyone but Michael gathered up their personal items and left the President's office without saying another word.

Michael asked his boss whether they should have their first strategy meeting tomorrow or at a later date.

"Let's rest tomorrow, if you don't mind," she told her new Chief-of-Staff.

"Certainly," he answered. "I'll jot down some key items I'd liked to propose over the next few days," he added.

"Sounds good to me," Sara said.

With that Michael said, "Good morning, ma'am," as he left the office and headed for his new quarters in the capitol building.

Sara retired to her master bedroom, showered and put on an extra, extra large Penn State t-shirt and slipped between the light blue silk sheets.

The new President awoke at 06:30, showered and dressed for the first full day as 'President of Western States of America.'

As Sara approached her office, Mrs. Ruth Bakker her personal secretary met hew new boss with a hot cup of Ceylon tea and two cookies and a couple of slices of almost burnt toast.

"Thank you, Ruth," she said, taking the large cup of tea and the small plate of toast and goodies.

"If you need me, ma'am, just whistle or call. I'll be setting your schedule for the coming week. You can review your schedule sometime this afternoon if you chose she added."

"Okay, Ruth."

Sara entered her office to begin her first full day as her country's first President. She pressed the intercom and Mrs. Bakker answered. "Ruth, please call Michael and have him come to my office as soon as he is available. Nothing earth shattering, tell him, but I would like to see him today."

"Right away, ma'am."

Within ten minutes, her Chief-of-Staff was standing tall before President Williamson.

"Yes, ma'am," he said as she motioned him to set down at the small table across the room from her huge Presidential desk.

"Good morning, Michael," she said as he seated himself at the oval table. "Do you want anything to drink or eat?" she asked.

"No, I'm fine, I had a quick bite earlier this morning," he answered.

"Buck, I need to pick a Vice President within this month of January. I need you to make a list of potential candidates for this high position. We need somebody who basically thinks like we do. One who has strong conservative values that encompass smaller government, less taxes and policies and laws that stays the hell out of the lives of all Western Americans."

"I have a short list already," he admitted, "but I'll add a few more names for your review."

"I'd like around a dozen names to review, if that's possible," she asked.

"I'll provide at least twelve, as you requested," he answered.

"Thank you, Michael."

"Ma'am if you don't mind, my name is Michael but my handle or nickname is Buck. Buck was a handle given to me when I was a kid because I loved watching the old Buck Rogers films from the thirties. My father got a hold of the old movies somehow and I watched everyone at least fifty times each."

"Well, from now on you'll be known throughout our capitol and this administration as only 'Buck'.

"That's fine ma'am All my life friends have called me Buck, so if people start calling me Michael, I'll be saying 'who?'"

"Good," Sara assured her new Chief-of-Staff.

"Ma'am, I've contacted Colonel Montgomery at his headquarters in Querétaro Providence Mexico. He said he was going to give you an update within a few days if that was acceptable. I told him that was fine."

"Okay," Sara told her C.O.S.

"Buck, would you please schedule a meeting here in Flagstaff with the four Governors as soon as possible. A couple of topics will be our new Federal Mint and the political structure of our country. Tell them we have some first samples of our folding money and some ideas on our coinage."

"I'll contact the group and set up the money meeting this afternoon, ma'am."

"Good," she answered. "Oh! Buck, I see your office is full of boxes. Why not spend the rest of the day unpacking all your staff form San Francisco and have a working office."

"I do have a lot of personal belongings to unpack." he admitted.

"That's settled," she said. "See ya tomorrow."

Buck waved as he exited the President's office.

The four Governors arrived in Flagstaff and quickly entered the capitol building to attend the first official meeting with President Williamson.

After the usual hellos and handshakes the Governors were seated in the large reception room. The huge table was round so no one could set at the head of the table.Everyone seated was equal.

Ladies and gentlemen, I don't think you know our new Treasury Secretary, Mr. William J. O'Neil.

Bill O'Neil stood up and said please remain seated, he reached his huge hand across the table and shook all the Governors' hands.

"Make sure you count your fingers," President Williamson told the group. "He has a grip like a bear trap." They all stretched their fingers and laughed. Sara continued, "Mr. O'Neil is about six foot, six inches tall and weighs over two hundred seventy-five pounds and comes from Texas. Oh! And he usually carries a loaded handgun, I'm told. Is that true, Bill?" she asked the Secretary.

"Yes, ma'am, but I left my weapon with your secretary before I entered your office."

"Thank you, Mr. Secretary."

"We have decided on the coinage and the paper money. This meeting is to finalize our denominations, scenes on the folding money and photos on the coins.

Bill, please pass out the samples of our coins and paper bills. These are stamped 'samples', so they're not spendable dollars," Sara added.

"Too bad Eric commented, I like this thousand dollar bill."

"The following are the scenes on our paper money:

$1.00 = Alamo	$50.00 = Golden Gate
$2.00= Redwood Forrest	$100.00 = Gold Rush (Sutter' Mill)
$5.00 = Monument Valley	$200.00 = Carlsbad Caverns
$10.00 = Grand Canyon	$500.00 = Desert Scene (organ pipe cactus)
$20.00 = Gila Cliff	$1000.00 = Johnson Space Center

"If you agree with the various scenes on our folding money, I will give the okay to start printing the ten different denominations."

All four Governors and the President gave their approval for the Treasury Dept. to begin printing the paper money for Western States of America.

"Okay, now the problem coin denomination. We have ten coins ready for production if this group will approve the selection of persons representing the old west."

Bill passed out the list of coins and their representatives of the old west.

Coins:

$0.05 = Charles Goodnight	$2.00 = Geronimo
$0.10 = Buffalo Bill Cody	$5.00 = Davy Crockett
$0.25 = Wild Bill Hickok	$10.00 = Jim Bowie
$0.50 = Annie Oakley	$20.00 = Jesse James
$1.00 = San Houston	$50.00 = Christopher (Kit) Carson

"Does this group think it's a good idea to have people like Jesse James and Geronimo who were born killers on our coins?" Governor Anderson asked.

"Yes, I do," Margo said quickly. "Because they represented the old west, good or bad. Outlaws and renegades were part of the untamed west whether we like it or not," she added.

The other Governors said we agree and they looked towards the President.

She nodded her approval.

"Thank you, ladies and gentlemen," the Treasury Secretary said. He added, "The various western scenes on the reverse side of the coins were picked from your four states. Do you have any problem with our choices?"

"I think they're just fine, Bill," the President said looking around the table. Everybody present gave their approval by nodding their heads.

"The Treasury Department will start printing and stamping our money starting tomorrow morning. We have the coin blanks and rag paper in huge quantities ready to do, ma'am.

Our new money is smart looking and will be extremely difficult to print and copy by forgers."

"We have incorporated many safety and security measures within our folding money. Silver threads, invisible codes and proof marks as well as other anti-copy features." The Secretary continued, "I really like the new twenty dollar and fifty dollar coins. Both are not only gold color, be are covered with real gold. Each of these coins are large and heavy and will be very popular with our countrymen. The silver coins in one, five and ten dollars are made of 99% silver from our own silver mines in two of our Western States. Our money will be sought after by the remaining forty-six states," the Treasury Secretary said with a smile.

"Once the new money is printed, it will be shipped to our Central Government Bank here in Flagstaff. As you know this new bank has six floors below ground and will store our printed and coined money as well as the gold and silver bullion that is the backbone of our government's financial system. Once the banks are reestablished throughout W.S. of A., the Central Bank in Flagstaff will start issuing banks our new money for general distribution to the public. We will be on the gold standard, backed by gold bullion."

The Secretary continued, "The original amounts of new money given to each current state bank will be determined by your regulatory group I've been told, ma'am."

"Yes, that's correct. Each bank will receive different amounts depending on their current total assets and other considerations and factors. This banking system will not be controlled by a Federal Reserve banking system that had nothing to do with the Federal Government. Our banking system will be controlled through our Central Bank here in the capitol and supervised by government employees.

I think we have covered about everything pertaining to our money and its distribution. I'd like to thank Treasury Secretary O'Neil for his tireless service in bringing our new money to reality under very difficult conditions and time restraints." Sara stood up shock his hand and walked with him into the outer foyer. After a short absence she returned to her seat and said, "Sufficient amounts of our money should be ready within the next two weeks. Secretary O'Neil said the printing office will be cranking 24/7 until the required quantities are met.

Old American Greenbacks will be turned in for new W.S. of A. dollars."

"Okay," Sara said with a sigh. "Now let's get down to our political issues. Our constitution isn't completed yet but we, or I should say this small group, must set the ground rules for this democracy. With only some seventy plus million citizens we don't want or need the law making body of our government as large as the other forty-six states. The old congress with its five hundred and thirty-five members was way too large even with 312 million citizens. That's why nothing ever got done, too many career politicians to deal with. I would like the total number of representatives of all types to be somewhere around seventy members. That total would include Governors, Senators and State Representatives. Each state would be run by a strong Governor. He or she would preside over all law making issues and have the final yes or no vote whether the bill becomes a law or not. I want very strong state governments and less federal government intervention. Items like social security, state and federal pensions will continue to be funded by the old United States. Lump sum buy outs might be possible in the near future. The quicker we can cut the ties with our old government, the better we'll be. I'll be working with their re-elected President to iron out hundreds of various items like social security and government pensions. I would like samples and ideas of state and government structures required to support our new government and to insure our citizens have a strong voice in our new country.

"The law making body of our country should be held to as few members as possible. We don't need hundreds of representatives gumming up the political system. I want to work with a group form the four states that is controllable as I said before. We don't need the old 535 Reps and Sens to deal with. We can't afford the old gridlock that existed in Washington that crippled our old country and ground the U.S. to a standstill.

"We need to have our political system in place within the next thirty days. We've promised our countrymen that the new government would be as small as humanly possible, and I will keep that promise as their first President," Sara assured the group. "During the next ninety days we have hundreds of items to address and quickly solve so this fledgling country can start showing the world we are going to be a first class democratic country run by the people.

"One last thing on our Presidency. Remember the term of office for our next and future Presidents must be for four years only. Our new constitution must make that perfectly clear. No more campaigning during their first term to obtain a second. We want our head of state to concentrate on the issues facing our new country and not on personal gain and another four years. Also it must be spelled out as plain as day our constitution that a sitting President can be recalled if the majority of the people think he or she is not representing our country good enough. In the old United States it was virtually impossible to remove a President no matter what the charge or what he was accused of. We must have a policy and law that allows the removal of any President or law maker that is unfit to serve and represent our county. This removal process should not take more than sixty days at the most, with provisions that if the crime is great enough, his or her removal could be within days. Our new constitution must be a document that will stand the test of time like our forefathers constructed and wrote in 1776. This document must be plain English so all persons in our new country can understand and absorb the whole meaning of our constitution.

"Our select committee, and ourselves, who will write our constitution must have current and long reaching insight on the problems with human development and social justice that must prevail for all. Our document must require our citizens to be strong, hardworking, law abiding, self-sufficient and not a social burden to the rest of society. Very few people in the Western States of America will be dining at the Government trough. There will be no welfare like the other America along with the dozens and dozens of additional federal give-away programs. Everyone capable of working will find a job, pay taxes and contribute to our Western society.

"With that I'd like to end this meeting, if everyone agrees. We can meet again within a few days unless some critical issue rears its ugly head. Do we all agree?" she asked that four Governors and their aides. They all agreed by shaking their heads in the yes motion.

"Good," she said. "We have so much work to accomplish in such a short period of time. But no matter what, we must keep a wary eye on Mexico, China and our old friends in Washington. We don't want to be blind-sided by any of them."

"Have a safe return trip and don't hesitate to call me if anything hits the fan," Sara advised.

The group left the room quickly and headed back to their respective states.

Sara sat in the now empty room wondering how in the world are they going to cover all the requirements necessary to forge a new country with the thousands of items that must be addressed to insure a democratic government surrounded by near hostile countries. She thought, "Oh well, so far we have pulled it off. But for how long?" she said in a low voice.

Sara called her new Communications Director Marian Wilcox and asked her to contact Beverly Wolcott and get her final decision on whether or not she will accept the position of Assistant to the President.

"I'll call her right away," the new Director told her boss.

"Thank you, Marian."

Both parties hung up.

The phone rang as Sara replaced the receiver and startled her because she was in deep thought about the drug war in Mexico.

"Hello," Sara answered.

"Ma'am President, this is Beverly Wolcott."

"Beverly, it's good to hear your voice again," Sara said quickly. "Have you decided whether to join our new administration?" she asked.

"Yes, I've made up my mind. I will take the position of your personal assistant, if you still want me that is."

"You bet I do, Beverly, I have known you for more years that I care to remember and you'll fit right into our organization like a glove. You're smart, good with computers and you keep your mouth shut with sensitive material and you're not afraid to tell me I'm full of beans from time to time."

"Now when can you come to Flagstaff and join our staff?" she quickly added.

"I can be in Flagstaff this coming Monday if that's all right with you, Madam President."

"Good," the President said, "see ya early Monday."

As Sara hung up she thought, "There's another important job filled, only a couple hundred to go."

Chapter 6 – First Woman President

Before President Williamson could get her thoughts together the phone rang again. Communications Director Wilcox informed the President that Colonel Montgomery was on the line from Mexico.

"Put him through, please."

"Good morning, Colonel."

"Good morning, Madam President."

"I was hoping you would call, Colonel, I haven't had an update in a while," she said.

"Yes, ma'am, I know, but we have been very busy tracking down the western drug cartel and its tentacles that reach throughout Mexico and the States. We now believe that the Chino cartel is the largest and most powerful drug cartel within Mexico and most probably the world, Madam President. For years they have kept their huge organization as quiet as possible. When they eliminate someone it is done quietly and the body or bodies are never found. These people are just listed as missing. No open warfare, just quiet killings and burial at sea. Nothing messy that makes the papers or local newscasts. But we're learning that their payroll extends to high government officials here in Mexico and the States. We're hearing stories that some border officials are involved, as well as some Washington types. Also, the American Navy has been fingered as well."

"We are planning a large raid on the cartel and we're calling it 'clean sweep,'"

"Madam President, I hope this is a secure line?" the Colonel asked.

"Well, Colonel, I'm not sure, so let's end this conversation and I'll check this out. Please call back in an hour."

"Yes, ma'am," he answered as he hung up the phone.

"I can't believe the phone line to the President isn't a secure line and monitored constantly," he thought.

President Williamson buzzed the switch board and asked the operator, "Are these five phone lines into my office secure?"

"No, ma'am, only phone line #1 is secure at present."

"Good god, the world can capture my conversations on the other four phone lines."

"I'm afraid so, Madam President," the operator answered.

"Get me Marian Wilcox as quickly as possible," the President said in a subdued voice.

Within five minutes the phone rang and the Communications Director was on the line.

"Good morning, Madam President, the capitol switchboard said you called, something about the phone lines?"

"Yes, Marian, I did. The switchboard operator told me that all the phone lines into my office are not secured. Is that correct?"

"Only line #1 is totally secure, Madam President."

"Why in god's name aren't they all secure?" the President asked as calmly as possible.

"We thought only one line would be sufficient for high level conversation."

"My god, girl, all lines coming into this office must be secure and monitored 24/7. All conversations between myself and all parties must be and will be confidential in nature. How long will it take to secure the remaining four phone lines?" the President asked.

"It shouldn't take more than a few hours, I would guess, Madam President."

"See that it's done immediately," the President ordered. "And call me when they're fully secured please."

"Yes, ma'am, right away."

President Williamson replaced the phone and thought, "So most of my phone calls could have been captured by almost anyone throughout the entire world. I need my Chief-of-Staff more than ever now. Details like this must be covered to protect this office," she pondered.

Colonel Montgomery called again and President Williamson told him the bad news and asked him to call back on her secure line #1.

Ten minutes later the Colonel called back and was assured that their phone line was secured.

"Colonel, I'm so sorry that your previous conversation was not secure. This was inexcusable on my part in not knowing and insisting that all lines coming into this high office was fully secured and monitored 24/7."

"Let's hope nobody heard our conversation, Madam President. The Mexican drug cartel would have a heads-up on our current operation if they heard our conversation."

"Is there anything you can do to change you plan of attack if our ill-fated conversation was overheard?" she asked.

"No. ma'am, I don't believe so, we'll have to chance it I'm afraid," the Colonel answered. "When our plans are finalized I'll contact you with our plan of attack against the Chino cartel. I will probably have a list of high level names for your viewing, along with a case file on each name mentioned sometime within the next week or so."

"Colonel, I would suggest when you have gathered all your info on the subject, that you personally bring that sensitive material here to Flagstaff and give that information to no one but me."

"Do you agree, Colonel?" the President quickly added.

"Yes, ma'am, I do. This material will be for your eyes only," he answered.

"Thank you, Colonel, and goodbye."

Both parties hung up their phones very slowly.

The President wondered, "Who the hell will be on that list supporting and being paid by this drug cartel? I guess I'll know in about two weeks," she thought.

The Colonel slowly pulled his hand away from the phone and wondered how the new President, and a woman to boot, would handle this scandal which involved the other President and his administration.

As the Full Bird Colonel was pondering the problem, his Mexican aide entered the room and reminded him that the meeting with General Rōjas and President Lazzara was in just ten minutes.

"Thank you for the heads up, Lieutenant."

"Yes, sir."

Colonel Montgomery headed for the meeting to finalize the assault on the Chino drug cartel. He was thinking, "Do I tell them of my conversation with President Williamson on a non-secure phone line, or do I let it slide?"

President Obama was giving his usual Saturday evening address on radio and when he finished he was given a folded note by his military aide.

After reading the note he exploded in a fit of anger that startled his waiting staff. "Who knows about this?" he asked his long-time aide.

"Millions," he told the President. "It was broadcast on all the T.V. networks and radio about fifteen minutes ago sir."

 rickshaw

President Obama pushed back from his desk and said, "My god, another group of states wants to secede from our union. Nine states in all," he said looking at the note. He read that the secession documentation was delivered to Congress and the Whitehouse within the past hour. He read out loud, "The following states want to secede. Alaska, Colorado, Idaho, Montana, Nevada, Oregon, Utah, Washington and Wyoming. They basically stated the same reason as the other four states. Too much government, not enough federal protection against illegal aliens and federal mandates that allows these aliens all rights and privileges that are equal or even better than American citizens."

Obama immediately asked his Communication Director to contact the nine Governors for a meeting tomorrow at the Whitehouse.

Once contacted, the nine Governors insisted that only the President and the Secretary-of-State be present at the meeting. Only eleven people attending this very important and critical meeting that may determine the very future of the almost United States of America.

The meeting took place in a small room in the Whitehouse with the nine Governors and the President with Maggie Wilson. President Obama started by saying, "You can't secede from our union. If you do, the United States will be no longer. Currently we only have forty-six states remaining. I cannot permit this exodus by your nine states. That would mean half of the country would be lost. Certain foreign powers would jump at the chance to wage war on the country that was just split in half. We would not be able to defend our remaining country against attacks from Russia or China. They might even join forces to defeat the remaining states. We would be doomed as a free nation."

Governor Adams of Wyoming said, "Mr. President, we have already made up our minds. All our state residents have agreed that seceding from Washington is the only answer to our many problems. Our states are going broke because of Washington's directives. Mr. President, let me rephrase that, we're not going broke, we are broke, or I should say broken. Our states' residents are taxed beyond their ability to pay. They must choose between paying high taxes or house payments and food. They feel like we do, we must get away from the grips of the

Washington money grabbers that think the money sent to Washington is theirs to spend and squander away as they see fit. Well, Mr. President, no more, we have had it, no more Washington two-step. We want out of your tightening grip on the people of our states and their hard earned wealth.

"We are not asking to leave the remaining union, we are together seceding from what's left of your dying union, sir. We will be meeting with President Williamson in a few days to inquire whether it's possible to join her new western country. That move would make a total of thirteen Western States under President Sara Williamson with a population of one hundred and sixty million plus inhabitants."

"Is that all?" President Obama said in a curt voice.

"Yes, sir, that is. We are seceding from the remaining Washington union as of yesterday," the Wyoming Governor informed the President. The Governor said, "There is nothing more to add unless the other Governors have something to add." The other eight Governors nodded in a 'no' fashion to his question.

With that parting statement the nine Governors exited the small room and headed back to their respective states to confer with their staff and inform the public.

After the last Governor left the room, President Obama said, "My god, what will the next three and a half years bring to my Presidency?" He sat back in his chair and asked his Secretary-of-State, "What the hell do we do now? I admit that I didn't do anything to stop Governor Williamson and the others from leaving the United States, but we can't stand by and let nine more states leave Washington. We must, at all cost, prevent their secession from the remaining union."

Secretary Wilson said, "Mr. President, just how do we accomplish that without starting a second civil war that will cause death and destruction that would open the gates for any number of foreign powers to walk in and take America as their grand prize, with very little effort I might add?"

"Maggie, please call a meeting as soon as possible with all my civilian and military staff. Let's have the meeting in the Pentagon War Room."

Upon hearing the news President Williamson was somewhat surprised. She had heard rumors some months ago that other western states were not happy with Washington and

their do nothing attitude towards dozens of national and state issues. "My god," she thought, "our country of seventy million could almost double if they secede from the union and ask to join the 'Western States of America'"

Sara quickly called her Chief-of-Staff and asked him to quietly and quickly get an emergency meeting with the four Governors to assemble in Flagstaff as quickly as possible. "Tell them that subject of the meeting is an additional nine states want to secede from the Washington union. That will certainly perk them up, Michael. Sorry, I mean Buck."

"Yes, Madam President, it certainly will."

"Remember, Buck, President Obama gave them no choice but to leave the union. He didn't lift a finger to protect the citizens along the Mexican border and the other non-border states were strapped with Washington mandates that cost states billions and billions of dollars to support the illegal bunch. My comments during the Presidential inauguration must have turned the nine Governors and their citizens to their decision to leave the union. I hoped that wasn't the case," President Williamson admitted.

President Obama and his military aide entered the Pentagon War Room and without a word sat at the head of the huge thirty-two foot table. The whole staff sat down in unison and the War Room was dead quiet for a full minute. The President slowly rose from his chair and placed his hands on the table and said, in a subdued voice, "Ladies and gentleman, what the hell do we do now? This situation is totally unacceptable that an additional nine western states want to secede from our administration and possibly join President Williamson and her Western States of America. As far as I'm concerned we cannot allow these nine states to part company from our union. If they join the W.S. of A., that would bring their total to thirteen Western States and about half our current population. It would damn near cut this country in half as far as land mass," the President said, shaking his head. "Okay, people what do we actually do now?"

General Wolford, Chairman of the Joint Chiefs stood up and said, "Mr. President, with our nation in question we must not allow these nine states to leave the fold and join W.S of A. We must use military force if they don't change their decision to secede. The states don't have a real military force like the W.S. of

A. have, so our forces could quickly subdue them with minimum losses on both sides," the General said.

"Thank you, General."

"Who's next?" the President asked.

Secretary-of-Defense Marshal stood up and walked to the huge map of the original United States with the Western States of America shown in a different color. "If we allow these other states to join the W.S. of A., this is what it would look like." The Secretary picked up a large jagged piece of paper and affixed it to the map with push pins. "This is what it would look like if we allow them to exit the union. Currently more than half our west coast is in W.S.A. hands, and now with Washington and Oregon leaving the union, the whole west coast would be under the control of the Western States of America. Remember our border with Mexico is completely out of our control and in the hands of W.S.A., and if these nine states leave, our border with Canada will be reduced by almost half.

"If we're not careful we'll only have a border with W.S of A. and nobody else. This must stop, Mr. President, and I mean stop right now. No more exiting our union." The Secretary returned to his seat and slowly sat down.

"Thank you, Mr. Secretary. Now you people understand why I asked Jon to remain during my second term."

A few military and civilian staff members clapped on the President's phrase of the holdover Secretary-of-Defense.

President Obama quickly asked for additional comments on the crisis at hand.

Vice President Goodwin stood up and said, "Ladies and gentlemen, let's be very careful and not go off half-cocked and do something that will spell doom for our country." The V.P. continued, "If the nine states join forces with W.S. of A., the combined thirteen states would represent a very strong military force and a civilian population that approaches half our population. We just can't order our military to wage war against the remaining half of the country. I'm sure our military wouldn't fire upon their neighbors and family members. Mr. President, my vote on this issue is to allow the nine states in question to secede from the Obama union if they so desire. An all-out war between the states is out of the question. Millions would die and what's left of America would be quickly overrun by foreign armies. We must prevent this bloodshed at all cost, Mr. President," with that the Vice President slowly sat back down.

More than half of the staff in the War Room stood up and clapped very loud for a full minute. After the clapping died down, the President said, "Thank you, Chuck.

"Any other comments?" the President asked.

"Yes, Mr. President, I have some comments I'd like to add," the National Security Advisor Jennings said as he slowly rose from his wheelchair.

"Please be seated, Mel," the President urged his long-time friend and classmate.

"No, Mr. President. I may not be able to walk but I can stand for short periods without much pain," he said. "But thank you for your concern about my welfare, sir. As your National Security Advisor my job is not only to advise you, Mr. Present on foreign affairs but also on domestic issues as well. So here goes. Mr. President, I fully agree with Vice President Goodwin that we should, without delay, allow these nine western states to leave our somewhat less of a union and join the country of Western States of America. The security of our remaining thirty-seven states should be our foremost concern, Mr. President.

"We should not forgo the security and well-being of our remaining citizens for the possible revenge for the humiliation to the office of the President and yourself, Mr. President. There is more at stake, Mr. President, than the prestige of your office. Let's turn these states loose to join the W.S. of A. or form their own government so we can start trading with this new country. The quicker we put this national issue behind us the better we're going to be, sir."

With that final comment, the National Security Advisor fell back into his wheelchair. "Sorry," he said, "I can't bend very well after standing. I have to just plop into my wheelchair."

"Thank you, Mr. Jennings, for your advice. Your points are well taken as usual, sir."

"Ladies and gentlemen, let's close this emergency meeting for today. Get with your staffs and come up with viable solutions to this national crisis," the President urged.

The War Room emptied quickly and the President sat alone in the musty subbasement of the Pentagon. He looked at the map of the old United States and wondered just how this chain of events could have been prevented. He thought, "I know how we could have stopped this national madness. We should have stopped the illegals from crossing our borders while protecting the border state citizens. For decades we allowed these illegal aliens to flow across our borders as well as allowing undesirable foreigners to enter our country legally. Once these people entered our country, they simply disappeared into the woodwork of society never to be seen again. How stupid we were," he thought.

One of the Marine Corps guards opened the huge concrete door of the War Room and asked, "Mr. President, are you okay?"

"Yes, Sergeant, I'm fine. Thank you for asking."

"You're welcome, Mr. President."

President Obama slowly exited the War Room and headed for the Oval Office.

Before entering the Oval Office he thought, "We must assemble what's left of Congress and get their take on the latest secession by more western states."

President Williamson entered the room and the four Governors and their staffs stood up to great their first President. "Ladies and gentlemen, please be seated, thank you for Western States of America Flag standing but that's not necessary in our little informal meetings."

WESTERN STATES OF AMERICA

Sara took her place at the head of the table and was about to open the meeting when a knock on the door followed by Sara's Chief-of-Staff entering the room and quickly said, "I'm sorry for the interruption, but Madam President, you have an important message." With that Michael handed his boss a folded paper.

Sara read the note and asked Buck if he had read the note.

"Yes, ma'am, I have."

"Please put the call through on line #1 and I'll place it on speaker phone."

"Right away," Buck answered as he left the room at warp #2.

"Well, boys and girls, this will be an interesting call, it's Wyoming Governor Brian Adams."

Line #1 lit up and Sara picked up the phone and said, "Hello Brian, what's up?"

"Madam President, you're such a jokester. I'm sure after the news today you can guess why I'm calling."

"Of course, Brian, go ahead. Oh! I'm putting you on speaker phone if that's okay with you. The four Governors of W.S.A. and their immediate staff members are with me."

"That's fine, Madam President. The more the merrier."

"I'm speaking for the Governors and citizens of nine western states when I say we would like to join the Western States of America and you as our President."

"Well, Brian, you certainly lay a lot on a girl on the first phone call."

The room broke out in laughter and President Williamson had to laugh as she shook her head.

"Brian, I'm sure you and the other Governors have thought a great deal on this subject and action you took earlier today and what you're asking now."

"Just like you did prior to seceding from the union, we thought long and hard about leaving the remaining union. By leaving the Obama Whitehouse, we now have a chance to survive, Madam President. We feel if we join forces with W.S.A., the combined total of thirteen western states would become a strong country that controls all the Mexican border and about half of the border with Canada."

"Brian, I'll put your proposal to my staff, the four Governors and the citizens of W.S.A. I'll get back to you after I confer with all parties involved," President Williamson assured the Wyoming Governor.

"Thank you, Madam President."

Both parties hung up.

"Well, people, we expected that call but not that quick, I might add. Okay, what are your thoughts?" she asked the group.

"The added nine states would certainly add a lot of land mass to our country," Governor Lane said quickly. She added, "Lots of land but not many citizens."

"Madam President, a quick check shows the nine states in question would add a total of 795,776 sq. miles if they join our county. That would bring our total land mass to 1,457,526 sq. miles and our total population to around ninety million people or approximately twenty-nine percent of the total population of the old fifty state union. That would leave President Obama with about two hundred and twenty million citizens and our ninety million would be a almost forty-one present of his total."

"The added twenty million people and large chunk of real estate would certainly make our country huge," President Williamson added.

Line #4 on the phone console lit up. Sara picked up the phone and the operator said, "Madam President, the Governor of Alaska is on the line."

"Put him through, please."

"Good afternoon, Governor, what can I do for you?"

"First of all, Madam President, I'd like to say good afternoon, and second I'd like to ask if Governor Adams from Wyoming has talked to you yet?"

"Yes, he has, Barry. Only about twenty minutes ago."

"Madam President, Governor Adams and I have talked for weeks on the secession topic and now the State of Alaska and its citizens want to join 'The Western States of America.'"

"My god, Barry, that makes a total of nine new states that want to join our country. You'll have to give me some time to talk with my staff and our citizens on this whole nine state issue."

"Yes, Madam President, I understand the magnitude of the issue, but the State of Alaska would like an answer within the next thirty days, if possible."

"Certainly, Barry, you will have our answer within that time frame."

"Thank you, Madam President." Both parties hung up.

"Well, if we added Alaska to the mix that will increase the lad mass to over 2,072,756 sq. miles," Governor Anderson said.

"These two phone calls today have really thrown a monkey wrench into our progress of establishing the W.S.A. a tight new country. Now our country had been asked to accept another group of nine states. This is mind boggling and will require a lot of thought," Sara told the group. "In some ways this will cut the continental country in half. We must not rush into any decision too quickly without covering all the bases and ramifications.

We didn't get to the original intent of this meeting, but now we have more issues to deal with. Please return to your states and start pondering the recent events. I want to get the opinion of our country's citizens as well," Sara stated.

The Flagstaff meeting ended and the four Governors and their aides quickly left the capitol for their individual states and many upcoming private and public meetings.

President Williamson headed for her office and as she was about to open the large door, her Chief-of-Staff Michael McCarney said, "Mexico President Lazzara called about an hour ago."

"Thank you, Buck, I'll call Pedro in a few minutes."

Sara entered her office and sat down in her chair with a plop. She was suddenly very tired. She thought, "What I need is a quick pick-me-up. She called to Ruth Bakker in the outer office and asked for some sugar cookies and a cup of strong Russian tea.

"Right away, ma'am," was the answer.

Within fifteen minutes a tray of sugar cookies with sprinkles and a large ornate tea pot filled with Sara's special Russian Nal'Chik tea was brought to Sara's office.

"Thank you, Ruth, I needed something sweet and something hot."

Ruth placed the large tray on Sara's desk and left the office without saying a word.

Sara enjoyed the refreshments and leaned back in her brown leather chair to think about the earlier events of the day. "My god," she thought, "this is turning into something bigger than we originally thought our breakaway would cause. Not with an additional nine states and some twenty million plus new citizens asking to join our W.S.A. it's getting out of hand. Right now we don't have the government in place to handle such an increase in territory, citizens and boundaries. This could turn into such a debacle that our original plan for our new country could be in jeopardy," she thought.

Sara snapped out of deep thought and asked the switchboard operator to please contact Mexico's President Lazzara.

Within three minutes, line #1 lit up and Sara was informed that President Lazzara would be on the line momentarily.

"Good afternoon, Madam President."

"Good afternoon, Mr. President, it's good to hear your voice again, sir."

"Thank you, Sara," the Mexican President answered.

"How can I help you, Mr. President?" she asked.

"I was wondering when you're planning to remove the bulk of your military force from along the entire border with Mexico?" he asked.

"Well, Mr. President, you certainly have kept your part of the bargain by stopping most illegal aliens from entering our country. Our military leaders along the border have told me that only a small number of Mexican nationals have slipped by your people and ours. Your military and civilian authorities have done a sterling job to this point. But before I authorize any withdrawal of our troops from the border, I will again need your assurance that your current policy will continue with the same level of commitment, Mr. President."

"Yes, Madam President, I will make a Presidential promise to you and your country that my government will continue to stop all Mexican nationals and other foreign nationals from attempting to enter your country. I will sign an agreement if necessary, Madam President."

"No, Mr. President, that's not necessary, your word is good enough for me."

"Thank you, Sara."

"You're welcome, Pedro. I will talk to my military leaders and get back to you within a few days, Mr. President."

"Very good, ma'am, I'll be waiting for your call," the Mexican President said.

Both parties said, "Goodbye."

"Well, that just adds another issue to deal with at this time," Sara thought, leaning back in her chair. "Will these national issues ever stop popping up? I guess not," she thought.

Sara rang for Chief-of-Staff, Buck, and related her conversation with Mexican President Lazzara. She told Buck to contact General Wittingham and have him call as soon as possible.

"I wonder how the border leaders will react to President Lazzara's request. I'll guess our military leaders will balk at the possibility of leaving the border to only border patrols."

In less than thirty minutes Lt. General Wittingham was on the phone.

"Good afternoon, General."

"Thank you, Madam President."

"General, about an hour ago I received a call from Mexican President Lazzara. He wanted to know when we were going to pull back the bulk of our military units from the entire border with Mexico. I would like you and your staff to ponder this request by the Mexican President, and come up with various scenarios, sir."

"Will do, Madam President. I'll get back to you shortly," the General assured his boss.

"Thank you, General."

Sara dialed the switchboard operator and asked her to contact the four Governors and have them on a conference call.

Within the hour, all four western state Governors were on the phone with President Williamson.

"Thank you for your quick response to my call.

"First: the Mexican President is asking when we plan on removing our troops from the border. I called General Wittingham and asked for his opinion.

"Second: let's ask the citizens of W.S.A. if they like the idea of an additional nine western states to join our country. Let's format a questionnaire that covers the main question of should they be allowed to leave President Obama's Washington and join our country. This questionnaire should also show the land mass involved and the population increase.

"Let's make this top priority. We should give these nine states and answer as quickly as possible. Are there any questions on the two topics I've outlined?"

"Yes, Madam President, what do the Secretary-of-State and Defense think about these two issues?" the Governor of Texas asked.

"I don't know, Marilyn, I haven't talked to either party yet, but I'll contact them shortly."

"Please be thinking about the first issue, and let's format that questionnaire and distribute them quickly throughout the country. Make sure the questionnaire is in paper form and computer on line."

"Thank you, my friends, I'll be talking to you very soon."

The conference call ended and the President sat there wondering what's next.

President Obama's meeting in the Pentagon War Room started at 18:00 sharp. The War Room was packed with all his military and civilian leaders and a small group of college professors that specialize in state's rights and laws, as well as complete understanding of the constitution.

The President opened the meeting by saying, "Ladies and gentlemen. Do we allow the eight states and now Alaska make it nine western states to leave the union and probably join the country of 'Western States of America'?"

Secretary-of-Defense Marshal said, "Mr. President, we should never allow these nine states to leave our union and join the W.S.A. or form their own country. We should use whatever force is necessary to prevent this exodus from happening. Even is war is required to stop this madness then so be it," the Secretary added.

Secretary-of-State Maggie Wilson stoop up and said, "Ladies and gentlemen, we should under no circumstances declare war on any portion of our union, Mr. President. This country is in real trouble and we can't afford a second civil war that would return this country to the sixteenth century and complete lawlessness. Roving gangs will rule this nation from east to west and Mexican nationals will flood into this country across the border to add to the lawless gangs roving the countryside. Complete anarchy will consume this once great nation," the Secretary concluded.

The room erupted in loud clapping and yelling in support of Secretary Wilson's statements.

"Thank you, please be seated, people. Please, please be seated," the President asked.

Vice President Goodwin said he'd like to add to Secretary Wilson's comments. "The first civil war of 1861-1865 caused the death of 620,000 lives the North and South reported. We know the death count wasn't very accurate back then and I'm sure the real count was somewhere between 650 and 675 thousand lives, not counting the tens of thousands of civilians that died during the war. If there is another civil war the death count will be in the millions, Mr. President, so let's set aside the thought of sending military forces against these nine states. We must get our own house in order. We cannot continue to supply one third of the country with government giveaways and encourage millions of illegal aliens to leave their country and come to this country for 'free living' provided by our administration. I'm part of the problem and I admit it, Mr. President."

"Who's next?" the President asked quickly.

The Chairman of the Joint Chiefs, General Phillip Wolford stood up and walked to the huge map of the continental 48 states and drew a line from Montana down to Texas and a circle around Alaska. "This land grab, Mr. President, represents a total of some two million square miles of American soil by these nine states who are leaving the republic. As a military officer I've sworn to uphold and defend the constitution against all foreign and domestic threat of the greatest magnitude. In closing sir, my recommendation is to fight this massive exodus." With that the Chairman returned to his seat.

The room was dead quiet. They respected the views of the Chairman and his forty plus years of military service and guidance.

"Anyone else?" President Obama asked the elite group.

The Air Force Commanding General Jefferson Taylor said, "Mr. President, I have a few comments."

"Ladies and gentlemen, we have a large number of old SAC bases stationed within these nine states. Not only the bases, but they also contain large quantities of nuclear weapons and nuclear tipped artillery rounds. Two of our finest nuclear labs are also within these states, and don't forget the numerous silos positioned within their borders that have our birds ready for national defense. And of course we shouldn't forget Norad Headquarters stationed in Thunder Mountain Colorado.

"Mr. President, we are in deep trouble if we lose these facilities, and if Alaska is allowed to secede we will lose our defense against an over pole attack by Russia or China.

"Just the idea of these additional nine states leaving our union is mind boggling at least. With this exodus, our country would be reduced to third world status within few years, and if our Russian friends take advantage of our loss we would cease to be a nation.

"Somehow, Mr. President, we must convince these nine states that leaving the union would eventually bring down the W.S.A. and the remaining States of America. If talking doesn't work, sir, then military action should stop this exodus." The Air Force General slowly sat down and the room continued to be silent.

"Thank you, General Taylor, I guess we're evenly divided on this secession issue. As Commander-in-Chief, I will make the final decision, but before I do, I want a variety of scenarios covering all aspects of the national issue."

"Please get with your staffs and come up with solutions as quickly as possible," the President urged the gathering. President Obama stood up and said, "This meeting is over." The hundred people in the War Room exited the bomb proof bunker and headed for their offices within the Pentagon.

President Obama and his National Security Advisor headed for the Oval Office.

The alien round-up within W.S.A. had found millions of undocumented illegal aliens. Their round-up, incarceration and deportation is costing untold millions. The federal and local authorities are very surprised at the amount of illegals that have entered this country from our northern neighbors Canada.

President Williamson, during an interview, said, "We will continue to round-up all unwanted, un-documented illegal aliens within this country. Along with the illegal issue we are stopping the welfare give-away and many other old government policies and federal giveaways that have driven our states to bankruptcy. These many social programs will end very shortly. We want our citizens to be self-sufficient and prosperous, not feeding for years at the public trough. All our villages, towns, cities and states will be self-sufficient and live within their means. No more bailouts if you fail, you fail, and that's it. These items and policies supported by our old government are part of the reason why we seceded from the union and started our new country. Remember socialism doesn't work, just look at the mess Europe is in because of years of social policies that have ruined many countries.

"Many European countries are now bankrupt and are requesting billions upon billions of bailout Euros. They should not be given a single Euro because they'll never pay back a single penny.

"Our country, under President Obama, had lead us into the grips of massive socialism. Socialism rewards the individuals that don't contribute anything to the national good. They don't work, they don't pay taxes, but they receive all sorts of government benefits. As President of Western States of America, we will not participate in national socialism."

"Don't you think you're going to the extreme?" the national interviewer asked the President.

"No, I don't, thank you, and this interview is over," President Williamson informed the impertinent young fluff. "Please leave before I call security and have you escorted out," Sara said in a loud voice. She was tired of these liberal reporters who want all illegals to be allowed citizenship and everybody on welfare or other government giveaways.

"No more interviews," she told her new Chief-of-Staff as she paced back and forth. "We have so much to do without being questioned and picked apart by some young fluff who represents the national media who collectively want our new country and theirs to fail and become a third world country. They feel we have taken everything of value form all the countries of the world, and now we should give back everything to the non-productive and unimaginative peoples of the world.

"Complete socialism is the prelude to full blown communism. Socialism doesn't work and neither does communism."

"Yes, ma'am, I'll keep all interviews at arms-length for the time being," Buck told his boss.

"Thank you," Sara answered as she sat back down at her desk.

"Madam President, a large quantity of questionnaires have been returned, and so far the 'No's' have a lead of four to one against the adding of these nine new dissatisfied states to our W.S. of A. They're saying we're making good headway in establishing our new country and by adding these extra new states it would set back our progress to square one again.

If this trend continues ma'am, we'll have a resounding No to adding these extra nine states to our fledgling country. Besides the Washington administration wouldn't allow that number of states to leave the Washington union without threatening to declare war to prevent their leaving. Too many federal facilities within these nine states. If Washington took some sort of military action to prevent their exodus, we surely would somehow be drawn into their conflict one way or another," Buck assured his boss.

"I'm certain you're correct, Buck, and as President I do not want these additional nine states to join our Western States of America. We have enough to worry about with our four states, our border problems, foreign governments and Washington. Let's not add additional grief to our many problems."

"I agree, ma'am."

President Williamson's Chief-of-Staff quietly left the room while Sara continued to ponder the many issues that confront her office.

Line #4 lit up and Sara pushed the button and said, "Yes."

Ruth Bakker said, "Colonel Montgomery is calling from somewhere in southern Mexico, Madam President."

"Thank you, Ruth. Put him through."

"Colonel, I'm glad you called. What's up, if I dare to ask, sir."

"Well, ma'am, I owe you an update on a variety of issues," the American Full Bird Colonel admitted.

"Please continue, Colonel," the President urged.

"The first item I'd like to discuss is the possibility that you might withdraw all your military forces away from the entire border. I've been told President Lazzara has asked for this move.

"I would not recommend you do that, Madam President. While I believe that President Lazzara will continue to keep his word on stopping the illegal entry of Mexican nationals, he is not very popular with many drug cartels, some government agencies and many high ranking public officials. There have been numerous attempts on his life over the past two months and if he should be removed from office by any number of ways the incoming new President might not be obligated to continue Lazzara's policy on border reform.

"You might consider pulling back certain units, but I'd continue to fly sorties 24/7 along the border photographing everything.

"Madam President, this is only a suggestion from on old Army dog."

"Please continue, Colonel."

"The second item, ma'am, is the Chino drug cartel. Very shortly we will be ready to strike against this very large and well-connected drug cartel. They have their own private army and even a small air force. They boast having over ten thousand members that conduct their deadly business throughout Mexico and every country in Central and South America as well as the U.S. and Canada.

"We are getting reports that many high Ranking American government officials are on the Chino payroll. We may have some specific names very shortly I've been told. When we have names and proof, I will personally deliver that list and report to you, Madam President."

"Colonel, once you have that list of probable names, you must guard that info as top secret pertaining to national security."

"That goes without saying, Madam President."

"The last thing is my assignment here in Mexico. It should be finished when we have broken the Chino cartel and put its members in our island jail. I'm sure it will take months to track down their foreign operatives and cut their extended supply lines. I've been told they have some eighty tons of stored drugs in various locations throughout Mexico alone. To locate these huge stashes and dry up the pipeline will take some time.

"Madam President, I would like to stay until we have crushed this massive organization and destroyed their huge quantity of deadly white powder."

"You stay in Mexico as long as you feel you're needed, Colonel.

"But please be very careful, sir, we can't afford to lose you, Colonel."

"I will be super cautious, I assure you, Madam President.

"I'll call again when I have that important list for your eyes only."

"Thank you Colonel, and good luck in your upcoming exercise."

"Goodbye, ma'am."

"Thank you again, Colonel."

Both parties hung up.

Sara sat back and thought, "I wonder who in the U.S. is on the list. Accusing some of the Washington elite will be a dangerous adventure to say the least. They won't appreciate an outsider accusing them of treasonous activity. We'll just have to see where the chips fall. I hope none of our people are fingered in the cartel sting," she mused.

Chapter 6 – First Woman President

Chief-of-Staff, Buck McCarney approached President Williamson's office with the final vote tally on whether the nine runaway states should join our Western States of America.

Mrs. Bakker told Buck to go right in, "Madam President is alone."

Buck told his boss that the final votes were in for the yes or no vote towards having the nine states join our country.

"Madam President, we have a total of 2,100,070 votes, and 445,779 voted yes and 1,654,291 voted no. Overwhelming the population if W.S. of A. wants no part of the seceding nine states. Their comments indicate we have a good start on creating a government with conservative values, with less taxes and the freedom to start new business without government red tape and a ton of restriction."

"That is certainly good news," the President said, clapping her hands. "I feel the same way. Please contact the other governors and give them the final tally and comments if you would, Buck."

"Yes, ma'am, right away."

"Well, now how do I break the news to Wyoming Governor Adams and the other eight states?"

Sara pressed the intercom and said," Ruth, please contact Marian and ask her to come to my office."

"Yes, ma'am."

The Communications Director was at the President's door within five minutes.

"Come in, Marian."

"You rang, ma'am," she said with a smile.

"Yes, I did," Sara said with a slight grin.

"Would you please contact Governor Adams of Wyoming and ask him to come to Flagstaff for a meeting with me."

"Certainly, Madam President."

"May I tell him the subject of the meeting?" Marian asked.

"Yes. The subject matter is their request to join the W.S. of A. upon seceding from the Washington union."

"I'll contact the Governor right away, ma'am."

Marian headed for the door when President Williamson said, "One more thing. Ask our four governors to attend the meeting with Governor Adams and myself. You set up the time and date, it makes no difference to me."

"Yes, ma'am, right away."

President Obama assembled his civilian staff for a 10:00 hundred meeting in the Whitehouse War Room. The Commander-in-chief started off the meeting by saying, "Gentlemen, we cannot allow these nine western states to leave our forty-six state union. Whatever it takes to convince them not to secede must be done. I need ideas and I need them today. We must come up with programs and tax relief incentives to woo them back."

Vice President Goodwin said, "Let's cut the federal gasoline tax in half. Also let's reduce the tax on individuals and corporations."

"Thank you, Charles. These are good ideas to start with, but we need a lot more than that to convince them to stay."

National Security Advisor Jennings said, "Let's strengthen our border with Canada and put new requirements on persons entering our northern states and two Pacific states. Let's purge these states of all unwanted and undocumented foreign invaders. My god, we sound like W.S. of A.," the National Security Advisor continued. "Mr. President, if you had done these things we're suggesting now, the four states that seceded would have surly remained in the union. But that's old history now."

"Thank you, Mel," the President told his long-time friend.

Secretary-of-Sate Wilson stood up and said, "Gentlemen we must allow these nine western states to determine their own destiny by allowing each state to vote whether or not to continue to fund programs like welfare, food stamps and a dozen other federal sponsored giveaways. Each state should sponsor whatever state funded programs they want. The national government should back off and allow these states in question to run their own states with a lot less interference from the federal government in Washington. Oh! And that statement includes the balance of our thirty-seven states."

Secretary-of-Defense Marshal said, "Mr. President, does this mean we won't take any military action against these nine breakaway states?"

"Yes, Mr. Secretary, that's exactly what we mean. No military action will take place against any of the states in question. Too many down side ramifications that would likely end this country as we know it today," President Obama quickly told the group. "We must contact Wyoming Governor Adams as quickly as possible and explain this various options and concessions we're willing to offer."

"Bob, please contact Governor Adams and ask him to come to Washington and discuss the secession issue."

"Yes, sir, right away," the Chief-of-Staff said as he exited the meeting at warp speed.

"Gentlemen, let's get busy with a list of concessions that might change the minds of these nine governors," the President urged. "I need a solid list of proposals to offer Governor Adams when he arrives."

Chief-of-Staff Mott returned within a few minutes and informed President Obama that Wyoming Governor Adams was on his way to see President Williamson in Flagstaff.

"Good god, he is trying to convince Sara that the nine runaway states should join up with the W.S. of A.? Leave a message with his staff that I still would like to see him in Washington as soon as possible."

"Yes, Mr. President. The Chief-of-Staff hurried from the room to inform Adams' staff."

Governor Adams arrived in Flagstaff and was quickly driven to President Williamson's newly completed office.

President Williamson welcomed the Wyoming Governor and spokesman for the nine seceding states. "Please sit over there in that green chair, no one has sat in that new chair. This furniture only arrived yesterday," she added.

Sara picked up the phone and asked Buck to have the four Governors join the meeting.

As the four Governors were seated, the President said, "Governor, I'm sure you know the Governors of California, Arizona, New Mexico and Texas."

"I know everyone but the new Governor of Arizona," he replied.

"Governor, may I introduce Margo Lane, the new Governor of Arizona and my replacement, I might add. Margo, this is Governor Adams of the great state of Wyoming." Both shook hands then returned to their seats.

"Well, Governors, this is your meeting," Sara told her guests.

"Thank you, Madam President. I'm sure all of you know exactly why I'm here representing the nine states who want to leave the Washington union for the same reasons the Western States of America was formed. We are asking that our nine

western states be allowed to join your new country, Madam President."

"Governor Adams, I'm sure your reasons to leaving the Obama Whitehouse are for many of the same reasons we left the Obama Whitehouse. But, Governor, we must decline your offer to join our country of W.S. of A. Now let me tell you why," Sara said quickly.

"The first thing is that by your exiting the remaining forty-six states it would basically split the country in half. The remaining thirty-eight states would lose half the Canadian border and lose the balance of the Pacific coast. The only access to foreign shipping would be the east coast and the southern states. The Obama administration would not allow the squeezing and non-access to the northwest and half of Canada from Washington State to the eastern part of Montana. Also you must consider the large number of military installations within your nine states. NORAD complex in Colorado, and the bases and early warning network within Alaska. And don't forget the millions of barrels of oil daily coming from Prudhoe Bay to the lower forty-six.

"Now for the biggest reason we must say no to your request. We as a fledging country have made good progress in forming our new nation. We have with the help of Mexican President Lazzara almost stopped the entire flow of illegal aliens from entering our country along the entire two thousand miles of border with Mexico. President Lazzara is clamping down on all the drug cartels within Mexico with our help. We as a new nation cannot take on the extra burden of adding nine additional states and millions of people to the W.S. of A. We have already established borders with our adjoining states and have even settled upon a capitol city which you know is Flagstaff, Arizona. As you can see, we have gone too far in establishing a new nation to just scrap almost everything and start again.

"For all these reasons and many more we must again say no to your request to join the Western States of America. As head of State, I'm truly sorry, Governor, but my word is final." Sara told the Wyoming Governor.

With that, Governor Adams stood up and said, "I too am sorry your answer is 'no'. I guess our nine states only have a couple of options remaining. One is to form a new country and government, and the second is to stay with the Obama

Whitehouse and be bleed to death by federal mandates and unpayable taxes."

Sara said, "Governor, I'm afraid your choices are few. I would talk to President Obama and ask for as many concessions as you can get. Remember, he cannot afford to lose nine states that would cut his remaining country in half. Maybe he would be willing to reduce or eliminate certain taxes and federal mandates to persuade you to reconsider and stay with Washington. The Western States of America wish you and your followers much luck in whatever course of action your group of nine decides to take."

"Thank you, Madam President, and your Governors present for at least hearing my proposal. When I heard the results from your questionnaire on the 'yes or no' for our joining the Western States of America, I thought your answer would be 'no'. But you understand we had to try anyway," Governor Adams admitted. He slowly stood up and shook hands with Sara and said, "Thank you again for hearing my story." The Governor quickly turned and exited the room.

"Well, that didn't last long," Sara admitted to the group.

"I don't envy them," Governor Anderson of New Mexico chimed in. "They're going to have a tough row to hoe now that we have rejected their request to join W.S.of A."

"Does anyone else have anything to add to this subject?" Sara asked.

"Yes, Madam President, I do."

"Go ahead, Margo," the President urged.

"Well ma'am, what if Obama's administration decided to wage war against these nine states?"

"I don't think he's that stupid," the Governor of Texas said quickly. "He would be exposed to foreign intervention while he was mounting a campaign against the nine. I would guess that Russia and China would probably join forces and attack all the continental United States from coast to coast. And of course that would draw our country into the battle."

"Let's hope Governor Adams and President Obama can come to some sort of agreement before it comes to all-out war," Sara said, shaking her head. "Before you all leave, I'd like to address another subject. As you know, President Lazzara has asked that we withdraw our troops from the entire length of the Rio Grande. So far he has upheld his promise to stop his countrymen from entering the border states illegally. A few days ago I received a call from Colonel Montgomery urging caution when we consider withdrawing our border forces. The Colonel feels that with Mexico in a state of flux in dealing with the numerous drug cartels and the fact that many assassination attempts have been made against President Lazzara, he may not survive his Presidency.

"If he dies, for whatever reason, the new President might feel differently about the border situation and reverse the agreement we had with President Lazzara. Colonel Montgomery is advising we pull back only a small force of support unites while maintaining the large force of combat units at ready.

"When you return home, meet with your military leaders and discuss the option of removing all units or just a token number. In the meantime, I'll contact General Wittingham and get his views on any withdrawal from our border. Thank you for attending Governor Adams' meeting and let me know as quickly as possible on the question of border withdrawal or not."

"Ruth, please contact Buck and ask him to join me in my conference room as soon as possible. Nothing urgent, Ruth, if he's tied up let me know."

"Yes, ma'am."

Sara waited for fifteen minutes then headed for the large conference room. She opened the pair of large heavy doors and spotted Buck sitting alone at the head of the huge table that could seat twenty-four.

Buck jumped up and started to move when Sara said, "Stay seated, you look good setting at the head spot."

"Sorry, ma'am, I wasn't thinking, or I should say I was in deep thought," Buck admitted.

"Remember when I asked you to make a list of candidates for Vice President?" Sara asked.

"Yes, ma'am, I have that list in question," Buck replied.

"How many names are on that list?" she asked her Chief-of-Staff.

"You asked for twelve names and I have twelve, ma'am. But I consider only three or four to be top candidates for V.P.," he added.

"Okay. Let's go over the list of names."

"Can I give you the top three first, Madam President?"

"Of course, Buck."

"First: Eric Richardson"

"Second: Lt. Gen. Charles Wittingham"

"Third: Kathleen Wilson Lopez"

"Forth: Paula Catherine Anderson"

"That's enough, Buck, those four are good enough. Normally there would be a selection committee to produce a list of candidates for the office of Vice President, but I alone want to pick my second in command without a lot of fanfare and delay," Sara admitted. "Who would be your first choice?" Sara asked her Chief-of-Staff.

"Well, ma'am, my first choice would be Governor Richardson from California. He thinks like we do, ma'am, and he has been the Governor of the second largest state for years. He has controlled spending throughout the state, which is a tough job considering all the movie liberals and hard core democrats throughout the entire state. He was responsible for repealing many laws the previous governor passed with the help of the state's numerous liberal judges. Eric purged the state of most of the liberal judges by passing a law supported by the people of California that allows the recall of any state official the public deems incompetent. He would be my first and only choice, Madam President."

"Thank you, Buck, for your comments. May I see the complete list?" Sara asked her C.O.S.

"Certainly," he said as he handed his boss the entire list of V.P. candidates.

"That's quite a list," she said scanning the balance of the names. "I'm surprised at a few names," she said quietly before handing the short list back to McCarney. "I'm intending to agree with you, Buck," she said leaning back in her chair. "Has anyone else seen this list?" she asked.

"Certainly not, Madam President, this list is top secret as far as I'm concerned," Buck answered. He continued, "I'm surprised you should even ask me that."

"Sorry, Buck, I shouldn't have asked you that. I'm sorry," Sara said shaking her head. "My trust in you is one hundred percent," she added.

"Thank you, ma'am. All's forgiven."

"Buck, I'll let you know my decision for Vice President in a couple of days."

"Yes, ma'am." Buck left the room without another word. He was visibly shaken by Sara's comment of questionable loyalty.

When the Chief-of-Staff left the room, Sara was very disturbed at her comment and choice of words toward her own staff watch dog.

Governor Adams' car was waiting with his aide de camp inside. As soon as he settled in the back seat his aide told him of the call from President Obama inviting him to the Whitehouse as soon as possible. "Is he going to feed us or eat us?" his aide asked.

"Your guess is as good as mine," the Governor answered.

"Call the airport and change our destination from Cheyenne to Washington D.C."

Upon arriving in Washington, a long back limo was waiting to drive Governor Adams and his aide quickly to the Whitehouse. Governor Adams was escorted to the Oval Office where President Obama and the Secretary-of-State Wilson were waiting.

"Thank you for coming so quickly," the President said. "I know you had to change your travel plans on short notice and I'm glad you're here. Please be seated, Governor. The black leather chair is the most comfortable, I've been told."

"Now let's get down to business and the reason I asked you here."

"First I must somehow prevent you and the other states from leaving the forty-six state union. When I say prevent, I don't mean by force and military action. We must prevent that at all cost, don't you agree, Governor?"

"Yes, Mr. President, I agree."

"I assume your meeting with President Williamson did not go well. Under the circumstances, if I were in her position I wouldn't want another nine states to add to their burden of creating a new country and government. You know your group of nine leave very few options, I'm sure you know them too well. On the other hand, you know Washington can't afford to lose another nine states. Half of the country would be lost and that would create a golden opportunity for China and or Russia to strike a fatal blow to the whole continental U.S. Both foreign powers have been waiting for just this type of crack in the union to finish off this country once and for all. Now, with that said, I want to propose some changes that I hope will change your mind about leaving our forty-six state union:

#1. We're willing to cut federal taxes by twenty-five percent.

#2. Cut federal tax on gasoline by fifty percent.

#3. Our military bases stationed within your states will be compensated the same as our foreign countries. This will amount to billions of dollars per year.

#4. We will supply federal funding for the round-up and deporting of all illegal aliens.

#5. As President I promise you this administration will back off even more on certain federal mandates. Your states will be allowed to determine the social programs they feel necessary for the well-being of their state citizens.

"Governor Adams, what do you think of these concessions I've proposed so far?" the President asked.

"Well, Mr. President, that certainly is a good start, but I'll have to confer with the other eight Governors before giving you an answer."

"Please get back to me as soon as possible," the President urged.

Governor Adams left the Whitehouse and headed for his home state of Wyoming.

Secretary-of-State Wilson said, "Mr. President, what are our chances of convincing these runaways to remain in the fold?"

The President thought for a minute and said, "I would say better than fifty-fifty. I don't believe they have much of a choice in the matter. But we'll just have to wait and see which way they choose. Make sure our top commanders know what we have proposed to the nine Governors."

"Yes, sir, I will, Mr. President."

President Williamson rang for Ruth Bakker and asked her to contact Eric Richardson and ask him to come to Flagstaff for a meeting.

"May I tell him the subject matter?" Ruth asked.

"No. Just ask him to come alone," Sara answered.

"Yes, ma'am, right away."

"Thank you, Ruth."

The next afternoon, Eric arrived in Flagstaff and was met by Sara's limo and driven quickly to the Arizona Whitehouse for his meeting with President Williamson.

Mrs. Bakker rang the President and said, "Governor Richardson is here, ma'am."

"Thank you, Ruth, send him in."

"Yes, ma'am."

The California Governor entered Sara's office and had a puzzled look on his face. Before Sara could say anything he asked, "How many are attending this meeting?"

"Only you and I," she quickly informed the Governor.

"Boy, this must be really important if it's just the two of us," he said.

"It is of the utmost importance, I assure you, Governor. Eric, I would like you to be my Vice President. I think you would be the perfect person for this very important job representing the 'Western States of America'.

"Now let me explain further. As you know in the past, most V.P.'s did very little and a lot of them were nothing more than figure heads at best. Most were kept in the dark and unaware of many national issues.

"But not this time. Between to two of us we'll be so busy it will make our heads spin. With creating a new government, our border problems, investing in Mexico and a thousand other projects, no one person can handle this amount of items. As Governor of California you have shown strong leadership in a largely democrat state while keeping your state finances in the black. Your inheritance was a state on the verge of bankruptcy, but within four years and against overwhelming odds, you turned the red ink into black. I know you can do the job of Vice President, and for your information I've not considered anyone else for this important job. Should anything happen to me, I know you would be an excellent President.

"Now I'm asking Governor, will you become the first V.P. of our country and represent 'The Western States of America'?"

"My God, Sara, I'm overwhelmed by your offer. Can I think this over, Madam President?"

"No, Eric. I want your answer today, please."

"Can I at least call my wife and confer with her on your unexpected offer?"

"Certainly, Eric, but I want your wife to keep this quiet until you have decided one way or another, you understand?" the President insisted.

"Yes, I understand. I'll call Margaret right away." He exited the office at warp speed to inform his better half of this opportunity to become Vice President.

After only thirty minutes Governor Richardson returned and said, "Madam President, I accept your offer to become the first Vice President of 'Western States of America'."

"I'm very happy that you have decided to accept my offer Eric. You'll have to move to Flagstaff just as soon as possible," she reminded her almost V.P.

"Yes, I know. How much time before you want me in Flagstaff?" he asked.

"Within a month at the outside," she answered. "But I want you sworn in as Vice President within the next few days or so," Sara insisted.

"Yes, ma'am, I agree."

"I'll call Kathleen Lopez, our Chief Justice, and see what her schedule is for the next few days."

"Just let me know when you want me here for the official swearing-in, Madam President. In the meantime I'm heading back to California and get things moving to sell our house. As you know, I don't live in the Governors' mansion. It was much too large for my wife and myself. We should be in Flagstaff within the month," he assured his new boss.

Governor Adams started off the meeting with the other eight state Governors by passing out the list of proposed changes offered by President Obama. Alaska Governor Torcello stood up and addressed the group of Governors and their aide de camps.

"Ladies and gentlemen, after reading this list of concessions the President is offering our states, I'm very dubious that his administration will allow these concessions to take place. How do we know he will keep his word and not prevent our seceding from his union by military action?"

"We don't know," Brian told the Alaska Governor. "But this list will save our states hundreds of billions of dollars each year and also give us huge income from the military installations within our states. All of you have had time to review the list of concessions, what do you think?" the Wyoming Governor asked.

The Governors of Washington and Oregon said that their leaving the federal government would close off the Pacific west coast and stop most imports to the Obama Whitehouse. "We can't believe the President and his generals would allow this to happen without a real fight."

An aide to Alaska Governor Torcello stood up and said, "May I address this group?"

"Please, go ahead," Brian told the aide.

"Gentlemen, these concessions proposed by our President are worth more than a trillion dollars to our nine states in just over two years. How can we not take advantage of this opportunity being offered? If President Obama doesn't uphold his end of the bargain, then we still can secede from the Washington union."

"Thank you," Brian told the Alaska aide.

"Well, gentlemen, we don't have much time. Can we take a vote on the Washington proposal at this time?" Brian asked the group. "Let's take a couple of hours then decide one way or another. We certainly don't have time to present this yes or no question to our state citizens. We represent them and must decide this one ourselves. Please confer with your people and we'll vote within the next two hours," Brian urged.

After two hours of arguing and much debate, the nine states were ready to vote. "We'll vote in alphabetical order," Brian said.

Alaska - yes
Colorado - no
Montana -no
Nevada - yes
Oregon - yes
Idaho - no
Utah   - no
Washington - yes
Wyoming -yes
The vote tally was 5 – yes   4 – no

"Then we accept the concessions proposed by Washington."

Chapter 6 - First Woman President

"Now there is one additional item we must agree upon," the Wyoming Governor told the group. "Along with everything else we must insist that these federal concessions be offered to the other thirty-seven states as well. All forty-six states must be treated equally or they might force President Obama to change his mind and modify his concessions to our nine states. Do we agree that all states should have the same relief for federal over taxation?" Brian waited a full minute before the remaining Governors nodded in approval.

"Thank you, gentlemen."

"I'll fly to Washington tomorrow, but first I want to speak to President Williamson and explain the various concessions offered by the Obama administration. I want her take on these proposal offerings and our demand that all states be allowed the same tax relief and federal help in removing all illegal aliens."

"Madam President, Wyoming Governor Adams is on line #4."

"Thank you, Ruth."

"Good morning, Brian, it's good to hear your voice again," she told her long-time friend from Wyoming.

"What can I do for you, Brian?"

"Madam President, I want to run something by you. I need your advice."

"Go ahead, Brian."

Brian explained the meeting with President Obama and the group of nine state Governors. He covered all the Whitehouse concessions that were offered in great detail. When he finally finished he said, "Well, what do you think, Sara?"

"Brian, I believe it's worth a gamble. Right now you'd be better off by staying united with Obama's administration rather than striking out on your own and trying to form a new nation. I don't believe the current government would allow your block of nine states to exit their union. They would have far too much to give up and would certainly lay themselves wide open to foreign intervention and even occupancy. I also like the idea of your insistence that all remaining states be given the same concessions as their offering you. Good move on your part, I might add, Brian."

"Thank you, Sara, I'm on my way to Washington as we speak. We'll talk again after I visit with the President," he assured his long-time friend.

"Thanks again, Madam President."

Both parties hung up.

Sara thought, "President Obama will surely have a stroke or at least a super fit when he hears Brian's request that all states be treated equally. I'd like to be a little mouse in the room and hear that conversation," she thought, shaking her head and showing a slight grin.

Sara was brought back to reality with a knock on the door.

"Come in," she said in a surprised voice.

"Madam President, Chief Justice Lopez just returned your call and said her docket was clear for the next week. She said just pick the date and time for swearing in Vice President Richardson."

"Thank you, Buck. How about having the swearing in this Sunday," Sara suggested.

"The quicker the better, Madam President."

"Then it's settled. But let's call Governor Richardson in California and ask him if this Sunday is acceptable to him and his family. If he says that he is okay with Sunday, then you'd better get busy setting all the wheels in motion for his inauguration here in the capitol building."

"I'll call him right away, ma'am."

President Lazzara was leaving his office in Mexico City when a large black van without plates sped past spraying dozens of rounds at the President and his small group of body guards and staff assistants. The speeding van passed quickly around a street statute and disappeared quickly into the noon day traffic. Five people lay dead on the steps and sidewalk but although President Lazzara was wounded twice, he was awake and alert. Within minutes he was rushed to the nearest hospital in guarded condition.

General Rōjas was informed of the attempted assassination with all available details within minutes at his Army headquarters in Querétaro. The General quickly told Colonel Montgomery and both men prepared to fly to Mexico City within the hour. Aboard the military jet Colonel Montgomery told his friend, "These cartel bastards are not getting away with this lawlessness anymore. We'll track these people down, no matter how long it takes, General."

After an hour flight they arrived at the military air base just outside Mexico City. Within thirty minutes they approached the hospital which was virtually surrounded by military units protecting President Lazzara and wounded members of his staff. General Rōjas and Colonel Montgomery were escorted into the hospital and directed to the top floor where the Mexican President was resting from surgery. The President was not fully awake form his surgery, but awake enough to tell his military chief to find the cartel members and bring them to quick justice.

The Chief Surgeon said, "Gentlemen that's enough, the President must rest. You can see him tomorrow."

"Take care, Mr. President, you can bet the Colonel and I will find these cowardly bastards who did this." Both men left the hospital and returned to the airbase just west of the city. "Let's return to the hospital around noon tomorrow," the Mexican Commanding General urged.

"Sounds good to me," his American Colonel and friend added, "noon is fine. But before that, let's shake the bushes and see what shakes loose. Get our undercover officers questioning all their snitches and informants and see if we can finger these bastards before the dust settles."

More than fifty undercover military officers and some one thousand local police hit the streets in search of any info that might lead them to the low life creatures. The word also went out to the small villages that are known to supply workers for the various cartels. A reward equal to one hundred thousand American green backs was offered to anyone who supplied the information that would lead to the arrest and conviction of said assassins and attempted assassins of Mexican President Lazzara.

"I'm sure someone will put claim to that much reward and turn against those bastards," Col. Montgomery told a group of Mexican officers waiting to see General Rōjas.

The next day around quarter to twelve General Rōjas and the Colonel entered the President's hospital room and were surprised to see their leader setting in a chair beside the bed. Both men saluted the President and were told to be seated.

"Thank you for coming back today," Pedro told his two favorite Army officers. "When the shooting started I could see the black van and the two gunmen who had dark masks covering their faces and firing automatic weapons from within the van. I assume they wanted to retain all their brass casings and not leave a trace."

"I think you're right, Mr. President, they wanted a clean get away and to leave no evidence."

"Now, gentlemen, what is our first action in order to apprehend these slime balls, as you Americans say?"

"I like your choice of words, Mr. President, very colorful indeed," the Colonel added with a smile. All three men had to laugh.

"Please don't make me laugh," the President urged, it really hurts when I laugh.

"Sorry, sir, but your American slang is expanding quite nicely," General Rōjas added.

"Mr. President, we have fifty undercover officers in the field as well as over a thousand federal and local law enforcement personnel beating the bushes for any information on the attempted assassination and murder of your body guards and staff members. We are also concentrating on the villages that supply manpower for the local cartels in hope for a lead to who and where, Mr. President."

"Thank you, I know you both will pull all stops to locate these people. Mexico cannot continue to tolerate these types of actions if we want to remain a free and law abiding nation. These drug cartels must be wiped out once and for all so our people can be free of intimidation, corruption, greed and indignity."

"Please, gentlemen, go and route out this cancer that has gripped the country from border to border and sea to sea. Their tight grip must be broken and never again be able to make a fist against our government. Now, my friends, I must again rest. Good luck in the hunt and find these assassins as quickly as possible," President Lazzara asked.

"Yes, sir – will do."

Both men saluted and left the room smartly. They headed for the military airport and the return trip to Army Headquarters in Querétaro. Once they arrived, they immediately called for a meeting with all their troops to fill them in as much as possible about the assassination of five staff members and the attempted assassination of their President. Once the troops were filled in on the attempt on the President's life, they were dismissed to resume their normal duties.

General Rōjas and Colonel Montgomery gathered up their staff officers and held a quick meeting in the headquarters war room. In perfect Spanish, the Colonel told the group that their attack on the Chino cartel is being moved up due to the attempted assassination attempt on President Lazzara. "Only the General knows the exact day and time of the attack. We agreed that one man would know the correct time for security reasons. We'll be privy to time and date only a few hours before shoving off. We can't afford a surprise when we enter the compound. If they are prepared and ready for us we'll take a real beating."

"That's all I have. Do you have anything to add, General?"

"Yes, I do, Colonel."

"Gentlemen, and of course you, too, Butch. We have found out only a short while ago that the Chino cartel was basically operating under the radar for many years. They are a powerhouse and have around one thousand civilian soldiers. We have also learned that their cartel has a monetary value of over twenty-eight billion Yankee dollars. This cartel has tentacles that stretch to South America and large areas of Europe as well.

"I don't think we have enough personnel to pull this off. You people are the best, but you'll be outnumbered by at least four to one, and I don't like those odds. We're going to draw an additional force of two hundred men from various units in the field. These men are equivalent to the Green Berets and the Rangers in the States. I've been told by the general staff that the two hundred men will be arriving within the week. As soon as they get here we'll have some joint maneuvers so we can evaluate these additional soldiers. I would also like you people to welcome these extra men into our unit, even though they'll only be attached for a couple of weeks.

"That's all I have Colonel. You may dismiss the men."

Sunday was a perfect day for swearing in the Vice President, it was full sunshine and just a beautiful day. About a thousand people came to the capitol for a look see at the first Vice President of the Western States of America. The actual swearing in only lasted about six minutes, but the congratulations, back slapping and hand shaking lasted more than two hours. That evening, President Williamson held a very swanky and formal party for the first V.P. that lasted until the wee hours Monday morning. The V.P. position was one of the last appointments filled by the Williamson administration. Only a few more appointments were needed, but none were critical to the young nation.

Colonel Montgomery stepped into General Rōjas' office at Army Headquarters and asked the General if he could do without him for a day or two.

"Certainly. This is a perfect time, we won't have the additional men for at least another week."

"General, I'm taking the list of American names who were on the Santiago cartel payroll to President Williamson for disposition. There will be <u>Hell</u> to pay when these names are revealed to the American people. I'm going to hand carry this list of names and place them into Sara's hands for safe keeping. Some individuals would kill if they knew this list existed. A lot of heads will certainly roll when this becomes known. Long prison terms will be the order of the day when all is said and done."

"Colonel, do you really believe that? I'll bet the men accused never see the inside of a cell anyplace. I'm convinced that nobody is held responsible for anything in your country, Colonel. The criminals literally get away with murder and are protected by the courts, slick lawyers and liberal judges. I'm sorry, Colonel, sometimes I talk when I should keep my big mouth shut.

"That's okay, General, you're ninety-nine percent correct in your statement. I'll be back within two or three days. Can I bring you anything from the States, General?"

"After the way I spouted off you would bring me back something form America?"

"Yes, sir, I would because I'm your friend and partner in the drug wars. Just name it and I'll get it for you, sir."

"Colonel, you're a good man and one hell of a soldier to boot. I've never met anyone like you before. Remember you are really the brains of this outfit, and I'm grateful you're assigned to my outfit."

"Thank you, General, but remember, you and I are a team and we trust one another completely. Without that trust we wouldn't be a successful team."

"You're right Colonel. Now get the hell out of here and I'll see 'ya in a few days. Oh! And I don't need anything from the States, thank you."

Colonel Montgomery flew out of Mexico City and headed for Flagstaff, Arizona and a meeting with President Williamson. He entered the capitol building and was directed to Sara's large office in the back of the large building. Colonel Montgomery stopped at Mrs. Bakker's desk and asked if Madam President was free.

"She is in a meeting, Colonel, please take a seat. She should be out within fifteen minutes or so."

The Colonel sat down and was admiring the furnishing of the recently completed capitol building when President Williamson entered the room and quickly walked up to the Colonel and shook his hand vigorously. "I'm sorry, Colonel, I completely forgot you were coming. I have been just swamped these past few weeks."

"It's good seeing you again, Madam President."

"Same here, Colonel."

"I assume you have a certain list you want me to view, Colonel."

"Yes, ma'am, I do. This list of names will have major ramifications throughout the Washington establishment and the country as a whole."

"Let's head for my outer office so I can view this very disturbing list of American names." Once inside Sara's office, they sat and Michael opened the briefcase and handed his President the list of names found inside the Santiago drug cartel complex. President Williamson started to scan the long list and was shocked at some of the prominent names listed and the amount of monies paid. Not only names listed, but the complete mailing address of each person listed. There isn't any mistake with the names, addresses and amounts paid from start to finish. Some had been paid for over ten years and were still receiving pay offs.

"Colonel, I'll take this list from here. I want to think about this for a while before I go public. I want to thank you, General Rōjas and of course President Lazzara for all your efforts in crushing many of the drug cartels within Mexico. Are you heading right back to Mexico?" Sara asked her favorite Full Bird Colonel.

"No, ma'am, I'm going to spend a couple of days in Yakima, Washington before I head back to Mexico City and Army Headquarters in *Querétaro*."

"Well, good luck, Colonel, and be very careful when dealing with the Chino cartel. I hear they have a small army at their disposal and have top notch weapons, equipment and communications."

"Yes that's correct, ma'am, they are well equipped but so are we," the Colonel added.

"Goodbye, ma'am, I'll call you again after our attack on the Chino cartel."

"Good luck, Colonel."

Colonel Montgomery left the capitol building and headed for Yakima, Washington by car.

After the Colonel left her office, Sara sat there going over the long list of government and state officials who were listed on the cartel payroll. She thought, "My god there are half dozen high profile officials who must be toppled and sent to jail for a long time. I can't believe the Attorney General of California, head of the State Police for Texas and head of the Border Patrol for New Mexico are among the hundred or so names on the list. Dozens of Washington, D.C. names and addresses are listed as well."

President Lazzara was up and around in his hospital room. The two bullet wounds were not life threatening but he was lucky due to the amount of shots fired at his group. The capitol police estimated some ninety to one hundred rounds were fired into President Lazzara's party.

The President picked up the phone and called General Rōjas at Army headquarters and told him that he wanted the remaining drug cartels within Mexico exposed and its members hunted down and killed. "These people are not going to overpower this country and drive our citizens into despair and lose all hopes and aspirations of all our citizens. As long as I'm President of Mexico, I will work every hour of every day towards stamping out every drug cartel, every individual drug pusher and help current users to shake their habits. If we don't take this hard stand right now against the drug lords and all their activities, our beautiful country will be lost and overrun by those unscrupulous individuals."

"General, let's go balls to the wall in our attack on this massive drug complex. It has taken years just to find the damn locations of this facility which is tucked away deep in the jungle on the banks of the Huaynamota River."

"Your attack on this complex must be a complete surprise and planned to the second, or a disaster will be the outcome. Please make sure you and Colonel Montgomery agree completely on the plan of attack and all phases of the operation. You'll need all the intel you can get to pull this attack off without massive loss of personnel. I hope the additional personnel you're borrowing from field units are up to your standards."

"I'm sure they will be, Mr. President, but to make sure, we're going to have joint maneuvers with both groups to insure smooth operations among the entire group before we attack this huge drug cartel."

"When are you holding these joint operations?" the President quickly asked.

"Within a week, sir."

"That's good, General. I don't have anything else and I'm sorry to rant and rave, but the boldness in the attempt on my life is the final straw."

"Good luck, General, and wish Colonel Montgomery good luck for me, also."

"Yes, Mr. President, I will. Thank you."

Both men hung up without another word.

Lt. General Wittingham and his staff finished their assessment of the request form Mexican President Lazzara on the issue of removing all American troops from the Mexican/American border. He called President Williamson and gave her his oral report on the two thousand mile request to remove all troops.

"Madam President, you asked my opinion on the request to remove our troops from our border with Mexico."

"Yes, I did, General, please continue," Sara urged her favorite General.

"I am dead against removing all our military from our border with Mexico. Even though Mexican President Lazzara seems to be keeping his word on stopping his countrymen from illegally entering our country, I think it would be foolhardy at this time to abandon our responsibility to protect our lengthy border especially now, ma'am, with respect to the attempted assassination of President Lazzara. If he should, heaven forbid, be taken out of the picture, the next Mexican President might not feel the same about our mutual border. I don't have a problem with removing a certain number of units that are not critically essential to the protection and defense of our border, but anything more than that would be very dangerous in my estimation, Madam President."

"Thank you, General. Your assessment is good enough for me. Go ahead and remove whatever units you feel comfortable in relieving from border duty and reassign."

185

"Yes, ma'am. A small number of units will be removed and reassigned within the week."

"When complete, let me know how many personnel have been removed from the border area," Sara asked.

"Will do, ma'am."

"Madam President, Secretary O'Neil is on line #4," Mrs. Bakker called from the doorway.

"Thank you, Ruth."

"Hi, Bill, what's up," Sara asked her Treasury Secretary.

"Madam President, the authorized amount of our new currency has been printed, checked and delivered to our four Chief State Banks. Now it's up to you, ma'am, when the exchange takes place between the U.S. greenbacks and our Western States of America currency. Do you still agree the exchange rate should be par for now?" Secretary O'Neil asked

"Yes, Bill, for now let's open the rate of exchange at par with the greenbacks." Sara continued, "But all other foreign exchange rates will be under the rates we established earlier this year. We can adjust any rate on the world market we feel is out of whack when necessary."

"Don't you agree, Bill?" the President asked

"Yes, ma'am, for now, I do agree."

"One more thing, Bill, do you feel your Treasury Department printed enough money?"

"Good god, I hope so. We printed 24/7 for over two months with the total exceeding five and a half trillion W.S. of A. dollars. That amount includes both coins and paper bills, Madam President, and the total amount is backed by our own gold reserve. We will not print any currency without being backed by gold from our own mines or gold we have purchased and stored in our own Fort Knox. As soon as we adhere to that criterion, Madam President we'll be on solid footing for all future government business," the Treasure Secretary stated firmly.

"Okay, Bill, let's inform the public this Friday that starting Monday morning the new W.S. of A. money will be distributed and exchanged through all the authorized state banks within our countries for states. Can the main banks distribute the money to the general banking facilities by Monday morning at 09:00 hours?" Sara asked.

"That gives us a little over five days, ma'am. We should be able to cover all banks by then if we go balls to the wall, he answered.

"Good, Bill, then see that it's done by Monday, if you would, please," Sara urged.

"Yes, ma'am I will."

Colonel Montgomery arrived at Army Headquarters in Querétaro, Mexico and was quickly directed to Mexico City for a meeting with President Lazzara. Upon arriving at the Presidential Palace overlooking Mexico City he was ushered immediately into the President's waiting room, and within five minutes the President entered the room with his arm bandaged and in a sling and his right side bound up to hold the large bandages. He walked with a silver cane but didn't seem to rely on it.

The American Full Bird Colonel snapped to attention and the Mexican President motioned for him to stay seated.

"Good to see you up and around, Mr. President."

"Thank you, Colonel. I've asked you here, my friend, to discuss a few things." With that opening statement President Lazzara very slowly and carefully sat down with the help of his long-time aide.

"That's better," he told his aide. "Thank you, I'm good for now." His aide quickly left the room.

"Colonel Montgomery, I'd like to discuss the upcoming raid and attack on the Chino cartel near the village of Nayar. With the latest intel we have received, it's quite clear they have a small army and large quantities of the latest military arms and equipment available. As you know, they have over one thousand armed bandits in a huge compound tucked away in the most dense jungle in all of Mexico. I'm very concerned about the welfare of your troops, Colonel. I know you have an additional two hundred men assigned to this mission for a grand total of only four hundred and fifty members in your attack force. And yes, I know they are the best of the best we have in Mexico, and you have expanded their special training to ensure they are top notch."

"That is correct, Mr. President, I'd put these men and Butch up against anybody in a combat situation."

"But, Colonel, you're outnumbered more than two to one and they've tucked away under dense cover just waiting for our government forces. Unless your attack is a complete surprise you could be wiped out, Colonel."

"That's true, Mr. President. If we don't enter into this military campaign with stealth, aggressiveness, split second timing and military prowess we could be in real trouble, sir. It's the responsibility of General Rōjas and myself to insure that we're totally prepared to pull off this military action."

"Well, Colonel, you're the military expert, and I respect your long and distinguished military career and special ability in dealing with our drug problems. When is your attack planned for, Colonel?"

"I don't know exactly, Mr. President, General Rōjas is the only one who knows the exact date and time of the operation. We wanted complete secrecy on this mission, sir."

"Very good, Colonel, I remember a certain relative of mine who cost us many lives and millions of pesos."

"Mr. President, you said you had another topic to discuss with me."

"Yes, I do. The other topic I'd like to cover is the American troops positioned along the entire length of the Rio Grande with Mexico. I have asked your President Williamson if she would consider removing all American military personnel from the U.S. side, only leaving border patrol personnel on duty."

"Mr. President, I'm only a Full Bird Colonel. There are a dozen high ranking Generals within the Western States of America. The Secretary-of-Defense and his Generals will make that assessment and advise the President, sir. Colonels like me don't make those kinds of major policy changes."

"I know you're right, Colonel, but I was hoping you'd speak to Sara on my behalf and support my position on removing all American forces from our mutual border. I'm basically concerned that some incident might arise that would provoke a military situation that would cost both Mexican and American lives. If the border states would pull back their forces, I'll make sure all our Mexican troops fall back at least ten kilometers from our common border."

"I would rather not intervene into that debate, Mr. President. I have my hands full with this assignment, Mr. President, I don't need to piss off my President while working for a foreign head of state, sir."

Chapter 6 – First Woman President

"Of course you're correct, my learned friend. Your loyalty to Sara and your country is admirable, Colonel. I apologize for trying to place you in danger with your country. As you can tell, I'm not one hundred percent in my thinking as of yet. Please forget that I even brought the subject up, Colonel."

"Yes, sir, I will, Mr. President."

President Lazzara called for his aide and slowly exited the room.

Colonel Montgomery left the Presidential Palace and caught a military scout plane for Army Headquarters in Querétaro. In just over an hour and ten minutes Colonel Montgomery landed at Army HQ and headed straight to General Rõjas' quarters for a Q & A session. Before the General could say hello, the Colonel asked whether he knew President Lazzara wanted to see him or not.

"Yes, I did my friend, but sometimes Presidents don't tell lowly Generals why they want to converse with certain Full Bird Colonels."

"Sorry, General, I didn't know why you didn't brief me before I left for Mexico City to see our leader. It was no secret, General, he is concerned that our forces against the Chino cartel isn't large enough. He figures we're outnumbered and probably out gunned as well. President Lazzara is truly worried about our well-being and after the attempt on his life he wants us to step up the time table on our attack. I told him for security reasons you're the only one who knows the actual date and time."

"Well, I guess we better get down to brass tacks as you Americans say, Colonel. I think you and I should agree on the time table to insure a smooth operation. The logistics of this venture must be near perfect or like you say, we'll get our ass kicked. I believe, Colonel, we have received about as much intel as we're going to receive from our spies in the sky and village residents near the compound on the river Huaynamota. Most of our planning has been done and the added special forces have melted into our unit quite well don't you agree, Colonel?"

"Yes, I do. The combined exercises went well and they seem well trained and should work and fight nicely with our personnel. On a lighter note, General, I'm glad Butch now has another female to ease the pain of being the only gal in our outfit."

"She does seem happier, doesn't she?" the General added.

"General, according to the latest weather prognostication from your weather center in Mexico City and our weather forecast center in Laredo, Texas, sometime around mid next week the moon will be totally blocked out due to heavy cloud cover and heavy rain. Almost perfect conditions for us to approach the jungle compound from both directions. One group approaching from Aqua Brava and the village Rosamorda to the west, and the second group will arrive by motor launch on the Huaynamota River to the east. From the river we must travel through heavy jungle for approximately three miles. From the western approach the group must travel slightly over sixty kilometers, the River San Pedro and many, many miles of mountainous jungle. The fight time, jump height, landing and jungle approach by the western group must be near perfect and with complete surprise. The eastern group will have it much easier getting to the jungle compound from the river side. They will enter the Huaynamota River some twenty kilometers south of Nayar Village and ride the waterway for about another twenty five kilometers before entering the jungle, striking west towards the Chino compound and hooking up with our western group before starting the attack. As usual, our biggest concern and threat is the 'cell phone'. One call from more than three hundred thousand people in the area would result in the slaughter and elimination of our whole military force."

"The only saving grace, General. is the fact that prior to our arrival at the compound, the Texas National Guard 10th Bomb Group will drop special delayed bombs and assorted ordinance that won't explode until they hit the hard ground. Being that the compound is under almost one hundred feet of jungle canopy. This type of bomb ordinance was the only answer. Without pinpointing the exact location by thermal infrared imagining, the bombing would have been impossible at best. You can't hit what you can't see, they say. As you know, General, it took a lot of doing by your President and his administration to finally agree to these type of military flights when necessary. But of course they would never know where and when due to complete national security. I'm sure it became more palatable to government officials because the co-pilots in the Texas bomber are all Mexican Air Force officers, and they alone will drop the special bomb ordinance on Mexican soil."

Chapter 6 - First Woman President

"General, will you authorize the attack during this inclement weather period?" the American Colonel asked his military partner.

"Yes, we should go during that period," the Mexican Commanding General informed his friend.

"Okay, let's start the final preparation, equipment alignment and check. We'll need these four or five days to get our act together to ensure a well-oiled machine."

The two hundred and sixty two thousand Western States of America banks and credit unions opened sharply at 09:00 Monday morning and the customer lines snaked around buildings for blocks. The changing of green backs into Western States of America coins and currency was something to behold. The colored currency with bills up to one thousand dollars were very popular and the coins with the western icons pictured were snapped up by the bag and roll.

Treasury Secretary O'Neil said, "Over three trillion dollars changed hands in one business day. The other forty six states and Washington, D.C. haven't even exchanged or purchased a W.S.A. cent yet." O'Neil quickly asked President Williamson for authorization to continue to print coin and currency as long as it can be backed by gold.

The President quickly gave permission to print an additional three and a half trillion W.S. of A. dollars and coinage. "Oh! Bill. How many dollars can we print with our current amount of gold on hand?"

"Without checking, I would guess we could print, stamp and distribute around a total of eight trillion. Of course, we can step up gold production and refining in our eight state mines and also purchase outside gold if necessary, Madam President."

"I think we better step up gold production, don't you, Bill?"

"Yes, ma'am, we'll start immediately."

"I knew our new currency would be a hit, but 3.5 trillion changing hands on the very first day of issue within our country alone. My god, what will be the demand when the foreign governments want our currency?" Sara thought. "We better have lots of gold reserve to back this high demand. If we don't we won't issue."

Governor Adams of Wyoming returned to Washington, D.C. to attend a meeting with President Obama and his staff after a two day battle with eight western state governors. During the

191

meeting, Governor Adams presented a signed document signed by six out of the nine states stating they would not secede from the union if certain concessions were met. President Obama and the Secretary-of-State reviewed the nine state document and informed Governor Adams they would sign their paper even with the demand that all concessions agreed to benefit the nine states in question would also be given to the other thirty-seven states.

Once the historical meeting was over and Governor Adams and his staff left for Wyoming, the President's administration had a big sigh of relief. The exodus of those nine states would have destroyed the union and opened the door to foreign invasion.

Before boarding his flight to Wyoming, Governor Adams called President Williamson and informed her that the nine states he represented had agreed to stay in the Washington, D.C. union. Sara was very glad to hear the good news. She realized her new country would be in grave danger if they had seceded from Obama's union.

Lt. General Wittingham issued the orders to relieve and remove approximately one quarter of the units presently assigned to border duty. Most of the relieved units were communication, transportation, medical units, artillery and some special service units. About a full division was pulled back from the Mexican border at the request of the Mexican President Lazzara.

Sara thanked her top General and said she would call the Mexican President and inform him of the partial pull back of forces from the border. She thought, "He won't like the partial pull back, but he will live with it, I'm sure." Once Sara and the General were finished, she called Marian Wilcox and asked her to contact Mexican President Lazzara as soon as possible.

In less than five minutes the Mexican President was on Line #3. "Good afternoon, Mr. President," Sara said quickly. "I hope you're feeling better."

"Thank you, Madam President, and yes, I am feeling much better today," the Mexican President answered in a strong voice. "What is the nature of this call?" he asked.

"Mr. President, I'm calling to inform you that we are removing a full division, as we speak, from the Mexican/American border. Now, I realize you wanted all our military forces removed from the border area, but for now this gesture will have to do, Mr. President."

Chapter 6 - First Woman President

"Sir, our border country of Western States of America still expects you to continue to uphold your promise to stop you nationals from illegally crossing our border and melting into our American society."

"Sara, I will continue to honor my commitment to you as President. As long as I'm alive my word is my bond, Madam President."

"I'm glad to hear that, Pedro, and we expect you to keep your promise to me and our country," Sara answered.

At 14:00 hours at the Whitehouse in Washington, D.C. President Obama started a press conference.

"Ladies and Gentlemen, for once I have some good news to report. After talking with Wyoming Governor Adams and the consent of the Governors of the states of Alaska, Washington, Colorado, Idaho, Utah, Nevada, Montana and Oregon, we have reached an agreement. The nine states that were planning to secede from our union have decided not to leave our Washington group. This is great news to me as your President. No matter what, we must stick together and preserve what's left of our union. As a solid union of forty-six tightly knitted states we can withstand any and all foreign intervention and invasion. If we come apart and divide any more from within, we won't survive as a nation. As your President, I'd like to say thank you to all the citizens of these nine states for choosing the right course and staying in the union. Certain foreign governments have been watching this unfold and were hoping our country would divide again in conflict and be subject to invasion and conquest.

"I'd like to cover one more subject this afternoon and that's the illegal alien problem and cost. The extremely high cost of supporting these illegal squatters had reached enormous proportions and is bankrupting your individual states and federal government. The hundreds of billions of dollars shelled out each and every month must stop. Currently, we have some twenty-seven federal and state programs that support these illegal aliens alone. They range from housing assistance to medical care to food stamps to transportation to unemployment benefits to free schooling and dozens of other federal and state giveaway policies and programs.

"Previous Presidents and their administrations did absolutely nothing to prevent the mass influx of unwanted foreign squatters and that applies to me and my administration as well. I have had over four and a half years to correct this problem but chose to ignore it. I admit my socialistic ideals that I've held all my life, along with the whole Democratic Party, have almost driven this great nation into a socialist state and even closer to communism. My democratic friends, associates and even my family will never forgive me for turning against them and their core socialist beliefs.

"No matter what, I must change for the betterment of our people and the nation as a whole. Other countries have tried leaning towards socialism and look what has happened to them. High unemployment, civil unrest, huge private and national debt while half the population is being supported by government giveaway programs and the other half is paying the whole bill while trying to absorb higher taxes on everything.

"While I stood by and did nothing for years, four states seceded from our union and worked with Mexico to stop the flood of illegal aliens from crossing our borders. Now, we don't have a border with Mexico, but President Williamson and her four states do. She accomplished that in a matter of months when we couldn't do it in forty plus years. My god, it's hard to believe that our heads were buried in the sand for that long.

"Shortly, I will be announcing the dates when most of the federal giveaway programs will stop. Not only will the funding for illegal aliens come to an end, but the presence of illegal aliens will also come to an end in this country. This means all undocumented illegal persons will be rounded up and sent back to Mexico and Canada. We are assuming the same policy that President Williamson and the Western States of America has adopted. With our forty-six states this will be a huge undertaking and will cost billions of dollars, but it must be done before this country is completely bankrupted and slips into third world status. Hardline immigration is the rule from now on. The social giveaways are coming to an abrupt end during my second and final term in office. Our country must not be pulled apart again by internal strife or a foreign invasion that would turn this country into a hell from which there is no escape. I know that I have increased our national debt by trillions of dollars in an attempt to bail out certain companies and organizations with the concept of redistributing wealth. Well, for the most part it did not work, and from now on we will strive towards living within our means as long as I'm your President. If you fail, then you fail.

No more bailouts at the expense of the American taxpayer. I realize if I talked like this before last November's Presidential election, I surely would have lost the Black and Hispanic vote and my Republican rival would have been your President. But, it's never too late to change direction and possibly save this nation, or what's left of it." he President continued, "No more lies, deception and cover ups will be forced down the throats of every American as standard operating procedure of this administration. Again, this is a new beginning and a new direction for myself and this administration. If any of my cabinet or other government officials don't like this change then submit your resignation immediately. I will work with the Republican Party and what's left of my Democratic Party after my change in direction to right some of the wrongs and re-establish old values that were the cornerstone of this nation.

"Thank you ladies and gentlemen." With that President Obama quickly left the press conference without taking a single question. The national press corps was stunned and, for the first time ever, speechless at what they had just heard form the most liberal President of all time.

As President Obama and Chief-of-Staff Mott headed for the Oval Office, the President said, "That's a big start in correcting runaway policies and spending while stopping the death spiral that would plunge this nation into an uncontrollable decline which there is no return. I'm going to receive a lot of flak, to say the least, and many hard line Democrats will never forgive me. They'll call me a turncoat and a dozen other less than flattering remarks."

"My god, Mr. President, what have you done?" the Chief-of-Staff said, opening the door to the Oval Office.

Once inside President Obama pushed the door shut and in a loud voice said, "Robert, are you staying as Chief-of-Staff or not? I want to know, here and now," the President said in anger.

"Yes, sir, I'll stay but it's going to be a very rocky ride for the next few months. There will be many desertions along the way, Mr. President."

"So be it, Robert, at this point I don't give a damn," he said, flopping into his old leather chair. "While you're recovering from my speech, would you please contact Mexican President Lazzara as soon as possible?"

"Yes sir, right away."

Within minutes the secure line rang and President Lazzara was on the line and he was hopping mad. Before President Obama could say hello, the Mexican head of state said "Mr. President what the hell are you doing? You're going to send back millions of my countrymen who have lived in your country for years?"

"Yes, I am Pedro, we're going to clean house and purge our country of all squatters that have caused so many problems and cost this administration and the American public hundreds of billions of dollars. We should have stopped this forty years ago, but the past Presidents and I didn't lift a finger to stop the flow of unwanted quests.

"Your government even passed out pamphlets and maps as well as instructed your people on how and where to cross the Rio Grande and desert to enter the United States. I have to admit, Mr. President, my administration did the same thing by telling your countrymen how to apply for our government welfare programs. Between your predecessor and myself, we must have caused an unknown number of death and the expenditures of huge amounts of money we don't have. But now, with the help of President Williamson and yourself, the flow of Mexican nationals entering the U.S. has all but stopped. This is a great start on your part, and now it's my turn to return all illegal aliens that are currently living throughout my forty-six state union.

"Mr. President you must be prepared for the return of millions of your wayward citizens.

"Now, I understand that the Western States of America and your country are considering some joint ventures in the near future?"

"Yes, that is correct," the Mexican President said in a low voice.

"If I'm still President after the dust settles, maybe our government might be willing to support some of your ventures. Once you have earmarked specific projects, we will contact W.S.A. and your government for your assorted requirements."

"I don't know how my country is going to provide housing and jobs for millions of returning nationals," the Mexican President told the American President.

Chapter 6 – First Woman President

"That is your problem," Obama told President Lazzara. Your government allowed this exodus to happen for decades and now these people are coming home to roost."

Without saying another word, President Lazzara slammed the phone down ending their conversation.

"Robert, I have a feeling the Mexican President is highly pissed. My ears are still ringing when he slammed the phone down. Hanging up on the President of the United States seems to be catching," he said shaking his head. "Bob, please gather up my military and civilian staff for a meeting here at the Whitehouse War Room as soon as possible. Let me know if anyone is refusing to attend. Also, I want to broadcast the entire proceedings within the War Room to the American public. I know this is unprecedented, but that's what I want. No T.V., just radio."

"Yes sir, I'll get right on it."

Within an hour the Chief-of-Staff reported to the President that the War Room meeting was on for 18:00 hours today.

Before heading to the basement War Room the Chief-of-Staff told the President that two cabinet members would not be present for the meeting. "The Secretary of the Treasury is on a fact finding mission in China, and the Secretary of the Interior is on vacation in France."

"That's fine, Robert, I'm sure they'll hear the proceedings no matter where they are."

President Obama entered the Whitehouse War Room at exactly 18:00 hours and was greeted by complete silence as he headed for his seat at the head of the long War Room table. "Please be seated," he told the thirty-five people standing in front of their chairs. The President continued to stand while looking around the table and to the many people lining the walls of the War Room. "I thought I'd just stand here so you people could get a look at your President who obviously has lost his democratic mind. After some soul searching I came to the conclusion that it was time to change and come clean to the American people and the world.

"Yes I won re-election last November but it was won by some unscrupulous methods and questionable voting irregularities.

"By all rights, ladies and gentlemen, I shouldn't have been elected, or I should say re-elected, as your forty-forth

President. I wanted the legal and illegal Hispanic vote during the election and I received about seventy-four percent of their votes. Let me be very clear," the President said in an elevated voice, "the only reason I got their votes was because of my many federal giveaway programs and the underlying promise of becoming American citizens. That also applied to the Black voters where I received almost ninety-four percent of their votes. Black Americans voted for me for many of the same reasons, the redistribution of wealth and the many giveaways that benefited the Black population. Let's face it people, I was the candy man who distributed goodies to both groups."

"Now, I want to clear up a couple of items. First the question that was asked right from the beginning."

"Where was I born?"

"I was born in Malaysia, in the coastal city of Kota Terengganu and not in Hawaii."

Someone in the room said, "Oh my god you should be impeached at once. You should not have been elected to the highest office in our land."

Without any comment the President continued, "The second item is whether I'm a Muslim or not. Yes, I am, I'm a life-long Black Muslim.

"So now you can see the deception I have imposed upon the American people and the world. Again, I have let down my family, my political party, my associates, my religion and the nation as a whole. I'm now at the mercy of Congress, the Supreme Court and the will of the American people.

"I won't take any questions or comments at this meeting. If anyone here wants to resign, retire or just plain quit after hearing this, please contact Chief-of-Staff Mott and we'll start the ball rolling." The President lowered his head, paused for a moment then continued, "During this meeting, I have come to the conclusion that rather than put this country through months of wrangling and speculation, I will submit my resignation as your President effective noon tomorrow. Thank you, ladies and gentlemen, it's been a pleasure to serve as your President. Somewhere along the trail I lost my way as a Muslim and a world citizen. For that, I'm so sorry. Please forgive me, and goodbye."

Without another word, President Obama quickly exited the Whitehouse War Room with his Marine Corps aide and Chief-of-Staff. The three headed for the Oval Office.

Chapter 6 – First Woman President

The War Room was dead quiet until the President left the room. Once the huge bomb proof double doors closed, all hell broke loose. Everybody started talking at once and the level of noise was deafening at best. The Marine guards opened the War Room doors and everyone scrambled for their offices in the Pentagon and Whitehouse.

Within minutes of the meeting, the T.V. networks and every radio station were broadcasting the news that President Obama would be resigning his office as of the next day at noon.

President Obama was met at the Oval Office door by Winnie Oaks, who was crying. She said, "Mr. President, without you the Democratic Party and all of us non-elected people will be finished."

The President gave her a hug and said, "I'm sorry but I must go Winnie." He kissed her on the forehand and went into the Oval Office. He flopped into his old worn leather chair and put his head in his hands upon his desk.

A knock at the door brought the President back to the present.

"Yes," he said. "Come in."

Vice President Goodwin entered the Oval Office and quickly sat down facing the large desk and President Obama.

Chuck said, "Mr. President, have you lost your mind? I can't believe what you have done to yourself, our party and the country."

"I couldn't continue to drive this nation toward the edge of the social and financial cliff that would put this country into a death spiral from which there would be no return. I couldn't continue to lie to the American people and myself. The public had to know the truth before we created a nation that followed in the footsteps of Greece, Spain and a dozen other socialistic countries.

"No matter what, as of tomorrow at high noon I'm no longer President, and you are."

When President Williamson heard the news that President Obama would be resigning as of noon the next day, she was dumb founded. Within minutes, her Chief-of-Staff and other staff members were in her office and asking what the hell was going on. Every phone line was lit up and flashing, but Sara told her Secretary Ruth to hold all calls for now.

"Well, people, I thought I had heard of everything, but this latest action by the President certainly takes the cake. Admitting to the world that his liberal agenda, policies, actions and beliefs were wrong is just unbelievable to me. His admission is totally against every fiber of his being," Sara told the group, shaking her head. She continued, "Now with V.P. Goodwin becoming President tomorrow, the question is what changes will he make or will he continue to press the agenda that Obama started. No matter what, this is a tremendous step backwards for the Democratic Party.

"This is a golden opportunity for the Washington Republicans to rise to the top and convince the American public that the democratic ideas and liberalism is not the right path for America to take. Redistribution of wealth, higher taxes and social programs that add millions more the government feeding trough is the path towards complete socialism. These forty million people will be devastated that their candy man has admitted he was wrong in his giveaways and everything else he believed in.

"We are seeing the biggest change and impact to the Democratic Party and a huge segment of the American population. God help us," Sara added.

"Will this change in Washington impact us?" Beverly Walcott asked her boss.

"Right now I don't see any major change that would affect our country, but remember, the change is just starting and complications certainly come to the forefront. Only time will tell."

Everybody was asking the "What if" question as they exited President Williamson's office to continue their daily routines.

"Ruth you can start putting the calls through," the Western States of America President told her long-time friend and secretary.

"Get ready for the tidal wave," Ruth said, closing the door.

The Republican hierarchy in Washington were stunned beyond belief when they learned President Obama was resigning the next day at noon. The Speaker-of-the-House was informed by Secretary-of-State Wilson that the President's hand written letter of resignation would be delivered to him sometime that afternoon.

Chapter 6 – First Woman President

At 15:30 the Secretary-of-State arrived at the Speaker's Office and Secretary Wilson handed the Speaker an envelope with the Seal of the President.

"Thank you, Madam Secretary."

As she turned and started to leave, the Speaker said, "Maggie could you stay for a minute?"

"Certainly," she answered.

The Speaker said, "Please be seated," and he pointed to the large overstuffed chair next to the large window.

Secretary Wilson walked over to the chair and just plopped down in visible exhaustion.

"I am completely dumb founded and surprised beyond belief, Maggie. Why at this stage, after winning a second term and having another four years as President? As you know, Maggie, I have fought hard and long against President Obama and his policies, ideas and general political philosophy. As our 44th President, I felt he was the worst man by far to hold that office. But putting that aside, most of the voters in this country, after four years of turmoil, uncontrollable spending and constantly lying to the American public, re-elected him to continue his giveaway programs and deception. I guess after forty-nine years in public office I really don't understand the American voter. High unemployment, higher taxes, Obama Care and a host of other problems didn't seem to bother the American electorate.

"With all this going for Obama, why did he all of a sudden come clean and bare his Muslim soul to the whole world?"

Secretary Wilson admitted that she had no idea, but it certainly isn't the Obama she had known for the past nine years. "What he said during his farewell radio speech was against every fiber of his being. I couldn't believe what I was hearing," she said throwing up her hands and shaking her head. "I just don't know what to tell you," she admitted to her long-time friend but political opposite. "I must get back to my office, I'm sure my staff is wondering 'where the hell is she?' I'm sorry I couldn't shed any light on President Obama's reasons to resign abruptly."

"That's okay, Maggie, we'll just have to wait and see where the chips fall."

Without another word the Secretary-of-State left the Speaker's office.

rickshaw

The Speaker of the House took the sealed envelope and headed for the emergency meeting with Congress to start within the hour.

When the Speaker and his aide entered the House Chamber, the noise level was unbearable. As he got to the high podium, he grabbed his gavel and started to pound repeatedly to gain the attention of the loud House members. After pounding repeatedly and yelling, "Ladies and gentlemen!" for an extended period, the noise level began to wean and the Speaker finally gained the attention and rule over the House Chamber. "Ladies and gentlemen, the hand written resignation from President Obama has arrived, and I will read his resignation at this time." The Speaker opened the sealed envelope, unfolded the single sheet of paper and read its contents.

To: Speaker of the House and the
Congress of the United States
As of noon today, September 15th I will resign the office of President of the United States.
It has been my pleasure to serve in that high office, but I have come to the realization that my policies and methods of leadership were not in the best of interest of all Americans. I sincerely wish I could have been a better President who represented not only the Black and Hispanic population but the hard working White population that made this country the world leader.
May God in heaven protect this nation from tyrannical individuals and would be kings.
Goodbye:

Barack Hussein Obama
President,
United States of America

After reading the letter of resignation to Congress, the Speaker sat back down and replaced the hand written letter in its envelope and instructed his aide to deliver the document to the Chief Justice of the Supreme Court.

The wheels started turning for the installation of the 45th President of the United States. Vice President Goodwin was to be sworn in as President at 12:01 pm September 15.

President Obama, his family, and two Secret Service agents will leave the Whitehouse before noon and will fly aboard

Chapter 6 – First Woman President

Air Force #2 to Hawaii where they own a large house high on a cliff overlooking the ocean.

President Obama and his family left the Whitehouse by an obscure exit and were quickly driven to the airport where Air Force #2 was ready for takeoff. As soon as the ex-President, his family and the Secret Service agents boarded the plane, it started to taxi down the runway for its long, non-stop flight to Hawaii.

The ex-President had requested that no Secret Service detail be assigned to him once they arrive in Hawaii.

The swearing in ceremony was quickly arranged so the next President could be sworn in as soon as possible. On the steps of the Supreme Court building, a small crowd of well-wishers and political types were gathered to witness the installation of V.P. Goodwin as the next President of the United States.

Chapter 7
JOINT VENTURES

Once the oath of office was given by the Chief Justice, the 45th President quickly left the ceremony and headed for the Whitehouse and the Oval Office. President Goodwin did not want the usual parties, dinners and social gatherings that are associated with the swearing in of a new President. The new President said in no uncertain terms that he did not want the goodies and pleasantries beseeched upon a new head of state. He wanted to get down to business as quickly as possible under the unusual circumstances of Obama's resignation.

When President Goodwin arrived at the Oval Office, he was met by various Obama staff members that did not attend the swearing in ceremony. After saying hello, he asked the Chief-of-Staff to join him in the Oval Office. Both men entered the most famous office in the world and President Goodwin slowly closed the door. "Please be seated, Robert."

Both men sat down and the new President asked the C.O.S., "What the hell do we do now to save the Democratic Party after what Obama admitted to the American people and the world? My god, he basically said we're all liars and can't be trusted on anything."

"Mr. President, I Have to admit that he was correct when he said we have given the American public the old smoke and mirror deception. We have lied on a variety of fronts and issues, Mr. President. When Obama was campaigning for President, and during his first term as President, he promised a whole pile of things while only coming through with a couple. He spent trillions of dollars, or I should say pissed away that amount, while saying we must reduce our national debt. Good god, Mr. President, he created the money pit," the Chief-of-Staff admitted.

"Well, Robert that was quite a mouth full," the new President said as he got up and went to the large window behind his desk. He continued, "We were on the verge of crushing the Republican Party and maybe even eliminating them altogether until President Obama gave his confession. That short speech, on a single hand written sheet of paper, may have destroyed the democratic liberal idea and even the Democratic Party. His final statements have certainly put me in the target crosshairs."

"Bob, I want you to set up an emergency meeting with the whole staff as quickly as possible. We must see how we can repair the damage created by President Obama. If there are any defections at this early stage please let me know," President Goodwin added.

"Where do you want the meeting, sir?"

"Here in the Whitehouse War Room, Robert."

"Yes, sir."

President Williamson was informed by Secretary-of-Defense Waterman that the Washington administration had informed Mexican President Lazzara that they were going to start returning the Mexican squatters to Mexican soil shortly.

"My god, Mr. Secretary, this added burden on Mexico will surely drive them beyond any chance of recovery. With our country returning thousands every month and now with Washington going to return millions back to Mexico, the fragile Mexican economy will certainly collapse from the sheer weight."

"Please ask Marian to contact President Lazzara as soon as she can, Ralph."

"Certainly, Madam President."

After more than an hour wait, President Lazzara returned Sara's call. "Madam President I have received enough calls from north of the border today. Every call spells more disaster for my country," the Mexican President said in a subdued voice.

"Mr. President, I'm calling because I heard that President Obama is going to start returning your illegal countrymen back to Mexico. But, Mr. President, right after that speech he decided to resign his Presidency. Right now, we don't know whether the new President Goodwin will continue with Obama's policy of returning your countrymen. If Obama's policy is continued, the added burden will put a tremendous strain on your administration and economy."

"The purpose of my call is to suggest that our previous conversation on possible Mexican-American joint ventures should be reopened."

"You're going to need millions of new jobs, Mr. President and our joint ventures could fit that bill," Sara offered.

Chapter 7 – Joint Ventures

"Yes, you're right, Sara," the Mexican President admitted. "But I'm so swamped with critical issues, I can hardly believe someone is actually trying to help my country."

"Pedro, even though we're sending back all your illegal aliens, we are still your neighbor and friend who wants your country to survive and prosper."

"Since we first talked on the subject of joint ventures, I've had a group of government officials and leading business men and women looking into the various industries and infrastructure projects that would benefit your entire country, Mr. President. I will get with that exploratory group and come up with a list of possible joint venture projects we would like to propose to your administration, and yourself, if that's acceptable, Mr. President."

"Certainly, Sara, we realistically don't have much of a choice if we're going to survive in this present climate we're in. I certainly don't want my country to fall back into total despair and lawlessness like in the nineteenth century. Madam President, we're close enough to that now," the Mexican President admitted.

"You're on the right track, Mr. President, you're keeping your promise of the border crossing and you're clamping down and eliminating drug cartels and drug running gangs that are holding your country hostage. With numerous joint ventures starting all over your country and the ability of your returning countrymen to fill these newly created jobs, the overall conditions within Mexico should change drastically for the better, Mr. President. I'd like to add one more thing. All this future prosperity is predicated on the elimination of the powerful drug lords and cartels. Unless they are destroyed, and soon, everything is lost, I'm afraid," Sara admitted.

"Yes, I realize that Sara," he answered, a little annoyed. "I'm sorry, but I don't know what else I can do more than I'm presently doing. It consumes most of my time, energy and limited resources that I have."

"Okay, give me a few days, Mr. President, and I'll contact you with a list of ventures I'd like you to consider with locations, costs and benefits to locations and environmental considerations. One other thing, once we agree upon a certain project we don't want or need certain government regs and blockages that hinder or slowdown the projects. It's also imperative that our engineers and yours work closely together to insure highest building standards and safety possible. There will be no slip-shod construction on these joint ventures."

"I agree, Madam President. While you're working on your project list I'll have my staff make a list of our own," the Mexican President said.

Both parties said goodbye and immediately notified their staffs that the word was go pertaining to joint ventures with Mexico. Chief-of-Staff McCarney headed up the group working on the lengthy list of joint venture projects for Mexico. Various members of the committee had travelled extensively throughout Mexico and had many friends within the Mexican government who had indicated certain needs throughout the country.

Buck mentioned to his boss some of the hundreds of projects ear marked for joint venture status such as water treatment plants, dams, highway improvements, desalination plants, hospitals, housing and a hundred other major projects that will benefit most Mexicans. "Madam President, the biggest overall project we have listed is the replacement of numerous village and large city sewer systems. We feel there are well over half a million needed projects throughout Mexico just to bring them into the twentieth century.

"When President Lazzara and his staff presents their wish list we'll compare our lists and choose either or. But I do believe, Madam President, that since we're going to finance the lion share of all costs, we should have the final say on which projects are worthy of completing. We also must be careful that old fashion pork projects don't weasel their way into the list of venture projects that only benefit very few."

"I agree completely, Buck, but let's wait until we review President Lazzara's wish list. One more thing, Buck, you and your group have estimated the overall cost of the current list of projects would surpass half a trillion dollars."

"Yes, ma'am, that figure is correct, but our committee feels that the five hundred billion figure is just a drop in the bucket for what is really needed throughout Mexico."

"Well, we're not going to solve all their problems and turn Mexico into the promised-land, but we can make life a little easier for all Mexicans by following many of these needed projects," President Williamson added.

Chapter 7 – Joint Ventures

Within just two days the Mexican President produced a wish list of projects he wanted to join together in a joint venture agreement.

President Williamson was very surprised that the list wasn't much larger than it was. Chief-of-Staff McCarney and his committee started comparing their lists before meeting with the Mexican government and deciding on hard projects.

In less than a week, Buck and his committee, along with members of the Army Corps of Engineers flew to Mexico City and met with top officials in Lazzara's administration. The first ten joint ventures were finalized and approved by both sides, and the financial arrangement was that the Western States of America would pay eighty percent of these first ten joint ventures and will provide a large number of civil engineers from the Army Corps of Engineers. These engineers and their families would live in Mexico while working on these many projects. Certain specialized materials and equipment not available in Mexico would be supplied by W.S. of A. The first ten projects are defined as the following:

- Sewer replacement in Mexico City and five other cities
- Roadway repair (approx. 800 miles)
- Bridge repairs (167 bridges)
- Hospitals; new (6)
- Dam construction; new (4), repair (6)
- Air ports; new (4), repair/improve (16)
- Desalination plants – Pacific (2) Atlantic (2)
- Housing units – house 200,000 families
- Water purification facilities; new (27), repair/upgrade (35)
- Railroad; new lines 450 miles, new box cars (500), new engines (4)

Colonel Adam Fuller, Head Civil Engineer of the ten joint ventures, and his staff estimated the overall cost of two hundred billion (200,000,000,000) dollars and that's with using ninety-nine percent Mexican labor. Some projects would take years to complete and require thousands of workers at each construction site. Sewer replacement/repair would take even longer than four years to complete. Each joint venture would have an Army Corps of Engineer project leader and it would take him and his staff, along with the Mexican counterpart, at least a month to review each site and determine what equipment and supplies were needed to complete the project. All necessary equipment and building supplies were to be purchased form Mexican businesses, unless the items are not available or the quality is not up to standard.

As the three-day meeting in Mexico City ended, most of the major questions and concerns were addressed and agreed upon by both sides. Both groups agreed on the first day that Colonel Brian Adams, Chief Civil Engineer of the Army Corps of Engineers, should be in overall charge of all ten joint ventures. Most of the Mexican top engineers had known Colonel Adams for years and many had consulted with Brian on countless Mexican projects.

Buck said, "Both sides must quickly assign their engineers and specialized manpower to each separate project. Each project will utilize as much local manpower as possible."

Before closing the meeting, the date for the next get together was set for one week in Mexico City. Buck told the group that within the next week a list must be accomplished by both groups. "The selection of project engineers and other managers required to handle the influx of material, personnel and etc. Travel arrangement alone will be a big issue especially in Mexico." Buck reminded the group that Secretary-of-the-Treasury, William J. O'Neil, and his selected group of financial people would be assigned to each project area along with the Mexican Treasurer and his people to keep track of all expenditures. "Remember," Secretary O'Neil said at the start, "there will be no cost overruns on any of these projects. A tight grip on all costs are imperative on these joint ventures."

The meeting broke up and the American team headed to the airport for the return trip to Flagstaff and a meeting with Secretary O'Neil and President Williamson.

Without delay, upon arriving in Flagstaff, Chief-of-Staff McCarney and Army Corps of Engineers Chief Field Engineer Colonel Brian Adams headed for the Flagstaff Whitehouse for a meeting with President Williamson and Secretary-of-the-Treasury O'Neil.

Chapter 7 – Joint Ventures

After introducing Colonel Adams, Buck quickly covered the Mexico City meeting and said, "All ten proposed joint venture projects have been agreed upon." The Chief-of-Staff said, "A mountain's worth of work had to be done during the next week by both sides. Current maps and satellite photos are needed before the engineering types can finish their individual assessment of each site," Buck added.

"Madam President, these ten joint venture projects will take at least five years to complete," Colonel Adams interjected. "Between the dam projects and the sewer reconstruction in the big cities, we'll be lucky to finish within our estimate of five years and as Chief Engineer responsible for construction of all ten joint ventures, I just want you both to know these are huge projects especially being in Mexico."

"Please explain your last comment," Secretary O'Neil asked their top military engineer.

"Yes, sir, I will. I have worked in Mexico some years ago as a consulting engineer and I saw first-hand the many unexpected problems that always came up to slow down the project or in many cases actually stopped the construction completely. Some examples were wage disputes, material deliveries, environmental concerns, pay offs not received or special very expensive permits that were required to continue. There were other problems beside these, but my main reason for mentioning these stoppable tactics is we cannot put up with type of ransom demands that will undermine our ability to construct these projects on time and within budget."

Colonel Adams continued, "Madam President we must have clear sailing on this and the complete agreement by President Lazzara and his administration. I would also like a direct line to President Lazzara and his civilian staff in case some unexpected problems crop up that require the top dog to solve quickly. This I must insist upon, Madam President. I don't want to go through a half dozen politicians to solve any problem on any of the ten construction sites."

"I don't like the word demand, Colonel, but I agree with your assessment of Mexican ransom. I will talk with President Lazzara and get your direct phone line to his office as you wish," Sara told Colonel Adams.

"Thank you, Madam President, that will make my job a lot easier on all fronts."

"I think that's all for now," Buck told the group, "I'll keep you both informed on our overall progress in the coming weeks." Buck headed to his near-by office and Bird Colonel Adams headed for the Army Headquarters building that is only about one third complete and his office.

President Williamson called Colonel Montgomery at Army Headquarters in Querétaro Province, Mexico. The American full Bird Colonel answered immediately and was asked if he could attend a meeting in Flagstaff with some Governors on a border issue.

"Is it what I think?" he asked

"Yes, it is, Colonel."

"Yes, ma'am, I'll be there. When?"

"How about tomorrow afternoon, late?" Sara asked. "Or is that too soon?" she added.

"I'll be there, Madam President."

"Good," she answered.

Colonel Montgomery made the necessary arrangements using military air craft to Mexico City then civilian airlines to Flagstaff.

Chapter 8
MORE CARTELL WARS

The next afternoon he arrived in the capitol and drove directly to the capitol building to attend the meeting scheduled for 18:00 hours.

The meeting started on time with President Williamson, the four state Governors, Chief-of-Staff McCarney and Colonel Montgomery.

Sara started off by relating the activities being done by the Mexican military and Colonel Montgomery towards the many drug cartels inside Mexico. She asked Colonel Montgomery to describe the drug raid on the Santiago cartel and what documentation was found at the scene.

The Colonel quickly told of the military raid on the jungle cartel and with great detail described the office, the filing cabinets and the locked box with the gold cover log book that contained the list of names and mailing addresses of persons being paid off. Along with the names was the amount paid each month and when the payments started. Among the many names included three names from the states of California, New Mexico and Texas. The position they held were Attorney General of California, Head of State Police in Texas and Head of Border Patrol in New Mexico.

"Thank you, Colonel."

"As President of W.S. of A. I want these three individuals arrested and immediately removed from office as quietly as possible. I want swift justice and these three dirt bags to spend the rest of their lives in jail. They have caused numerous deaths in co-operating with the Mexican drug cartels by allowing drugs to freely flow into our border states and beyond. Between these captured records, the cash payments delivered to these individuals plus their bank records and foreign accounts we should have proof positive of their guilt.

"I have talked with Chief Justice Kathleen Lopez and she said we are on solid legal footing, so as we build our case I want these three jailed without allowing any chance of posting bail. If they post bail these three will disappear forever. Please handle this as discretely as possible," Sara asked the state Governors.

They nodded their heads up and down in the 'yes' motion.

"One more thing," Sara said, "we want to prosecute these three individuals in one trial held in federal court here in Flagstaff. I would also suggest transferring these scum bags to the federal prison at Winslow, that way they'll be close to the courtroom. Oh! And for your info, there are many more American names the Santiago cartel listed as pay off receivers. But I'm only concerned with people that are in our four states. The rest of the names can be handled by President Goodwin and his administration."

"Thank you for coming on such short notice and if you run into any problems, don't hesitate to call me or Chief Justice Lopez." With that the meeting ended and the four Governors headed for home. Colonel Montgomery left the capitol and headed for is headquarters in Mexico.

"Secretary-of-the-Treasury O'Neil is on line #2" Mrs. Bakker informed President Williamson.

"Good afternoon, Bill, what's up," Sara asked her long-time friend and school mate.

"Good afternoon to you Madam President. I just wanted to inform you that all the banks within W.S. of A. have received their allotment of new currency. Many large banks had to receive more than one shipment of our new currency because of the high demand. The overall demand by the public was overwhelming, as you know. I was surprised at the amount of greenbacks the public held at home. My staff and I guessed they might have held somewhere between 250 to 500 billion, but we were way off. It amounted to just under a trillion dollars held outside the banking system. I guess the public still doesn't trust their government and the banking system. They lost billions a few years ago and have long memories when it comes to losing money."

"I'm going to try and change their minds and have trust in our new government and banking system. That amount of money should be available to our government and private citizens upon demand and not weaseled away in a mattress."

"I agree, Bill, that's a huge amount of cash being held due to total mistrust of government. Let's work on changing that public perception of their government," Sara asked her Treasury Secretary.

"I certainly will, Madam President."

Colonel Montgomery arrived at Army Headquarters outside Querétaro, Mexico and was immediately confronted by General Rōjas and his aide. "Welcome back, Colonel, we must talk as quickly as possible, but I'm sure you're tired from your trip to Arizona."

"Thank you General, but I'm fine, sir. The trip back was uneventful and on time. I'm ready when you are, General."

"Okay, my friend, let's go to my office were we can talk in private and security." They headed for the General's office and Colonel Montgomery was wondering what the hell was so important or so urgent. General Rōjas opened his office door and asked his aide to remain outside and not allow anyone to access his office. Once inside both sat down and relaxed for a minute before General Rōjas said, "Colonel, President Lazzara called this morning and asked if we could possible attack the Chino cartel within the next day of two. He didn't say, but I think he has received some additional intel that he won't share, but longer delays could be costly in his eyes. I told him I wanted to converse with you before making any commitment on a date. The weather conditions we discussed a week ago will arrive at our target site within the next 24 to 48 hours," General Rōjas said, lighting his special Cuban cigar with a very unique sweet smell. "I think we can brief our men, go over the latest intel, prepare our air craft and watercraft and alert the Texas National Guard for their bomb run within the next day or two. Can we do this, Colonel, within that 24-48 hour window the Mexican General asked?"

"Yes, I believe we can, General, but we must start the ball rolling right now," the Colonel said, standing up.

"I agree, Colonel, I'll call a staff meeting for 18:00 hours this evening then we'll assemble the men for a quick briefing at 20:00 hours, and I'd like you to alert the 10th Bomb Group with the date and time of their bombing run."

"That's fine, sir, I'll alert the Texas group within the hour with the specifics."

At 18:00 the General's staff officers assembled in his office for a detailed briefing on the upcoming operation against the Chino drug cartel. The only item left out was the date and time. He warned the group that phone calls and cell phone usage would not be authorized. "Anyone caught calling out will be

arrested and held for court martial proceedings." He added, "Secrecy is the formula for success in this type of operation."

"Do you have anything to add, Colonel, the General asked?"

"No, sir, nothing," the Colonel answered.

The General stood up and said, "Gentlemen, that's all for now, there is a formation at 20:00 hours for all Spl Ops personnel." The staff officers quickly exited the office and the Mexican commanding General and American Special Ops Colonel just stood there wondering if they would be able to pull this operation off without losing half or more of their unit.

Colonel Montgomery broke the silence by saying, "If President Lazzara is worried, then so should we, my friend."

At 20:00 hours sharp, the four hundred and fifty members of the Special Ops Company were standing at attention waiting for General Rōjas and the American Colonel to finally divulge the target they had trained for: The night jumps, repelling from high jungle canopy and using new night time location equipment and other aides to distinguish them from the enemy.

General Rōjas shouted, "At ease. Now I'm going to ask Colonel Montgomery to brief you on the coming operation and all its pitfalls."

The American Colonel stepped forward and explained in perfect Spanish the target, jungle location and the number of armed cartel members they should expect to engage. He also told them about the Texas National Guard 10th Bomb Group and the type of ordinance they would be dropping prior to their attack. The Colonel also explained that the location sensors that would be dropped at night to pin point the cartel's exact location. "The Chino cartel won't even realize they have been pinpointed. The two point incursion was explained in detail with emphases on split second timing by both attacking forces. Your officers will be passing out detail maps tomorrow for your review. Between now and tomorrow I want you to double and triple check your equipment and make sure the safeties are working on all you weapons. We don't want an accidental shot fired to alert the cartel we're coming. Remember, our goal is zero causalities, but we know there will be some deaths in an operation like this, so if anyone wants out of this operation for personal reasons, please step forward. You'll just be held here until the operation is completed then transferred to another outfit with no ramifications of any kind." With that, two members of the Spl Ops Company stepped forward.

"Take the two men to the arms room and place them under house arrest until our operation is over," the Colonel ordered.

"Company attention."

"Dismissed."

Once the company dispersed the Colonel asked his aide Captain Ortiz to inquire why these two men declined to participate in this operation.

The Captain returned and said one man indicated his wife just gave birth to twins and he already has three children at home and doesn't want to leave her with five little children if he should be killed in the raid.

The second man said his wife is currently in the hospital with a life threatening illness and he has four children to care for.

"Thank you Captain, please make sure they understand it's okay they are dropping out of this operation for understandable reasons," the Colonel insisted.

"I will, Colonel, sir."

Long into the night the members of the Spl. Ops group checked and double checked their mountain of special equipment and studied the target area maps to insure every member of the unit is completely familiar with the jungle terrain.

General Rōjas called for a company assembly at 09:00 hours. After calling the company to attention, the General said that Colonel Montgomery would give additional details of the coming raid.

"At ease, troopers," the American Colonel yelled in English. He smiled and shook his head as he forgot to speak in Spanish. All members of the unit had to laugh at his language mistake. Once the Colonel regained his composure he continued in Spanish. "Like in our training we will be divided into two attacking forces. One attacking form the west and the other group coming from the river and entering from the east. Just like it shows on your maps.

"Group #1 will be commanded my me, and we'll fly in two C-135 Globe Masters and be jumping for a hillside clearing east

 rickshaw

of Rosamorada and just west of the river San Pedro which is approximately fifteen kilometers from the cartel location. Our long trek is through thick jungle, high hills, one river and many small streams. We will be parachuting into our LZ some six hours before General Rōjas and his group hits the silk.

"The General and group #2 will fly in two C-135s and jump for a clearing just one mile west of the village Nayar with their equipment and the special boats needed for their trip down stream to their jump off point. Once they leave the river they only have a little over three miles to the target area.

"Group #1, my group, will exit from here at 19:30 hours this evening and with the flight time of about one hour and forty-five minutes should arrive at our LZ at 20:45 hours. We'll low level jump and should be ready to force march within thirty minutes. I didn't mention this before, but we have a small group of local men who will cut a trail through the jungle. They'll quickly make a path for us to make the fifteen kilometers within the six hour window. To cover that distance in six hours is a feat in itself, but we are jungle savvy and we've done it before. Even with our extra equipment, the added help provided by the local natives should make it possible to reach our objective by 03:00 hours.

"I know some of you in my group were concerned about crossing the San Pedro River, but that shouldn't be a problem because boats will be provided by locals. Also, a crossing has been found where fording is possible if boats are not available. At the fording point the water is only three to four feet deep and the San Pedro is only one hundred feet wide. So crossing the river shouldn't be a problem unless there is a downpour or deluge.

"Group #2 lead by General Rōjas will leave at 22:30 hours and arrive at their LZ around midnight.

"I think we are well prepared for this assignment and our extensive training has molded this fractured group into a well-organized and cohesive fighting unit. Myself and General Rōjas are very proud to lead you fine soldiers into battle against a scourge that must be stamped out of your society.

"Group #1 should regroup with your equipment at 19:00 hours for your flight at 19:30 hours. Group #2 should likewise assemble at 22:00 hours for their departure at 22:30 hours. Even though we're leaving at different times, both groups should be in position by 03:00 hours. Between now and departure try and get some sleep or at least some rest and quiet time."

"Company attention."

"Dismissed."

The Special Ops group quickly dispersed and headed for their quarters.

Colonel Montgomery and General Rōjas headed for the headquarters building and some final preparation for this evening's long awaited attack on the Chino drug cartel and complex. Montgomery called the Texas National Guard for one last check on the operational timing of their bomb run. General Rōjas contacted the local native group responsible for marking the drop zone, cutting a path through the jungle and providing the river craft to cross the San Pedro.

After fifteen minutes, both officers were satisfied they were about as ready as humanly possible. Without saying a word, both men left headquarters and headed for their quarters to obtain some sleep, if possible. When Colonel Montgomery reached his quarters he called the National Weather Bureau for an update.

The Mexican Weather Bureau confirmed their prediction from a week ago that a storm front would start to move in the drop zones around early evening and should provide heavy cloud cover for this evening's drops. Only a small amount of rain was expected during the next twelve hours, but the wind speed could reach thirty to thirty-five kilometers per hour during the operation. The Colonel thanked them and as he hung-up the phone he thought, "I hope that amount of wind speed doesn't affect the bomb run." He again called the Texas National Guard Bomb Group and inquired whether the wind speed of thirty-five kilometers could affect their bomb run and accuracy.

The Commanding Officer of the 10th Bomb Wing assured the Colonel that wind speeds of that amount would not impede their ability to hit the target dead center.

"Thank you, sir," Colonel Montgomery said as he replaced the phone. He moved over to the leather sofa, laid down and within a couple of minutes he was fast asleep.

Chief Justice Kathleen Lopez called President Williamson and informed the President that the Supreme Court building, for

all intent, had been completed. "Only a few minor things have to be finished, Madam President."

"That's great news," the President told her tong-time friend, "That's one more federal building completed. That makes Capital,

Treasury and Supreme buildings now finished and ready for business. I pass by the Immigration, Transportation and Military Octagon building every day and they are close to completion. We'll have a full fledge capitol in no time," she told Justice Lopez.

"Yes, Madam President, Flagstaff is starting to take shape as our capitol. Beautiful buildings, lots of trees, grass and flora along with the mirror ponds make our capitol very lovely," Justice Lopez admitted.

"We have had hundreds and even thousands of workers pouring over the construction sites 24/7 to complete these many government buildings as quickly as possible," the President added.

"Thank you, Kathleen for your update."

"Yes ma'am."

Both women hung-up their phones without another word.

Chief-of-Staff McCarney (Buck) appeared in the open doorway and President Williamson motioned him to come in.

"Good morning, Buck, what brings you here this early?"

"Morning, ma'am. I just wanted to report some new figures on the influx of new citizens entering Western States of America. Since our founding, over one million Americans have left the Washington beltway mob and entered our new country. In the last ninety days some one thousand persons have relocated every day to our country. Most to California and Texas. I've been talking to each Governor and they are concerned about the rising number that are entering their states each and every day. If this continues, we'll be swamped with displaced Americans and not illegal aliens.

"We may have to limit the number of persons allowed to relocate in our new country. This could develop into a different kind of immigration problem. We must address this issue as quickly as possible, Madam President. ould you agree to discuss this issue with their new President Goodwin?" the Chief—of-Staff asked. "His new administration must make the necessary changes that President Obama had promised the nine Governors and make the population of the forty-six remaining states satisfied with the new President. As the new Democratic President, he should make a multitude of changes to benefit all the states' citizens. If he doesn't change, or stop the massive social issues that are bankrupting his country and slowly dragging their country into the abyss of despair, Goodwin will be a one term President.

"Buck, I've known this problem has existed for some time, but I didn't realize it was that serious. One million persons added to our population each year is too many. We can't support that influx of persons year after year," she added.

"You're right Buck, this is growing into a massive people problem that I must address with our staff as well as President Goodwin. I'll call the new President as early as tomorrow. Just make sure I have all the facts and figures before I call him, Buck."

"You'll have all the necessary data by this afternoon, Sara." With that Buck turned and left the President's office.

Sara had to smile at Buck's resistance to call her name, Sara.

Mexico's Vice President Raoul Aquirre met the Chinese delegation at the airport outside Mexico City and quickly drove the six miles to the Presidential Palace under heavy guard provided by the Mexican State Police. Chinese Premier Choi Sin Woo and his party were escorted into the huge reception area where President Lazzara and his wife and other members of his government were waiting. After the introductions and pleasantries, the Chinese Premier, his interpreter, President Lazzara and his Chinese speaking Mexican national left the reception area and entered a small but very ornate room filled with murals of Mexican history and glass display cases filled with Aztec gold figures, masks and statues. Once seated Mexican President Lazzara quickly asked Choi the real purpose of his non-official state visit to Mexico.

Once the translation was complete, the Chinese leader said he was here in Mexico to offer any assistance to help the Mexican government with their massive drug problem and even the American problem.

Pedro asked, "What American problem are you referring to?"

Choi's interpreter translated and before he finished, the Chinese Premier said, "The border problem, Mr. President. The Americans have many divisions stretched across the entire length of the Mexican/American border. This is an act of aggression, Mr. President, and the Chinese people would like to help in eliminating that standing problem."

"Just how would you eliminate 'the problem,' as you put it?" Pedro asked.

Once the translator stopped, Choi said, "We would, with your government's permission, station Chinese troops on Mexican soil to face the American forces along the entire two thousand mile border. About ten or twelve divisions of Chinese soldiers should convince the Americans to retreat from the border and stay out of Mexican business."

President Lazzara stoop up and said, "My god, Choi, the Americans would not stand still for that. They would consider that as a foreign threat to the U.S. and would strike long before your Chinese troops stepped on Mexican soil, let alone assemble at the border."

Choi leaned back in his chair and said, "The Americans of today have lost their will to fight and are satisfied to only occupy and send out patrols rather than attack with many divisions to secure a fast and lasting victory. These Americans are too soft. They're becoming bogged down with their social issues that are putting them into a pit of debt that they can't climb out of. The Democratic preoccupation with social justice and equality for all will cost the Americans everything while dragging them down to third world status. Our military intelligence feel that Americans will rattle their swords but do nothing to stop our forces from helping you eliminate the border problem."

Choi continued, "The American military forces are stretched beyond thin around the world while fighting a holy war in Afghanistan, a war of which they cannot win. Many countries have tried to conquer the Afghan people and have ended in defeat. Just ask the Russians how they did after years of fighting. The Americans do not know how to win in the 21st century. Back in the forties during the Second World War, the American people were committed to unity and the overall cause to win. Everyone would sacrifice anything in order to give their fighting men a better chance to win. But today is a much different story indeed. Most Americans are in the game of life only to see what they can get for little or nothing. It's all me, me, me, what's in it for me."

"Just look at all the politicians that are corrupt and sent to jail. Look at all the Wall Street people who are fleecing the American public of billions of dollars. The American public is completely different form seventy years ago. The pride of being an American has fallen by the wayside and the unity as a nation had been broken such as the breakaway states that became the country 'Western States of America.' I rest my case on the American issue, Mr. President. Now the other issue I came to discuss is your every expanding drug problem. In China we have opium houses or dens. Drugs are sold and used within these establishments only. Drugs are not sold on the street corner or in dark alleys. If a Chinese citizen is caught selling hard drugs he or she is taken away and, in short order, shot. Controlled drug houses are one thing, but open selling to the general public is forbidden. We have drug control units that provide protection to the general population. These units inspect the authorized dens and make sure opium and other drugs are not allowed to leave these establishments."

"You see Mr. President, we understand the drug problem and know how to control the disease. But your country has not learned how to play the game yet."

"And just how would you help our helpless country?" President Lazzara added sarcastically.

"I understand you're frustrated in trying to cope with this national problem but we can help control your drug problem."

"Choi, you keep saying you can help but haven't yet said just how you would accomplish this."

"Mr. President, the first thing we would do is start eliminating the chemical supplies. This would put pressure on the cartels to find other suppliers for chemicals to process their poison. This search for substitute supplies and chemicals would make them visible and open for detection. Then the drug enforcement squads would move in and make the cartel and its members irrelevant and out of business. The cartel leaders would be photographed and pictured in local and national papers with the time and date of their coming execution. All cartel leaders

and first tier members will be executed. This will be a strong deterring factor for others wanting to be drug dealers.

"That, Mr. President, is how we deal with various drug problems in other countries. We are currently in twelve foreign countries using this method to reduce and eliminate their overall drug problem. I could have sent my Vice Chairman or the head of our drug control unit, but your drug problem is the largest in the world and it affects millions and millions of people worldwide. This drug distribution must stop, Mr. President, and I'm here to offer our help to solve this drug issue.

"If you and your government agree, the Chinese people will send enough personnel to hunt down the cartel members and shut down their various operations throughout Mexico. As your probably not aware, Mr. President, we have thousands of Chinese citizens who speak fluent Spanish.

"On the border issue. If you want to ease the tension that currently exists at the border with the U.S., we can man the border with Chinese troops and that should stabilize the border issue. You know the Mexican military wouldn't stand a chance against the overall military might of the American forces. But the sudden appearance of Chinese troops along the entire border with the U.S. would cause the Americans to back off instead of chancing a confrontation with the Chinese military. They will be scared to death at our appearance on the border and stand down. They have no stomach to engage in a Third World War with our Chinese military. We could defeat the American military many times over I assure you, Mr. President."

"You really think the U.S. government would stand still when Chinese troops appear at their two thousand mile border? My god, Choi, they would pull out all stops to annihilate your Chinese forces and at the same time kill thousands upon thousands of Mexican nationals in the ensuing battle."

"I don't want to hear any more of your solutions to our problems, sir. Our meeting is over. I'll see that you're driven back to the airport and safely put aboard your waiting Chinese aircraft."

"Thank you for seeing me, Mr. President, but remember our offer to help with your national issues still stands. If in the near future you need our help, just call through channels and I'll get your message." With that the Chinese Premier and his interpreter left the Presidential Palace and were driven to the Mexico City International Airport.

President Lazzara went to his office and stared out the window while thinking, "The nerve of the Chinese Premier coming to Mexico and expecting me to allow thousands of Chinese troops to enter our country and man our border and roam throughout my country killing suspected drug dealers. It wouldn't be long before China overran our country and gained a solid foothold in Central America." He shook his head as he remembered that China now controls the Panama Canal and portions of Panama itself. "If Mexico fell under the dragon's spell, it wouldn't be long before Guatemala, El Salvador, Honduras, Nicaragua, Costa Rico, Belize and Petén became a Chinese land grab. Once they occupied Mexico and the other Central American countries, they would turn north to conquer the U.S. and Canada then slither south to overrun the countries of South America and eventually control North and South America.

I'm sure that's their long range plan that looks out some fifty to one hundred years. The Chinese people are very patient and will wait long periods to accomplish their overall goals." President Lazzara turned away from the window and went to his desk and sat down. He said out loud, "As long as I'm President of Mexico, I'll never allow Chinese troops to enter Mexico under the pretexts of helping my country. My god, they are bold. For the leader of the largest communist country to come to my Mexico and offer their protective services to save Mexico is unbelievable at best. Chairman Woo must feel that Mexico is the key to his overall plan to dominate North and South America. For the leader of one point three billion Chinese to come alone without fanfare is something in itself. I will notify my staff of the Chairman's proposals and my total rejection."

Communication Director Marian Wilcox called President Williamson and said, "President Goodwin can meet with you tomorrow afternoon at 4:00 o'clock, if that's okay with you, ma'am."

"Yes, Marian, that's fine. Tell him I'll be there at 16:00 hours tomorrow."

"I'll inform him right away, Madam President."

"Thank you, Marian."

President Williamson arrived in Washington and was quickly driven to the Whitehouse. An aide to the President greeted Sara and ushered her through the Whitehouse and into a room off the Oval Office. The aide said that President Goodwin would be available in just a few minutes.

After a short wait, the door to the Oval Office opened and the new President said, "Good afternoon Madam President, please come in." Sara entered the Oval Office and was motioned to take a seat.

"May I call you Sara?" President Goodwin asked his quest.

"Certainly you may," she answered. But before we get started, may I say congratulations on becoming the 45th President, even though it happened with the surprising resignation of President Obama."

"Thank you, Sara. Your Communication Director said the subject you wanted to discuss was the number of Americans that are leaving our forty-six states and electing to relocate within your Western States of America. Am I correct in my assumption Madam President?"

"Yes, sir that is correct, Mr. President. It's one of the subjects."

"Please call me Chuck," he told his guest with a cool voice.

"Fine, Chuck," she answered. "I've been told that a thousand individuals each week are applying for entry and relocation into our country. At this time we cannot accept, house or afford this number of people wanting to leave your country. We will be forced to deny entry to most of these applicants. Mr. President, you should look into the reasons for their wanting to leave your forty-six state paradise."

"You're being a little facetious, aren't you, Sara?"

"More than a little, Chuck," she answered while displaying a slight smile.

"I think you'll find their reasons are exactly the same as the reasons why we seceded from your union. Unless you address these problems, more people and even some states will again consider leaving your union. You do whatever you want, Mr. President, but this problem will not go away. It will continue to build and build until you experience massive civil unrest that could balloon into a full blown civil war."

"Now, for the second reason I'm here, Charles. When Mexico's military raided and broke-up the Santiago cartel in Central Mexico, they came into possession of a list of names that were receiving cash payments for turning a blind eye or in some way aiding the distribution and sale of various drugs to the U.S. I have that list, Mr. President."

"The Western States of America had some names on this list and we have since arrested and removed these individuals from office. These people will spend many years in federal prison for their indiscretion that caused untold number of deaths in Mexico, the U.S. and lord knows how many other countries. Mr. President, you have some names on this list. About eight or nine names of people located inside the Washington beltway and are currently in your administration."

"I'll give you this list and you can do whatever you want with it. These people were paid huge sums of money delivered in person and paid in American greenbacks. This list also contains the amounts paid in cash for their ability to allow the cartels poison to spread throughout your country."

"Who knows about this list?" President Goodwin asked as he rose from his chair and walked to the bay window and looked out over the Whitehouse lawn.

"Only a few, Mr. President. Mexican President Lazzara, his Commanding General, American Colonel Montgomery, my Chief-of-Staff, myself and of course the senior members of the Santiago cartel and the many runners here in America. That means a total of around one hundred people who know the list exists, and the names listed. Most of the cartel members in Mexico are either dead or in jail. But that leaves the payoff runners here in the states that probably won't be caught."

"That's all I have, Mr. President, but I'm sure that's enough to occupy your interest for a day or two. If you want to discuss either issue again feel free to call," Sara offered.

"Thank you, Madam President, I want to think about the two issues before I do anything."

With that comment President Williamson placed the list in question on the desk and without another word left the Oval Office and headed for Ronald Reagan Washington National Airport and the trip home to Flagstaff.

 rickshaw

Colonel Montgomery watched as his attack force quickly bordered the two huge C-135 Globe Masters with all their electronic equipment, weapons, special boats and six all-terrain vehicles mounted with special designated Gatling guns. The ATVs could go almost anywhere and would be invaluable during the attack on the cartel.

Two hundred and forty-seven men and one woman were loaded into two planes in less than thirty minutes and were cleared for take-off. At exactly 19:30 hours, the two planes cleared the runway and headed for their LZ at Rosamorada. The weather was cooperating. No moon with a complete overcast and a slight mist. With these weather conditions and darkness it made it almost perfect for their low level jump.

The Spl. Ops personnel were dead quiet as they sat lined up against both sides of the plane's fuselage. Talking would be difficult due to the level of noise produced by the four prop engines. They knew this low level jump and trek through the jungle would end in a fire fight against a well-armed force. They also wondered if the cartel and their small army knew they were coming tomorrow morning. If they were tipped off somehow and prepared, a large number of the force would never return to Querétaro.

After a little more than an hour and a half, the stand-by order was given by the jump master and all one hundred and twenty-five troopers and Colonel Montgomery jumped to their feet. Each man started checking the man next to him to insure his chute and attached equipment was tight and secured properly. Then the jump master gave the order to hook-up and all personnel clamped their static lines to the jump cable. There were two cables on each side to accommodate the entire group. Sixty-two men on one side and sixty men and one women on the other. Once everybody was attached to the jump cable, the rear landing ramp started to open and the jungle below was a dark green blur as they flew past only three hundred feet above the jungle canopy.

The green jump light started flashing and the Spl. Ops troop moved in a belly to back tight line to the open ramp and jumped. At only three hundred feet they were on the ground in less than a minute. Both planes were empty of troops in just two minutes, and most of Colonel Montgomery's force hit the two mile long LZ. Four men got tangled in the canopy along the edge of the landing zone, and one trooper was killed when he hit a tree and broke his neck.

The two C-135s came around again and dropped the especial canvas boats, ATVs and all ordinance. It took less than forty-five minutes to gather up the equipment and assemble the entire unit around their Colonel. Their individual electronic locator-finders worked like a charm in the total darkness of the jungle floor and clearing. The local guides arrived on time and after conferring with Colonel Montgomery, started clearing a path for his men and equipment. The six ATVs were fired up and equipment loaded for the fifteen kilometer trek through marsh, hills, river and jungle.

Group #2 assembled at 22:00 hours and were given their last minute instructions by General Rōjas. After wishing them success in their mission, he said, "Let's board." With that command, the one hundred and ninety-nine men and one woman started boarding the pair of C-135s with their personal equipment, boats, 4.2 mortars and over a ton of various ordinance.

At 22:37 hours both planes lifted off the runway and headed west for the village of Nayar and their LZ. In just one hour and twenty minutes, the order to stand and hook-up was given and all two hundred Spl. Ops elite jumped up and hooked their static lines to the jump cable. After one last chute and equipment check, all were ready for their low level night jump.

The rear ramp opened and almost immediately the green jump light started blinking. Both lines of troopers exited the planes and were on the ground in less than a minute.

Just before they jumped the weather turned a little. A cross wind of thirty to thirty-five miles per hour developed and a heavy rain started to drench their landing zone. Even with a low level jump of only three hundred feet, the wind was strong enough to scatter them over a mile and a half. Some troopers hit the clearing, others drifted into the jungle and a few ended up in the river. The two planes made their second pass coming up wind and dropped their load dead center in the clearing. It took over an hour to gather up his scattered forces, assemble his boats, lead the equipment and head down the Huaynamota River to their landing point.

 rickshaw

After an hour of paddling, General Rōjas and his force of two hundred arrived at their predetermined landing site. They quietly unpacked their gear, pulled the canvas boats from the river and covered them with brush, vines and jungle ferns. They gathered around their General, and again he told them to make sure the safeties on their weapons were on.

As the group entered the jungle, the rain became more intense. It was coming down in sheets. The General thought, "This hard rain is a god send, it will cover our advance in a wet coat of silence." The two hundred heavy armed Spl. Ops personnel walked in silence as they headed for the Chino complex.

An advance squad with metal detectors led the way, clearing a path for any land or tree mines. General Rōjas lifted the cover on his watch that concealed the illuminated dial and checked the time. He figured they were only about twenty minutes behind schedule and if all went well, they should arrive at their assembly point east of the compound at 03:20 hours. As he walked with his men, the jungle floor became a soggy march and more difficult to walk while carrying heavy packs and weapons. After coming one mile he ordered a halt and a brief rest. After a ten minute break, the group of two hundred packed up and hit the trail for their final leg of their trek. In an hour and a half the General's group arrived at their designated assemble point.

Colonel Montgomery and his elite group arrived at their final assembly point at 03:25 hours. The entire force was dead on their feet and welcomed the rest before the Texas National Guard Bomb Group started dropping their special ordinance on the Chino compound. Once the bombing started it should only last about ten minutes then they would attack with a force of two hundred from the east and a force of two hundred forty-eight from the west. When they attack, the special ATVs with their Gatling guns will lead the way from the west.

The four B-1 (E-Class) Attack Bombers left their airbase in Lubbock, Texas and headed south to Mexico's Zacatecas Providence and the Chino compound near the village of Nayar. Their last time to the Mexico target is one hour and forty-five minutes at thirty-five thousand feet.

Each plane carries a bomb load of ten, one thousand pound delay fuse bombs that explode within a few seconds after hitting the ground. This type of ordinance can plow through the jungle canopy without exploding before they hit solid ground. When the air strike gets within thirty miles of the target, they would drop to one thousand feet for their final approach. The heavy rain and brisk wind would not affect the accuracy of their strike.

The Spl. Ops group had electronically painted the target and the B-1 bombers would hone in on that signal and deliver their ordinance for a bull's eye strike. They were scheduled to arrive at their drop zone at approximately 03:30 hours and make two bomb runs each within ten minutes. The devastation should cover a half mile square and destroy everything above and below ground.

Texas Governor Marilyn LaCrosse and Governor Conrad Schiller of California entered the President's office and were directed to their seats by President Williamson who was on the phone. Sara said, "Goodbye," and replaced the phone. "Sorry about that," she said. "I have asked both of you here to Flagstaff to talk about oil, gas and drilling. Before we start can I offer you both something to eat or drink?"

"Madam President, I'm starved. I would like something," Governor Conrad said with a smile.

"How about you, Marilyn?" the President asked.

"Yes, ma'am, I could eat something if it's not a problem."

"Not at all," Sara answered. She pressed the intercom and asked Ruth to please bring in some tea, soft drinks and a plate of cookies.

Mrs. Bakker said, "It will be about ten minutes, Madam President."

"That's fine, Ruth."

"While we're waiting for some chow, let's get started," Sara said. "As you both know, our supply of oil is just adequate in our four states. We have very little gasoline, diesel fuel and home heating oil in reserve. We must pump more oil to satisfy our growing appetite. We have thousands of oil wells that were capped years ago in both California and Texas. I want to uncap the wells and start pumping again. Besides uncapping these wells, I want to extract more oil from the gulf and off shore of

California. Now, when I say 'off shore' I mean at least fifty miles off shore. No one on the shore should be able to see any oil rigs. We need to drill, drill and drill more oil wells. No matter what any President or Senator says we need more oil to run our economy for decades to come. We have more oil in the ground than most Middle East countries. Of known reserves, we have trillions of barrels of oil just sitting there waiting to be tapped. In just two known reserves there are more than five hundred and two billion barrels in each. But due to government regulations and restrictions, these oil reserves are not being tapped. Since these government regs don't apply to our country, we will drill for oil whereever we want. Now, there are certain National Parks, preserves and land areas that are off limits to drilling. Even though we need a huge amount of oil, we will not jeopardize pristine wilderness areas for the sake of more oil.

"Please get with your oil experts and oil companies and urge them to reopen their capped wells. Just between the three of us, if they refuse to uncap and resume drilling, I might consider nationalizing the oil industry as the last resort. But let's hope it doesn't come to that," President Williamson told the two Governors. "This administration will issue oil drilling leases to all domestic oil companies after reviewing their location, safety precautions and other pertinent issues."

"Is there any question about what I want in respect to oil drilling?" Sara asked both Governors.

"None, Madam President, we have been discussing this very issue over the past month. With your backing, we'll get started immediately," Governor LaCrosse assured her President. "Sorry ma'am, no time for chow."

"That's okay," Sara said, standing up and walking over to the two Governors. She shook their hands with a surprisingly firm grip.

Both Governors quickly left the capitol building and headed for the airport and their return tips to California and Texas. Before catching their flights, Marilyn and Conrad discussed the oil issue and came to the conclusion that the oil industry within their states would certainly resist their request to uncap their numerous low producing oil wells. "I guess we'll just have to convince the oil company brass that they should open their capped oil wells and start pumping again. They must

232

understand what will happen if they don't start pumping their old capped wells or resist drilling new wells in the Gulf and off shore of California. Remember Conrad, our country is still under Martial Law and President Williamson has unlimited government powers. She will ask the oil companies to increase substantially their oil production and also lower the price of a barrel of sweet crude or she will threaten to nationalize the whole oil industry."

"To nationalize the oil industry would be a huge mistake," Marilyn told her counterpart from California. "Our state citizens might then say, like the union of forty-six, our new government is interfering with private business."

"We must talk Sara out of that threat," Conrad answered.

"We should gather up our oil experts and see what can be done to increase oil output. Maybe we can increase that flow of oil without tapping the thousand small wells scattered through Texas, Oklahoma, California and Pennsylvania. Let's set up a meeting next week to address the oil issue. We can hold the meetings in my state or yours, I don't care," Marilyn admitted.

"No matter where we meet, it will take a full week to gather up the knowledgeable people for Texas and California, as well as acquire the necessary data to make sound judgments and recommendations to President Williamson. Talk to your people then we'll get together and decide where to hold these meetings," Conrad suggested. "Maybe we should ask Sara to contact President Goodwin and ask him if the Governors of Oklahoma and Pennsylvania should attend our meeting."

"I'm sure our oil companies will balk at the idea of uncapping their old low producing wells. They will contend that it will cost more to extract the oil from those wells than it's worth."

When Marilyn got to her office in the Governor's mansion in Austin she immediately placed a call to Flagstaff and President Williamson. To her surprise the President was in her office and the call was put through immediately.

"Hi, Marilyn, you got to Austin at warp speed, what's up?" Sara asked.

"Madam President, we're gathering all our oil and gas experts from California and Texas for a meeting next week. Governor Schiller and I were wondering whether you should call

President Goodwin and ask him to allow the oil people in Oklahoma and Pennsylvania to attend our oil meetings next week."

"No, Marilyn, I don't want to call Goodwin. I want our country to be oil independent of the now Goodwin union and eventually all foreign sources. We'll pump oil and gas from our current wells within our states, the gulf and off shore."

"Remember, Marilyn, the oil speculators control the overall price of oil coming from foreign wells. They worry about every little thing, whether the Strait of Hormuz will be blocked by Iran, or a supertanker runs aground, or terrorist's hi-jack a tanker, or some foreign leader in the Middle East is disposed and the country's wells are set ablaze. And there are dozens of other reasons that effect the price per barrel."

"We will not be controlled by the Wall Street speculators because we are an independent country, and we will do what we want to control the price of our own oil. We have enough known oil to fuel the needs of our driving public, and with the expanding drilling in the Gulf and off shore in the Pacific, we'll have an abundance of crude. In the meantime, Mexico and Canada are willing to deliver oil to our country at less than world prices. Even though we're at odds with Mexico on various issues, President Lazzara is trying to improve relations with our country and border states."

"We should remember the way we currently divide a barrel of crude. Presently we use the 3-2-1 crack spread by refineries to produce various fuels. One barrel of crude (42.5 gals) using the crack spread produces (3) bbls of gasoline, (2) bbls of diesel and (1) bbl. of various by-products. If the crack spread was (6), then one barrel of oil would yield (255) gals of gasoline. Remember 100 percent of a barrel of oil is used. Everything from fuel to thousands of other products that are based on crude such as common aspirin. We cannot be without oil in our present economy. Many people continue to harp on oil dependency and how we must get away from its dependency. Well we can't. Alternate fuel is one thing, but the thousands of other products that are based on crude must continue."

"Marilyn, when you and Conrad decide on a date, time and location, would you mind if I address that group?" Sara asked.

"Madam President, you're always welcome to participate in our state meetings. I'll notify your office when the date is finalized," the Texas Governor told her President.

"Thank you, Marilyn."

Both parties hung up.

After a quick cup of green tea, Marilyn placed a call to the California Governor. Conrad had not arrived at the Governor's residence in Sacramento yet, but one of his aides assured the Texas Governor she'd give Conrad the message the minute he returned.

Marilyn hung up and sat back thinking about all the issues that are currently on her plate and the many other issues that will continue to pile on. After that brief interlude she picked up the phone and asked her top aide to join her.

Once the aide was seated, Marilyn asked her to contact all the oil companies in Texas and ask that their oil experts attend a state meeting next week. The exact day, time and location will be provided in the next day or two. "Also contact the leading companies that provide the images from space for possible oil deposits on land and in the Gulf. I want every expert in the oil and gas industry to attend our meeting next week. Let me know if anyone or company balks at this short notice."

"Okay, that's it. You have a lot of work to do in the next few hours."

The aide stood up and said, "Yes, ma'am, I'll get right on it." She exited the Governor's office at high speed with a big task at hand.

The light on Governor LaCrosse's phone started blinking and Marilyn answered with, "Yes."

"Marilyn, its Conrad. I just got to my office and was told you called."

"Yes, Conrad, I wanted you to know about my conversation with President Williamson earlier today. She does not want to call President Goodwin on the oil meeting next week. Sara wants this meeting to pertain to our own oil needs, reserves, wells and future drilling sites on land and off shore."

During the next forty-eight hours straight, some sixty-three oil companies large and small in California, Texas, New Mexico and Arizona were alerted to the important upcoming meeting. Not only were the specific oil and gas companies

notified, but every known oil and gas expert in the Western States of America. The meeting was scheduled for next Thursday at 18:00 hours at the Fairmont San Francisco hotel ballroom in San Francisco. This huge ballroom could accommodate up to twelve hundred guests and the oil and gas industry will certainly fill the ornate room.

Most of the oil executives answering the meeting call were worried that President Williamson might impose certain regs because of martial law.

The huge ballroom was packed to capacity when Chief-of-Staff Buck McCarney stepped to the glass podium and said, "Ladies and gentlemen, the President of Western States of America." As President Williamson stepped up to the podium wearing a beautiful red suit that hugged her perfect figure like a second skin, the entire twelve hundred guests stood up and gave their first President a standing ovation that lasted a full two and a half minutes. President Williamson raised her arms to quiet the ballroom gathering and slowly they returned to their seats.

"Thank you so very much. I hope after my speech you still feel the same. My speech will be short and sweet but very important to the progress of our fledging country."

"We need more oil and gas. Our current demands are being met, but just barely. We see an increasing demand looming up very shortly. I want every oil company to look at their entire well inventory and determine how they can increase their oil and natural gas output. This includes the small but important independent oil producers. I want old capped wells to be reopened and start producing again. I know some wells are slow producers and can cost more to extract the oil than the oil is currently worth, but let's drain these wells dry and move on.

"Not only do I want known wells uncapped and pumped, but I want more drilling in the Gulf and off shore of California from Imperial Beach in the south, to Prince Island in the north. I know you're not happy with the idea of uncapping a large number of low producing wells, but we need every gallon of oil we can squeeze from these low producers. Drain them dry, cement them shut and move on. As your President I must alert the country of this pending shortage that will limit our ability to move forward at warp speed. Please ask your R&D people to step up their search for oil. If necessary, our numerous satellites can be used to hunt for possible drilling sites.

"I told you oil and gas experts that my speech would be short and sweet. I don't know how sweet my message was, but it was short. Remember I came here today to inform you of our pending shortages and not to threaten the oil and gas industry. My staff who is sponsoring this important meeting will be available during the next three days to help with drilling leases and contracts and any other requirements that your government can provide. If I can be of any help, please don't hesitate to call upon me." With that President Williamson stepped back from the podium and waved to the packed ballroom. The entire room with its twelve hundred guests stood up and clapped loudly for their first President. While they clapped with great enthusiasm, they did not like the overall message put forth by their President.

Thirty miles from their target, the lead pilot contacted General Rōjas to ensure both Spl. Ops groups were in position within the safety zone. The Mexican General assured the bomber pilot that both groups were on station and ready for action. At 03:28 hours the first B-1 bomber was lined up with their painted target and started their first of two bomb runs. The second bomber was off the wing tip of the lead plane as they passed the jungle canopy at only one thousand feet.

Both bombers with Mexican co-pilots started to drop their payloads dead on their jungle target. Each plane dropped five bombs on the first pass and banked slowly to the right and circled around for their second and last ordinance run. When the first group of ten, one thousand pound bombs hit the jungle floor the explosions were deafening and the ground shook for miles. Secondary explosions were occurring above and below ground. As the second group of ten delayed bombs hit the ground inside the massive compound the jungle was bright as day for a mile in all directions. Huge explosions continued for three minutes after the bombs had ignited the vast quantity of processing chemicals and the large cache of ammunition.

Once the secondary explosions died down, both Spl. Ops groups started their attack.

Colonel Montgomery's ATVs were armed with two mini Gatling guns that could spew out more than four thousand rounds per minute.

 rickshaw

They led the way into the vast compound spraying thousands of rounds as they moved throughout the bombed out buildings, huge bomb craters and collapsed underground rooms.

As the surviving cartel members came out of their holes, they were quickly eliminated. As the battle continued, the weather got worse, it rained only like it rains in the jungle. Sheets of rain resembling a well of water pelted the attacking forces, but didn't slow them down.

Both Spl. Ops groups moved quickly from their ten o'clock and two o'clock positions forcing the remaining cartel members into a funnel that was a killing field. The bombing and ground attack caused the death of two hundred and twelve Chino cartel members while capturing fifty-three. Of the fifty-three, thirty-one were wounded.

Colonel Montgomery's group lost four killed and sixteen wounded. Three of the wounded were critical. His favorite commando, "Butch," received an arm wound, but nothing serious. Butch drove the lead ATV in the attack and is credited with killing more than forty cartel members. General Rōjas' group sustained six dead, twenty-four wounded and one missing. Considering there were more than two hundred and sixty-five known members before the attack, the Spl. Ops losses were ten killed and forty troopers wounded. Without the bombing run and the foul weather, the Mexican Spl. Ops group would have sustained much heavier losses.

Twenty tons of coke was destroyed at various stages of production and more than seventy million in American green backs were seized along with a truck load of weapons, ammunition, chemical supplies and payroll records.

The remaining buildings that were not completely destroyed were systemically wired with C-4 explosives and collectively blown up. Nothing remained of the huge complex but smoking piles of rubble.

General Rōjas and the American Colonel collected their dead comrades in arms and transported the many wounded via the small airstrip outside the compound. The remaining troops, along with their gear, headed for the River Huaynamota and the waiting boats to transport them to a LZ down river where four C-130s were waiting to return them to Army Headquarters in Querétaro. Once all the troopers were returned to base, services for their dead comrades were held. Some troopers were buried on base and others were returned to the families or other relatives and friends.

General Rōjas called for a quick formation of the whole Spl. Ops battalion in front of the headquarters building.

"Attention" the General ordered.

The whole battalion snapped to attention.

"At ease," the General quickly added.

"I know you're all dog tired and I won't keep you long. But Colonel Montgomery and I want to say 'job well done.'"

"Now for some more good news. Everyone in this Spl. Ops battalion will be advanced by one grade in rank. That includes officers and enlisted alike." The entire battalion hooped and hollered and jumped with joy at the advance in rank.

The General held up his arms and the group quickly settled down. "Now, the second bit of good news for the Mexican Army personnel that joined the Spl. Ops group for the assault on the Chino cartel complex.

"Most of you will be returning to your regular outfit within the next few days, but anyone who wants to join our Spl. Ops team as a permanent member in dealing with the national problem of illegal drugs, just submit your name to Colonel Montgomery and we will review your request.

"You people were hand-picked from many units within our entire army and are the best. Without your special qualifications and expertise the success of the raid on the Chino complex would have cost the lives of many more Spl. Ops personnel. Thank you for your service."

"Battalion – Attention."

"Dismissed."

The entire battalion quickly headed for their barracks and a well-deserved rest.

Colonel Montgomery and General Rōjas entered the headquarters building and headed straight for their office. Once inside, the American Colonel said, "I think there is some medals that should be awarded."

"I agree," the General said quickly, "but first I'll run this by President Lazzara."

"After talking with the Mexican President," General Rōjas said, "he authorized us to distribute whatever medals necessary.

He also reminded us that we're due in Mexico City within the next few days." After two days of resting, the Spl. Ops battalion was called to formation by General Rōjas at 18:00 hours.

The General called the battalion to "attention", and then to "at ease."

"Colonel Montgomery and I have assembled this unit for the purpose of awarding medals to a few of you or your unselfish duty during our attack on the Chino cartel. Colonel Montgomery will present the first and highest award."

"Colonel."

"Thank you, General."

"Would Maria Ortiz, better known as "Butch," please step forward."

Maria weaved her way through the formation and stood in front of her Colonel.

Maria stood almost five feet tall and the Colonel at six feet four. She smiled as she looked up at him.

"Maria, your country is happy to award you 'The Medal of Military Merit First Class.' You are to wear this medal over your breast." The Colonel handed the medal to her and said in a low voice, "You should affix this to your uniform.

Maria was small in stature but was heavy chested and the American Colonel did not want to attempt the placing of the ribbon on her uniform. She gave him a broad smile as she took the 'Medal of Merit' and pinned it on her uniform. The Mexican eagle hanging from the ribbon couldn't lay flat because of her large breasts.

She saluted and was about to turn when Colonel Montgomery said, "Not so fast, I'm not finished."

"Sorry, Sir."

"Besides the 'Medal of Military Merit first class' (Condecoracion al Merito Militor), you have also been awarded the 'Anti-Narcotics Campaign Medal of Merit, first class.' (Condecoracion par Merito en Campana Contra el Narcotracico)."

He again handed the medal to Maria so she could attach the ribbon along-side the M.M.M. award on her chest.

"How is your arm?" the Colonel asked in a low voice.

"Fine, sir, but it hurts like hell."

The Colonel looked up and at the whole battalion and said, "Butch is a fine example of the Spl. Ops personnel who leads the way during the attack without fear of injury or death."

The whole battalion starting clapping.

Colonel Montgomery looked at Butch and said, "Well-done, young lady."

Maria stepped close to the Colonel and on tip toes gave him a kiss on the cheek. She turned around and returned to her place in formation.

The American Colonel turned and said, "General."

General Rōjas stepped forward and said "Would Lt. Lopez please come forward, or I should say, Captain Lopez."

The new Captain stepped forward and saluted the General.

"Captain, I'm pleased to award you the 'Anti-Narcotic Campaign Medal of Merit' First Class, for your outstanding leadership and courage under fire during the attack on the Chino complex." General Rōjas stepped forward and pinned the large decoration on the Captain's chest. The General saluted and the new Captain returned his salute then turned and returned to the formation.

General Rōjas said, "Would Corporal Ceron please step forward."

Corporal Gilberto Ceron made his way from the back of the large formation and stood at attention in front of the top General in the Mexican Army.

General Rōjas said, "Corporal Ceron was a member of the various Mexican units that supplied their best personnel to join the Spl. Ops group in the attack on the Chino cartel near the village of Nayar."

"Corporal Ceron led a group into battle and is credited with killing and rounding up a large number of cartel members. Even after sustaining two wounds, he continued to lead his group until the mission was complete. His leadership and action is of the highest order. Your government awards you the 'Medal of Military Merit' first class (Condecoracion al Merito Militar)."

General Rōjas pinned the medal on the new Corporal and Gilberto beamed from ear to ear. The Corporal saluted and quickly returned to the formation while the battalion gave him a very noisy ovation.

The American Colonel stepped forward and said, "That's all the awards for the Chino compound attack. But let me say, every one of you deserve a medal for bravery and military expertise."

The Colonel continued, "For myself, General Rōjas and your President Pedro Lazzara, we say 'Job well done.' We have struck a blow to the Chino cartel that sent them back to the Stone Age. The remedy is not complete, but we will find the members that were absent during our attack. Remember, there are many more drug organizations that are holding your beautiful country hostage. We must stamp out this scum that has a death grip on the throat of Mexican freedom. In the near future we'll again have a list of drug targets to attack and stamp out. For now, relax and enjoy the temporary lull because it won't last."

"General, do you have anything to add?" the American Colonel asked his Mexican leader.

"No, Colonel, I think you have covered it nicely."

"Battalion – attention," the Col. Yelled.

"Dismissed."

After a solid two weeks of being fully open to truck and foot traffic, the backup of tractor trailers approaching the two thousand miles of border was starting to ease. The thousands of Mexican vehicles were being processed as quickly as possible and the transfer of goods to U.S. trucking was gaining momentum.

"Madam President, you have a call on line #4, I believe its Mexican President Lazzara."

"Thank you, Ruth."

"Good afternoon, Mr. President."

"Yes, good afternoon, Sara."

"Sara, I'm just calling to let you know that the tensions are easing on my side of our border. I'm happy that the U.S. and Mexican customs are working together to eliminate the huge backlog of vehicles."

"Mr. President, I know the border officials on both sides are working 24/7 and will continue until the number of crossings return to pre-shutdown numbers."

"Sara, there is another subject I'd like to touch upon if you have the time," the Mexican President asked.

"Certainly, Mr. President. Go ahead please."

"As you know our attack on the Chino drug cartel was a great success. Our General Rōjas and your Colonel Montgomery have done a suburb job in closing down a significant amount of drug activity within Mexico. Under our new drug enforcement laws which passed by unanimous votes by all parties, convicted drug dealers will be given a death sentence which will be carried out within thirty days. To help these new laws, my government is offering substantial cash rewards for information leading to the arrest and conviction of drug dealers and pushers.

"If possible Sara, I'd like to hold your Colonel Montgomery over for another month or two. We have some scattered pockets of drug activity that must be eliminated. I thought you should talk to Colonel Montgomery and see if this arrangement is satisfactory with him."

"Certainly, Mr. President, I'll call him as soon as I can. Colonel Montgomery indicated some time ago that his assignment in Mexico will take a little more time. So I'm sure he will agree to your request, Mr. President."

"I hope you're correct, Madam President, we need his military expertise a while longer in our national struggle."

"I'll call you as soon as the Colonel and I have discussed your request, Mr. President."

"Thank you, Sara."

Both parties hung up.

Sara pressed the intercom and asked Ruth to contact Colonel Montgomery at Army Headquarters in Querétaro, Mexico.

"Yes, ma'am right away."

Col. Montgomery was in his office at Army Headquarters going over maps of southern Mexico with a few of his Mexican staff officers when the call came in from President Williamson.

"Gentlemen, would you please excuse me while I take this call."

His Mexican staff quickly exited the office leaving their American Colonel to answer the call.

"Good afternoon, Colonel Montgomery," the Western States of America President greeted her favorite Colonel.

"Good afternoon, Madam President. It's good to hear your voice again."

"Colonel, I'll get right to my call."

"President Lazzara called earlier today and asked if your assignment in Mexico could be extended a few months longer. I told him it was strictly up to you, Colonel."

"Madam President, I have no intention of leaving Mexico and this assignment until our Spl. Ops group had eliminated most of the drug cartels and their chemical suppliers. We have put a dent in the drug trade, but we're not through yet. With the help of the Mexican public and the new strict drug laws, we'll bring to justice hundreds of drug dealers and street pushers. Currently I'm looking at some drug areas in southern Mexico close to the Guatemala border. We have more work to do, Madam President. We can't put a time limit on this type of operation. It will take a 24/7 activity to stamp out this national drug problem. I've heard that the price of coke and marijuana has tripled because of shortages from Mexico. The price escalation is certainly good news, but I'm sure the crime rate will spike due to the shortage of available drugs.

"Madam President, please tell President Lazzara that I'm not going anywhere and I'll stay in Mexico until both of you feel I'm no longer needed."

"Thank you, Colonel, our Mexican friend will be happy to hear your answer and your dedication to duty."

"Let's just say I'll be here until I'm no longer needed," Colonel Montgomery assured his boss.

"Do you have anything for me?" Sara asked.

"Nothing right now, but I'll give you a report in a week or so on our current and projected activities, if that's okay with you, Madam President."

"That's fine, Colonel, let me know if you or your Spl. Ops group needs anything."

"I will," he answered.

Both hung up.

President Goodwin and his National Security Advisor Mr. Jennings said, "We are reviewing the list of persons who received kickback drug money from a Mexican drug cartel. They sat in the Oval Office shaking their heads as they scanned the list of very prominent figures within state and federal governments. A few were appointed by President Obama but most by previous Presidents. "

President Goodwin said, "The list was provided by President Williamson. She obtained the list from Army Colonel Michael Montgomery whose Spl. Ops group is attacking the drug cartels throughout Mexico. The Colonel found the list along with other paperwork after destroying the drug cartel and their compound. As you can see Mel, we not only have the names, but full addresses and amounts paid with dates. Most were paid in cash and delivered by Mexican courier. Pretty compelling evidence," the President added. "We must keep this under wraps as best we can. We can't afford a blockbuster scandal at this time," the President continued.

"Mr. President, you know damn well that this will hit the papers and airways somehow. There are always leaks, Mr. President, and no one can prevent them," the National Security Advisor reminded his boss.

"You're right, of course," President Goodwin admitted.

"Now, how do we handle this sticky situations without blowing the lid off this boiling pot?" the President asked.

"Mr. President, you should address the American people on all networks and lay it out plain and simple. These bastards must be exposed and promptly removed from office and remanded to federal facilities awaiting trial. Just think how many lives were lost because of these treasonous individuals," Mr. Addison said in a raised voice. "As I see it, Mr. President, before your T.V. appearance, these people must be removed if still in office and held to show the American people that your administration will not tolerate drug cartel kickbacks. Also these names should be made public. They must be under lock and key before their names are made public," he added.

"Yes, I agree Tim, so let's have Bob Mott contact all the major networks for time and date that's sometime within the next few days. We need time to round up these lawbreakers, but not much," the President added.

During the next twenty-four hours, a total of thirty-seven people were arrested and held on federal warrants for accepting foreign bribes from drug cartels in Mexico that led to hundreds, and maybe even thousands of deaths on both sides of the border. These arrested individuals ranged from a state senator, two congressmen, state police officials, border supervisors and many management positions in between. If found guilty by a federal

court, these named individuals wouls surely face life in prison. Their names would be made public during the President's upcoming speech. President Goodwin would not only read the names, but they would be flashed on the T.V. for all Americans to see.

The evidence against these people was overwhelming and undisputed. Names, addresses, amounts, bank account numbers, cartel records and even the Mexican runners who delivered the cash payments to these despicable American citizens. This scum would pay the price for the untold lives lost over the years by drug cartel murders and wholesale poisoning of millions of human beings.

With President Lazzara's new policy of paying for information leading to the arrest and conviction of drug dealers and street pushers, Mexican cartel leaders and their members were being turned in by Mexican citizens by the hundreds. The largest of the drug cartels had been broken up, but there were still many smaller cartels and organizations that were producing and spreading their poison to the United States and throughout the world.

The Mexican public had been held hostage for years under the threat of death from the all-powerful drug cartels and their paid informants. Now it was their turn to put the drug lords and street pushers in jail for the rest of their lives.

The Mexican government would pay as much as a thousand dollars for the conviction of these criminals, and to the average Mexican citizen, these sums of money were a huge amount in their lives.

President Goodwin was straightening papers on his three hundred year old desk when the T.V. director said, "Mr. President, you're on in 5-4-3-2-1."

"Good evening, America.

"I have asked for this time to disclose acts of treason against our country by some thirty-seven individuals who are American citizens, but have caused hundred and maybe even thousands of deaths in Mexico, the United States and throughout the world.

"These individuals have received pay off money to help and assist the various drug cartels sell and distribute hard drugs. All thirty-seven people have been arrested and are currently being held in federal custody awaiting trial. The bribes received by these individuals totaled over twenty-eight million dollars over the past seven and a half years. We have the dates and amounts paid to these people as well as addresses, bank records and even the Mexican cartel members who delivered the payoff monies to these thirty-seven individuals. If convicted, they will never see a sun rise or sun set outside the walls of a federal prison. If I had my way, these people would be shot for these treasonous and despicable acts.

"I'm not going to read the names of the people involved, but their names will be flashed across the T.V. screen for all Americans and the world to see. I have asked the Attorney General to prosecute these individuals under the acts of treason laws of the United States, which carry the death penalty.

"As the Mexican government under President Lazzara's direction flushes out the many drug cartels and its members, I'm sure additional individuals in many countries will be exposed, arrested and prosecuted for their high crimes."

Buck approached the outer office and asked Mrs. Bakker if the boss was in. Ruth buzzed the President and informed her that the Chief-of-Staff wanted her ear.

"Send him in," Sara answered.

Buck knocked on the door and entered before the President could say 'come in.' "Madam President, have you heard what the Republican Party leaders in Washington are saying as we speak?"

"No, Buck I have not," she quickly answered.

"They're having a press conference and ripping the Democratic Party to pieces. They are jumping on the comments by ex-President Obama that almost everything about the Democratic Party was a pack of lies. The Speaker of the House is saying 'how could the national media and the liberal American voter re-elect President Obama when the Republican Party and many conservative talk show hosts have been talking about the constant cover-ups and lies for more than four and a half years.' Let's listen to the Speaker."

"From fast and furious guards aboard war ships without loaded weapons, Marine Corps personnel guarding our ambassador without ammo and not allowed to even show a weapon, border guards not allowed to shoot illegal aliens no matter what transpires. The Obama administration has made the military into a wishy-washy force due to the many 'do nothing' rules of engagement, there are hundreds of incidents that lack basic common sense and the unwillingness by his administration to enforce laws that are supposed to protect the American people. A justice system that refuses to arrest the Black Panther members that threatened voters at polling stations. The administration top cop said that he would not arrest any black violators. Blacks in the Democratic administration won't prosecute other black law breakers, you talk about racism by our black elected and appointed leaders."

The Speaker continued, "Now that the Obama dictatorship is over, I hope the American people can some to their senses and realize the mistake they made in electing a person who had not a single qualification become our 44th President. Let's face the truth, the only reason Obama was elected twice is because he is <u>Black</u>. A feeling of guilt by many Americans that the blacks have been given a raw deal for the past hour hundred years. White, Black or Brown the best person with the best qualifications should be elected to our highest office. We all know the Santa Clause giveaways by Obama insured his winning a second term. Regardless of the continuous lies, Presidential decrees that bypassed Congress and the numerous government giveaways to millions of uninformed Americans, the American public elected Obama twice. It's beyond belief that a large group of Americans both smart and uninformed would be hoodwinked into voting for the worst man to hold the office of President of the United States."

The Republican Speaker of the House continued to speak to the American people and the world.

"Now that I've got that off my chest, let's put all the Obama reign behind us. We must not let the past four and a half years continue to drag this great nation into the socialist state we were heading.

"Even though President Goodwin is a Democrat and must put up with the fallout from the come clean speech by ex-President Obama, he certainly has a chance to reverse the many policies put in place by his predecessor. At the same time, I would hope our new President would clean house and appoint well qualified individuals to help him straighten out this national mess. If he doesn't and continues down the same path as Obama was heading, we are doomed as a nation and our country would surely be attacked in the near future by China, Russia or a combination of both.

"Socialism is a sure recipe for national disaster. Big governments and dozens of federal giveaways to the bottom feeders would continue to make half the population of this country beholden to their government master. These bottom feeding recipients are not hungry, not without cars, not without cell phones, not without welfare, not without W.I.C., not without housing assistance or any other social requirement the liberal Democratic government has provided. These uneducated and uninformed Americans are happy to gain substance at the government trough and continue to contribute nothing to the well-being and advancement of this once great nation.

"I apologize for talking so long, but we must now regroup a move towards a more stable economy and re-establish the values and truthfulness that this country was founded upon. I'm appealing to all Americans to change. Please step back and look at what you have done by electing and re-electing a person like Barack Hussein Obama. We have a chance now to correct all the mistakes and ills of his previous administration.

"Now it depends on our new President and the Democratic administration to change directions, step back and reverse the trend towards total socialism.

"Thank you, ladies and gentlemen, the Republican Party stands ready to work with President Goodwin and his administration. We will help him return to the non-socialistic type of government and strive towards a smaller government with less interference into our private lives." With that the Republican Speaker left the podium and headed for his office.

"Well, Buck, that was some speech by the Republican Speaker of the House. He really laid it on the line and told it like it is. Now I wonder how the Democrat Party is going to respond," Sara asked her Chief-of-Staff.

"Only god knows," Buck answered.

Sara's secure line #4 started blinking and Buck got up to leave the President's office when Sara motioned for him to stay seated.

President Williamson picked up the phone and after a short wait said, "Yes Governor. Please continue but do you mind if I put you on speaker phone. Only I and my Chief-of-Staff are present. Okay, please continue," Sara told the Alaska Governor.

"Madam President and Buck, I have just informed President Goodwin and Congress that the state of Alaska is seceding from the union of forty-six as of today. We want no part of the old Obama administration and the Goodwin establishment alike. Our state has no debt and our residents want no part of the lower forty-six state regime. We want you to be alerted as quickly as possible, Madam President."

"Thank you, Governor, for your consideration. If there is anything we can do to help you, please do not hesitate to call me directly, sir."

"Thank you, Madam President, I'll keep you informed."

Both parties hung up.

"Oh! My god, Sara, I mean, Madam President. Another state has left the fold. President Goodwin now has a plate full after only a few days in office. I wouldn't want his job for all the money in the world," the Chief-of-Staff admitted to his boss.

"No matter what, the new President is now in a no win situation, at best," Sara admitted.

In less than an hour the national media had learned of the defection from the union by the largest state Alaska. The Goodwin Whitehouse was inundated by more than six hundred thousand calls from all remaining forty-five states and hundreds of overseas calls wondering what the hell was going on. After hearing the secession by Alaska, dozens of countries were asking if the Obama commitment to their countries was still going to be honored by the Goodwin Whitehouse.

President Goodwin informed the Whitehouse switchboard to hold all calls.

Sara asked Bev Wolcott to contact the four Governors and arrange a quick phone meeting for some time that day.

"Yes, ma'am, I'll get right on it."

Before President Williamson could digest the earlier events the secure line #4 lit up again. Sara said, "President Williamson."

Chapter 8 – More Cartel Wars

"Madam President, this is Governor Torcello, again. I forgot to mention that Alaska will continue to supply crude oil to your country."

"Thank you, Governor, but I knew you would keep your word about supplying sweet crude to our country. I think you and the citizens of Alaska have made the right decision about seceding from the Washington union at this time. I believe the future of the remaining forty-five states is questionable at best," Sara admitted. "The Western States of America stands ready to help Alaska in any way necessary for you to become a new country," Sara offered.

"Thank you, Madam President, the people of Alaska and myself appreciate your support. I'll be talking to you again soon, I'm sure," he admitted.

As Sara replaced the secure phone she said, "My god, Buck, what is going to happen next with the Washington mob?"

"Your guess is as good as mine," Buck answered. "One thing for sure, it will certainly get worse and not better. With Alaska leaving now, I wonder how many more states will decide to venture out of the union and form another new country. The Goodwin administration certainly has its hands full now. With their beloved leader confessing his wrong doings and lies to the whole world and quietly slipping away to Hawaii, and now the Alaska departure. The Democratic Party's grip on the voting public will certainly be less now, don't you think, Madam President?"

"I'm not so sure, Buck, remember the people who voted for their messiah, Obama, will now expect their new Democratic President to continue the Obama giveaways and social programs that makes them dependent on the free government feeding trough. These people are poor, uninformed and stupid educated who are well off but have this feeling that the United States has been unfair to minorities and illegal aliens. While the changes implemented and even planned by the Democratic Party don't affect these high paid individuals, they don't care how if it affects the remaining hard working Americans. Only time will tell what pans out," Sara added.

"Buck, would you please get with Bev and see when I can talk to the four Governors?"

"Yes, ma'am."

Buck left the room to find Bev Wolcott.

Within an hour, the Governors of California, Arizona, New Mexico and Texas were on a conference call to the Flagstaff Whitehouse and President Williamson.

Buck entered the President's office and said, "The four Governors are on secure line #1 Madam President."

"Thank you, Buck."

"Please stay, if you would?" she asked.

"Certainly," he answered.

Sara picked up the phone and pressed number #1 saying, "Good afternoon, ladies and gentlemen. I'm sure you have already heard the news that Alaska has seceded from the Washington union as of today."

All four answered, "Yes."

"The Governor of Alaska called a short while ago to let me know that they have informed Washington on their decision to leave the union. He also assured me that the flow of crude from Alaska would continue as promised. That certainly is good news, we need all the oil we can get. This latest action by Alaska is a great blow to the Goodwin administration and the party as a whole. This could be the final straw that breaks the Washington grip on the population of the forty-five remaining states," Sara told the group.

Governor Lane of Arizona said," Madam President, do you think this will affect us in a negative way."

"No, I don't, Margo, but let's be prepared for anything that the Washington group might conger up. One good thing Alaska is far enough away from Washington that an armed force by the Goodwin Whitehouse is very unlikely. Remember Washington doesn't supply Alaska. Alaska gives the lower states petroleum, natural gas, feed crops, dairy products, fish of all kinds, lumber, gold, silver and long list of other commodities. Alaska has over 615,000 sq. miles of relativity unexplored wilderness, even today. The real hidden wealth of Alaska is yet to be realized. She is an uncut diamond of known and unknown beauty."

"Now I'd like to change the subject to oil," Sara told the group of four. "Marilyn how is the planning for your new refinery and tank farm coming??"

"Well, Madam President, we have the final location nailed down and the final construction plans are about ninety percent complete. But before we start the actual construction, we're waiting for the final approval from your oil minister and the four state environmental agency."

"Just where is the huge refining location?" Sara asked.

"Ma'am, it's located about eighty miles southwest of Houston on Matagorda Bay where the Gulf water is at least forty feet deep. The ocean oil tankers won't have any trouble docking. Right now, the state of Texas owns a block of land nine square miles. We'll have plenty of room to construct a safe and secure refinery and a state of the art tank farm and docking facility. The oil storage tanks will have double hulls and will be buried partially to insure better safety while setting in a saucer shaped pit, lined to insure no petroleum product will leak into the ground."

"We need to start construction on that site at once," Sara told the Texas Governor. "I'll call the oil ministry and the environmental agency and put a bee in their bonnet."

"Thank you, ma'am."

"Now, Conrad, how are you coming with your new refinery?" Sara asked the new California Governor.

"Madam President, the ground breaking started this week and the construction will be a 24/7 project until it's completed. Our current estimate is operational within 2.6 years. The location is between Smith River and Fort Dick. It's just twelve miles south of the Oregon and California border. The site covers more than six square miles for the refinery and tank farm. The dock will be in deep water, so ocean going tankers and assorted vessels will have no problem in berthing. Also, a pipeline extension from Alaska can be easily constructed by way of the Pacific Ocean," the Governor added.

"Marilyn, your facility first. What is your estimation of the final cost?" President Williamson asked the Texas Governor.

"Madam President, our oil experts and construction gurus are telling me that the final cost will be 4.6 billion dollars and no cost overruns."

"Thank you, Marilyn."

"How about your facility, Conrad?"

"Madam President, our cost is twofold. Without extending the Alaska pipeline to our California facility, the cost estimate is 3.95 billion. With the pipeline added, the final cost should be close to 6.3 billion dollars." The Governor continued, "The high cost of the pipeline is due to the special pipe required if it's laid in the Pacific about a mile off shore. This pipe is double walled and very flexible. It's made of stainless steel and natural rubber to insure the safe transfer of crude underwater. This pipe will withstand ground movement that would rupture standard pipe. Our engineers are looking at both routes for the crude pipeline, land vs ocean. The cost of a land pipeline, above and below ground, is still being evaluated. We know there is a huge cost in gaining the right-of-way throughout private land and city property. At first glance we like the ocean route over the land placement of the oil pipeline. Without question, the Pacific Ocean route is cheaper than a land route above or below ground. But a final decision will not be made until all the facts and figures are in and scrutinized, over and over."

"Thank you for the refinery updates," President Williamson told the two Governors. "Also continue to push the many oil companies to pump their low producing wells dry and encourage them to drill offshore in the Gulf and Pacific Rim. Here in the capitol our energy department has drilling permits for most areas of the California coast and the Texas gulf. We need all the oil we can pump and all the crude Alaska is willing to send us."

"One last thing. Please be aware and alert on the Alaska situation and make sure your military forces are informed with the latest info and updates."

"That's all I have," Sara told the group, "Does anyone have anything for me?" she asked.

"Yes, ma'am I do," the California Governor said quickly.

"When do you think we can pull back the rest of our military from our border with Mexico? The California border is very short as you know, and I would like to."

"You're Commander-in-Chief for the California forces, but the four state military force was formed and assigned to border duty by me. As your President, these National Guard and Reserve units were called to duty by Federal Authority. As your President elect I was empowered to activate our combined state forces to protest our citizens from the flood of illegal aliens. For now, you state military personnel are under federal jurisdiction," President Williamson informed California's new Governor. "Are we clear on this matter?" Sara asked with a hint of annoyance.

"Yes, ma'am. Crystal clear."

"Does anyone else have anything?" Sara asked

There was complete silence.

"Thank you, and goodbye."

President Goodwin was hopping mad when he called the Secretary-of-Defense and asked him to arrange an emergency meeting for the whole staff as soon as possible. He suggested the meeting on the Alaska secession should he held in the Pentagon War Room at 14:00 hrs. sharp.

Within minutes, President Goodwin left the Oval Office and walked to the waiting chopper for the short flight to the Pentagon.

The emergency meeting started on time, and the famous War Room was packed wall to wall with standing room only. Everyone seated stood up when President Goodwin entered the room, but returned to their seats when the President motioned the group to be seated.

"This latest action by the state of Alaska is the last straw. Our country cannot afford these states to just leave our union and form their own countries. If we allow Alaska to leave, our northern guard against the Russians will pass to another country. Along with losing our northern guard we will lose a wealth of goods coming from Alaska. Huge quantities of oil, lumber, fish, gold, silver and a thousand other products will be lost as a state to state transfer and sale.

"If this seceding by other states continues, our country will be picked apart and become a hodge-podge of states with very little power, and the United States will become somewhere between a second and third class country. Well, people, I'm open to all suggestions, but no matter what we decide, it must be quick and decisive." The President slowly sat down.

The Secretary-of-State stood up and said, "Mr. President, we must not allow the state of Alaska to secede from our union. If necessary we should fight to keep Alaska within our fold. Their National Guard and Reserve Units within Alaska are negligible, sir. Their real strength is their Air Force. They have several wings but very little land forces. They do have large quantities of surface to air and air to air missiles which include nuclear. We must contact the Alaska Governor and issue an ultimatum to him and the people of Alaska. Either return to our forty-six state union or be prepared for all-out war. We must not let this expand to more states leaving this nation. Mr. President, I vote for military action against the renegade state of Alaska." With that statement, the Secretary sat down slowly.

General Wolford, Chairman of the Joint Chiefs stood up and said, "Mr. President, Secretary Marshal is my civilian boss but I completely disagree with him. We must somehow convince the Governor and the residence of Alaska that to leave the union is a no win situation for both of us." The General continued, "And to declare war on Alaska is crazy and certainly an unacceptable solution to the problem. To fight among ourselves is not the answer, other states would join their cause and we would be engulfed in another civil war. As far as I see it, we only have two options. First, let them leave and form their own country. Second, convince them that leaving our union is not the answer. And attacking Alaska is certainly not an option as far as I'm concerned," the top General told the packed War Room.

A few military and civilian leaders stood up and clapped at the non-military stand made by Chairman Wolford.

Secretary-of-State Wilson stood up and said, "Mr. President, you should contact Governor Torcello as soon as possible and lay out the various options that our government has, and the few options that are available to the state of Alaska and its people. We cannot waste time and energy by holding meetings that spawn little results while the remaining states ponder the Alaska secession. Please contact the Alaska Governor, Mr. President, and do it now, sir." With that Secretary Wilson sat back down.

More than half the people in the War Room stood up clapped and whistled at the remarks by Secretary Wilson.

President Goodwin quickly stood up and motioned to the standing members to return to their seats.

"Thank you, ladies and gentlemen, for your remarks and suggestions. I agree with Madam Secretary that I should call the Alaska Governor today. When this meeting is over, I will call the Governor and discuss the various options. No matter what, we must somehow end this crisis of states leaving our union to form their own country."

President Williamson asked for air time to explain the various changes in the new government of the Western States of America. As the appointed time approached the T.V. director showed his fingers 5,4,3,2,1 and "You're on," he said to Sara.

The President looked straight into the camera and in a strong clear voice said, "Good afternoon, ladies and gentlemen of the Western States of America. I have asked for this time to remind our citizens of the changes we have made to the giveaway policies of the Washington mob. As a separate and new country, we no longer have the 'lunch box' giveaways such as welfare, food stamps, free meals in school, housing assistance, free cell phones, WIC programs and dozens upon dozens of other state and federal programs that allow millions of free loaders to feed at the government trough. Washington may continue these social giveaways that enslave a large group of its citizens, but our country will not."

Sara continued, "We want a country with full employment, and if you, as a resident of the Western States of America don't want to work and pull your weight, then you should leave this country and return to the Washington Santa Clause social giveaway type of country. Another big change is our federal income tax filing. As an individual you only need to file your federal income tax on a 3"x5" card. This was made possible because of the seventeen percent user tax that applies to every citizen of Western States of America.

"Like I have said repeatedly, we have made dozens of changes from the Washington giveaways that made millions of citizens completely dependent on government hand-outs. We will continue the Social Security payments to all Western States of America citizens who reach the age of 65. Not 67 or 70 like Washington. Remember, all monies designated for Social Security by your employer and yourself will be kept in a separate account by this administration, and twice a year we will inform all our citizens of the total funds that are currently in the Social Security account. I want total and complete transparency in this account, and we'll show the amounts paid per month for the previous six months. You can see this account grow and provide

security for all individuals sixty-five and older. We have separate accounts for disability and other special needs by our citizens.

"Now changing topics. We currently have a different immigration problem besides the Mexican influx. So many individuals and families are leaving the union of forty-five and settling in our four states that current housing and job availability are being strained to the limit. While we want to accommodate all persons who want to become citizens of the W.S. of A., we must slow down this influx of new persons. A thousand newcomers per week in California alone are causing real problems for our new government, so we're going to limit the number of new citizens allowed to enter our country.

"This is only a temporary reduction in the number of individuals allowed to enter our country. This reduction will allow our new nation to catch its breath.

"One other topic I'd like to touch upon is our new oil and gas refineries being built in California and Texas. When their two facilities are up and running in a couple of years, we will be very close to complete independence of Middle East foreign oil. When I say 'foreign' I don't mean our neighbors in Canada and Mexico or Alaska when they become a new country. We will continue to purchase petroleum from these three countries. Our overall goal, besides being oil independent, is to have sufficient quantities to drastically reduce the cost of a gallon of gasoline and home heating oil. This is a top priority for my administration," President Williamson added.

"There are a hundred other topics I could cover, but I'm out of time today. But we'll have more of these FYI sessions in the near future," Sara concluded. "Thank you, ladies and gentlemen, and good afternoon."

President Williamson sat back and the T.V. director said, "Cut." The three cameras went silent and the many bright lights went dark.

"My, the lights are hot," Sara mentioned as she wiped her forehead. "I was starting to sweat," she admitted to Buck as she left her office for the ladies room to freshen up.

General Rōjas entered Colonel Montgomery's office at Army Headquarters in Querétaro and informed his American counterpart that they have located the San Marcos cartel. "That's good news, sir. Where is it located?" the Colonel asked his Mexican friend.

"Near the City of Ciudad Cuauhtémoc in Chiapas Provence, near highway #190 in southern Mexico. It's located right on the border with Guatemala. The cartel is in the middle of no man's land that covers over one hundred and fifty square kilometers of very thick jungle. They will be hard to surprise and very difficult to attack," the Mexican General admitted.

"The Guatemala government won't appreciate our attack on their border. Guatemala and Mexico have been at odds for years," the General admitted. "Not only drugs, but a host of other issues," the Commanding General confessed to his military friend. "We will need President Lazzara's help in this one, I assure you," he said shaking his head.

"What do we know about the San Marcos cartel?" Colonel Montgomery asked.

"They have a sprawling compound that is run by a Mexican drug lord and high ranking Guatemala Army Officers. This will be a stinker to attack, as you Americans say," the General said with a slight smile.

"How many members are in the cartel?" Michael asked.

"Colonel, we think it's made up of one hundred and fifty Mexican nationals and somewhere around seventy-five or eighty Guatemala military and civilian personnel. The problem is that the Guatemala Army has armed the cartel with a wide array of military arms which includes armored vehicles, surface to air missiles and a long list of sophisticated equipment like radar, a wide circle of listening posts and a large force of armed guards that roam the countryside carrying cell phones. We can't use your Air National Guard Air Force to bomb this target, Guatemala would surely declare was on Mexico and scream bloody murder to the U.N. This cartel is a big one. They supply drugs and weapons to many Central and South American countries and even ship their poison to Asia and Europe."

"Colonel, I don't know how to even start to formulate a plan of attack on this cartel," the Mexican General admitted.

"That sounds like a real nightmare," Colonel Montgomery answered. "We should talk to President Lazzara as soon as possible," the Colonel added.

"I agree," the General said reaching for the phone.

 rickshaw

After waiting an hour the Mexican President was on the line and agreed the three should meet in a day or so.

General Rōjas and Colonel Montgomery flew to Mexico City the next day and arrived at the Presidential Palace just before noon. They were ushered into the large waiting room without delay and had just sat down when President Lazzara entered the room. Both officers quickly stood up and saluted the Mexican leader.

"Good morning, gentlemen. Please be seated. It's good to see you both again," the President said, shaking their hands. "You said on the phone your people located the San Marcos drug cartel somewhere in southern Mexico."

"Yes, sir. In the City of Ciudad Cuauhtémoc, which is right on the border with Guatemala," the General told his boss.

"Gentlemen, I know that border city, I spent a year there many years ago. That town back then was a real hot spot, as I remember. A lot of Guatemala civilians and military work there. Just to the west of the city is a huge area that they call 'no man's land.' You could hide a division or more let alone a drug cartel," the President added.

"That could be a real problem, gentlemen, the city is about seventy-five percent Guatemalan and twenty-five percent Mexican. That area west of highway #190 is some of the heaviest jungle in Central America, you can't see three feet in front of you, and I've been told the snakes and spiders are huge in that area. Some of the spider webs can trap small jungle animals and some of the longest snakes in the world have come out of that area. It certainly is a nasty place, gentlemen, and it will take an army to eliminate this cartel."

"Now with that said, let's discuss the political aspects of this problem," the President said, standing up and walking to the huge cloth map of Mexico and Central America. He pointed to the City of Ciudad Cuauhtémoc and said, "Even though the city is in Mexico it is populated mostly by Guatemala citizens. It's somewhat like Laredo, Texas where the population is somewhere around ninety-eight percent Mexican. I have heard that the Guatemala military have a presence in the city, but I have not had a single complaint about Guatemalan presence there. As President, I don't like the idea of another country's military camping within our country and I would say Mexico has more pressing problems but with the discovery of a large drug cartel within Mexico and being helped by Guatemala military personnel, I want this cartel eliminated. I will call the President of Guatemala and voice my complaint."

"Mr. President, I don't think that's a good idea," the American Colonel said quickly. Before the Mexican President could answer, General Rōjas said, "Sir, the President of Guatemala could be involved with the drug cartel and we don't want to alert the cartel that we have located their base of operations."

"Gentlemen, I agree, but we must be careful and handle this operation with caution. I don't want or need another border problem. One is enough. Before you act, I want to review your plan of attack. This is somewhat different, being on our border."

"Yes, sir. When we have worked out the details we'll give you a look see, Mr. President."

"Thank you, gentlemen, and have a safe trip home."

Both officers headed for the military airport and the return trip to Army Headquarters in Querétaro. Once aboard their flight, the two officers sat quietly thinking about just how they would plan the attack on the San Marcos compound.

Once they arrived at Army Headquarters they quickly headed for their planning room full of huge maps of Mexico and Central America. Once inside the large secure room they sat down and looked at each other, and General Rōjas said, "Colonel, how the hell are we going to complete this very important mission?"

"General, I need to return to the Western States of America and confer with General Wittingham and his staff. We need additional help on this one," the Colonel admitted.

"Go ahead, Colonel, I need to check on our border troops and other military matters I have neglected for some time."

"Yes, sir, but I want you to accompany me to Arizona as well."

"Do I really need to attend your meetings with your top General and his staff?"

"Yes, General you do. We should confer with General Wittingham, and President Williamson as well."

"Okay. I'll call President Lazzara and ask his permission to leave Mexico." General Rōjas left for his office to call the

President. Within five minutes, he had permission to accompany the Colonel but insisted that the General travel in civilian clothes.

The next day both men headed for Arizona and the capitol of the Western States of America in Flagstaff. They arrived at the capitol and quickly drove to the capitol building and President Williamson's office.

Sara met her favorite Colonel and the Mexican top General before they reached her new office. "You must be exhausted," she said, shaking their hands. Both men tried to salute but she held their hands down.

"Yes, ma'am, we are a little tired from our two flights," Colonel Montgomery admitted.

"General Wittingham will arrive this evening from California, so why don't we call the meeting for 09:00 tomorrow morning, if that's okay with both of you?" Sara asked he two guests.

"That's fine with me," the Full Bird answered, "how about you General?" he asked.

"This is your trip, Colonel, I'm just along for the ride, as you Americas say."

"Madam President, that's not true. General Rōjas is our leader in Mexico, and our Special Ops Company would not exist or function without the General."

"You're right, Colonel," Sara said quickly. "General Rōjas is paramount in the war against drugs within Mexico and outside his country."

"Thank you, Madam President, I appreciate your confidence. But your Colonel is a master of planning and executing our attacks on the various drug cartels, and I'm happy to be working alongside him," the Mexican General told the American President.

General Wittingham arrived at the capitol building at 16:00 and quickly went to President Williamson's office, which is now known as the Blue and Gold Room. Sara met her top General and both headed for the large conference room and the waiting Colonel and Mexican General.

Once Sara introduced General Rōjas to General Wittingham, they sat down and she asked Colonel Montgomery to brief her top General on the problems with the newly discovered San Marcos drug cartel new the border with Guatemala.

Colonel Montgomery talked non-stop for thirty minutes explaining the possible political ramifications, the jungle location and the cartel association with the Guatemala military. He continued, "This compound is isolated and protected by radar, listening devices and surrounded by a hundred members with cell phones. So chances of a surprise attack by ground forces is about nil at best," the Colonel admitted.

"General Rōjas, do you have anything to add or suggest?" President Williamson asked the Mexican General.

"Yes, ma'am, I do," the General answered.

"Colonel Montgomery and I have talked to President Lazzara and he has great reservations on how we will attack the compound without huge civilian losses and also the fact that the Guatemala military is active inside Mexico. He doesn't want an international incident on the border with Guatemala if it can be prevented."

"Thank you, General, we will take all that into consideration when making suggestions to the both of you on how to approach this problem and eliminate the San Marcos cartel," the President assured the Mexican top General.

"Thank you for your concern and assurances, Madam President."

Colonel Montgomery stood up and unfolded a large map of southern Mexico and Central America. General Rōjas pointed to the city of Ciudad Cuauhtémoc on the border with Guatemala. The General pointed to the area west of highway #190 where the San Marcos cartel is located. He said, "The area has some of the thickest jungle in all of Mexico. You can't even see the buildings from the air," the Mexican General added. "We know the exact location and receive additional info daily because we have one of our agents currently working there. He has been there for the past two months and is transmitting info by a very old and very dangerous method. He is using a special breed of carrier pigeons and a local runner sometimes. If they even suspect him, is a dead man. He is well aware of the danger and will give his life if necessary, I'm told. Remember, we must eliminate the cartel without causing large numbers of civilian deaths. President

Lazzara is very concerned about the cartel's location so close to the border."

General Wittingham picked up the secure phone and authorized the re-alignment of a tasker bird to photograph the area in question. Within two hours the bird was taking pictures of the jungle location and in less than thirty minutes the Flagstaff Whitehouse was receiving the color pictures of the drug cartel site.

After scanning the nearly five hundred infrared pictures, the group headed for their version of the Pentagon. The Flagstaff military facility was in the shape of a wagon wheel with spokes leading to the hub, or center.

Once they arrived, the group of three and the President headed for the planning room. This room was huge and the walls were lined with physical maps and large T.V. screens next to each map. Each screen could zero in on any area of the physical map and picked up the smallest details. Almost the heads or tails view could be seen with this special equipment.

General Wittingham went around the room introducing his planning staff to the President, Colonel Montgomery and Mexican General Rōjas. Once the pleasantries were finished, the group surrounded a large table and the many photos were spread out for all to see. General Wittingham asked Colonel Montgomery to explain the various details again to the planning staff.

Once again the American Full Bird explained the very unique setting and special political considerations that must be realized before this operation can take place. The Colonel continued, "Gentlemen, before our final plan is deemed operational, General Rōjas and Mexican President Lazzara must approve the operation. One other thing, General Rōjas will be in charge and full command of the whole operation from start to finish. That must be understood from the get go," the Colonel stressed.

The six members of General Wittingham's planning staff quickly reviewed the infrared photos, and within an hour the Lt. Col. in charge of the planning staff told the President and her group that they believed they had a solution to the problem.

"That was fast," President Williamson answered.

Colonel Montgomery and General Rōjas looked at each other with some doubt in their expressions.

"Well, ma'am, there are so many problems and restrictions with the area in question, we feel there is only one way to eliminate the San Marcos cartel and its members. With our solution there is only one drawback the Light Colonel admitted. The civilians working in and around the San Marco compound would be killed. Let's face it, if you attack the compound with ground forces you'll lose somewhere in excess of fifty percent of your forces."

General Wittingham said, "Go ahead, Colonel, give us the details."

"Yes, sir."

"We recommend a non-nuclear air vacuum bomb. When detonated it reaches almost five thousand (5000 F) degrees and evaporates everything within a mile radius of ground zero. It blasts outward then sucks in all air from as far as a mile away killing everything in a micro-second. It's a controlled blast that kills quickly and destroys everything within the blast zone. You can have an air burst or ground contact blast. With the thick jungle we recommend an air blast at about five hundred feet for the best effect. The explosion will not extend to the city limits of Ciudad Cuauhtémoc and endanger the residents. But, again, it will kill the two hundred or so local civilians employed at the drug compound. Not only Mexican and Guatemala civilians, but any Guatemala military personnel that will be present."

"How about any shock waves," Colonel Montgomery asked?

"Yes, sir, the shock waves will extend outwards for about three miles and the city will certainly feel the shock waves but experience no physical damage. Just window rattling," the Light Colonel added.

"What type of plane would be required to drop this air vacuum bomb?" the Mexican General asked

"Sir, the plane could be as small as the old C-47 or a C-130 prop type. The bomb itself is rather large, about eight feet long and almost five feet in diameter and it weighs about twenty-five hundred pounds."

"One more thing," the Light Colonel offered. "The many infrared pictures showed some thirty individuals coming and going between the many buildings and about twenty people ringing the compound as far as half a mile away. We estimate another one hundred and fifty persons could be working inside the compound buildings."

"That's about right," General Rōjas added. "Our inside man estimated that the cartel employs around two hundred to two fifty civilians."

"Remember, the photos also showed some military vehicles were present when the pictures were taken," as the Light Colonel pointed to the odd shaped vehicles.

"The presence of Guatemala military will certainly add to the difficulty for President Lazzara to make a final decision to attack or not using the air vacuum bomb," General Wittingham told the group.

President Williamson asked General Rōjas if he would approve the suggested plan to eliminate the San Marcos cartel.

"Yes, I would, reluctantly, Madam President. I don't like the idea of killing so many Mexican and Guatemalan civilians, but I don't have any problem killing the Guatemalan military that are currently inside Mexico. If President Lazzara okay's this plan of attack, I'll have to move a fairly large force of my military personnel close to the city in case the Guatemala government wants revenge for the loss of their source of income."

"Colonel, are you in agreement with the idea of using the high temp air vacuum device?" General Wittingham asked the Special Ops officer.

"Yes sir. It seems to be the only way to eliminate the cartel without sustaining huge losses of our forces."

"Okay. If we're all in agreement with this plan of attack, I'll draw up the final report and you'll have a copy within the next two hours," General Wittingham told the group.

Two hours and ten minutes later, the report was completed and all members were given a copy. General Rōjas had an extra copy to give to President Lazzara for his approval or rejection.

Colonel Montgomery and General Rōjas left the Flagstaff Whitehouse and headed for the airport and the return trip to Mexico City and a meeting with the Mexican President.

The Special Ops. Officers arrived at Mexico City but couldn't land for almost an hour due to the intense fog, or actually, super high levels of pollution. Once they landed and headed for the Presidential Palace, the car head light could hardly penetrate the dense pollution at ground level. They safely arrived at the Palace and were quickly ushered into the large ornate waiting room. Almost immediately, the Mexican President entered the room and shook hands with both officers before they could even salute the President.

"Gentlemen, please be seated. I'm glad to see you both again," the Mexican President told his two favorite officers. "General, on the phone you mentioned you had a plan of attack for the elimination of the Sam Marcos cartel new our border with Guatemala."

"Yes, Mr. President, we do. The American plan is not perfect, but we feel it's the only way to eliminate this drug cartel in one quick strike. The plan does have its drawbacks, as you'll see when you read it."

General Rōjas handed his President the two reports and sat back down.

"Gentlemen, I will retire to my office and read the report. Please wait her, I won't be long." With that, the Mexican President exited the room and the two officers relaxed and waited for the President to return.

After only thirty minutes the President returned and both officers snapped to attention as he entered the waiting room. The Mexican President motioned them to be seated as he laid both copies of the report on the small table and sat down.

"I have read the report prepared by General Wittingham, and I have some comments and suggestions. First, I like the idea of your vacuum bomb that is limited to a one mile diameter blast zone. Second, I like the fact that the City of Ciudad Cuauhtémoc will not be damaged by this non-nuclear device. Now for some of the drawbacks. The potential loss of two hundred and fifty Mexican and Guatemalan civilians bothers me terribly," the President admitted. "But if they elect to work for an illegal drug cartel my concern is much less."

"The presence of Guatemala military personnel and the possibility of some Guatemala government officials operating inside our country disturbs me greatly, but if they are eliminated along with the San Marcos drug cartel, then so be it. I can defend that, if the Guatemala government raises hell over their deaths."

"I also have some reservations, as you do, but I like the overall idea," the President stated. "I will give my complete

support to this plan of attack, but I do have some requirements I must insist upon," he added.

"First: The plane that drops this non-nuclear device must be piloted by a Mexican Airman and have a Mexican Navigator as well. But the co-pilot can be American, if you wish.

"Second: The plane must have a Mexican flag painted on both sides of the fuselage and, it's probably a good idea to have the plane painted in camouflage.

"Third: General Rōjas, you should be prepared to have a large force of military personnel close to the border with Guatemala before the attack starts in case the Guatemala government wants revenge for the attack.

"Forth: If the Guatemala military attacks our forces, you have my go ahead to repel their forces with everything at your disposal, General. Their military should not be inside Mexico, and if they are, they won't be for long," the President stressed.

"Gentlemen, please relay my terms to President Williamson and General Wittingham. I'm sure they will agree, the terms are not earth shattering the Mexican President told the two Spl. Ops officers. Also, for security reasons I think you better keep the specific details of the upcoming raid within the Spl. Ops. Group and the American High Command. Thank you, Mr. President, we will pass on your suggestions and terms to President Williamson and her staff," General Rōjas answered.

Both officers saluted the Mexican President and quickly left the Presidential Palace and headed for the airport and a flight back to Army Headquarters at Querétaro. When they arrived at HQ both men headed for their so called war room and a secure phone.

Colonel Montgomery immediately called General Wittingham's headquarters at the Wagon Wheel in Flagstaff and explained the various terms and conditions that President Lazzara wanted. After the short explanation, the Colonel hung up the phone and said, "General, we have started the ball rolling. You have a lot of planning and decisions to make tomorrow," the Colonel added, "but how about we get some sleep and tackle this problem in the morning, if that's okay with you?" the American Full Bird asked the Mexican General and his friend.

"You bet, Colonel, let's get some shut eye, as you Yanks say."

Chapter 8 – More Cartel Wars

The Colonel said, "Oh brother," as both men headed to the BOQ and a short rest before the morning light.

"Madam President, the Governor of California is on line #3" Mrs. Bakker called from the outer office.

"Thank you, Ruth."

President Williamson picked up the secure phone and before she could answer, the Governor said, "Good afternoon, Madam President."

"Good afternoon, Conrad, it's good to hear your voice again," Sara told the new Governor.

"Ma'am, we have completed the monorail study, and we would like to discuss this project with someone, but I admit I don't know who to contact."

"Our Transportation Agency is now up and running, and the man to call is Greg Wong, the Director of Transportation. He is a great guy and he'll arrange a meeting with your people whenever you want. I'm sure he will want the Secretary of the Treasury to attend your meeting, but that's up to him," Sara added.

"Thank you, Madam President, I'll call Mr. Wong this afternoon and arrange a meeting. Thanks again."

"Madam President, your Chief-of-Staff is here to see you, and he is driving me nuts," Mrs. Bakker told her boss.

"Send him in, Ruth."

Buck entered the President's office and Sara asked her C.O.S., "Why are you driving my secretary crazy?"

"She makes the best peanut butter cookies and I always try to con her out of a few," Buck admitted.

"Did it work?" Sara asked.

"Not really ma'am, but she did breakdown and give me three of her famous cookies."

"Your sweet tooth will be your undoing," the President said, shaking her head.

"Most likely, Madam President."

"You wanted to see me, Buck?" the President asked.

"Madam President, I feel you should contact President Goodwin and talk to him face to face on the Alaska situation. Whatever President Goodwin and Washington decides to do about the state of Alaska, it should not affect us directly or indirectly, Madam President."

"Buck, when we're alone, please call me 'Sara.' I get tired of being called 'Madam President' by everybody."

"Certainly ------- Sara."

"That's much better, thank you," she said with a smile. "Please continue, Buck," she asked.

"Well, Sara, if Washington decided to attack Alaska and force the state back into the Washington fold, we will certainly be drawn into the war. Alaska is no match for the Washington military, but the way to Alaska is through California, Oregon and Washington State. As you know, Sara, we can't just stand by and allow the Goodwin mob to run rough shod over a state who had the constitutional right to secede from the union if their government no longer protects the state citizens or demands more taxes and imposes more and more government regulations and restrictions. This continuous erosion of personal rights by the federal government has driven millions of citizens from the Washington mob and will continue to do so unless the federal government changes its liberal policies and socialistic ideals."

"I thank you're right, Buck, I will call President Goodwin today and see if he can spare a few minutes for me in Washington as soon as possible."

"Thank you, Sara. We need a solid pledge from Washington that military action against Alaska will not take place. If it does, I believe more states will seek independence."

President Williamson immediately called the Washington Whitehouse and President Goodwin said he would see Sara the next day.

Sara and Chief-of-Staff Buck left Flagstaff and headed for Washington. They arrived late in the afternoon and were met by the Whitehouse Chief-of-Staff Robert Mott and quickly headed for the Whitehouse and the meeting between both Presidents.

Sara and Buck were seated in the waiting room just outside the Oval Office and were told President Goodwin would be available shortly.

After waiting patiently for more than two hours, the Western States of America President and her Chief-of-Staff were steaming at the length of wait for President Goodwin. During the two hours of waiting, not a single person entered the waiting room to mention a possible delay. Finally, Sara told Buck they were leaving. As they left the waiting room and passed the

President's Secretary, Mrs. Winnie Oaks, Sara informed her, "President Goodwin has insulted the Office of the Western States of America and their President." With that, Sara and Buck exited the Whitehouse and called a Washington cab to take them to the Ronald Reagan Washington National Airport and their return trip to Flagstaff. During the return flight, President Williamson hardly said a word, but Buck knew she was steaming and about to explode over the inexcusable insult towards her, and most importantly, the President of Western States of America.

When they arrived in Flagstaff, they were met by General Wittingham, and the three quickly proceeded to the Flagstaff Whitehouse and Sara's office.

"Madam President, I heard what President Goodwin and his staff did to you in Washington," the General blurted out. "That kind of conduct towards a President of a foreign country is unheard of," General Wittingham told his President. "His name may not be Obama, but he is certainly exactly like him in many ways," the General admitted. "Believe me, I know these people, Madam President, and they are still uptight over your leaving the union and creating the W.S. of A. They will never forgive the four states for seceding their beloved union. Now that Alaska want to secede as well, Washington will become even more dangerous, I believe."

"What would you suggest?" Sara asked.

"I would contact the Governor of Alaska and offer our united support of the Western States of America. And I would also notify Washington to that effect, Madam President. Basically, if the Washington mob and their military attack Alaska, we will offer our assistance to Alaska. Alaska has the constitutional right to secede if they wish," the General added.

"Well, General, that's a mouth full, sir," Sara told her ranking General officer.

"What do you think Washington would do if we throw our full support to Alaska and their cause?" Sara asked.

"Nothing, Madam President. Washington cannot afford a conflict with our four states and Alaska. If they elect to wage war on the five western states, the remaining forty-five states might decide to leave the union and join our cause. The remaining states are fed up with the heavy handed federal government that demands more in taxes to distribute to the fifty percent that are

bottom feeders. I've said it a hundred times, Madam President, between food stamps, welfare, WIC, cell phones and a hundred other federal government and state giveaway programs, the liberal Washington Democrat and Republican mob is going to drive more states away from their union."

The General continued, "We must never be like the liberal Washington, Madam President. We should fight to the death, if necessary, to preserve our conservative way of life. Our laws should be upheld, no more concessions, no more plea bargaining for criminals and no more early outs for these scumbags. Most of all, we must uphold the death penalty in all four states in the Western States of America."

"Sorry. I didn't mean to grandstand, but the way President Goodwin treated the both of you today is typical of the liberal left," the General concluded.

"Thank you, General, I needed that speech before I call Washington tomorrow morning," Sara said as she pushed back in her favorite chair and removed her shoes. "Sorry, boys, but my feet are killing me."

"If there isn't anything else, ma'am, I'll turn in for the night," the Three Star General asked.

"Nothing more tonight, Charles, and thanks again. I value your advice and your opinion above all others," the President told him.

"Goodnight, Madam President." The General left the President's office and headed for the Flagstaff Military Wagon Wheel.

"I'm tired as well," the Chief-of-Staff said as he slowly got up and headed for the door. As he opened the door he said, "Remember, Sara, play nice with the kids in Washington when you call them tomorrow."

"Get out of here," Sara said as she threatened to throw something at him. "See ya early tomorrow," she said as he closed the door. The President sat there thinking of what she was going to say to that skunk, President Goodwin, in the morning.

Sara picked up her shoes and exited her office walking in bare feet to her apartment and bedroom in the rear of the Capitol Building. As she passed a Marine Guard, he smiled and gave her a very smart salute.

She smiled and whispered, "Thank you," as she passed.

Sara was up at 06:10, had a long shower, fixed her hair and dressed in a dark blue business suit with a V-neck blouse. She had a quick breakfast in the President's dining room then headed for her office in the very front of the Flagstaff Whitehouse.

At 09:00 sharp, Sara asked Mrs. Bakker to contact Chief-of-Staff Robert Mott and ask him to have President Goodwin return her call as soon as possible.

"Madam President, Mr. Mott said he would ask President Goodwin to call you shortly."

"Thank you, Ruth."

Within the hour President Goodwin was on secure line #1.

"Good morning, Madam President," he said as she picked up the phone.

"Good morning to you, Mr. President."

"I'm very sorry I missed you yesterday afternoon," he said quickly. "I was in a meeting with a West African President and....."

Sara didn't let him finish. "Mr. President, my Chief-of-Staff and I sat in your waiting room for two hours and twelve minutes without a single person entering the room to ask if we needed anything or to explain just why you were indisposed. I am the President of the Western States of America and should be treated as such. I don't care if you don't like Sara Williamson, but you should respect the office that I hold."

"I am very sorry, Madam President, I assure you it won't happen again."

"The reason for my visit yesterday was to discuss the Alaska situation and possible solutions to the matter. Now with Alaska seceding from your union, that makes a total of five states that have left the Washington union. If, Mr. President, you continue to press your liberal ideas and socialistic government, more states will certainly leave, I assure you. President Obama started down the path of National Socialism and the destruction of America and now you're making it even worse. You are bordering on civil war, my friend. We have even heard rumblings of desertion among your military ranks," Sara was shaking her head at the phone. "You better settle this problem with Alaska in an amicable way, Mr. President. Do not wage war against Alaska, my country will not stand by and watch the destruction of Alaskan cities and other western states along the way. One other thing, Mr. President, don't forget Canada. They're not going to stand by and let your military forces cut across Lower Canada to reach Alaska. Another thing I have heard, Mr. President, is that Hawaii, Oregon and Washington are fed up with your taxes and many mandates as well. If these three states secede, you'll then lose the whole west coast as well as the whole border with Mexico. You then have lost more than thirty-five hundred miles of coast and border because of your liberal Democratic ideas and left wing philosophy. You're losing your country, Mr. President, and you better wake up before it's too late," Sara said in a loud voice.

"Are you giving me an ultimatum?" President Goodwin said in a sarcastic voice.

"You're damn right I am," Sara answered. "If you're planning on attacking Alaska, my country will defend our northern neighbor with all our military can muster," she added.

With that last statement, Sara slammed the phone down and uttered, "That stupid bastard." She pounded the desk with her fist and sat back in her chair thinking how bad and how far down the slippery slope the Washington mob has brought the union. "I'm afraid a civil war is coming under the cover of socialism and liberalism where big brother is running every phase of their lives. Liberty and justice fall by the wayside and eventually anarchy and destruction form within prevails across the land," she thought.

"My god, why can't the Obama/Goodwin voting people in their country see the madness that is happening? The bottom feeders that represent fifty percent of their population are just too stupid to realize the burden they are putting on the other half of the population that are paying all the bills. Let's face it," she thought, "the trough feeders are being fed and paid so they are happy and will continue to vote for their Santa Clause as long as the goodies keep coming."

Sara pushed the intercom button and asked Mrs. Bakker to contact Buck and ask him to come to the office as soon as possible.

"Right away," Ruth answered.

Chapter 8 – More Cartel Wars

Within fifteen minutes the Chief-of-Staff was standing tall in the President's office.

"Have a seat, Buck. Try the new brown leather chair with the built in foot rest, it just came a few days ago and it needs someone to break it in," she told her C.O.S.

"Buck, I want you to hear my conversation I had earlier with President Goodwin." Sara pushed the play button on the phone recorder and the whole conversation was played for the Chief-of-Staff. When the recording was finished Buck said, "Wow, you really put it to him."

"You bet I did," Sara answered.

"What I need you to do is contact General Wittingham and play my conversation with Goodwin for him and instruct him to place our military on alert status number #3, yellow, as soon as possible. No telling what President Goodwin and his military puppets will do about Alaska in the coming days and weeks," she added.

"Yes, ma'am, I'll contact the General right away."

"Thank you, Buck," she said, walking him to the door. She added, "If the General has any questions, have him call me direct."

"Will do, ma'am."

"The Lt. Governor of Alaska called and said the Governor was in the airport outside Juneau and would return your call within the hour. He was flying to Whitehorse in Canada but his flight was delayed by weather in Whitehorse," Beverly informed her boss.

"Thank you, Beverly."

The Alaska Governor called within ninety minutes and said that he had tried twice to fly to Whitehorse but had to turn back because of inclement weather. "Mostly fog," he added.

"Governor, I'd like to play for you the conversation I had earlier today with President Goodwin, if that's okay?" Sara asked.

"Certainly, Madam President."

Sara played the tape and when it finished, she added her comments after she hung up on President Goodwin.

"It sounded like you were rather pissed, Madam President," the Governor said quickly.

"Yes, I was," Sara answered. "If the Washington mob wages war on your state of Alaska, our combined military forces will help you repel these bastards. As President I promise you the full support of the Western States of America in your endeavor to secede from the union and establish a country of your own," Sara assured the Alaska Governor.

"Thank you, Madam President, I'm sure we'll need all the help we can get before all is said and done. But I have one question?" the Governor asked.

"Go ahead," Sara answered.

"Now that the people of Alaska have voted to secede from the Washington union, and we have officially notified the Whitehouse and Congress, my question to you, ma'am, is why can't we join your Western States of America as your fifth and largest state?"

"Well, that's a good question, Governor, but remember, the citizens of Western States of America voted some months ago not to allow the state of Alaska to join our country. At the time, I also agreed with our citizens, but now it's somewhat different. There is a strong possibility that Hawaii, Oregon and Washington State might also decide to break away from the Washington union."

"If the three states I've mentioned do leave the union, then the Western States of America will strongly consider your request."

"That's fair enough," the Alaska Governor said. "Is there anything else?" he asked.

"Yes, there is," Sara answered. "First, make sure your forces are on alert, and don't be conned by any promises Washington might offer. Second, have you alerted the Canadian government on your decision to secede from the union and form your own government and country?"

"Yes, on both questions. Our ground forces, Air Force reserve units and Coast Guard patrol units are on high alert as we speak. We also have a group of small satellites that alerts our military of all movements coming from the lower U.S. and Russia as well. I have contacted the Canadian government by phone and was on my way today to discuss the matter with the Canadian Premier in Whitehorse. But as you know, the snow and fog kept me from that important appointment. The Premier indicated that he would contact Washington and strongly insist they respect the Canadian border when dealing with Alaska. He also told me he had alerted the Canadian military as a precaution."

"That's excellent," Sara told the Alaska Governor. "I do believe you have covered all the bases so far. Now it's up to Washington to make up their mind on whether to let Alaska go and form its own country or start a war that could easily encompass the entire nation. Let's keep in constant contact," she offered. "If you require anything, please don't hesitate to ask."

"Most certainly, Madam President. And thank you and your citizens of W.S. of A. for their support."

Both parties hung up without saying the usual goodbye.

President Williamson pushed back from her desk and leaned back in her chair thinking, "What the hell is next? It seems like one disaster after another lately. The dark clouds of war are starting to form over North America. War between the remaining states could breakout at any time, and foreign intervention during this period could destroy the union."

"The Western States of America must be prepared," she thought. "Not only from Washington, but from China and/or Russia. If Russia and China combine their forces and jointly attack the continental U.S., the demise of that one great nation is assured. Man for man we couldn't win any battle, but the use of tactical nukes and the powerful vacuum bombs would level the playing field while being attacked by the Chinese hordes. Supplying their huge military would certainly be a problem, but like their troops in Korea, they could live week after week on a very small amount of rice and a little piece of meat. Most likely they would land their troops in Central America and move north through Mexico and into the continental United States."

Mrs. Bakker surprised the President when she came in with a tray of sugar cookies and a large cup of very strong Russian tea. "I thought you might need a little pick me up, ma'am."

"Thank you, Ruth, you're very thoughtful, and I am a little hungry," she admitted. "After I eat the goodies, please hold all calls for an hour. I'm very tired so I might take a short snooze, so unless World War III breaks out or a huge wave washes over Washington, I don't want to be disturbed."

"Yes, ma'am, I will keep the political wolves away from your door for at least an hour," Ruth assured the President. Ruth quietly left the office and slowly closed the door without making a sound.

rickshaw

Two hours later the President opened her office door and informed Ruth she was back and ready to continue the fight. "That short snooze helped a great deal," the President told her friend and Secretary. Sara left the door open and returned to her desk and placed a call to military Headquarters at the Wagon Wheel and asked if Secretary-of-Defense Waterman had returned from his extensive trip to Formosa and the state of Hawaii. The Under Secretary said, "Yes, ma'am, Secretary Waterman returned less than two hours ago."

"Has he been brought up to speed on my conversation with President Goodwin?" Sara asked.

"Yes, Madam President, General Wittingham and Chief-of-Staff McCarney are here, and they have played the tape with your conversation and after comments to Secretary Waterman."

"When the Defense Secretary is available, please have him call me. Nothing earth shattering, just have him call when he is available," Sara asked.

"Certainly, Madam President."

General Rōjas entered the officers mess at 06:15 and Colonel Montgomery was already seated and having breakfast alone. The Colonel saw the Mexican General and motioned to him to join him for breakfast. Before the General could even place his metal tray down on the table, the American Full Bird said, "I hope you slept well, General, we're going to have a very busy day."

The General smiled and said, "It was more like a short nap rather than a night's sleep," he answered, setting his tray down and sliding next to his favorite American Colonel.

After a full breakfast, both officers headed for the Headquarters Building and their conference room and so called map room. They sat at the large table and started to plan for the attack on the San Marcos drug compound.

General Rōjas started by saying, "The date and time of this operation should coincide with the weather conditions that ensure one hundred percent destruction at ground zero." The General continued, "This so called 'vacuum bomb' should have good to perfect weather without any possibility of rain during the blast, I've been told."

"That is correct," the Colonel added, "the vacuum concept works much better in good old hot sunny weather. Being the weather on the border with Guatemala is always very hot, there shouldn't be much of a problem picking a certain day and time."

"Remember, the daily rain usually comes around three o'clock in the afternoon in that region, so if we detonate this device between twelve and two we should be good," the General added.

"Let's contact your weather people in Mexico City and my people at Randolph and come up with a hot stretch of weather, at least four days from which to pick a drop day. When I contact Randolph I'll talk with the assigned co-pilot and get his fight time and other particulars of the flight. I do know the mileage from Randolph to the target is approximately one thousand fifty miles as the crow flies. But the exact route will be up to your Mexican pilot and his navigator as specified by President Lazzara," the American Colonel made perfectly clear.

"I'll call Montgomery and talk to Colonel Ortiz on his upcoming mission. He is a great pilot," the General added. "Of course, he'll pick his own navigator for this important flight to eliminate the San Marcos drug cartel and compound. Ortiz can fly about every type of aircraft; props, jets, single engine or four. He told me once he liked to fly the old 747-400 wide body because it flies itself and you're just around for the ride. Besides being a good pilot he is a ball-breaker, as you Americans say. And to add another plus, he speaks perfect English, which will certainly help this mission."

"He sounds perfect for this mission," Colonel Montgomery told his Mexican partner.

"I believe he's our man," the General answered.

"Now, what day of the week should we pick? I like Thursday because their manufacturing facility should be going full bore to produce as much product as possible before the upcoming weekend. Do you have a specific day in mind?" the General asked.

"Not really," the American Colonel answered. "I like your reasoning for Thursday," he admitted.

After talking to Colonel Ortiz in Monterey, the designated officer and his navigator were scheduled to leave for Randolph Air Force base in San Antonio within the next day or so for pre-flight indoctrination and possibly a test flight in the prop C-132.

 rickshaw

"Now we just have to pick which Thursday to drop our surprise package and then determine just how to get our forces into position prior to the drop without tipping our hand," the General added.

"I'm not sure we need to move the whole Spl. Ops Company to the border with Guatemala," the American Colonel said, rubbing his chin. "With that much devastation caused by the vacuum device, there shouldn't be many left to roundup. Maybe we should only send a small force rather than our whole Spl. Ops Company," the Colonel asked.

"But what if the Guatemala government or the local authorities send in their military or police to re-coop their losses by salvaging what's left." the top Mexican General answered.

"President Lazzara has left the details of the attack up to you, my friend."

"And you, too," General Rōjas quickly told his American counterpart.

"How about if we send a single bus load of our Spl. Ops people disguised as tourists, and have their backup force positioned within a short hop by choppers? With helicopters, they could be at ground zero in less than thirty minutes. At the same time we could have the Mexican Air Force on station in case they're needed. According to our spy in the sky photos, there is a clearing just large enough twenty-five miles south of Latrinitaria that can support a group of ten or twelve choppers. That area might be a little moist, but it's within a half hour flight time of ground zero. Instead of landing skids or wheels on the helicopters, we'll have them equipped with pontoons just in case the landing site is soft to wet. What do you think?" the American Colonel asked.

"Do you think the bus load of our people will be enough to initially hold back any force that might come from Guatemala after the blast?" the General asked his friend.

"Yes. The bus load of thirty troopers should be enough to hold back any force until the choppers arrive. Remember, after the blast it will take a period before they know what happened and can muster up a force to cross into Mexico. That assumes, General, that they don't already have a sizable force already inside Mexico. If they do, there will be a fight. But on the other hand, if that Guatemalan force is in or around the San Marcos compound, the blast will take care of them. Now, where can we put our bus load once they arrive near Ciudad Cuauhtémoc prior to the drop?"

"Our man, Felix, inside San Marcos said there is a Playa Del Mar just outside the city on Rt. #190. It's between Presa de la Angostura and the city, which is about six kilometers from the center of town. That's a perfect distance from town as not to arouse suspicion. Of course, our troops will be dressed in civilian clothes while traveling to Ciudad Cuauhtémoc. They'll change into their military uniforms once the party starts," the General said with a slight smile. The General continued, "We'll need about one hundred and twenty troopers for the ten or telve choppers and another thirty for the bus trip."

"What do you think?" the General asked.

"I agree with the numbers," the Colonel answered. "The bus should look beat-up like any other Mexican bus but have a new engine, transmission and tires. It must not breakdown on the way. I would also advise we send a second tour bus a few minutes behind the one carrying our forces as insurance. This operation is too important for a breakdown to cause the death of a single trooper," the American Colonel stated. He continued, "I think we should get your staff officers together and up to speed on the overall plan of attack."

"I agree," the General said, picking up the phone and setting the staff meeting for 14:00 that afternoon.

The meeting started on time, and the six staff officers were in attendance and patiently waiting for their next assignment against a drug cartel somewhere in Mexico. One Major said he was tired of watching training films and mundane camp duties, and his men indicated they were itching for a fight.

"I'm glad to hear that, Major," the General told the rest of his staff. "There is one small problem, we only need about one hundred and fifty men for this very important assignment."

General Rōjas for the next hour covered the many aspects of the attack on the unnamed drug cartel. He also went into great detail about the 'vacuum bomb' and its area of destruction while mentioning that about one hundred and twenty men will fly in choppers and another thirty trooper will be going by bus. The General even told the group about the C-132 and its Mexican pilot and navigator. The only critical information not disclosed was the name and location of the cartel and the possibility of Guatemala's intervention into Mexican territory. He told his officers that their destination and other vital info would be divulged just prior to boarding their transports. "Now, since we don't need the whole Spl. Ops Company, we'll need volunteers for this assignment. You may tell your troops everything I have told you and that's all. Please, no speculation on the final target. One more thing," the General quickly inserted, "we're on full alert as of right now."

"Inform your people and get back to Colonel Montgomery on the names of the volunteers as quickly as you can. The Colonel will decide who goes by chopper and who travels by bus. He will also instruct you on the necessary equipment needed for this unusual assignment."

"Do you have anything to add?" General Rōjas asked his American friend.

"No, sir. You have covered about everything, I believe," he answered.

"That's about it for now, gentlemen."

The entire staff stood up, saluted their commander and quickly left to inform their troops of the upcoming assignment.

"One more thing, General, the weather reports from Randolph and Mexico City are both saying that this coming Thursday will be very hot, dry and have cloudless skies," the Colonel reported.

"Good. Just the ticket, as you Americans say," the General answered with a little laugh. "Perfect weather for our little surprise party," he added.

"What about your man, Felix?" Colonel Montgomery asked. "How can we warn him before the bomb is dropped?"

"We can't. He has known for some time that the attack is coming, but not when. Felix has terminal lung cancer from smoking those terrible Honduran cigars that are full of weeds and not much tobacco. It's the chemicals in those weeds that gave him stage four cancer. He told me not to worry about him, if he is killed in the attack then so be it. Felix has no family and he said he is what you call 'expendable.' He is a very brave man and not afraid to die. Felix is very religious and will take death in whatever form the good lord decides, he told me some months ago."

282

"How about Felix's contact in Ciudad Cuauhtémoc?" the Colonel asked.

"You mean Juanita? Juanita is not only his outside contact but she is also his short-wave radio besides," the General said with a smile.

"Very good, General, the least number of people that know his assignment, the safer he is," the Colonel admitted.

"Now, our large choppers cannot fly the total of six hundred and fifty miles to the target site loaded, so I assume you have an LZ somewhere in between."

"I thought you might never ask, Colonel."

"Well, General, I didn't think you wanted me to mention that during your staff meeting."

"Correct, my learned friend."

"Now let me know what you think about this idea and plan. First, there is a small very private airstrip at Playa Vicenta with a 4500' concrete runway. I have landed there a couple of times and the runway is in pretty good shape. The air field is owned and operated by an ex-colonel who I've known for almost twenty years. He won't ask any questions, I can assure you."

"The airstrip is about three hundred and fifty miles from Querétaro and a little over halfway to Ciudad Cuauhtémoc. Let me show you on the wall map." The General pointed to its location and said, "As you can see, it's between highway 175 to the west and Rt. #185 to the east. It sets between rolling hills and is surrounded by heavy jungle. Very isolated and perfect for our half way landing and jumping off point towards our final LZ."

"Second. How about we fly the twelve helicopters to Playa Vicenta empty, and bring the troops in by C-119 flying boxcar. This C-119 is special, it has JATO (jet assisted take off) on each wing and a three parachute launching rig to help the place stop on short runways. It can land on the length of a soccer field and with the help of JATO can take off even in less runway."

"Well, Colonel, what do you think of my plan so far?" the Mexican General asked.

"I like the overall plan so far," Colonel Montgomery stated.

"One thing I would add, the choppers should have extra fuel tanks installed. With twelve men and equipment in each

bird, the helo will burn an extra amount of fuel in the last fully loaded stretch of three hundred miles to Ciudad Cuauhtémoc."

"You're right, Colonel, we can't take a chance of running out of fuel and having to land short of our final LZ. Not only will they be equipped with pontoons but additional fuel tanks as well. These extra tanks will be jettisoned when empty. The choppers will use these tanks first, I assume?" the General asked.

"Yes sir, that is correct."

"These new choppers should have no trouble traveling the last leg with a full tank of fuel. These birds fully loaded can fly between 400 and 425 miles with no problem. But I still like the idea of sending the two extra birds in case of trouble. Now, just when do we start this train moving? The birds will fly at 135 miles per hour and without much headwind should arrive at their last LZ in about two and a half hours. Once the bomb is detonated the ten choppers will take off from the Presa de la Angostura area and fly to the San Marcos compound and clean up what's left of the drug cartel members. There will be numerous civilian deaths during the initial bomb detonation, there could be as many as two hundred our man Felix has estimated. That's a lot of civilian deaths, but it can't be helped. That drug cartel works seven days a week so an attack on the weekend wouldn't be much benefit," the American Colonel added.

"At the same time the birds head for the bomb zone, the bus load of troopers will travel the six miles down Rt. #190 for the City of Ciudad Cuauhtémoc and stop any escaping members while being on guard against any intervention from the Guatemalan government and any foreign military that may be inside Mexico illegally. Now the timing must be perfect," the Colonel advised the Mexican General.

"Okay, let's plot all the necessary moves to establish the exact timing of each move." the General advised.

#1. What time does the C-132 leave Randolph?
Thurs. 10:00am
#2. What time Thursday do we drop the bomb?
Thurs. 1:30pm
#3. When do the 12 choppers leave Querétaro?
Thurs. 06:00am

#4. When should the choppers arrive at Playa Vicenta?
Thurs. 09:15am
#5. When do the choppers leave Playa Vicenta for the final LZ at Presa de la Angostura?
Thurs. 10:00am
#6. When do the civilian dressed troopers leave the final LZ and travel by sub to Playa?
After bomb drop
#7. After the explosion how long before the choppers arrive, and the bus arrives in Ciudad Cuauhtémoc?
Approx. 20 min. each
#8. What time does the C-119 flying boxcar leave Querétaro with troopers for Playa Vicenta?
07:00 hours approx. 1.40 min flight

As the Mexican General and the American Full Bird Colonel were plotting the various flight schedules and comparing their estimates with the air speeds and mileage info given by the people at Randolph, a Captain entered the map room and advised his General that a message was just received form Randolph stating the Colonel Ortiz and his crew were ready for their flight south. "Also, that the package in question has been loaded and secured on the C-132 and is ready on the flight line awaiting your order to rock and roll, sir."

"It that all, Captain?"

"Yes, sir, that's all we received."

"Thank you, Captain."

The Captain saluted smartly and quickly exited the map room.

"We better have a company formation to see how many volunteers we have collected for this mission. I'm very curious to see how many of our Spl. Ops people volunteer for this unknown mission," the American Colonel said as they exited the map room to call a gathering of this elite unit.

Once the company was assembled and called to attention, the General said, "At ease. I know your officers have spelled out the main goal somewhat, and explained the workings of the so called vacuum bomb, but not where we're going and against whom."

 **rickshaw**

"But before I go any further, would the one hundred and fifty volunteers step forward, please."

With that order, the entire company of two hundred and fifty spl ops personnel stepped forward.

"Well, I see we have a rather large problem. But I must admit, a very pleasant one. I know all of you are tired of laying around and are ready for a fight, but this fight can only involve a small force of one hundred and fifty Spl. Ops people."

With that, trooper Butch, the only female in the company, took two paces forward and said, "Sir I'm volunteering for this assignment because I want to get away from these fat and lazy men, sir."

The whole company laughed.

The General smiled and said, "Butch, you are a rose among weeds, and your request is granted. You're our first volunteer for this mission."

Butch saluted and said, "Thank you, sir."

"Since you all wanted to participate in this adventure, I'll ask your officers and Colonel Montgomery to pick the remaining one hundred and forty-nine men. We'll convene again when the selected group has been picked. At that time, Colonel Montgomery and I will make you aware of the complete mission, target and possible complications that might rear its ugly head."

"Company attention."

"Dismissed."

The officers gathered the men and started to pick the individuals for their specific and unique skills. Colonel Montgomery said he must approve all the volunteers picked for this assignment. The Colonel asked every man where he was born in Mexico and where his relatives were living.

The men were very surprised and curious at the questioning, but understand there must be a very good reason for it. They have learned over the months together and under combat conditions to completely trust the tall Full Bird Colonel from north of the border.

Within an hour, the remaining one hundred and forty-nine men were selected. There were seven troopers questioned that were either born very close to the Guatemala border or had close relatives near there. One Spl. Ops trooper was even born in the City of Ciudad Cuauhtémoc itself and still had relatives living there. The Colonel was glad that he questioned the men first. Even after the individual questioning, at the final briefing, they will be asked if the deaths of fellow Mexican civilians working for the drug cartel is a major problem because there will be a large number of civilian deaths when that special vacuum device is exploded in the compound. Almost all the civilian workers, men and women working at that time inside the cartel complex would be evaporated.

General Rōjas was informed that all the volunteers had been picked and only the one hundred and fifty men and Butch were assembled for your briefing.

The assembled group was told to stand easy and that Colonel Montgomery would give the briefing.

The American Colonel gave the group of Spl. Ops volunteers the whole scoop, and twice emphasized the number of civilian deaths that were going to take place at ground zero. "If anyone here has a problem with the large number of civilian deaths in this operation, please step forward. Nothing will be said, held against you or even asked why. Your decision is yours and yours alone."

With that, two Spl. Ops troopers stepped forward. "Thank you, gentlemen, for being honest to yourselves on having personal reservations. I will pick your replacements. You may leave the formation."

Both men walked quickly from the formation and returned to their barracks.

The Colonel addressed the group again, "We are traveling very light this time. But we will carry lots of ammo and plenty of hand grenades. We'll wear the usual jungle camo with Spl. Ops ID front and back so we don't shoot each other. I will travel in the lead chopper and General Rōjas will ride in the bus heading for the city proper. President Lazzara wanted General Rōjas to be close to the Guatemala border in case extra forces are needed to repel foreign troops. Once more thing I forgot to mention, a group of Mexican Air Force fighter jets will be crossing the area in case something goes wrong and we need them." Their whole group yelled with approval.

"Now before we break up this info party, remember, not a word about the final destination and other details about this mission. No cell phone calls, please. You're on the honor system as before, and as you know, I have complete trust in each and every one of you," the American Colonel told his Mexican military Spl. Ops Company.

With that last statement by their American co-commander, the entire company clapped and yelled, "Viva!" To the delight of the American Colonel.

"Thank you," the Colonel said with a smile.

"One more thing, be ready at a moment's notice."

"Company – attention."

"Dismissed."

Without a sound, the entire company left the formation and headed for their barracks to collect their equipment and get ready to move out.

General Rōjas walked up to Colonel Montgomery and said, "Colonel, your Spanish is first class and is almost as good as mine. I said 'almost as good.'" They both laughed and headed for the map room again. "Now everything is set, General, only your word go will start the ball rolling."

The light on the intercom started blinking and President Williamson said, "Yes, Ruth."

"Madam President, Buck is here to see you."

"Good. Send him in, Ruth."

"Madam President, I have some good news for a change to report," the Chief-of-Staff said quickly.

"Good, what is it?" she asked.

"Our gasoline and fuel oil prices are moving down significantly since the big increase in production has hit the refineries and distribution centers. So much oil is being pumped that our current refineries can't handle the extra load, but as usual, Canada has come through and offered to refine any extra oil we want to divert north. The current price this morning was $2.35 per gallon and we expect the price to even drop lower in the next week or so."

"That's great news, Buck. But I wish our two refineries were up and running to process this increase in oil production," she quickly added.

"With construction going on 24/7, they should be completed in approximately twenty-six months, I've been told," Buck answered.

Chapter 8 - More Cartel Wars

"Now, Madam President, the second part of potentially good news. Maybe," he added.

"The Governors of Hawaii, Oregon and Washington State have contacted me with a request for a meeting with you for the purpose of joining the W.S. of A. All three states are liberal and Washington state is ultra-liberal but the three have had enough of Goodwin's Washington and their policies and mandates that are costing these states billions upon billions of dollars they don't have. And to raise taxes to pay for these mandatory programs is not practical or warranted."

Buck continued, "There are many good reasons to add them to our country, and also there are as many reasons not to bring these liberal states into the fold," Buck told his President.

"Continue," she insisted.

"Their three new states added to our country would seal off the west coast completely from Washington, D.C. and deprive them of direct line of sight to China, Taiwan, Japan, South Korea and the Philippines. I'm sure President Goodwin and his mob wouldn't put up with that west coast loss and our gain," he added. "Washington needs all three of these liberal states to hold the so called union together, and you can bet he will do anything including military intervention to stop this exodus. He will insist this bleeding of states must stop at all cost, ma'am. Now, add the loss of his border with Mexico and now the possible loss of the whole west coast, his Presidency is about over. The balance of the remaining forty-three states wouldn't be able to fiancé the huge appetite of Washington. And don't forget the Alaska problem, if they secede from their union that would leave only forty-two states for Washington to screw with. Another problem, Sara, if they are allowed to join the Western States of America and want to continue with their very liberal ideas and ideology, it would certainly conflict with our founding principles for leaving Washington in the first place. I feel those three states would cause more trouble than they're worth to our country."

"That's my quick assessment, ma'am. Now when do you want to meet with the three Governors?"

"Okay, Buck. Tell then I'll meet them in three days here in Flagstaff. You set the time of the meeting and I'll rearrange my schedule to match."

"Thank you, ma'am."

 rickshaw

The Governors of Hawaii, Oregon and Washington State sent representatives to Washington, D.C. carrying the official documentation saying they were seceding from the Goodwin union as of the first of the month. In a lengthy letter to President Goodwin and the Speaker-of-the House, they explained in great detail just why they had no choice but to leave the Washington union. Even though the three states are very liberal, they feel the current path that Washington is taking will result in total socialism and the eventual demise of our great nation. The residents of these three states have realized that hard line liberalism is not the answer and they are turning towards conservatism. They also indicated in their letter that they wanted to join the new country of Western States of America under President Williamson.

Chapter 9
MORE SECESSIONS

President Goodwin was in his office when Chief-of-Staff Mott came barging in with the official notification that Hawaii, Oregon and Washington State were seceding from the D.C. union.

Upon reading the official document, President Goodwin pounded the two hundred year old desk, stood up and threw the ribbon bound secession document across the room. The President was beyond the boiling point after reading the document and the attached letter explaining their reasons for seceding.

After setting back down, he instructed his Chief-of-Staff to gather up his entire staff, the Joint Chiefs and various key military personnel, and call National Security Advisor Jennings who is in Chicago speaking at Loyola University. "I need him to attend our meeting tomorrow. If he can't get a flight send a plane to fetch him," the President ordered.

"What time do you want the meeting, Mr. President?"

"Tomorrow afternoon at 15:00," he answered.

"Yes, sir. I'll get right on it Mr. President."

President Williamson asked Mrs. Bakker to call the Chief-of-Staff and ask him to come to her office.

The Chief-of-Staff was standing tall in front of his boss within five minutes.

"My god, Buck, that was fast," Sara told her C.O.S.

"I was very close," he answered.

"I wanted to confirm the time of our meeting tomorrow with the Governors of Hawaii, Oregon and Washington," she asked.

"I contacted the three Governors and they will be arriving here in Flagstaff tomorrow around noon. I've scheduled the meeting for 14:00, if that's okay with you, Madam President?"

"The time is fine, I have cleared the whole afternoon in case the meeting becomes a marathon session. There is one more thing, Buck, I want you to contact the Governor of Alaska and ask him to attend the meeting. Apologize to him for the short notice, but we need him here to attend this very important

 **rickshaw**

meeting. If he can't make the meeting tomorrow, we'll postpone the meeting until he can attend."

"I'll contact him right away," Buck answered as he headed for the door.

"Thank you," Sara called after him.

Buck contacted the Alaska Governor who was about to fly to Ottawa for a meeting with the Canadian Parliament, but he said he would forgo the trip to Ottawa and fly to Flagstaff for the meeting. "I will arrive in Flagstaff tomorrow A.M. in case you want to discuss anything before the meeting."

The meeting Thursday with the Governors of Alaska, Hawaii, Oregon, Washington, the Chief-of-Staff, Secretary-of-State Anderson, Secretary-of-the-Treasury O'Neil and President Williamson started on time.

President Williamson started by saying, "Welcome to our capitol here in Flagstaff. As you could see on your drive here from the new airport, we are constructing our government buildings 24/7. Within the next year to a year and a half we'll have most of our federal buildings completed. Now, you didn't come here today to hear my visitors' presentation on our new capitol. Who will start?" she asked.

The Governor of Alaska said he would start by saying that Alaska feels the same way the four states that made up the Western States of America felt when they seceded from the Obama liberal union. "Our reasons are exactly the same, Madam President. My being here, Madam, is very simple, the people of Alaska want to join your W.S. of A. and be part of your conservative government where the people are heard loud and clear, and the government is limited and the states are strong. That's it in a nut shell, Madam President."

"Thank you, Barry. Whose next?" she asked.

"I'll speak for Hawaii, Oregon and Washington State," the Governor of Washington said, standing up to address the group. "You're well aware that our three states are overwhelmingly Democratic, Madam President, and out-number the Republican and Independent parties by at least three to one. We were very happy when Obama won the Presidential election the first time. But after his first term and six months into his second term as President, it became very clear that our President was a full blown socialist that was dangerously close to a communist dictator who is bent on changing our great nation into a third class country that had lost all its fundamental principles, such as the basic freedom allowed by our constitution.

"Obama and now President Goodwin have driven our states into bankruptcy with their heavy taxes, mandates and nickel and dime bites into the dwindling income of our state citizens. Madam President, our three states cannot continue to live under these conditions and want to leave the Washington, D.C. union as quickly as possible. We cannot survive by ourselves, we need your combined four states that make up your fine country, as well as your combined military might to insure our survival. If you add our three states and maybe even the great state of Alaska, that block of eight western states would represent a very strong and consolidated group and country."

"Does anyone else have any comments?" Sara asked the group.

"Yes, I do," Secretary-of-State Anderson said quickly. "I like the overall concept of the four states joining our country, and I especially like the state of Alaska joining us because of their conservative views.

"But I have great concerns about the other three very liberal states joining our country. I'm afraid they will continue to be liberal and will try to divide our country as the D.C. union did. Our four states and Alaska are conservative, and we don't need the aggravation of liberal ideas and policies again. We finally cut our ties with liberalism and don't want to return," the Secretary said with noticeable strong conviction.

"Madam President, may I add my two cents?" the Chief-of-Staff asked.

"Most certainly, Buck."

"I agree with Secretary Anderson, we don't need these three Obama thinking states to join our conservative country. I know these liberals, they won't change and will certainly try to convert our citizens to their liberal ideas. If we put this idea to a vote, I'm sure our citizens would vote a resounding 'no' to their joining our country."

"I would like to add something, Madam President," the Secretary-of-the-Treasury asked.

"Go ahead, Mr. Secretary."

 rickshaw

"I like the idea of adding the four states to our country in one respect. By adding these states the west coast would be solidly in our hands and completely cut off from the Goodwin administration and liberal government. We would then control not only the entire west coast, but the entire length of the border with Mexico. That's over thirty-five hundred miles of Pacific shore line and southern border control. Also, we would have direct access to Canada though Washington State. And by adding Alaska to our fold, the wealth of Alaska in their gold deposits and numerous other minerals along with fishing would benefit our country immensely. Remember, the near border with Russia is an added plus for military reasons," the Secretary added.

"Madam President, after hearing all your concerns about our three states being very liberal, I would like to remind you again that our citizens have overwhelmingly voted to leave the Goodwin union. Our liberal ideas were sliding towards total socialism and coming very close in some cases to communism while our President was becoming a dictator that did not represent the citizens of our country. We may not be conservative yet, but we're no longer the liberal left we once were. If you agree to permit our three states to join the Western States of America, I promise you that our citizens will be very grateful and fit right in with your philosophy of smaller government, strong states' rights and a federal government in Flagstaff that listens to the people of W.S. of A. We have seen what the socialistic governments of Europe and South America have created when their leaders have become all powerful, and even dictators."

Governor Winslow continued, 'We can bring a lot of good things to your new country, Madam President, and for one will follow your leadership as we progress deeper into the twenty-first century."

"Thank you, Governor Winslow. That was well put, and I appreciate your candor. Does the Governor of Hawaii or Oregon have anything to add to our discussion?" President Williamson asked.

"No, Madam President, we're satisfied with what Governor Winslow has said. But we are thankful for the opportunity to discuss the possibility of joining your country. Here in Hawaii, we are starting to lean towards the middle rather than extreme left. Liberalism is not the path to our future here in the beautiful Islands of Hawaii, I might add."

Oregon Governor Lila McPherson said, "Ma'am, we welcome a vote by your citizens on whether or not to allow our states to join your Western States of America."

"That's fair enough," President Williamson told the group. "I'll talk with our Governors, and if they agree, we'll present the admission question to our citizens. But before that vote can take place, there are some liberal laws you have passed that must be repealed if you are to join our conservative country." President Williamson insisted. "My Chief-of-Staff, Michael McCarney, will send you that short list of current laws in your various states that must be overturned quickly. When the list is presented there will be no discussion, just your action on our request."

"I have enjoyed our little get together and let's see what develops in the near future. This matter must be settled quickly for all parties concerned President Williamson advised the group. Have a safe trip home and convey our concerns to your constituents." With that the meeting ended and the four Governors started to leave when President Williamson motioned to Governor Torcello to stay behind.

When the Governors of Hawaii, Oregon and Washington State left the room, Buck closed the door and asked Governor Torcello to please be seated, "President Williamson would like a word with you."

Sara walked the three Governors to the main lobby and said goodbye again. She returned to her office and both secretaries, Buck and Governor Torcello were waiting patiently.

"Thank you, Barry, for waiting," President Williamson told the Alaska Chief Executive. "I wanted a quick word," she said. "No matter what happens with the three liberal states in question, I would strongly support the idea that Alaska be allowed to join our country. First I'll contact our four state Governors and if they like the idea, we'll propose the idea of Alaska joining the Western States of America to our citizens. We'll ask our population to contact their representatives and voice their opinion. Is that satisfactory?" she asked Governor Torcello

 rickshaw

"Yes, ma'am it is, and thank you for asking me to join your meeting here today."

"We're glad you could change your plans so quickly and join us for this important meeting here in Flagstaff," the President added.

"Madam President, I must leave right away. I still have a meeting in Ottawa as soon as I can get there. My office and the people of Alaska will be waiting for your decision." He shook hands with all present and quickly exited the room and headed for the local airport.

"Well, people, what do you think? Will our citizens say 'yes' or 'no' to the Alaska issue?"

Secretary-of-State Anderson said, "I like the idea of Alaska joining our country and I believe our population will vote yes as well. On the other hand, the question of Hawaii, Oregon and Washington joining our government is very questionable in my view. I would say the vote would be a resounding 'no,' Madam President."

"Anybody else?" Sara asked

Secretary-of-the-Treasury O'Neil said, "Madam President, the addition of the state of Alaska to our country would certainly be a significant gain in land mass, as well as a huge gain in natural resources such as oil, wood, fish, gold, silver, copper, platinum, uranium and a dozen other minerals. We should admit Alaska as soon as possible, Madam President."

"Thank you, William. Buck, how about you?" the President asked.

"I agree with both Secretaries, Madam President. The Alaska request 'yes' and the Hawaii, Oregon and Washington request a solid 'no.'"

"Buck, would you please contact the Governors of California, Arizona, New Mexico and Texas? Explain our meeting with the Governors and especially cover our combined feelings on the Alaska request to join the W.S. of A. Ask them to contact me directly if they have any specific questions or concerns."

After the Chief-of-Staff left the room to contact the state Governors, President Williamson asked Secretary O'Neil about the supply of gold bullion in the treasury.

"Actually, very good," he answered. "That last gold vein they discovered in mine #3, if I remember correctly, ran for almost a hundred yards. That strike was very productive and the purity ran around eighty-three percent. To answer your question, ma'am, we have approximately one hundred and twenty tons of gold. That's almost four million ounces, which represents a little over six trillion dollars' worth. Also, we have another very large shipment of the yellow metal due this month and that twenty ton will add another trillion dollars to our treasury," he added.

"That's great news," Sara answered. "We must stay on the gold standard. Paper I.O.U.s jammed in a drawer as payment are worthless, and we don't want that. The Washington, D.C. union collected trillions of dollars' worth of these paper I.O.U.s, but we don't want any of that type of smoke and mirror finance," she added. "How much of a cushion do we have," Sara asked.

"Somewhere around a trillion right now, but we'll have another trillion this month," the Secretary answered. "We should stay ahead of the game as long as the four mines continue to produce at their present rate," he added. "Now, if we allow Alaska to join the Western States of America, their gold production would certainly enhance our coffers. One more thing on the gold subject, ma'am, I've been told that large deposits of gold have been discovered between the towns of Purgatory and White Eye along the Yukon Flats. They said some nuggets were actually found above ground along the shallow creek. Rich veins were found in the hills around Dall Mountain north of Purgatory. Without counting any Alaska gold, we should be good for at least eighteen months or more," the Secretary offered.

"Refresh my memory, Bill, how much of a dent will our joint ventures with Mexico cause? I've seen your financial report but I don't remember the specifics," Sara admitted.

"Not much, ma'am. We have enough available cash to start all ten projects and we'll be floating a small amount of federal bonds to cover almost half the joint ventures," he reported.

"That's great, Mr. Secretary."

"I'm tired," the President admitted, "let's call it quits for today." The two cabinet Secretaries left the President's office without a word.

Before Sara closed the door she told Mrs. Bakker to call it a day. "We all need rest," she told her long-time friend and personal secretary. She closed the door slowly and returned to her brown leather chair and sat down with a plop. She kicked off her shoes and put her sore feet up on the large desk, closed her eyes and stretched out. As she sat there, she was thinking, "Each new day brings more and more pressing problems. No rest for the wicked, as they say," she thought.

Army Headquarters Querétaro, Mexico

"General, I believe it's about time, don't you agree?" the American Colonel asked.

"Yes, I do Colonel. Please inform Randolph that I'm authorizing the whole shebang to start tomorrow morning at 10:00. Tell them to leave at 10:00 sharp and drop our surprise package at exactly 13:30. And be sure to tell them good luck he added. Also inform our one hundred and fifty Spl. Ops volunteers that we'll be leaving tomorrow morning at 07:00 for our flight to Playa Vicenta in our C-119 flying carpet."

"Yes, sir, General. I'll inform Randolph Air Base right away and I will have our staff officers inform our Spl. Ops volunteers to form up at 06:30 tomorrow morning with all their gear and be ready to rock and roll."

"I'll get another weather report, just to make sure our cartel drop zone is rain free for tomorrow afternoon."

"Good idea, Colonel."

"Also, I'll alert the commander of our chopper group to prepare to leave for Playa Vicenta at 06:00 tomorrow. I think that about covers our alert duties," the Commanding Mexican General added.

"How about your man Felix? Is there any way we could alert him?" the American Full Bird asked.

"Yes, there is, we could contact him though Juanita but that is very risky. If we call and he is not near the radio, someone might hear the hum or see the light flashing on the front display. I guess it depends on where Juanita is hidden. Remember, Colonel, he is not a well man and doesn't lave long to live, I've been told. But Felix is a friend, and I don't want him killed if we can help it. We owe him a lot, my friend."

"Let's take a chance, General, we'll place a call through Juanita late this evening and see if we can alert him in time."

"Why not, Colonel, we certainly owe him everything on this venture. He has been gathering intel for months on this cartel while being in ill health. His info on personnel, production and shipping destinations will help in upcoming operations against other drug cartels and suppliers. Let's try and contact him around 23:00 this evening," the General suggested.

At 23:10, General Rōjas and Colonel Montgomery entered the Headquarters communications center and asked the three radio operators to take a long coffee break.

General Rōjas sat down at the console and started turning the dial to the appropriate wave length. After turning up the volume he started by saying a code phrase, "My darling, Juanita, – are you there?" he asked. No answer. He repeated the code words again and still no reply. Let's wait fifteen minutes and try again the General suggested.

At 23:30 the General tried again to reach his undercover man Felix, but again there was no answer. He pushed the chair away from the transmitter and said, "Where the hell can he be at this hour?"

"Maybe Felix is working the second shift and doesn't get through until eleven o'clock. How far from the compound does he live?" Colonel Montgomery asked.

"I have no idea, Colonel, we didn't want any connection with him and that included where he was staying, for security reasons. We had too many security leaks to gamble with his life back then."

"Okay. Let's try again at 01:30, and if he doesn't answer, at least we tried," the American Colonel offered.

"Fine, we'll meet back here in an hour."

The three radio operators returned from their forced coffee break and General Rōjas said that he and the Colonel would return in one hour.

As the two officers were leaving the communications center, Colonel Montgomery said, "General, what if Felix knows we called, won't he return the call?"

"No, he won't. The only time he will answer is if he is present when we call. No return calls, by design," the General added. "See ya in an hour, Colonel."

At 01:30 sharp both officers re-entered the com center and again asked the radio operators to leave. The General tried again to reach their inside man Felix with no answer. He was about to switch channels when the answering code, "Juanita loves you," was received loud and clear.

"My god, Felix, where the hell have you been?" the General asked. "We thought the worst, of course, my friend."

"General, I'm being watched 24/7. I don't know how they would know my mission, but something is definitely going on. At work I'm being relegated to minor jobs outside the main building without access to virtually anything. Something is adrift, sir. Another thing, General, the security all around the compound and surrounding country side has been increased. More motion detectors, roving guards with dogs and mobile units with S.T.A. missiles and even some post with the new variety of shoulder fired surface to air missiles that can bring down a plane up to a distance of five miles. Their new missiles are super accurate and travel just below the speed of sound, I've been told. They are ready for something, General. Do you have something planned that I should know about?" Felix asked.

"Yes, my friend, there is something. At 13:30 this afternoon, a special type of vacuum high explosive device will be detonated above the compound and will inflict total destruction for a radius of one mile in all directions. It will explode outward then suck in all the oxygen and incinerate every living thing. The temperature at ground zero will exceed three thousand five hundred degrees Celsius, so make sure you're a few miles away before one thirty this afternoon."

"As you're aware, General, they tell me I have only a few more months to live, and in a month or so I'll need hospitalization until the end. Now, in case I can't get away from the compound in time this afternoon, I don't want you to feel bad for me, sir. I have had a great life and have enjoyed every minute of it. I have my faith, General, and if God wants me evaporated by this bomb, then so be it. Please be careful, General, they're planning something or preparing for something. I wish you and your men much success in this operation, and wipe every last one of these scum bags from the earth. It's just too bad that all these innocent civilians must perish along with them. Most of the civilians are hard working with families and are working for the drug cartel because that's where the work is.

"Another thing. There are a lot of Guatemala military personnel inside the main building and also inside Ciudad Cuauhtémoc proper. They are a nasty bunch, General, be careful in dealing with them. 'Shoot first, ask questions later' should be your guide, sir.

"Goodbye General, I hope in a small way I have helped to eradicate these despicable human beings."

"Thank you, Felix, we're in you debt. We'll meet again someday my friend – goodbye." The General hit the power switch and the radio transmitter went dead. "There goes a true friend, Colonel. He has a stern warning for us, he indicated they may be waiting for something to happen and they are beefing up their security. He also confirmed that Guatemala military personnel are inside the compound as well as the city itself. That could be a real problem for President Lazzara if we kill Guatemala military personnel."

"General, we must inform President Lazzara as quickly as possible about the probability that Guatemala military forces are inside the Marcos compound and even stationed inside the City of Ciudad Cuauhtémoc itself," Colonel Montgomery insisted. He continued, "One thing your man did not tell us was just how many Guatemalan troops were inside Mexico. We don't know whether there is twenty or two hundred Guatemala forces protecting the drug cartel and their distribution routes, General. We may attack with our small force and find ourselves out manned and probably out gunned as well. I don't like this new twist of uncertainly, General. This new intel could mean a disaster for our Spl. Ops group. Between the heavily armed cartel members and now the Guatemala military adding their firepower to the mix, we could be in serious trouble."

"Yes, Colonel, I agree. I'll call President Lazzara right away," he answered.

Once inside the com center, General Rōjas placed and emergency call to President Lazzara in Mexico City.

Within thirty minutes the Mexican President was returning his Commanding General's call.

On a secure line the General said, "Mr. President, we have some new and disturbing information on the San Marcos cartel. We have been told that some quantity of Guatemalan military personnel are in the drug compound and even present inside our border town of Ciudad Cuauhtémoc itself. Mr. President, we're about to give the okay to attack the cartel tomorrow afternoon

with a small force of only one hundred and fifty Spl. Ops personnel."

"My god, General, it's hard to believe that foreign troops are actually working and stationed inside Mexico without our military and government knowledge. Even more disturbing is the fact that both you and I don't know about this foreign invasion of our country. Where is the closest military unit?" the President asked.

"Mr. President, we have a very small military detachment at the coastal City of Tapachula, which is about eighty kilometers from Ciudad Cuauhtémoc. I was told years ago that this military unit was only a barracks type service organization."

"What the hell does that really mean?" the disgruntled Mexican President asked.

"Sir, that means they are stationed on their base and that's about all. They perform minor military duties when ordered and only possess small arms and have very few military vehicles."

"When your southern attack is completed, go down there and relieve that base commander, and close that military facility if you deem necessary, General."

"Yes, Mr. President."

"General, have you alerted all parties on this upcoming operation?"

"All parties except the Mexican Air Force that will fly support in case the operation gets out of hand, sir. They only need to know the exact location and time we want them on station, Mr. President."

"Along with your fighter cover, why don't you have a company of paratroopers available in the area ready to drop in case your little war on drugs expands beyond your control, General?" Before General Rōjas could answer the President asked, "What does Colonel Montgomery think of the new development where Guatemala military troops may be involved?"

"The Colonel is right here, Mr. President. you can ask him yourself."

"Colonel Montgomery, Mr. President."

"Good to hear your voice again, Colonel. Do you think we should continue with this operation or cancel it for now?"

"Mr. President, with your Air Force available in the area and your idea of having a company of jumpers ready to go if we need them, makes me feel a little better, sir. Without those two factors I would have said 'cancel,' Mr. President."

"Thank you, Colonel."

The American Colonel handed the General the phone and shook his head up and down to designate an affirmative answer.

"Go ahead, Mr. President."

"I agree with Colonel Montgomery, let's proceed with your operation, Marcos, General. Please keep me informed on the Guatemalan military intervention, and call me if I'm needed, General. Good luck, and God bless you and your forces." With that, President Lazzara hung up.

"I'll call our Mexican Air Force fighter group and pass on the time and area to patrol before and after the bomb drop."

"After alerting them, I'll contact our nearest Army Airborne unit for immediate activation. Like the fighter group we want them close, but not too close."

"Let's not have the fighters or the C-130s full of airborne troops any closer than twenty-five or thirty miles from ground zero. We certainly don't want these two groups to alert the cartel or impede our own plan of attack," Colonel Montgomery advised.

"I agree, my friend. After my calls, we better get some rest because our day starts in only a few hours, and I'm sure today will be a real bitch," the General said, dialing the phone.

Mrs. Bakker entered President Williamson's office and said, "Ma'am, President Goodwin is on secure line #4, but the switchboard is holding the call in case you don't want to talk to him."

"That's okay, Ruth, tell the switchboard to pipe the call through. Only God knows what he is up to," Sara told her secretary and friend.

Sara pushed the button on the main console and said, "Good evening, Mr. President, what do I owe this call to, sir. Just why are you calling me?" Sara said quickly.

"Madam President, I'm calling because I'm very concerned about the state of Alaska. Governor Torcello has filed for secession effective immediately. We cannot allow this treasonous State of Alaska to leave our union and join the Western States of America. To add to this problem, I've been informed that Hawaii, Oregon and Washington State have contacted your administration for the possibility of joining your country, Madam President."

"Why are you calling me," Sara asked, "You should be talking to the four state Governors, not me, sir."

"I'm talking to you, Madam President, because I want to warn you against taking these four states into your fold," President Goodwin said in a threatening voice.

"You dare to threaten me and my country, you pompous ass. I will accept any state or country into my 'fold,' as you call it, whenever I wish, sir. Your country is doomed, Mr. President, but you're too damn stupid to see or admit it. If you try to interfere with our country's internal affairs, Mr. President, you will regret your actions," Sara said in a voice just below screaming. Sara was so mad that she slammed the phone down and it slid off her desk, taking a stack of papers with it. Mrs. Bakker heard the loud bang and came running into Sara's office.

Sara was picking up the phone and some scattered papers while saying, "That stupid bastard, if he thinks I'll take his threats laying down, he is very mistaken."

"Are you all right, Madam President?" Ruth asked her boss.

"No, I'm not Ruth, I'm just pissed at the so called President who resides in Washington," she answered.

"How about a hot cup of Russian tea?" Ruth asked.

"Sounds good to me. Along with the tea also bring me a bottle of scotch and no glass, I'll drink straight from the bottle," Sara answered with a slight smile.

"Really, ma'am?"

"Not hardly, Ruth, just the tea will be fine."

"Right away, ma'am."

When Ruth returned with the Russian tea and a plate of oatmeal cookies, Sara asked her to contact Buck and ask him to see her as soon as possible.

Buck knocked and entered the President's office and said, "Could I join you in a scotch, Madam President?"

"Ruth is a blabber mouth. There are no secrets around here, I can tell you," Sara said shaking her head.

"I assume you had a crappy conversation with President Goodwin." Buck said with a slight smile.

"You can joke, mister, but that Washington jerk is on a path towards war, I'm afraid," the President admitted. "There is no telling what he will do to prevent these states from leaving his Washington union. Buck, I want you to ask General Wittingham to alert the Governors of our four states and advise the Governors of Alaska, Hawaii, Oregon and Washington State as well. At least we should be prepared for anything this mad man might do towards his four rebellious states. I don't want our country drawn into his fight, but we may not be an outsider in this issue."

"Buck, ask the General if he would advise our forces to go on alert at this time. Tell the General that it's his call."

"Yes, ma'am, I'll get right on it."

Buck headed for his office to call General Wittingham at Wagon Wheel Headquarters. Buck was at his desk and about to pick up the secure phone when he decided to drive to military headquarters at the Wagon Wheel structure in greater Flagstaff and talk to the General in person. After making a dozen calls, Buck contacted the President.

"Madam President, the following people will be at your meeting tomorrow at noon. The Secretaries of Defense, Treasury and State, V.P. Richardson, along with our four Governors and Lt. General Wittingham and his aide-de-camp. Did I miss anyone?" Buck asked.

"No, they will do," she answered. "I just want all parties on the same page in case the D.C. mad man goes off the deep end and tries to stop the states from seceding his dying union. We must be prepared for anything," she insisted, "and I mean anything," she repeated. "You did miss one person," the President added.

"Who, ma'am?" the Chief-of-Staff asked.

"You, of course," she answered.

"Yes, ma'am, there will be an even dozen at your meeting tomorrow."

"Thank you, Buck, see ya at noon tomorrow, unless the shit hits to fan before the meeting starts."

Both hung up without another word.

President Williamson entered the large bomb proof war room one hundred and ninety feet below ground level with a covering of almost twenty feet of hardened reinforced concrete

below the new military headquarters called 'the Wagon Wheel.' The large room hummed with the electronic sound of hundreds of computers and every kind of monitoring device known to man. She walked to the head of the huge table and stood there looking over the assembled group. The long table could seat thirty, but for this meeting only a full dozen seats were occupied.

Sara slowly sat down and said, "Thank you, ladies and gentlemen, for coming on such short notice, but I felt the problem needed your comments and overall input.

"First, as you know, the State of Alaska, through Governor Torcello has asked me to allow their great state to join the Western States of America."

"Second. The states of Hawaii, Oregon and Washington through Governor Winslow have also asked to join our country. Their reasons for leaving the old Obama and the new Goodwin government are basically the same as ours. The Goodwin liberal spend, tax and giveaway government has driven these very liberal states into bankruptcy. They no longer can afford the social programs that are creating millions of government trough feeders who contribute almost nothing to the well-being of their state, but do provide a huge voting block for the socialist government who gives them everything."

President Williamson continued, "I do like the idea of Alaska joining our country, but I have reservations about allowing the very, very liberal states of Hawaii, Oregon and Washington to join the Western States of America. Could these far left liberal states fit in with our conservative way of thinking with smaller government with very few social giveaways? Policies like Social Security, various disability benefits and unemployment are the few government policies that our conservative federal government will provide. There may be one or two I have forgotten, but nothing like the Obama/Goodwin socialistic giveaway that makes their citizens beholden to their Democratic government that provided everything from cell phones to housing and even transportation, in some cases.

"Millions of their citizens are being held in bondage because of these social giveaways that keep them feeding at the government trough throughout their entire life. No need to work and contribute towards the good of all Americans as long as the social majority keep supplying all their worldly needs. Just like a dozen or more countries in Europe, the socialistic government of President Goodwin is sliding down the slope towards insolvency and complete government collapse. Thank god we no longer are attached to that form of so called Democratic government," Sara added.

Vice President Richardson said, "Madam President, I'll start off this very important question of granting statehood in our country. I also like the idea of Alaska joining our four state country for the many reasons we all know. But on the question whether the states of Hawaii, Oregon and Washington be allowed to join our country, I'm on the fence. They are so liberal, I can't imagine they will change their social spots and fit right into our smaller form of government," the V.P. added.

Secretary-of-Defense Waterman stood up and said, "Madam President, I'm afraid if we allow the four states in question to join our nation, the Goodwin government may, in dealing with these runaway states, find it necessary to attack our country as well. His military leaders may see this as an opportunity to settle the score for all the states who have seceded and are thinking about leaving his union, Madam President. But with that said, I do like the possibility of Alaska joining our country," the Defense Secretary added.

"Thank you, Mr. Secretary. Who's next?"

"I would like to add my two cents, Madam President."

"Go ahead, Madam Secretary."

Secretary-of-State Paula Catherine Anderson stood up and slowly walked over to the large cloth map of North America. She pointed to our four Western States and said, "If we add Oregon and Washington, we will have full control of the Pacific West Coast and have direct access to our northern friends in Canada. And if we add that beautiful state of Alaska to our country, that would complete the western piece of our national puzzle. You could even throw in the aloha state for good measure.

"Madam President, I also like the idea that if we're going to allow these liberal states to join our fold, they must repeal a whole array of social laws. I can't see them doing that, but we'll have to wait and see. If they did change their socialistic ideas and started to lean towards the right, then I would be in favor of their admittance, Madam President."

 rickshaw

"Thank you, Madam Secretary."

"General Wittingham, I'd like to hear your comments on this important subject," President Williamson asked her Commanding General.

"Well, ma'am, by admitting the four states, we certainly would be in a position of strength all around. We would have the whole west coast and the only door to the Far East as well as Alaska to the north and the two thousand miles of border with our southern neighbors. This combo would give us great strength in its unity, Madam President. I would like to see these extra pieces of our national puzzle slide into place. We certainly would have a much stronger country and could defend our borders a lot easier, ma'am.

"Setting aside their liberal views, I feel if they are willing to change I would support their joining our own union, Madam President."

"Thank you, General, well put, sir."

Texas Governor LaCrosse said, "Madam President, there is one thing I don't like, Madam President, and that's the fact that Alaska is much bigger than my state of Texas."

Some clapping and a few started booing.

"Thank you, Marilyn, for your unsolicited comment."

"You're welcome, Madam President."

Margo Lane, Governor of Arizona, said, "Madam President, I think we should take a straw poll on the question of admitting Alaska and the other three states. Like I said, maybe not nationally, but a good sample of our citizens. You can decide one way or the other, ma'am, but I believe you should hear from our constituents as well."

"I agree, Margo. Buck, if you don't have any objections, I'd like you to form a small group and create a voting document with only two questions. One on the possible admission of the state of Alaska, and the second on the admission of the other three states."

"Certainly, Madam President, I would be happy to take on that assignment," Buck said, rolling his eyes.

"Thank you, Buck, for volunteering."

"You and your select group can determine the sample of the population you want to ask these questions and the number of surveys necessary to give us a true sample of our voting population."

"Madam President, on the survey could we ask for comments as well?" the Chief-of-Staff asked.

"Certainly, Buck. I'm just interested in the two basic questions. Admit the states, or not," President Williamson added.

"I guess we have voiced our opinions on the admission of these four states and I know how you feel, now let's see how our country as a whole feels. Talk to your staffs and everybody else you come in contact with and get their overall opinion. I would like the surveys put on line within the next week and all results within a fortnight, if possible," Sara asked.

"I'd like to thank all of you for coming on such short notice and remember these decisions will affect our country for many years to come, so we better be correct in our final decision. War or peace could be in the balance if our action on Alaska, Hawaii, Oregon and Washington State isn't the right one."

The meeting broke up and all members except Buck slowly left the underground bunker and headed for the surface. The Chief-of-Staff was immediately on the phone contacting the people he wanted on the survey development team. After only fifteen minutes, Buck had contacted the six people he wanted. All persons he had called said 'yes,' they would help develop the important survey and put it out on the internet and other electronic answering media. Even a phone number would be provided for people who don't have access to computers and etc.

05:00 seemed to come early because the American Colonel finally went to sleep at 01:00 and four hours of sleep is better than none. He quickly showered, dressed and headed for the officers' mess for a quick breakfast. Upon entering the mess, he was surprised to see General Rōjas was already eating breakfast. Then General motioned the Colonel to join him and his aide.

As Colonel Montgomery sat down he said, "General, why didn't you wake me?"

"You needed the rest, my American friend," he answered.

"I'm sure we're both tired, General, but we have a full and very important day to start in an hour or so."

"Yes, we do, Colonel, and I'm still very concerned about the action we're about to authorize. There are too many unanswered questions and many unknown factors that could cost our Spl. Ops forces many casualties. After your breakfast, Colonel, meet me in the map room, and we'll give the various units the go signal to start our attack."

"Yes, sir, I'll meet you in ten," Colonel Montgomery said gulping down his coffee.

General Rōjas asked his American Full Bird whether he had anything to discuss before he gives the signal to start the attack on the San Marcos cartel.

"Not really, General, I just wish we know more about how many Guatemala military personnel are inside the cartel compound and positioned inside the City of Ciudad Cuauhtémoc itself. But it's too late to cancel, sir, let's give the signal to go, General."

General Rōjas called the com center and ordered them to call the various units and give them the go signal. "Remember, they are required to return your call within five minutes to confirm they received and understood your go signal. Let me know if any unit didn't confirm your call," the General added.

"Yes, sir will do."

"Well, Colonel, we're on our way at last. Let's have Major Alvarez call the company formation and check their gear prior to boarding the flying box cars for departure at 07:00."

"Sounds good to me, General. I'm going to grab my gear and maps and head for the helo pads. I'll fly with the twelve empty choppers to Playa Vicenta and wait for the C-119s and our troops." "Good luck, Colonel, keep in close contact, but no names."

"Yes, mother," the Colonel answered.

All twelve choppers left Army Headquarters at 06:00 sharp and headed for their first LZ at Playa Vicenta which is almost halfway to their final landing zoned close to the San Marcos compound.

The two C-119s were warming up on the runway while the one hundred and fifty Spl. Ops personnel started boarding the two flying boxcars. At 07:05 the two loaded planes lifted off the runway, circled Querétaro once and headed south east to Playa Vicenta and the waiting choppers.

The twelve empty choppers and Colonel Montgomery arrived at Playa Vicenta only eight minutes late. While waiting for the Spl. Ops troops to arrive, they refueled and did some minor maintenance.

The two C-119 prop cargo planes and General Rōjas arrived on time and landed on the short runway with the aid of their three parachute braking system. Once the Spl. Ops personnel and their equipment was unloaded, the planes went to the very end of the runway and revved their prop engines to the highest RPMs and started down the runway. They went to the end of the runway and took off with a hundred feet to spare. They didn't need to use their J.A.T.O. for liftoff with both planes empty.

After a quick meal and piss call, the Spl. Ops troopers climbed aboard the ten choppers and lifted off at 09:58 and headed south for their final LZ at Presa de la Angostura. The two empty choppers left ten minutes later, in case any helicopter had mechanical trouble of any kind.

General Rōjas received word that the C-132 with its special package was in the air and on route to their drop zone.

The ten loaded choppers arrived at Presa de la Angostura on time and landed with a splash. It was a good thing that the helps were equipped with pontoons, because the LZ was a little on the damp side.

The thirty troopers and General Rōjas dressed in civilian clothes had to slosh through ankle deep water while heading for the dirt road a quarter of a kilometer away. The road was high and dry where the ornately decorated bus was waiting. The remaining one hundred and twenty Spl. Ops troopers waited inside their helos for the bomb drop and their short flight to the San Marcos compound.

The time was exactly 09:59:28 when the vacuum device exploded in the middle of the San Marcos compound just six kilometers away. The shock wave was felt by the waiting helicopters, and they could see the rising smoke and feel the sound of air being sucked towards the blast zone.

After one minute, the ten choppers lifted off and headed towards ground zero and their drop zone. At the same time, the bus load of troopers and General Rōjas headed for the square in the center of Ciudad Cuauhtémoc.

 rickshaw

The vacuum device was dropped from only one thousand feet and exploded on contact with the ground creating a fire ball thirty-five hundred degrees that exploded outward then sucked in all the oxygen from as far as one mile away. The many buildings inside the compound were completely destroyed as well as the jungle vegetation within half a mile in all directions. Any persons above ground at ground zero were instantly evaporated and the underground facilities were void of any oxygen and death was almost instant.

The choppers landed in the clearing created by the blast, and the troopers quickly exited their whirly birds and started their sweeping of the scorched area where buildings once stood and where almost two hundred Mexican civilians and cartel members once worked producing large quantities of coke and other by-products. Only a few cartel members staggered from their below ground facilities and were quickly rounded up without firing a single shot. After the sweep was completed and the whole area secured, Butch complained to Colonel Montgomery that she didn't get a chance to fire a single shot.

"Isn't that great?" the Colonel asked the only woman member of the Spl. Ops Company.

"Yes, sir, I guess so," she answered.

Colonel Montgomery contacted the jet fighters circling the area and told them the compound was destroyed and the area was secure and that they were not needed. But instructed them to stay close in case General Rōjas needed their help. He also contacted the plane load of paratroopers and told them the same story. He tried to contact General Rōjas but didn't receive an answer.

General Rōjas and his small group quickly drove to the city center square to set up a defensive position. When he exited the bus, he was asked by some shoppers what was that loud noise and black cloud of smoke to the north. Before the General answered their question, he quickly asked if there were any foreign soldiers nearby.

"Yes, General, there are many soldiers from Guatemala in the city and the outskirts. We have wondered for years why our government in Mexico City has allowed these foreign troops to operate inside our Mexico."

Chapter 9 – More Secessions

"Please take shelter," the General advised the small group of civilians that gathered around the bus. As the group ran for cover, the General asked the Sergeant carrying the command radio to stay close.

Within five minutes, a group of Guatemalan military driving a jeep entered the large square and stopped when they spotted the Spl. Ops personnel carrying automatic weapons. The man next to the driver was on a field phone calling for assistance, and within less than a minute a truck load of Guatemalan soldiers were pulling along-side the jeep. The soldiers dressed in camo scattered for cover, and once they had protection behind the shop walls and fences, they started to fire at the bus with automatic weapons.

General Rōjas grabbed the field phone and called Colonel Montgomery and explained the situation and asked him to come to his aide. The Colonel said he would fly his chopper gun ship to the town square and see if he could even the odds. He estimated his ETA at five to seven minutes.

Colonel Montgomery put the gun ship down smack dab in the middle of the square and hovered ten feet above the ground. He waved the gun ship from side to side spraying machine gun fire at the entrance of the plaza, then moved the chopper about fifty feet above the plaza floor and told the General through his loud speaker to move forward. General Rōjas and his small force left their protective positions and quickly moved through the plaza towards the square entrance.

Five choppers landed outside the plaza gate and the Spl. Ops troopers sealed off any escape route. The Guatemalan forces realized they were being fired on from two sides and quickly put down their weapons and raised their arms.

Colonel Montgomery flew over the walled plaza and landed along-side the other choppers at the entrance.

Once the captured Guatemalan army personnel were safely gathered up and put into a bus, Colonel Montgomery and General Rōjas sat down and discussed their next moves.

The General's small force of thirty only had three men wounded and no deaths. But the Guatemala military suffered six dead, eight wounded and the remaining sixteen captured.

Colonel Montgomery's large force were also lucky as well. One man burned slightly by flaming debris, but no deaths in the attack.

The Colonel started by saying, "First we should call President Lazzara and give him the details of today's events, then we should find the Mayor and the Chief of Police and arrest them both for treason. Why did they allow foreign troops to reside inside their city and come and go between the cartel compound? General, we must still destroy the underground rooms, bunkers and storage areas as well as thousands of pounds of coke and tons of processing supplies. And also a storeroom full of American greenbacks that must exceed one hundred million, at least. You and I could retire in great comfort with that little stash," the American Full Bird said, shaking his head.

After that, we should travel to Tapachula on route #200 must thirteen kilometers from the coast and only eight kilometers from here and see just why the Army Camp Commander did nothing to stop the foreign troops from entering Mexico. He didn't even report the existence of foreign troops residing inside the city of Ciudad Cuauhtémoc or the existence of a drug cartel. I smell money, General, what do you think?" the Colonel asked.

"I think you're right, Colonel, but before we do anything, I'll call President Lazzara and fill him in on the operation and also our little problem with the Guatemalan military that exists inside Mexico."

"While you're doing that, General, I'll return to the compound area and supervise the destruction of all underground structures and their content. Also, I want to find out where they bought their processing supplies. The chemical companies or their distributers should be our next targets.

"Also tell your President that a windfall of over one hundred million dollars in American greenbacks are now available for his government's use. That will certainly make his day, General.

"One more thought," the American Full Bird said, looking at a map of southern Mexico. "With Tapachula only a stones' throw from the Pacific Ocean, it would make an excellent route for shipping and distributing their drugs to the U.S. and throughout the world. When we talk to the military commander in Tapachula, it might open a large box of worms that could involve a lot of military, civilian and government officials," the Colonel warns.

"You could be right, my American friend. I'll also mention that to the President, among the other things," the General promised.

"See ya later," the Colonel said, heading for his chopper and the short flight to the San Marcos dead zone.

Colonel Montgomery looked over the inventory of material found underground and was surprised at the amount of coke, arms, ammunition, money and processing supplies found intact.

"We're going to need a lot of C-4," he told his Mexican aide-de-camp.

"Start planting the explosive charges right away," he ordered. "The quicker we destroy this stuff, the better I'll feel," Colonel Montgomery admitted. He asked his aide to find Butch and have her report to him immediately.

"Yes, sir."

Within five minutes, the recipient of Mexico's second highest military award was standing tall in front of her American Commander.

"Colonel, sir, you asked for me," she said saluting smartly.

"Yes, Butch, I did."

"I want you to take charge of the American green backs found underground. I want an accurate count and the money packed in waterproof bags and put aboard my chopper. Post two guards around the helo until we take off. When I say 'yes,' we, I mean, I want you to accompany the money until it's delivered to President Lazzara in person.

"Can you do this?" he asked the only female in the Spl. Ops Company.

"No sweat," she added in English with a smile.

"Guard this money with great caution," he advised, "and don't trust anyone except the two of us," he said with a broad smile. "Take whatever automatic weapons you feel comfortable with, and I'd also advised you carry a high capacity pistol as backup."

",Yes sir. Is there anything else?" she asked.

"No, that's all."

Butch saluted and headed towards the underground room full of American greenbacks, all in one hundred dollar bills and in neat bundles of ten thousand dollars.

General Rōjas arrived at ground zero and was surprised at the amount of the destruction that stretched outward for one half mile in all directions. He related the conversation with President Lazzara and told Colonel Montgomery that they had a free-hand in dealing with the city officials in Ciudad Cuauhtémoc and the military post of Tapachula. "The President feels the same as you, Colonel, he thinks money is the key to everything in both cases. He asked if we needed any additional forces to help in the upcoming mission.

"I told him we had sufficient forces to handle both problems, and I asked him to hold off contacting the Guatemala government for at least a day, while we finish our roundup. The President agreed, but only for a day.

"First let's find out where the City Manager and his Chief of Police work and live. Once they are in custody, I'll install one of our ranking officers in each position until we can appoint a trusted civilian. We might have to bring in someone from another province to run the city government," the General added. "We'll hold these two city officials under arrest without bail until our investigation is complete."

Within an hour, Spl. Ops personnel had arrested both men at city hall, and they were put in their own jail for the time being. Other members of the city government were also being rounded up and jailed. Many citizens of Ciudad Cuauhtémoc quickly came forward to help the Spl. Ops troops arrest the city employees that had allowed the Guatemalan military to function in the city and inside Mexico itself.

Colonel Montgomery said, "Now that the first phase of operation round-up is complete, let's head for Tapachula and talk to the Camp Commander. I'm sure someone from here has already called the Army Commander and alerted him. We could have a fight on our hands," the American Full Bird added. "Also, General, I think we should heave forty or fifty of our troops here in the city to maintain order and be ready for any counter attack by Guatemalan forces. I would also suggest that you contact that plane load of paratroopers and have them land near the city and take up defensive positions along the border with Guatemala."

"Sounds good to me, Colonel. I'll contact Central Command and give the order for the Airborne troops to land here and help our Spl. Ops personnel guard the city and watch the border."

"While you're making your call, General, I'll get the choppers ready and brief the men for the flight to Tapachula." Col. Montgomery rounded up the Spl. Ops personnel selected to fly to the Army Camp and laid out their plan of attack.

General Rōjas joined the Colonel and the eight choppers with ninety-five men aboard headed, without further delay, for the City of Tapachula.

Butch and four troopers headed for Playa Vicenta in the Colonel's gun ship where they would transfer the money bundles worth one hundred million and change to the waiting C-119 flying boxcar and the trip to Mexico City and the President's Palace.

With only a twenty-three minute flight from Ciudad Cuauhtémoc, the eight choppers landed between the small town of Tuxtla Chico on the border and Tapachula. Their LZ was only two kilometers from the army garrison just outside Tapachula.

The Colonel contacted the other pilots and relayed the plan to land the choppers in the parade ground smack dab in the center of the compound. He also said, "Be prepared for almost anything, they may have been forewarned of our coming. And good luck," he added.

The choppers spiraled up to almost a mile before covering the short distance to the army compound then dropped quickly into the center of the parade field while Spl. Ops troops exited the choppers and surrounded the main building and a building that looked like a barracks.

Army Garrison personnel were running in all directions not knowing what was happening or what to do.

General Rōjas and Colonel Montgomery, along with troopers, burst into the headquarters building and disarmed all personnel they met. Colonel Rodrigues, Base Commander, was in his office with a civilian and a Guatemalan naval officer when the door flew open and the Colonel/General combo ordered the three to be seated.

The base C.O. said, "General, what is the meaning of this intrusion?"

"You are under arrest, Colonel, and so are your two friends, I might add."

"I'm a Guatemalan navy officer, you can't arrest me," he said in defiance. "I'm not a Mexican citizen, so I'm exempt from your military authority."

"You might be a foreign naval officer but you're also very stupid," the Commanding General informed his unauthorized foreign military officer.

"Just why are you here?" the American Colonel asked.

"The army is shipping some cargo north, and they asked me if I would transport the items," he said in a low voice.

"Just what are these so called items?" the General asked.

"I don't know, you'll have to ask Colonel Rodrigues, he hasn't told me yet," the foreign military officer told General Rōjas.

"Why would a Mexican Army officer ask a Guatemalan naval officer to move goods somewhere north? Why not have the Mexican Army ask our Navy or civilian cargo ships to move these unknown items? Colonel I'd like to hear your answer," the General asked.

"I refuse to answer," the C.O. answered.

"Fine. Put the Colonel in irons, and also tie up the two strangers as well, and find the Executive Officer and put him under arrest."

"We'll take these four people back to Army Headquarters at Querétaro for intensive questioning," the General told the group. "I'll appoint one of our ranking officers to take temporary command of this post until we can get to the bottom of this mess."

"We should also leave a strong force here and disarm every member of this command until things are sorted out and we can determine just who knew what," Col. Montgomery suggested.

"Certainly, Colonel, I'm sure many more Army personnel and many civilians working on base will be implicated as well."

Once the garrison was disarmed, and all personnel restricted to barracks, the attacking force headed for the waiting choppers with their prisoners and took off for Playa Viucenta, their first LZ before returning to Querétaro. The remaining Spl. Ops forces left behind closed and locked the main gate while posting guards throughout the entire base.

A district civilian judge, also with an appointed military judge from Mexico City would help sort out the foreign presence and intervention by Guatemala and its association with a Mexican Army Base Commander. Shipping of drugs and huge amounts of money was suspected by Col. Montgomery and General Rōjas.

Before starting his return trip to Playa Vicenta, the General called President Lazzara and informed him that the Base Commander and his friends were under arrest and the Army base was locked down until the many questions were answered by all investigating parties. He also said that they would most likely be in Mexico City by the next day with guests and a plane load of money.

Chief-of-Staff McCarney (Buck) entered President Williamson's office and sat down in his favorite leather chair. "Well, Madam President, we have the overall reports of our citizen voting on the admitting one conservative state or admitting three liberal states."

"Personally, I'm very surprised ma'am."

"Here are the totals:
Voting Alaska to join the W.S. of A.

Yes:	12.3 Mil.
No:	4.7 Mil.

Voting Hawaii, Oregon and Washington State to join the W.S. of A.

Yes:	9.1 Mil.
No:	7.9 Mil.

Comments: The yes voters said yes, only if certain laws approved by their states were appealed and the three Governors and State Senators were replaced at once by more conservative or moderate officials instead of the staunch liberals currently in power. The voters feel that the population of these three states

would not respond to their demands to change from left-wing liberals to conservatism of any kind.

"So you see, Madam President, we still have a mixed bag and no real answer. The 'yes' vote on the three states means 'maybe' and not 'yes.' The only clear agreement among the voters was to allow Alaska to join our country." Buck added as he passed the voting results to President Williamson. "Maybe we should impose a deadline for the states to repeal the list of liberal laws that are strangling their citizens and violating the Second Amendment and others as well. Also, hold state wide elections to replace their Governors and State Senators in Washington."

"Did you contact our Governors with the voting results?" Sara asked

"No, ma'am, I wanted you to hear the results first," Buck answered.

"Thank you, Buck, I appreciate that. Now please call the Governors and give them the official results, and tell them I'm in favor of allowing Alaska to join our country immediately. If they have any questions or concerns have them call me right away. Do you agree Buck?" Sara asked.

"Yes, ma'am I do. Alaska will be a great addition to our country and to the defense of the west coast and North America. We shouldn't linger on admitting them either, the quicker the better before President Goodwin and his Washington mob think the best answer in stopping Alaska from seceding is by using force. Once we admit Alaska, Washington will be helpless to act against Alaska and our county combined."

"I hope you're right, but remember the Washington mob are a bunch of very irrational people at best," Sara told her Chief-of-Staff. She continued, "I don't trust Defense Secretary Marshal and his top Generals, as I was surprised they did nothing when we took over the border with Mexico. No matter what, Buck, I still think they are very unpredictable and capable of doing anything to maintain a hold on the remaining states. Goodwin knows if they lose any more states to our country, their so called united group of states will be lost forever. We must not sell him short," Sara continued, "when his country's back is against the wall he is the most dangerous."

"As soon as you have talked to our Governors, give me a call. I want to call Governor Torcello and tell him our overwhelming decision by vote to admit Alaska to our Western States of America as our fifth and largest state," Sara said with obvious excitement.

"Yes, ma'am, I'll get right on it." Buck disappeared from her office at warp speed.

Within twenty minutes Buck was on the phone to President Williamson informing her that the governors of California, Arizona, New Mexico and Texas were in total agreement with the President's opinion that Alaska should be allowed to join our country as its fifth state.

Sara thanked her Chief-of-Staff and quickly pressed the button on the intercom and asked Mrs. Bakker to contact Alaska Governor Torcello as quickly as possible.

The Alaska Governor was on the phone in a matter of minutes and was delighted upon hearing the news of the voting public and President Williamson's decision to admit that grand state of Alaska.

Sara told Governor Torcello to inform the citizens of Alaska that The Western States of America had voted overwhelmingly to admit their state to our country. "They will be our fifth and largest state in the world's newest country." She told the Governor that she must call President Goodwin and give him fair warning not to start the second Civil War because various states want out of his Washington Social and spend club.

"I'll get back to you, Governor, with the details and date of your admittance to the Western States of America."

"Thank you, Madam President, the citizens of Alaska will be very happy upon hearing the good news of you decision to allow our state to join your country."

"I'm happy as well," Sara told Governor Torcello. Both parties hung up.

Sara called the Whitehouse direct and asked to speak to President Goodwin. The Whitehouse operator referred the call to Whitehouse Chief-of-Staff Robert Mott who in turn told Sara that President Goodwin was in a meeting but would return her call as soon as possible.

Sara thanked the C.O.S. and slowly hung up the phone as she was wondering whether the President was really in a meeting or if it was the usual brush off. "I'll give him the benefit of the doubt," Sara said out loud.

In a little over an hour, Mrs. Bakker informed Sara that President Goodwin was on secure line #2.

"Thank you, Ruth, put him through."

The light started blinking and Sara picked up the phone and said, "Good afternoon, Mr. President."

"Madam President, it's your dime," he answered curtly.

"Mr. President, I'm informing you and your Congress that the Western States of America have voted to allow the state of Alaska to join our country. The purpose of my call is two-fold, Mr. President. The first is to inform you that you're losing the state of Alaska, and the second is to officially warn you and your administration that any military action against Alaska will be considered military action and an act of war against the Western States of America."

"Madam President, you dare to steal away my state of Alaska and then threaten me if I take any action against the secession of one our states? Who the hell are you to tell me what to do about Alaska?" the Washington President said in a high state of anger.

"You can yell and scream all you want, Mr. President, but Alaska is joining our country and we will defend that decision, sir."

President Goodwin mumbled something then slammed down the phone abruptly ending their conversation.

Sara replaced the phone and had to smile. She thought, "Goodwin will go ballistic the more it sinks in that another state has seceded from his union and decided to join the Western States of America." Sara reached for the intercom and asked Ruth to contact Mexican President Lazzara as quickly as possible.

President Lazzara returned Sara's call within minutes.

"Mr. President, thank you for returning my call so quickly," Sara said.

"Madam President, I was actually reaching for the phone when your call came through," the Mexican President admitted.

"Mr. President, I wanted you and your government to be the first foreign country to learn that the state of Alaska has seceded from the Washington union and will be joining the Western States of America as its fifth state. I wanted you personally to be aware of the Alaska situation in case President

Goodwin and his Washington mob start some sort of military action against Alaska and the Western States of America.

"Your country and ours have a special bond, Mr. President, that has developed since your taking office as President of Mexico."

"Thank you, Madam President, I also feel that a strong bond between Mexico and the Western States of America does now exist. I believe your adding the state of Alaska to your country is a good move," the Mexican President added. "As we speak, Sara, I'm looking at a map of the whole fifty states, and I can see another move that would complete you country's position in North America."

"What do you see, Mr. President?" Sara asked.

"You should add the states of Washington and Oregon to your country, then you would control the whole west coast from Canada to our Mexico as well as the entire border with us," the Mexican President quickly added.

"You're very perceptive, Mr. President, we have kicked around that possibility, but both the states in question are almost one hundred percent liberal with very liberal laws that certainly would not fit into our new conservative five state government and country. We even thought about adding Hawaii as well, but they are as liberal as the other two states."

"Madam President, I have one question. Weren't your states of California and Arizona staunch liberal before you were elected President and replaced numerous public officials along with dozens of judges and other liberals with conservative thinking officials?"

"Yes, Mr. President, both California and Arizona have changed from very liberal to very conservative. Less government and less social programs that prop up the segment of our population that feel their government should pay for everything so they're not required to work and support themselves and their families."Everybody is required to work unless they're elderly or disabled. Free passage through life at the expense of the working public is not the way we do business in the Western States of America.

"We don't want anything to do with the old policies of the Obama/Goodwin Whitehouse and their one hundred or so social programs and giveaways administered through dozens of

agencies that created a group of Americans that reached fifty million non-producers.

"If the states of Washington and Oregon are going to join our country, they must repeal numerous laws that are on the books as well as other changes we have suggested. Mr. President, their social liberal policies will eventually bring the Whitehouse government to its knees. It's only a matter of time before their total collapse."

"Madam President, I'd like to thank you for the heads-up on the Alaska state situation," the Mexican President told his American counterpart and friend.

Chapter 10
CIVIL DISORDER

"Now, my American friend, I'd like to help you in a small but very significant way," the Mexican President said slowly. I am informing the Goodwin Whitehouse and the Congress that if any military action is taken against Alaska and or the Western States of America, the country of Mexico will be compelled to declare war against Goodwin's America. Mexico is becoming stable once more since the W.S of A. has controlled the border and assisted Mexico in stamping out the drug cartels that threatened to overrun Mexico and turn it into a lawless drug producing state the enslaves its entire population."

President Lazzara continued, "Also your joint ventures are creating thousands upon thousands of good paying jobs throughout Mexico. Even though you're purging you country of all illegal aliens and returning as many as ten to twelve thousand Mexican nationals each month, these returning people are quickly finding new jobs with the many joint ventures scattered throughout Mexico. Your country is even helping build new housing and other programs that assist our returning citizens.

"As President of Mexico, I do not want my neighboring country that shares a two thousand mile border with Mexico to be attacked by the Washington Whitehouse. That includes the three states in question as well," he added. "My country cannot have another set-back, after decades of drug cartel control over every phase of our social lives. We must take a military stand along with your Western States of America," the Mexican President said in a raised voice.

"I will call President Goodwin within the hour and repeat my promise to you, Madam President. He will be shocked and stunned at Mexican's stand I'm sure, he added."

"Thank you, Mr. President, for your firm stand on our Alaska and the other three state secession and possible admission into our W.S. of A. Mr. President, Washington will go crazy after you call President Goodwin and Congress," Sara added.

"It will be very interesting," President Lazzara answered.

 rickshaw

"Thank you, Madam President, for all your help. I'm going to call the Whitehouse now."

"Goodbye, Mr. President, and good luck with your call to Washington."

After hanging up the phone, President Lazzara asked his Communication Officer to contact the American Whitehouse and President Goodwin as quickly as possible.

Within five minutes the Whitehouse switchboard answered and transferred the call to Chief-of-Staff Robert Mott.

"Good afternoon, Mr. President," the C.O.S. said quickly.

"Mr. Mott, I would like to speak to President Goodwin on a matter of great importance to my country and his."

"I'm sorry, Mr. President, but President Goodwin is currently meeting with some Congressional leaders, but I will inform him of your call, sir."

The Mexican president said, "Thank you," and promptly hung up.

Within twenty minutes, the phone in the Mexican President's office rang, and he slowly picked up the ornate phone and said, "Hello."

"Good afternoon, Mr. President, this is President Goodwin returning your call. Your message to my Chief-of-Staff sounded urgent, sir."

"Yes, it is, Mr. President. After a long and detailed conversation with President Williamson, I'm calling to inform you and your Congress that if you use military action against the Western States of America, Alaska or the three states trying to secede from your collapsing union, my country of Mexico will declare war against your America."

There was a long silence before President Goodwin said, "Mr. President, you must be joking or you have lost your mind," the American President told his Mexican counterpart.

"No, Mr. President, I am in full control of my mind, and an official letter from my government will be delivered to your Whitehouse and your Congress by tomorrow, sir."

"While our military is very small compared to yours, Mr. President, we have over seven hundred and fifty thousand men and women presently under arms with another hundred thousand in reserve. We have a well-equipped Army and Navy and Air Force. As you know, we have the latest F-24 fighter jet and new missiles that have pin point accuracy."

"We would lose a military fight with your armed forces, but believe me, Mr. President, our forces would raise hell with your troops and large cities. Our military, combined with the Western States of America, would certainly be a formidable military force to deal with, Mr. President. This is a warning from a foreign government, be very careful in dealing with those seceding states and W.S. of A."

"You or your country is in no position to dictate orders to me or my country," President Goodwin said in a raised voice.

Without wanting to hear the American President's ranting, President Lazzara quietly hung up the phone.

President Lazzara immediately called General Rōjas and ordered him to place the Mexican armed forces on standby alert.

President Goodwin was hopping mad, he quickly called Mr. Jennings, his National Security Advisor and repeated the phone call he had with Mexican President Lazzara. In turn, Jennings alerted the Chairman of the Joint Chiefs who immediately called a meeting in the Pentagon War Room.

When President Goodwin entered the subterranean War Room he was surpised that only the military chiefs were present along with the National Security Advisor, the Secretary-of-Sate Wilson and the Chief-of-Staff Mott were present. As the President was walking towards his seat at the head of the massive Brazilian table, he stopped and said, "I'm surprised at the very few participants attending this very important meeting."

General Wolford said, "Mr. President, a threat by Mexico hardly warrants a full staff meeting."

"I disagree, General, the threat by President Lazzara is a very serious matter and is most disturbing that a foreign government is siding with the Western States of America and threatening military action when the matter in question is an internal matter between Washington and a group of states wanting to secede from our union."

Secretary-of-Defense Marshal entered the massive War Room and quickly sat at his assigned seat. "Sorry, Mr. President, I was caught in a traffic jam in the famous Washington roundabout and couldn't get out until the capital police come to my rescue."

 rickshaw

"I'm glad you're here, Mr. Secretary. I need your assessment of this new twist by Mexico and the Western States of America."

"Thank you, Mr. President. I think this unusual stand by our southern neighbor Mexico is a far bigger threat than of our military is willing to admit. While our military forces dwarf the Mexican military, they could, in junction with the Western States of America forces, provide a strong military force that could inflict great damage to our forces and major cities. Without going into a host of reasons and speculations, I believe we as a nation should allow these three or four western states to secede and leave the Washington union."

"Mr. President, we must change our liberal thinking and ideas or we will lose many more states. If we lost additional states, this nation will collapse and become a third world country. We need to rescue the remaining states by rescinding the many social laws that have strapped the states and brought them to insolvency."

"Madam Secretary. What is your position on this latest action by Mexico?"

"Simply, Mr. President, I totally agree with the comments by Secretary Marshal. Either we change our overall philosophy and allow the remaining states to control their own destiny or we'll lose the grand country to anarchy and lawlessness."

"Thank you, ladies and gentlemen. I want an emergency meeting with the full Congress before this escalates into a full blown military action."

Secretary-of-State Wilson said she would arrange a meeting with both Houses for tomorrow afternoon.

The War Room meeting broke up and the President headed for the helo pad and the short flight to the Whitehouse.

President Williamson called General Wittingham and told him about the conversation she had with Mexican President Lazzara. The General knew something was adrift because he just received word that the Mexican military was just put on standby alert.

"I was about to call you, Madam President, to inquire just what the hell is going on. I was thinking about raising the alert status to level #2 (blue) alert status."

"General, I think that's a good idea and a safe move under the latest move by Mexico and the unknown action the Washington mob may take."

"Instead of level #2 General, let's go to level #3 (yellow) and test our overall readiness," Sara offered.

"Yes, I agree, Madam President, yellow alert status it is." General Wittingham made the call and alert level #3 was initiated immediately.

The states of Oregon, Washington and Hawaii informed President Williamson that they would repeal any and all laws that the Western States of America deems necessary in order to join the W.S. of A. With that good news and commitment by the seceding states, President Williamson would inform Washington and both Houses of Congress that the Western States of America would be acquiring the states of Oregon, Washington Hawaii and Alaska. With these acquisitions, the total population of W.S. of A. would balloon to seventy-six million five hundred and twenty-one thousand persons. That's about twenty-six percent of the original fifty state population.

With the move, the Western States of America now controls the entire west coast from San Diego, California to Point Barrow, Alaska, with the exception of six hundred miles of coast line in Canada; as well as the entire two thousand mile border with Mexico. As Sara thought about these new acquisitions and expanded geographic boundaries her country now enjoys, she was thinking, "What's next?"

Sara called Mrs. Bakker and asked her to contact Washington and President Goodwin as soon as possible.

In a little over an hour, the call came in from Washington. Chief-of-Staff Mott said President Goodwin would be available shortly. After another five minute wait, Goodwin was on the line with Sara.

"Madam President, I'm sure you're calling in regards to Mexican President Lazzara's unbelievable statement that Mexico will declare war on my country if we interfere with the secession of another four states."

"Yes, Mr. President that is exactly why I'm calling. While I don't like the idea of threatening war, I can understand why the Mexican President does not want the Western States of America dragged into a conflict between the states in question and

Washington. Mexico has made significant advances in the past two years and they don't want anything to cause them to slip back into the drug controlled society that existed then. With my country's help we have stamped out many large drug cartels and helped purge the Mexican government of the corruption that ran rampant for decades. The thousands of drug related murders have dropped to a trickle compared to the drug controlled days in the past. Along with helping to stamp out the drug problem we have entered into ten joint ventures with Mexico that have created tens of thousands of good paying jobs for the average Mexican citizen. And, Mr. President, this is while the W.S. of A. is purging our country of all illegal aliens. Another thing. We are also helping the Mexican government provide adequate housing for the returning nationals while supplying various farm equipment such as tractors, plows, mowers and etc.

"So you can see, Mr. President, the Western States of America and Mexico do not want anything to upset or change the fine relationship that exists between our two countries. You could have had the same relationship with Mexico if your predecessor and yourself were willing to invest in the future of Mexico instead of allowing open borders with millions of illegals slipping across the border into America without knowing who came across, where they were or what they were doing. If you had invested into the Mexican society instead of pouring trillions of American dollars into the many government and state giveaway programs that welcomed the Mexican illegal to flood across the border to receive almost everything free of charge. It was the American tax payer money you were giving away, not Obama's money or yours, Mr. President.

"In closing sir, I must warn you and ask you to be very careful when making your decision on the course of action you'll take with the states in question, my country and Mexico."

With that closing statement, Sara softly replaced the receiver and ended the call to President Goodwin. She pushed her chair back from the desk and thought, "Old Charlie Goodwin will have a barrel full to tell Congress after the call from Mexico and me."

President Goodwin opened the emergency meeting with Congressional leaders and his combined staff by relating the two phone calls from Presidents Lazzara and Williamson. Then he said, "Can you imagine the arrogance of the Mexican President who threatened war against our country if we act militarily against the four seceding states of the Western States of America? President Lazzara's little piss ant country wouldn't last a couple of days in combat with our force," he blurted out.

Before the President could continue, Representative Mark Wilder form Ohio stood up and said, "Mr. President, as Chairman of the Military Appropriations Committee, I must remind you and our military leaders present that in the past five years alone we have equipped Mexico with over five hundred of our latest helicopters and two hundred of our best all weather F-24 supersonic jets, plus other assorted air craft. Also we have provided them with one hundred and fifty of our newest sixty-five ton battle wagon with 120mm cannon that can hit a target traveling at fifty miles per hour from a range of over three miles. This list of arms we have given Mexico are only the ones I remember, Mr. President. I'm sure we have given them various missiles and systems that equal ours, sir."

Representative Wilder slowly sat back down.

Secretary-of-Defense Marshal said, "Mr. President, ladies and gentlemen, I agree with Congressman Wilder's assessment of certain arms given to Mexico and I know about ninety-nine percent of the military hardware given to or purchased by Mexico. Believe me, the list is a mile long and combined with the military power of just the four states of W.S. of A., their combined forces are huge. Between Mexico and the Western States of America they could raise one million men and women with ease. We would win the war, but our country would be reduced to No world status. There would be no winners in that war, Mr. President, and when the dust settled our country would be open for Russia, China or any third world nation to reside within our borders. To prevent untold bloodshed, Mr. President, we must allow these four western states to secede from our so called union. With the exodus of these four states we must change whatever it takes to hold onto the remaining forty-two states. Our liberal ideas of big government and endless social programs must go by way of the do-do. Liberal ideas should be extinct as the do-do bird."

"Thank you, Mr. Secretary."

 rickshaw

"Now, I'd like to hear from our military leaders. General Wolford, I'd like to hear your assessment of the matter at hand."

"Certainly, Mr. President. The Chairman of the Joint Chiefs stood up and asked his aide to put up a very large map of North America with all the states in various colors on a tripod so all could see the huge map clearly."

The General with his eight stars gleaming on his epaulets and another eight stars on his shirt collars was very impressing walking towards the map of North America. The General drew a black line from the eastern border of Washington State, through Oregon, California over to Arizona, New Mexico and Texas. He said, "That is one very large chunk of our original fifty state union that is now the Western States of America."

"We are now basically cut off and isolated completely from the west coast and cut off from Mexico completely. Our nation has been reduced by over twenty-five percent in land mass and population during these recent changes. Militarily, it has been a complete disaster at best with our many bases inside the four original states that seceded from the union. These bases are theoretically still ours, but I'm not so sure, Mr. President. If push comes to shove will they stand fast and be loyal to Washington, or will they join the Western States of America to join the conservative style of government that is less intrusive with very few social giveaway programs that strap the individual states?"

"Mr. President, in my opinion, we have no choice but to allow the four states in question to leave our fractured union and join W.S. of A. Our country, sir, has been reduced and damaged beyond comprehension and I feel it's too late to do anything, especially militarily, Mr. President."

"Some members in this room may disagree with my assessment and recommended military action against these western states and possibly even the Western States of America, but that would be a monumental disaster for all parties. When the dust clears, gentlemen, there would be no winners and both countries along with Mexico would be in massive ruin."

With that final comment, the Four Star General with almost forty years of spotless service to his country, shook his head and returned to his seat.

Chapter 10 - Civil Disorder

"Thank you, General Wolford, that was quite a mouth full. Now I'd like to hear from Air Force Lt. General Allen."

General Allen slowly stood up and said," Mr. President, I don't think you want to hear my overall opinion on this issue during this meeting, sir."

"On the contrary, General, I want your personal views on this very important issue."

"As a high ranking military officer, I'm under the command and direction of elected and non-elected government officials, Mr. President."

"Spill it, General, let's have it with the bark off," the President ordered his Air Force Commanding General.

"Yes, sir."

"Your liberal government has driven this once great country very close to open war with Mexico, the Western States of America and even some states."

"Your liberal democratic government along with millions of liberal judges and officials throughout the country has given trillions of dollars to special interests, illegal aliens and social programs that have created a class of bottom feeders that contribute absolutely nothing to the overall advancement of this national. You are forcing states to leave the Washington union. Mr. President, and if you're not careful sir you're going to lose many more states. Your many social programs are causing trillions of dollars in debt that cannot be repaid. States will be filing bankruptcy and anarchy and lawlessness will follow.

"I believe I have said enough, Mr. President, in fact I'm sure my military career is now over because of my soul searching during this meeting." The Air force Lt. General sat down and looked at the President.

"Not true, General, I'm glad you spoke your mind. Remember, I asked for your comments."

"Well, I don't think we need any more speakers on the subject, the President admitted. I guess the general consensus is, that to stop these additional states from seceding and joining the W.S. of A. is not the prudent course of action. I will invoke a series of Presidential executive orders to repeal a series of laws that have demanded social justice to a wide variety of lower class American citizens as well as illegal aliens.

"My actions tomorrow will put millions of Americans and illegal persons without any government assistance. But this must be done once and for all. There will be a ninety day grace period before the welfare, housing assistance, food stamps, WIC and dozens of other social programs are eliminated for good. The people effected must find work or get help from their families, churches and etc. The welfare country of America will cease to exist after ninety days.

"The tens of thousands of agency workers affected by these executive orders within the federal and state government will have the opportunity to transfer into other agencies or leave government. Along with the executive orders I am ordering the Secretary-of-Defense to put our military and reserve forces on alert to help prevent any civil unrest from developing in our large cities.

"Before I announce the changes on T.V., I will call Mexican President Lazzara and President Williamson and explain two things.

"First: That Washington will not take any military action or any other action against the four states of W.S. of A.

"Second: As of tomorrow, I will issue executive orders that will eliminate most social giveaway programs after ninety days.

"When we place our military and reserve on alert, I don't want either President to get the wrong idea and panic."

"Wait a minute," the President said, standing up. "Maybe I better make my calls to the Presidents right away. You know how leaks have a way of spreading the word before the official announcement."

As the Pentagon meeting was breaking up, President Goodwin was already on the phone calling Mexico first, then the Western States of America President Sara Williamson. His conversation with the Mexican President only lasted five minutes, but the call was received as good news by his southern neighbor. His second call to President Williamson lasted almost fifteen minutes with his assurance that Washington was okay with the secession of the states in question and the acquisition of same by the Western States of America.

Sara told President Goodwin she was happy that Washington had not resorted to any military action that would have brought disaster to all parties. Sara immediately informed her Chief-of-Staff, Buck, who in turn relayed her comments to all four states and the military through Secretary-of-Defense Waterman.

The states of Oregon, Washington and Hawaii have agreed that the Flagstaff Whitehouse would appoint the two Senators from each state once they were admitted into the W.S. of A. Once the Senate seats are filled general elections will be held within the three states in question and Alaska they would be admitted into the Western States of America as the fifth, sixth, seventh and eighth states in thirty days from today.

Sara called Mexican President Lazzara, and they discussed the call from Washington and agreed that the pressure has subsided now that Goodwin has backed off and agreed to allow all four states to secede and join the W.S. of A. Sara said, "One more thing, Mr. President. How much longer will you need Colonel Montgomery?"

"I don't exactly know, Madam President, I'll have to consult with General Rōjas and your Colonel."

"If you can spare him, Mr. President, I need him to take over border security from Washington State to Texarkana and the entire border with Mexico and the whole west coast from San Diego, California to Bellingham, Washington. Our border now extends more than six thousand, four hundred miles long. It's too much for one man, but I want and need him to take the job and head up the yet to be named and manned agency."

"I'll get back to you as soon as I talk to both men," the Mexican President assured his northern counterpart.

"Thank you, Mr. President."

Both parties hung up.

President Lazzara called Army Headquarters in Querétaro and asked General Rōjas and American Full Bird Colonel Montgomery to come to Mexico City in the next day or so.

"Certainly, Mr. President, we'll be at the palace tomorrow afternoon around four o'clock, if that's okay?" General Rōjas asked.

"That's fine, General, see you tomorrow."

The flight from Headquarters at Querétaro to Mexico City was a flight from hell. The weather was terrible, high winds, driving rain and hundreds of lightning strikes and one hit the tail section of the military transport the Mexican General and American Colonel were in. The lightning blew a large section of the horizontal stabilizer off and damaged the vertical stabilizer. The plane was very unstable and the pilot had great difficulty in holding the plane level. With the damaged horizontal stabilizer, the plane couldn't gain elevation and slowly started to lose altitude.

The pilot told General Rōjas the damaged plane could not make the airport at Mexico City and they would have to make an emergency landing very soon.

The co-pilot called out an S.O.S. for any station that could hear them in the electrical storm while the pilot tried to keep the aircraft in the air.

An answer to their emergency call came from a small town just thirty miles north of Mexico City.

"Do you have an airport?" the co-pilot asked quickly.

"Yes, we do, Army Leader One. It's a grass runway that runs for sixteen hundred meters. Usually it's firm and flat but it's been raining for the past three days and there is standing water on the runway. You are cleared to land if you want to chance it, Army Leader One. The runway is north to south, the elevation is thirteen hundred and thirty-three meters with current winds swirling at fifty kilometers per hour with heavy rain and some lightning. We have very few lights on the runway but we'll have them on, Army Leader One."

"Could you have available vehicles shine their lights across the runway?" the co-pilot asked. "Yes, sir, Army Leader One, we'll have all available vehicles lined up and ready to light up the runway. What is your ETA?"

"I'm guessing at ten minutes, max," the pilot answered.

"Ten-four, Army Leader One. Good luck."

After about eight minutes of struggling to keep the army transport in the air the co-pilot spotted the ground lights through the rain and clouds.

"We're going to have only one chance to land this army bird," the pilot informed his passengers, "so tighten your seat belts and prepare for a crash landing on a soggy grass field."

Army Leader One started descending faster than usual, but the pilot could not slow the rate of descent with the damaged tail section. The plane approached the grass runway with its landing gear up so the wheels wouldn't dig into the wet field and flip the aircraft. The plane dropped hard on the wet and muddy runway and skidded sideways for a hundred meters before smashing into a row of parked trucks with their lights on.

When the plane came to a rest, the pilot gave a sigh of relief and quickly opened the emergency exit and the two pilots and their passengers quickly exited the damaged aircraft.

An emergency vehicle picked up the crew and passengers and drove them to the airport tower for medical help, if needed, and to dry off.

President Lazzara was informed that Army Leader One had crashed during a huge electrical storm but received no other details.

After a hot cup of Mexican coffee and a quick chat with Colonel Montgomery, General Rōjas asked if he could use the phone. The Mexican Commanding General called Mexico City and got the President's aide. He gave him all the details of the flight and crash at Zumpango.

The General also praised the flight crew of Army Leader One for keeping the damaged aircraft in the air and maintaining control during a very difficult landing under very adverse conditions.

The President's aide said a vehicle would be dispatched to Zumpango as soon as possible, he assured the General.

"Thank you, Captain. Please tell the President that all parties on the fight are fine. No injuries at all."

"Yes, General, I will tell him."

The General hung up and told Colonel Montgomery that transportation was being arranged for their short trip to the Presidential Palace in Mexico City.

"Good," the American Colonel answered, "I need a bath and some clean, dry clothes."

Within two hours, a staff car and jeep arrived at the Zumpango airport.

General Rōjas and Colonel Montgomery entered the waiting staff car while the two pilots were driven to Mexico City by jeep. Before leaving the airfield, General Rōjas assured the airport director that the damaged aircraft would be removed and the grass runway restored to its original condition.

They arrived at the President's Palace at nine P.M. and were ushered into the President's waiting room without delay. Almost immediately, President Lazzara entered the room followed by his aide, Captain Ortiz. Both officers snapped to attention and saluted smartly.

"Please gentlemen, please be seated. You must be dog tired and shaken form you crash landing north of the city. Thank god both of you were unhurt. That goes for the two pilots as well," he added.

"Thank you, Mr. President, we were very lucky to escape uninjured," Colonel Montgomery admitted.

"Well, gentlemen, the reason I asked you both here was because President Williamson asked me a question I could not answer. She asked if you, Colonel, could be spared from your drug control duties here in Mexico to be assigned other important duties in your country."

"General Rōjas, I need your opinion. Can we afford to have Colonel Montgomery leave this important assignment in drug control?"

"Yes, I believe we can, Mr. President, we now have a pretty good handle on drug enforcement and the general population is helping to I.D. drug lords and pushers. Your cash for info program has been a big help, Mr. President. I feel we currently have the drug industry on the run because the whistle blowers are being paid large cash awards."

"What do you think, Colonel?" the Mexican President asked.

"I agree with the General. We have eliminated the largest of the cartels and are now concentrating on the smaller drug outfits and IDing the pushers and any corrupt officials."

"Well, Mr. President, I knew this day would come. Either we would stop the drug cartels and limit the distribution of drugs to a trickle, or I would be assassinated as an American in your country. With God's help, I have survived the many skirmishes the General and I have led into the jungle hideouts. We both have been extremely lucky, Mr. President."

"When would you turn me loose," the Colonel asked?

"Right away, if that's alright with General Rōjas."

"That's fine with me, Mr. President, the sooner the better. He is affecting my usual perfect Spanish. His American phrases are creeping into my flawless Spanish and my officers and troops are looking at me in wonderment."

The four men laughed.

"Let's drink to our American Colonel's departure," the President suggested.

The President's aide quickly left the room and returned in no time with a tray, four glasses and a bottle of American whiskey. The Captain filled the four glasses and the President said, "I salute you, my American friend." The four shot glasses were quickly emptied and refilled again.

General Rōjas said, raising his glass, "Without your military prowess, direction and expertise in all phases of combat, we couldn't have made the gains in drug control that we accomplished."

"Here-here!" the other three men shouted as they gulped down the American whiskey.

"Thank you, my very best friends. I will keep in contact and always remember the first class treatment you afforded me. This may be a foreign country, but it is certainly considered my second home. The Mexican people are great and I will always remember this tour as the highlight of my military career."

President Lazzara shook the Colonel's hand vigorously and the General gave his friend a big strong hug.

"Do you want to leave for the states from Mexico City or from Army Headquarters in Querétaro?", the President asked.

"I would like to leave from Querétaro, if that's okay with you, Mr. President. I should say goodbye to our troops rather than just slip away."

"Certainly, Colonel. Goodbye, and God bless," the President said, giving the American Colonel a smart salute.

"Thank you, Mr. President."

Both officers left the Palace and headed for the airport, if they could find it through the thick environmental fog that engulfed the entire city.

President Lazzara called the Flagstaff Whitehouse and informed President Williamson that Colonel Montgomery would be in Flagstaff within the next few days.

"Thank you, Mr. President."

"No, Madam President. Thank you for sending my country an American officer of the highest standard and

integrity. He is certainly one of a kind, I might add. I'm in your debt, Sara, and I mean it, my friend."

"Thanks again," the Mexican leader said as he hung up the phone.

Both officers arrived at Army Headquarters around midnight and quickly showered and hit the sack. They were up at 06:00 and headed for the officers' mess to enjoy a very hardy breakfast. General Rōjas suggested they have a company formation at 09:00.

"Sounds good to me, sir."

The General asked the Company Commander to form up the entire company at the agreed time for a goodbye speech by Colonel Montgomery.

At 09:00 sharp the entire Special Ops Company was standing at parade rest for the American Colonel to arrive. One minute later, the tall American Full Bird Colonel stepped up on the raised platform and said, "Attention," very loud in Spanish. The company snapped to attention in unison.

"At ease," the Colonel yelled.

"As you already know, I'm leaving the Headquarters and our Spl. Ops Company to take another military assignment somewhere in the Western States of America. I have enjoyed working with you to stamp out the drug cartels here in Mexico and its distribution worldwide. You're a great bunch of dedicated soldiers and I have trusted all of you with my life many times during the past year. Your officers and Commanding General Rōjas have no fear in leading you fine people into battle. If in the future another battle presents itself, I want you people by my side."

"Goodbye, my friends."

Sergeant Maria Ortiz (Butch) broke ranks, hopped up on the raised platform and jumped up spreading her legs and wrapping them around the Colonel's waist and planted a long and hard kiss on his lips. The Colonel could feel the warmth from Butch's very large breasts pressing against his chest. Butch was only five feet tall with thick soled combat boots on, but had huge tits for such a small gal.

She released her hold on the surprised Colonel, dropped to the platform, looked up at the tall Colonel, and smiled as she saluted, then turned and returned to her position within the company formation.

"Wow!" The Colonel said in a loud voice, "Now that is my kind of soldier."

The whole Spl. Ops Company started clapping and yelling their approval of their only female soldier.

The Colonel waved as he left the formation and headed for the H. Q. Building. General Rōjas said, "President Lazzara has sent his personal jet to fly you to Flagstaff."

The American Colonel saluted his Commanding Officer and said goodbye to his friend and headed for the flight line and the waiting new Jet Star "World Traveler" – JS-12 and his flight home.

During s session of Congress, President Goodwin entered the Chamber and asked if he could speak to the assembled members of Congress. The Speaker of the House said, "Certainly, Mr. President." The speaker approached the podium, pounded his one hundred year old gavel and said, "Ladies and gentlemen, the President of the United States."

President Goodwin said, "Thank you, Mr. Speaker, but I'm not sure the word United should be used. I have asked for this time to speak on behalf of liberalism. I understand you're not happy with my executive order to end welfare and other federal and state giveaway programs."

A voice form the Chamber yelled, "You're going to kill a lot of Americans with your executive order, Mr. President."

The Speaker stepped in front of the President and pounded his gavel saying, "No more outbursts, please. This is the President, show respect."

The President continued. "If we don't change our socialistic ideals and make Americans responsible for themselves and their families, this country if doomed."

"With our very liberal ideas comes our liberal judges, liberal courts, liberal government and state officials and a very liberal Supreme Court. There is too much government, too many taxes and too many criminals being let off with only a slap on the wrist. Nobody is held responsible for anything they do. Our justice system is in shambles and the laws on the books are not being enforced. We have no death penalty and killers are given only five to seven years in jail and are out on the street in only four with good behavior.

"We're becoming too passive, too liberal and too wishy-washy on everything. We have no backbone anymore and are known throughout the world as a do nothing country and a soft touch for every Muslim group that wants to take over a country. We always seem to back the wrong side. Foreign governments can kill our soldiers and diplomats and we basically do nothing. We talk up a storm and rattle our swords but in the end do absolutely nothing to settle the score.

"So far, eight of our states have seceded from our union because of our liberalism and the social programs that are producing trillions of dollars in federal and state debt. Our debt will continue to rise unless we change our philosophy right now. I have started by stopping the welfare giveaway program that will save this government some six hundred billion dollars per year. We must clamp down on our spending and that also means the foreign gifts that have cost our tax payers trillions of hard earned dollars throughout the years, and long term commitments will cost another trillion unless we cut the money cord here and now.

"As your President, I must warn you that any further secession by states will bring this Washington union to its knees, and open this country to foreign intervention and control. I'm not saying we must change to conservatism, but we must temper our liberal ideas a great deal.

"We must offer our remaining states solutions to their many problems that we have caused. Action on your part is the only solution.

"If we lose another state because of inaction, because of a do nothing Congress, I will resign as your President."

The Congressional Chamber erupted into a noise level that was deafening.

The Speaker of the House pounded his gavel for a full minute before the House regained order.

President Goodwin continued, "As your President, I cannot allow this great country to be pounded into the ground by law makers who don't care anything about the American people and only care about their survival and the power of their office. We must start by cutting taxes and allowing the individual states to control their own destiny. There will be no more bailouts, if you fail then you fail, no such thing as 'too big to fail.'

"Thank you, ladies and gentlemen, for this opportunity to speak to this assembled Congress. I'll be waiting for your suggestions and they must be coming quickly or I'll have more executive orders of my own." The President left the podium and headed for the Whitehouse. Only a few Congress members clapped as the Chief Executive left the chambers.

Colonel Montgomery arrived in Flagstaff and was greeted by Chief-of-Staff McCarney (Buck) who drove the returning Colonel the few miles to the Flagstaff Whitehouse and a meeting with President Williamson. The Chief-of-Staff escorted the Colonel to the President's office, opened the door and motioned the Colonel to enter and shut the door behind him.

President Williamson walked over and said, "Colonel, I'm so glad to see you safe and sound," while shaking his hand.

"Thank you, Madam President, it's good to be home. I liked my assignment in Mexico but it's always nice to come home."

"President Lazzara thinks you are a national hero. He can't say enough good things about you, Colonel."

"That's nice to hear, but General Rōjas and his troops did most of the work and took most of the risk, Madam President."

"Well, I'm glad you're home, Colonel. Now I suppose you're wondering why I asked President Lazzara if he could turn you loose."

"Yes, ma'am, I am."

"Please be seated, Colonel. Sara pointed to the large brown chair."

"After a month's leave, I would like you to form up and head an agency that is responsible for our border security. That involves over six thousand four hundred miles of border, Colonel." Sara continued, "Why don't you take your well-deserved leave and decide whether you want to assume this huge responsibility as Security Chief of our lengthy borders."

"Madam President, I don't need thirty days to decide. I would be honored to form a new government agency for the protection of our vast borders."

"Thank you, Colonel. I was hoping you would take this very difficult assignment. I want this new agency to be run by a

high ranking Army officer with impeccable credentials," she quickly added. "Your new rank will be Major General, I'm happy to say," President Williamson told the astonished new General.

"Normally, I'd have the Secretary-of-Defense present you with these new stars, but your agency and yourself will report only to this office. You only have one boss and that's me, General." With that, the Commander-in-Chief handed the ex-colonel four pair of Major Stars.

General Montgomery took the stars and said, "Ma'am I don't know what to say," he muttered.

"You don't have to say anything, General, your accepting this new assignment is thanks enough."

"This requires a salute, Madam President." The Army's newest General stepped back and gave his Commander-in-Chief a very smart salute.

President Williamson returned the salute.

After being congratulated a hundred times by Sara's staff, General Montgomery left the Flagstaff Whitehouse, headed for the airport and a flight to San Francisco and a month of R. & R.

The continuous drain of qualified workers in aviation, automotive, electronics, specialized manufacturing, medical, science research and dozens of other vocations are creating extreme shortages within the labor market in the forty-two states. The labor force is migrating to the Western States of America where federal and state taxes are low and opportunities are endless.

President Goodwin has appealed to Sara for strict entry policies to prevent the labor drain that is becoming critical.

Sara agreed to look into the massive exodus from the mid-west states of Colorado, Wyoming, Montana and both Dakotas. She is very fearful that other states will want to secede and join the expanding W.S. of A.

Sara called a quick meeting with her small staff and relayed the request from President Goodwin on the brain drain from his western states.

Chief-of-Staff (Buck) told the group that the Washington President was correct. "A steady stream of professional and non-professional people were leaving his fractured union by the thousands every day. I would recommend Madam President that we do nothing to stop this influx of needed vocations. I wouldn't restrict the entry of any person who wants to become a citizen of our country."

"Thank you, Buck. Who is next?"

Secretary-of-State Anderson spoke up and said, "I agree with Buck, but I feel we should put some limits on the total number of persons allowed to enter our country. If we continue to allow these professionals and anyone else to migrate into our country, I'm afraid that many more states will demand secession from Washington and want to join our country. If that presents itself, Madam President, then our problems with those states and Washington will be critical. Military action could be realized, I'm afraid," the Secretary admitted.

Secretary-of-Defense Waterman said, "Madam President."

"Yes, Mr. Secretary. Go ahead, sir."

"I agree mostly with Buck, let anyone from the forty-two states who has skills be allowed to enter our country and become citizens after a period of residency. Let's be very clear, we don't want the old crowd of welfare recipients. We want and need hard working individuals who will work and help our country prosper and grow."

"Thank you, Mr. Secretary."

"Anyone else?" the President asked.

"Yes, Madam President, I'd like to make a short statement," the Secretary-of-the-Treasury asked.

"Certainly, Bill, go ahead."

"I basically disagree with all comments given thus far," the Secretary told the surprised group. "I think our vast borders should be closed and sealed tight as a drum. We don't need another ten to fifteen million additional people to reside in our new country. If we allow our country to continue to expand and accept any states that want to secede from Washington, we will become a large nation with millions of liberal voters that could spell disaster for our conservative government and the country. Our country should be closed to accepting any more states, Madam President."

"Thank you, Mr. Secretary. I must admit I'm surprised at your comments," the President added.

"Well, ma'am, that's how I feel," the Secretary admitted.

 rickshaw

"If there are no further comments, let's end this session," the President suggested. "I believe I've heard enough to make a decision about the brain drain the Washington group is complaining about," Sara told the group.

"All day long, the Washington Whitehouse has been inundated with requests for federal assistance to help the states national guard and reserve forces to control the civilian unrest that has developed in many states. So far, ten states have experienced civil unrest and state officials have called repeatedly to Washington for help.

"After receiving a hundred calls, the President called an emergency meeting at the Whitehouse with National Security Advisor Jennings, the military Joint Chiefs along with the Secretaries of Defense and State. President Goodwin opened the meeting by saying, "If this civil unrest continues to spread to other states, the chance of a nationwide riot is a very strong possibility. We must stop the civil disobedience at once, or we'll have a full blown civil war on our hands," the President admitted. "If a civil war erupts, gentlemen, this country will be finished. Lawlessness will rule the land," he added.

"How many states are experiencing civil unrest?" General Wolford, Chairman of the Joint Chiefs asked.

"Currently, there are ten, General. Here is the list. Illinois, Indiana, Ohio, New York, New Jersey, Mississippi, Alabama, Georgia, Louisiana and Virginia. These states and some others have very large populations of uneducated citizens, Blacks and Hispanics who were on welfare and other federal and state assistance programs. I've been told the Black population that was on welfare are the main ones rioting and destroying property in the major cities. These wanton acts of violence must be stopped at once. No matter what, this government will not continue to support large numbers of Blacks and Hispanics. And that includes a substantial number of White bottom feeders as well," the President added.

"As Secretary of Defense, I am authorizing you, sir, to call up and deploy as many federal troops and reserve units necessary to stop this uprising and prevent it's spreading throughout the country. Have your commanders set up road blocks and shoot looters if necessary to stop these acts of violence."

"We should invoke Martial Law, Mr. President, so we can put certain restrictions on the civilian population such as curfews and travel restrictions. Also, imprisonment without bail and other restrictions that would normally hamper our forces. I would also suggest, Mr. President, that the Martial Law be imposed throughout the whole country, because I'm sure additional states will be added to your current list," the National Security Chief advised.

"Yes, I think you're right. I'll go on nationwide T.V. and invoke a countrywide Martial Law restriction." The President turned to his Chief-of-Staff Mott and asked him to contact all the major T.V. and radio networks and ask for fifteen minutes worth of air time within the next hour. "Please ask first, Robert, then if they refuse, demand the time."

"Yes, sir. Right away."

"Gentlemen, I want a very strong show of force in these affected cities. We must pull out all stops to prevent this tide of destruction and mayhem from continuing and spreading to other states," the President warned the group.

An aide to the Secretary-of-State gave her a folded piece of paper and Maggie unfolded the note and quickly read its contents. The Secretary stood up and said, "Mr. President, the District of Columbia is experiencing acts of violence throughout the entire district. The note says the Capitol Police cannot handle the large number of people demonstrating and marching on the Capitol."

"Thank you, Maggie. That's very disturbing news, to say the least," the President said, shaking his head.

President Goodwin pointed to Defense Secretary Marshal and said, "Mr. Secretary, I want federal troops to surround the Whitehouse and other federal buildings throughout the Capitol District. Use heavy armor and anything else you feel necessary to quell this uprising."

The Defense Secretary and Chairman Wolford were immediately on the phone barking orders in specific code word and phrases.

Every phone on the long table started blinking their red lights, but no one picked up their phones because of the President and the orders he issued to the Defense Secretary Marshal.

 rickshaw

Chief-of-Staff Mott reentered the Whitehouse War Room and told the President, "All the networks have granted you as much time for your speech as you need, sir. They just wanted to know when, Mr. President."

"Call them back and tell them within the next fifteen minutes," the President said in a raised voice.

"Yes, sir."

The T.V. camera and radio mikes were set up in record time and the President was sitting in the Oval Office behind his famous desk waiting for the network director to give him the go signal.

The camera lights came on and the director said, "Mr. President, 5-4-3-2-you're on, sir."

"Ladies and gentlemen. I have asked for this T.V. and radio time to discuss this civil disobedience that is happening in many states and here in the Capitol District. Your government will not stand for these civil uprisings and senseless destruction of government, state and private property.

"As of now I am invoking Martial Law throughout the entire country. The various restrictions for curfews and travel will be printed across your screen when I finish.

"I have ordered our armed forces to take whatever measures are necessary to halt these acts of violence, which includes shooting looters. Anybody caught looting will be considered an enemy of the state and will be shot. No rounding the looters up and throwing them in jail, just an on the spot death sentence. I don't know just why these people are rioting, but I'll guess it's because I have stopped the welfare system and a dozen other federal and state giveaway programs. Let me be very clear, the bottom feeders that for decades ate at the government trough will have to straighten up, find work and be responsible citizens and pay taxes like everybody else. I don't want to hear 'my children will starve,' they are your children, you had them and now you take care of them. It's your responsibility.

"In the Western States of America, President Williamson's government has no federal or state welfare type giveaways. We will follow her lead and do the same. If someone is injured or has critical health issues and can't work, they will be covered and aided by the Social Security System.

Chapter 10 – Civil Disorder

"While Martial Law is in effect, harsh punishment will be dished out to all violators. Long sentences will be given to law breakers with no intervention by slick liberal lawyers. Quick court decisions and long term jail sentences.

"As your elected President, I will not allow this country to succumb to anarchy and lawlessness. Federal troops along with National Guard and Reserve forces will be putting an end to this civil unrest.

"While my administration is doing away with the many giveaways, we are currently looking into cutting federal taxes, reducing gas prices and filing tax returns on a 3"x5" card. About eighty-five percent of our citizens will be able to file the card method. Along with these changes, we're looking into other things to make our citizenry freer to follow their dreams and goals. It may sound like we're throwing away our liberal ideas, and in some ways we are. We're not going to turn over and become conservatives, but somewhere in between.

"I'm asking for calm during this period of civil unrest. Your government will use all necessary force to stop this civil disturbance. Thank you, ladies and gentlemen. Please stay in your homes and obey the local and federal authorities."

"Cut," the T.V. director said, waving his arms. The cameras went blank and the hot lights went out. "Are you alright, Mr. President?" the director asked.

"Yes, I'm okay, but those camera lights were so hot I think I got a sunburn," the President told the T.V. crew.

"They certainly are hot, Mr. President, you could really work up a sweat if exposed for a long period."

Once the T.V. crews had gathered up their equipment and exited the Oval Office, the President and his Chief-of-Staff along with his Full Bird aide headed for the basement War Room. Once inside the huge room he asked his military aide to contact the Defense Secretary as well as the Chairman of the Joint Chiefs. "I want a minute by minute update on the deployment of federal troops in the major cities."

Within ten minutes, both the Defense Secretary and General Wolford were on a secure line filling their Commander-in-Chief in on the deployment of federal troops. The Secretary said that full deployment to the cities with riots would take the better part of a day.

"Twenty-four hours is not good enough," the President yelled into the phone. "You get those troops into position within the next few hours," the President demanded. "Hundreds of lives depends on the swiftness of our deployment," he added.

"We'll do the best we can, Mr. President, this is a huge undertaking to position troops in so many places at once," the General admitted.

As the President was on the phone, additional states were asking for federal assistance to stop the tide of protesters moving through the large cities smashing windows, burning cars and buses. Shots are being heard throughout the inner cities and many deaths are being reported.

After hearing the very disturbing news coming from Washington and other states, President Williamson called an emergency meeting to be held in the newly completed military complex called the Wagon Wheel. Sara arrived at the complex and took the elevator down to the subterranean War Room. As she entered the War Room she was greeted by the Secretaries of Defense and State as well as various military leaders, their aides and Chief-of-Staff McCarney.

The War Room was constructed almost three hundred feet below a nearby mountain peak that rises over twelve thousand feet just north of the capitol.

As Sara walked towards her seat at the head of the forty foot table, all members stood up and started to clap loudly in approval of their first woman President.

Sara was taken aback by this gesture and a little embarrassed as she sat down in the President's chair.

"Thank you, ladies and gentlemen, I appreciate that. This is the first time I have sat in this War Room under unstable and critical circumstances," she said with a sigh. "I was hoping this room would collect dust and not be used, but I was obviously very wrong," she admitted.

"The first order of business is to raise our level of readiness. I think we should go "Blue" (level 2) alert status," the President thought.

"No, ma'am I disagree." Commanding General Wittingham stood up and said, "Under the current conditions, Madam President, I feel we should jump immediately to Yellow (level #3) elevated status."

Chapter 10 – Civil Disorder

"Please explain," Sara asked.

"We have over one hundred Air Force, Army and Marine bases with our country that are not ours. And that doesn't count the various firing and missile ranges and storage facilities. Within the past few hours these bases and camps have sprung to life and are moving men and material from our country to various parts within the forty-two states. As a military Commander with almost forty years of military service, I do not like the idea of foreign troops stationed on bases that are not ours inside our country, Madam President. Over one hundred thousand military personnel are stationed throughout our country that belong to Washington. This is very dangerous to our national security and the very existence of our nation, Madam President. And now that rioting and civil unrest is griping Washington and a large number of their states, my concerns for our country is growing," the Three Star General admitted.

"You're right, General, raise our alert status to Yellow immediately," the President ordered.

"Yes, ma'am."

General Wittingham got the okay nod from the Defense Secretary and placed the call to elevate the alert status to all forces in the country.

"I believe we should also close our borders with the states to the east," the President suggested.

"I agree," the Secretary-of-State admitted, "but as General Wittingham notes, what about their forces within our borders, Madam President?"

"I'll call President Goodwin right away and tell him his military personnel can assemble their equipment and leave their bases for positions within you forty-two states, but our borders will be closed to civilian traffic."

General Wittingham stood up again and said, "One more thing, Madam President, before you call President Goodwin. Not only should we close our borders because there may be a surge of persons wanting to escape the escalating civil unrest, but I would recommend that we move some of our forces to our border crossings with the Washington states."

"I agree, General, make it happen," the President ordered.

"Yes, ma'am."

"Let's end the meeting for now, but please keep me in contact with Buck in case we need to reconvene at a moment's notice."

The War Room emptied quickly, but Sara asked Vice President Richardson to stay behind while she placed a call to President Goodwin. Sara called Mrs. Bakker and asked her to contact President Goodwin without delay.

While waiting for her call, she said, "Eric, we could be in for a fight before this unrest is over. We must not let it spill over our borders and involve our citizens."

The red phone rang, and Sara quickly picked it up and said, "President Williamson."

"This is President Goodwin, what do you want, Madam President, I'm very busy with the rioting that is spreading, I might add."

"I'll be brief, Mr. President. Your military bases within my country are being put on high alert and transporting men and material eastward to help in riot control I'm guessing."

"Once your administration has regained control of your country, I want discussions with you and your Congress on how and when these hundred plus military bases within my country can be closed, moved or turned over to Western States of America's control. We cannot allow foreign troops to be based within our country, Mr. President. We have come to the conclusion, sir, that we don't want anything to do with your Whitehouse and country. The sooner we break all ties with you, the better my country will be. Am I making myself clear, Mr. President?" she asked.

"Perfectly clear, Madam President," he quickly answered. "But what you're asking, or demanding, Madam President, is impossible, I'm afraid. We will maintain those hundred plus bases whether you like it or not," he added.

"If you're looking for a war, Mr. President, you might have bitten off more than you can chew," Sara warned him. "With your civil unrest expanding, deteriorating relations with the Western States of America and the threat of war from Mexico, your future doesn't look very bright, Mr. President."

Without another word the Washington President hung up abruptly.

Chapter 10 – Civil Disorder

Sara replaced the phone slowly and said, "He is highly pissed," she told V.P. Richardson. "I have just added to his many problems," Sara admitted.

"His bases within our country are going to be a real problem and a hard nut to crack without escalating into a military conflict," Sara added.

Sara picked up the phone and asked Mrs. Bakker to contact General Wittingham at the Wagon Wheel and ask him to join her and Vice President Richardson as soon as possible.

The General knocked and entered the equivalent of the Oval Office and was motioned to a leather chair by the President. "Thank you, General, for coming right over. Before the ranking General Officer could answer, the President continued. She related her short conversation with President Goodwin and added her concerns that a civil war could breakout at any time and if that happened, the possibility of foreign intervention would be greatly increased.

"General, we must decide on our position and course of action in dealing with the one hundred plus military installations which includes some huge Army bases like Fort Ord, Fort Bliss, Fort Hood, Camp Pendleton and a long list of other Army, Navy, Marine and Air Force bases that are scattered throughout our country. The size of the air bases alone is troubling," Sara added. "General, we have few options as I see it. We can surround the large bases and demand they surrender and join our forces, and if they refuse we'll attack and take the base by force."

"Madam President."

"Yes, General. You have something to add?" President Williamson asked.

"Yes, ma'am, I do."

"For starters, Madam President, we cannot surround the large Army bases scattered throughout our country. They are huge and in some cases cover hundreds of square miles and are manned by thousands of well-armed troops. Surrounding these bases is not an option, in my opinion, Madam President."

"I agree with the General, Madam President, the manpower required to surround these huge bases is far greater than the military force we currently have," Vice President Richardson added.

 rickshaw

"You're right, gentlemen," the President admitted. "If we can't possibly surround these large bases we must somehow convince them to leave the Goodwin government and join our country. What if they refuse?" she added.

"We offer them safe passage to President Goodwin's states or risk an all-out war with the Western States of America," the General answered.

"Madam President. The whole military sees the handwriting on the wall and they don't like what they see. Every man and woman can see their government slipping towards the abyss and they are helpless to stop it. The bulk of the military are caught between loyalty to their government and wanting to do the right thing when they know the Washington leaders are dead wrong and steering the nation towards self-destruction. The military may be looking for a way out, Madam President, and maybe we can bridge that gap," the General offered.

"General, would you and your staff develop a plan to present to the military leaders of the large bases, a straight talking and crystal clear proposal without ambiguity? At the same time develop a secondary plan of attack in case they stay and fight."

"Yes, ma'am, we'll have the proposal sometime tomorrow for your review, and we already have a plan of attack in case these bases stay with the Goodwin Whitehouse. We now have the ability to fire our artillery and have the rounds guided to their target with pin point accuracy under satellite control. Our artillery pieces can fire up to twenty miles and one satellite can handle up to fifty rounds a minute with unbelievable accuracy. You add our long range artillery plus our Air Force, Madam President, and you have a very strong attack force," the General said with confidence.

"One more thing. We have almost four thousand artillery pieces in position around the largest military bases and some weapon depots. The spy in the sky can detect troop concentrations and material buildup such as tanks, airplanes and other motorized vehicles. I'm told that each gun site has a stock pile of five hundred rounds and additional shells can be supplied within two hours or less.

"My staff anticipated six months ago that in the future we might have to attack these military installations inside our country if the shit hit the fan in Washington. Madam President, our ordnance and weapons development units have come up with a few new artillery rounds that can level a small city block and weapons dropped by air that will kill every living soul for a radius of half a mile. We may be a small country with a small military, Madam President, but we have a very modern and well developed arsenal of weapons."

"Well, General, that is comforting to know and I certainly hope we don't have to flex our military muscle, but we must in some manner convince their military within our borders to either leave, or join us. If our efforts fail and war breaks out between Washington and the Western States of America, we will surely lose in the end. We can last a few rounds, but when the fight is over we will lose everything. All our work and effort to create this wonderful country would come crashing down and be lost forever. We cannot allow our citizens to be put through the rigors of war when we have worked so hard to bring to this world a country that can provide unlimited opportunities and national safety for all," the President concluded.

"Well put, Madam President. I will do my best to convince our military friends to join the newest and best conservative government on earth," General Wittingham told their first President and her Vice President Richardson.

"Before you leave, General, for the Wagon Wheel, I want to give President Goodwin a better offer and a temporary solution to our problem here at home." Sara asked Mrs. Bakker to contact Washington again and ask for President Goodwin.

To Sara's surprise, the Washington President called back in short order. The light stated blinking and Sara quickly picked up the secure phone and said, "Thank you, Mr. President, for returning my second call."

"Madam President, I can't keep answering your many calls."

Before he could continue, Sara said, "Mr. President, I have another solution to the problem of your military facilities within my country. Like I said earlier, I want all your military bases removed from my country. But with the current conditions in your country, I have a modified solution I believe you'll like, sir."

"Please, be brief," he asked.

"You have some one hundred and ten bases of various sizes within our country and I still want them removed or abandoned. But I am proposing a two-fold solution, Mr. President. First I would require that a large number of your small bases, posts and depots be closed within the next six months, and all large military facilities be closed and abandoned within the next ten years. If you agree with this proposal, our relationship with you administration and Washington will jump a hundred fold, Mr. President."

There was a long pause, almost a minute went by before President Goodwin answered.

"Your proposal is very interesting, Madam President, but I must confer with my military leaders and my staff before I can give you an answer. I do like the idea at first glance," he said. "You'll have my answer within a few days, Madam President."

"Only a couple more things, Mr. President. Presently you are paying my government almost a half-trillion dollars per year for the use of these bases within my country. That huge sum of money could be used to close and relocate these military facilities to new locations of your choice. You could upgrade, consolidate and make more effective use of these facilities within your own country.

"And the last thing Mr. President, during your civil unrest all our borders with your country will be closed. Your military personnel from the bases inside my country can leave to assist in your problem, but your civilian population will be barred from entering the Western States of America. Also, remember President Lazzara has the better part of one million troops positioned along our border in case the Western States of America is attacked by your forces, Mr. President."

"Thank you, Madam President, for your offer, advice and warning," the President answered in an agitated voice.

Without another word both Chief Executives hung up.

Sara turned in her chair and said, "Well, gentlemen, what did you think of my offer to Washington?"

"I like it, Madam President, that would give us time to plan effectively and monitor the closing of numerous small camps, bases and depots," the Vice President added.

"Your comments, General."

Chapter 10 – Civil Disorder

"I like the basic idea, ma'am. Now we won't need to send scads of messages to every facility with few options and the threat of war the General answered." He continued, "I would guess that many small bases will be gutted because they're needed somewhere within the forty-two states to enforce nationwide Martial Law. With their personnel and equipment gone, the base closing could be speeded up when the present crisis is over. There will be benefits to this solution of yours," the General said rubbing his chin in thought.

"Not too fast, gentlemen, we must wait for his answer," the President cautioned.

General Wittingham got up from his chair and went to the large window overlooking the enclosed garden and said, in a low voice, "Madam President, he will jump at this delaying offer by our government. He will lose bases here and there and have years to plan his military strategy which may not be to our nation's benefit. Who knows what the next administration might do during the next ten years. Giving them that much time may not have been the best course of action, Madam President."

"Thank you, Charles, I always value your comments and insight on our military and governmental problems."

General Wittingham nodded his head in recognition. "Madam President, the reports coming in from the east are not good, riots have broken out in all but a couple of states. The loss of life is climbing by the hour and property damage within the large cities is reaching into the billions of dollars. Army units are having difficulty controlling the increasing number of rioters. Ninety percent of the rioters are Black and illegal aliens I've been told. The end of their welfare and other government handouts is sparking the unrest. Even people with jobs are rioting because they're still paying the bills to support the millions of individuals who don't work and don't pay any federal and even some state taxes."

"Gentlemen, we must keep a watchful eye on the raising civil unrest to our east," Sara warned. "We must make sure our eastern borders are sealed tight as a drum, we don't want that flood of individuals trying to escape the Goodwin Whitehouse."

"Madam President, I think we should move more of our forces to our eastern borders to insure the safety of our citizens

and show some military might as well," General Wittingham suggested.

"I agree, General, but I'd like to suggest a real kicker to the situation. Let's add some Mexican troops to our forces along the Texas border with Louisiana, Arkansas and Oklahoma. It would send a strong message to the Washington military that we're not alone in defending our borders. President Lazzara has offered Mexican troops to support our military, if needed. I think we should accept his very generous offer to have his forces join our military in defense of our borders."

"That is a real twist, Madam President. If we combine the two forces, will the Mexican troops be under our orders?" the General asked.

"Yes, but with conditions," Sara answered. "We'll breakup the border with the three states into sections controlled by one of our officers and his Mexican counterpart. These two officers will share the overall responsibility for that sector, but if push comes to shove, the Western States of America officer will have the last word."

"Madam President, the Mexicans assigned to border duty are already within ten miles or less from the Rio Grande. Before we allow them to cross the Rio Grande we should have our forces already positioned along the entire Texas border with the three states. We should also have the section drawn out and mapped so there is no confusion as to who is in charge of what sector of the border."

"That's fine, General, do what you think is best. Okay, gentlemen, let's end this meeting, and I'll call President Lazzara and fill him in on our proposals." Sara quickly put in a call for the Mexican President.

Pedro Lazzara returned her call within the hour and after hearing all the details, approved the overall plan that included two divisions of Mexican troops that will be spread along the Texas border with the connecting states. "The Mexican forces will stay in Mexico until all General Wittingham's troops are in position and ready to accept the Mexican forces. Sara and General Wittingham estimate they'll be ready and in position within the next two or three days."

For the next two days thousands of troops started moving through Texas to their assigned sectors along the border.

Chapter 10 – Civil Disorder

On the third day of the troop movement, President Williamson called her friend, Mexican President Lazzara, and informed him that her troops were in position and ready to accept the thirty thousand Mexican forces authorized by his government.

The Mexican President informed Sara that General Rōjas would command the two divisions assigned to the Texas border. "Who will be your commander?" Pedro asked

"We haven't made a final decision yet, but I'll appoint someone by tomorrow," she promised.

"May I make a suggestion, Madam President?"

"Certainly, Mr. President."

"If possible, Madam President, I would like Colonel Montgomery put in charge of defending your Texas border. Your Colonel Montgomery and General Rōjas have worked together through many combat situations in dealing with the drug cartels here in Mexico.

"These two fine officers are a winning combination and will stop any military force from entering Texas."

"I will consider your request, Mr. President, and get back to you shortly," Sara promised.

Both Presidents said goodbye.

Sara called Buck and asked him to contact Maj. General Montgomery and ask him to come to Flagstaff as soon as possible.

General Montgomery had just finished his thirty day leave in California and was about to start his new job as head of National Security when he received the call from Sara's Chief-of-Staff. After Buck had relayed the message from President Williamson, Michael hung up and thought, "what the hell happened?"

The Major General arrived in Flagstaff the next day and was greeted by Buck who drove them directly to the Flagstaff Whitehouse and a meeting with President Williamson.

Sara met with the newest General at the door and before he could even salute, she grabbed his arm and ushered him to the nearest chair.

"Thank you for coming right away," she said with a smile.

"You're the President, ma'am, and when you request my presence here in Flagstaff, I come as fast as possible," he answered.

"Well, I appreciate your speed in coming," she responded.

"Now for the reason I have asked you here today. As you know we are moving troops to our eastern and southern borders with the adjoining Goodwin states. Along with our military, we are adding two divisions of Mexican troops along the Texas border with Louisiana, Arkansas and Oklahoma. The spreading lawlessness is now engulfing every one of the forty-two states. The Whitehouse military is having a tough time trying to control the national uprising. President Goodwin is even bringing back some of his troops from foreign countries to bolster his ZI forces."

President Williamson continued, "As you know, Michael, hundreds of American civilians have died during this uprising and the amount of dollars lost in this wanton destruction is staggering. Whole city blocks are burned to the ground and gunman shooting at anybody and anything that moves.

Michael, we don't want this rioting to spill over into our country. We think Texas is in the greatest danger from citizens in the border states trying to escape the carnage. We must not allow these people to enter our country at all cost," Sara insisted.

"Now, getting back to why I have asked you here."

"When President Lazzara offered his troops to join our forces, he appointed General Rōjas to command the two full Mexican divisions assigned to guard our Texas border. He also suggested that you be put in command of our forces guarding the entire Texas border with Louisiana, Arkansas and Oklahoma. With the thirty thousand Mexican troops and our forces, we'll have over seventy thousand men and women guarding our frontier. The Mexican President said you and General Rōjas have worked so well in cleaning up the drug cartels in Mexico, he feels a joint command between the two of you would be a real plus in Mexican-American relations.

"Now you haven't started your new job yet, but this certainly is in line with that job," Sara added. "Besides it would only be a temporary assignment," the President said quickly.

Chapter 10 – Civil Disorder

"Madam President. If an all-out civil war breaks out, then this so called temporary assignment would certainly change?" the General questioned.

"That is true," President Williamson told her newest Major General. "I'm not ordering you to take this assignment, Michael, it's strictly up to you."

"It's true, ma'am, General Rōjas and I work well together, but if push comes to shove, who will have the final word? When I was in Mexico General Rōjas had the last word."

"You will have the final word for all Mexican and American forces along the border," the President promised.

"Does President Lazzara and General Rōjas know this arrangement?" the General asked his boss.

"Not yet," Sara answered. "I'll call President Lazzara and get his okay that a duel command is possible, but any final decisions will be made by yourself, General."

"If President Lazzara and General Rōjas agree, I will gladly take command of both forces guarding our Texas border," the General consented shaking his head.

"Stay put while I make the call to our Mexican friend." Sara placed the call and almost immediately the phone rang and the Mexican President was on the line.

Sara told the Mexican President, "General Montgomery is in my office and he has accepted the Texas border assignment, as long as General Rōjas and you agree that is a stalemate occurs, the final decision rests with General Montgomery."

"Certainly, Madam President, we wouldn't have it any other way," President Lazzara assured the Western States of America President.

"May I speak to my old friend, Colonel Montgomery?" the Mexican president asked. "I should have said, General Montgomery," the President corrected.

"Certainly, Mr. President."

Sara handed Michael the phone and said, "President Lazzara would like a word with you."

"Good afternoon, Mr. President."

"It's good to hear you voice again," the Mexican President told his American friend.

"Same here, sir."

 rickshaw

"I know you and General Rōjas will work well together as you're good friends and good combat officers under fire. You had a question about command. You, my boy, have the last word in any decisions that affect the Mexican forces. I will stand behind your orders, General, as I know you'll have both the American and Mexican troops' wellbeing at the forefront."

"Thank you, sir. General Rōjas and I make a good team," the American Major General assured the President.

"One more thing, General, a certain young lady will be assigned to General Rōjas' staff. You named her 'Butch', as I remember. Butch, as you call her, is a Second Lt. now with a chest full of medals I might add. You pinned a few on her as I recall, General."

"Yes sir. Very carefully, I might add."

"I remember you said 'medals don't lay flat when pinned on her chest'" the President said with a slight chuckle.

"No, sir, they don't," Montgomery said with a smile.

"As you know, General, our forces are positioned within seven or eight kilometers of our border. General Rōjas assures me they are ready and waiting for your transportation officers to escort them across your border and assign them to their sector of responsibility. I'm guessing it will take the better part of a week to move these two divisions to their positions and set up camp. As far as equipment goes, I believe we have the latest arms and gadgets needed in warfare."

"If your forces lack anything, Mr. President, I'll see they get it, sir."

"Thank you, General."

"Did you want to talk to President Williamson again, Mr. President?"

"No. I'm done," the Mexican President answered.

Both parties said goodbye in Spanish.

"Well, General, you have a lot of work to do within the next week. Just getting the Mexican divisions across our border and getting them into position is a monumental task in its self," she said. "Where is your combined headquarters going to be?" Sara asked,

"I would like to set up headquarters just outside Sherman, which is only sixty-five miles north of Dallas and just twelve miles from our border with Oklahoma. There is a small airport just south of Sherman which has a half dozen buildings and a hard runway that can handle most military aircraft. I know the owner and he'll be happy for the activity and excitement. I've known Bert for over twenty-five years and he will welcome our arrival with open arms."

The General continued, "I'll contact General Rōjas and steer him and his staff to Sherman on route #95. But before that, I better cement the plans by calling Bert and alerting him of his pending guests."

General Montgomery left Sara's office and headed for the Wagon Wheel and a meeting with General Wittingham. During the next two days, General Montgomery assembled his staff and contacted his friend General Rōjas. He also made arrangements for the Mexican Commanding General and his small staff to fly straight to their headquarters in Sherman, Texas. After speaking earlier to Bert, Montgomery sent a small group to Sherman for the purpose of sweeping out the cobwebs and setting up their headquarters with the necessary communications and security.

Within two days, General Montgomery and his staff, along with General Rōjas and his small staff arrived at the small airport south of Sherman at the same time. Confusion was the order of the day as the two Generals and their staffs unloaded their gear and personal belongings to their living quarters. After a round of introductions and a couple of hours of rest, both groups headed for the headquarters building where General Rōjas and his people would occupy one half of the building, and General Montgomery and his staff settled into the other half. The main building was large enough to house both groups along with all the communication equipment and special gear necessary to run a temporary military headquarters.

General Montgomery and General Rōjas held a quick meeting without any of their staff. They discussed the pending arrival of the Mexican forces to be assigned to the four positions along the Texas border. Each section alone the border runs approximately two hundred and twenty-five miles.

On a personal and military note General Montgomery said to his friend of many military campaigns, "As you know, General, I'm only a Major General, and you're a Four Star Commanding General in Mexico."

 rickshaw

Before Montgomery could continue his friend said, "Yes Michael. I'm a Four Star General in Mexico, not in the Western States of America. As friends, our military rank doesn't matter, we have a job to do and we'll work together to accomplish any task that confronts us, my friend."

Both men shook hand and said, "Let's get to work."

Michael met with Bert and decided upon a monetary amount per day for the use of his facility. Bert insisted he didn't want any money but Michael insisted. They briefly ran over the past quarter century and their accomplishments and failures, which were many.

Bert said, "Michael, if you need anything or want to change, tear down or build anything, just do it."

"Thank you, my friend."

"Anything for Texas," Bert answered with a broad grin.

In less than four days the entire length of the Texas border was finally protected by the seventy thousand plus military forces from Texas and Mexico. Each of the four sections would be manned by no less then seventeen thousand five hundred men and women.

Both Generals continued to meet with their respective staffs and plan various scenarios in case of attack by Washington or the influx of civilians trying to escape for madness.

Michael left his staff and entered his office to get a little rest. He sat in the softest chair he could find and suddenly a knock on the door. He got up and opened the door, and was surprised to see a brand new Second Lt. standing there saluting.

"Butch, my god, I'm so glad to see you," he said quickly.

"Don't I deserve a return salute?" she said with a big smile.

"You certainly do, Lt." He gave her a smart salute and said, "Come on in." He closed the door and Butch walked up to him and motioned for him to bend over. Michael leaned over, and Butch planted a big kiss on his cheek and gave him a bear hug. They separated and the General said, I see you have added to your medals."

"Yes, sir. After you gave me a meda,l General, they added two more," she admitted. "I only wore them for you, General," she added.

Chapter 10 – Civil Disorder

"Well, they look good on you, Butch," he told his favorite female soldier.

She said, "The problem is, sir, they don't lay flat when I wear them." After saying that she burst out laughing and turned a beautiful shade of red.

"Yes, Butch, I know your problem," he admitted.

"Please be seated," he told the only female he led into combat with the Spl. Ops Company in Mexico.

"What has been happening since I left Spl. Ops?" he asked.

"Well, sir, we attacked two small drug cartels and arrested more than a dozen government official receiving cash payoffs. It's been pretty dull for the most part," she admitted. "Many of us wished you would have stayed with Spl. Ops. You're planning and hands on fighting skills, along with General Rōjas, was a winning team," she said.

"Thank you, Butch, I appreciate your comments."

"Well, Colonel. Sorry, I mean, General. I must get back before General Rōjas thinks I'm overstaying my visit."

She stood up at attention and smartly saluted her American General.

He returned her salute and gave her a wink. She smiled and returned his wink with a smile.

She left his office, and he returned to his chair thinking about what a great gal Butch was and how much he admired her for her fighting skills. He admitted to himself that he must be careful in dealing with her, he had very strong feelings towards the Mexican beauty. The old Colonel liked her the minute he laid eyes on her. She was a tiger and first class combat soldier who possessed no fear of death. "She is a better soldier than ninety percent of her comrades. I can imagine a full division of soldiers like Maria Ortiz. We wouldn't lose a single battle," he mused. "I really like that woman, but I must not let personal feelings interfere with my duties to W.S. of A.," he thought, shaking his head. "I can't stop thinking about Maria, she is going to drive me to drink if I'm not careful. I wonder if she has any feelings for me. You old work horse," he thought, "you're old enough to be her father. Why in the world would she be interested in an old Army dog like me?"

 rickshaw

General Montgomery quickly put his romantic notions aside and placed a call to Flagstaff and President Williamson. Chief-of-Staff McCarney (Buck) answered the phone and said that the President was in a meeting with the general staff at the Wagon Wheel. Buck said, "They are assessing the latest development that a large number of regular Army and Reserve personnel are refusing to fire upon the civilian rioters and looters. That disobeying of direct orders is adding more fuel to the fire, I'm afraid," the Chief-of-Staff admitted.

"Have Madam President call me when she can," the General asked. "I just want to bring her up to date on our move to the border with our Mexican troops."

President Williamson returned the General's call after returning from the Wagon Wheel.

General Montgomery covered the move and disbursement of the Mexican troops along the Texas border. He also described the four zones that protect the entire length of the Texas border, and said each zone would have more than division of American and Mexican troops. "Each of the four zones will cover about two hundred and twenty-five miles of border, and will be commanded by a General officer with his second in command, with most likely be a Mexican General officer who speaks English. We are in position, Madam President, and ready for almost anything. Between our mobile artillery, new tanks, ground forces, attack helicopters, supersonic fighters and other assorted aircraft with spy in the sky satellite coverage, I feel we are ready, Madam President."

Sara thanked Major General Montgomery for the detailed update on the border build up and filled him in on the earlier meeting with General Wittingham and his staff on the latest problem facing President Goodwin and the Whitehouse. "My staff will keep your headquarters posted of any changes," the President assured General Montgomery.

"One more thing General, as you know we feel our Texas border is the most vulnerable for citizens tired of Goodwin's policies and the uprisings and numerous deaths that are consuming their dying nation. The balance of our borders are protected by one hundred and fifty thousand troops, plus law enforcement personnel that bring our border forces up to two hundred and ten thousand guarding our Idaho, Nevada, Utah and Colorado borders. When you add your Texas forces then we have some two hundred and eighty thousand men and women watching and protecting our frontier," President Williamson added.

"Let's hope that a civil war doesn't materialize and cooler heads prevail, so our forces are not needed to protect our country, Madam President."

"I agree, General, but that's asking a lot, I'm afraid. I don't have anything else," Sara said, "do you have anything to add," she asked?

"No, ma'am."

"Goodbye, General."

Both ended their conversation and slowly hung up.

President Williamson turned to Buck and said, "I'm tired of making all the decisions for our country. It's not right that I alone make all the calls. Our government must be run by our elected representatives and not just its President," she said pounding her desk. "When this Goodwin crisis is finally over and conditions normalize, I want to assemble the Senators and Congressmen that have been elected to get this new government on a strong footing. I must concentrate on the mechanics of government and see that each state has the number of officials necessary to run their individual states."

"I agree, Madam President. You tell me when, and I'll call the first meeting of our reps," Buck offered. "The Government Hall across for the Wagon Wheel will be completed within the next three to four weeks the construction company president told me yesterday at the update meeting. Within that time frame, the four newly acquired northern states will have the required elections and their representatives in place."

"That's good news, Buck. Now, if this current crisis is resolved by then and the Great Hall is completed within a month, then maybe we can have our First Congress in our new building. As president of the Western States of America, I hope this uprising is put down quickly and both countries can get back to peaceful endeavors. These next few days will determine whether President Goodwin's country will survive or become a third rate, third world country," Sara told her Chief-of-Staff.

President Goodwin was at his desk in the Oval Office when Secretary-of-Defense Marshal came in and said, "Mr. President, I have a sliver of good news."

"With rioting just outside my window, any part of good news is welcome, Mr. Secretary."

"Sir. With almost a million servicemen and women called into service because of the zone of interior uprising we're starting to see some results. With our federal troops roaming the big city streets and imposing strict curfews with death penalties for rioters and looters. We're not screwing around this time, Mr. President, our military and law enforcement personnel are shooting first and asking questions second. No more wishy-washy arrests and holding them releasing later on. Quick justice and death is the new rule of the day, Mr. President."

"How about the federal troops that refused to fire on civilians when ordered?" the President asked.

"They have been arrested and are being held in various federal facilities throughout the country, Mr. President. I do believe that trend of defying direct orders is over, sir,"

"Disasterous for any military organization, if unchecked," the President added.

"The latest death toll has risen to eighteen hundred and forty-seven, and most deaths were committed by civilians toward civilians. Hundreds of looters were shot and many more will be shot if looting continues," the Defense Secretary stated.

"Mr. Secretary. I want the national uprising stopped immediately!" President Goodwin shouted. "I mean today, Jon, not tomorrow or next week but today. Call Phil Wolford and have him call his commanders in the field, and tell them to do whatever is necessary to stop this national madness. It must stop now," the President insisted.

"Yes, sir, right away, Mr. President."

"I will go on T.V. within the hour and demand that all aggression by all persons must stop immediately," he said to an empty Oval Office. The Defense Secretary was long gone.

"Mister President, you're on in five." The T.V. director pointed to the President and mouthed, "You're on."

"Ladies and gentlemen. I'm appealing to you, Mr. And Mrs. America. This national uprising must stop immediately. Too many deaths and billions of your dollars have been wasted during this civil unrest. The changes in social programs I have initiated will stand. You know that your government cannot continue to foot the bill for millions upon millions of persons that are non-producers. If physically you can work, then you must work. Your local and federal governments are not going to continue to support you and your family while you set on your fat ass and watch T.V. and drink beer. Our country has far too many deadbeats and non-producers that pay no income tax and contribute nothing to the national good. I want a free society, not a police state. But if these riots and lawless acts continue, I'll turn this nation and country into an armed camp, if that is what it takes.

"No matter what, this civil unrest will stop immediately. Some of our beautiful large cities have been trashed and will take years to rebuild because of you wanton lawlessness. I said earlier that your social giveaways wouldn't stop for months, but since your people have no regard for the law, your local and government handouts will stop as of today. Naturally, disabled persons will continue to receive benefits, but all others must find work and pay their way like everybody else. That's all I have, ladies and gentlemen, you decide your future."

"That's a wrap, Mr. President."

"Well, Mr. President, you gave them a choice. An armed camp or a society that works and provides everything through hard work. Either the rioting will increase or the bottom feeders will buckle down and provided for their families," Chief-of-Staff Mott summed up the speech.

"We'll know shortly," the President added.

"Mr. Secretary. I want a meeting with all your military chiefs this afternoon at the Pentagon."

"What time, Mr. President?"

"18:00 hrs.," he answered.

"I'll inform them right away, Mr. President."

The Pentagon War Room was jam packed when President Goodwin arrived and headed for his place at the head of the huge table.

"Be seated, gentlemen.

"You saw or heard my speech to the American people this afternoon. Like I told them, this uprising, rioting and lawless acts of violence must stop immediately.

"Gentlemen. Whatever it takes to stop this madness do it. Our nation is being torn apart by these acts of lawlessness. Use whatever force necessary to squelch this civil unrest. If anyone in this room cannot in good conscience carry of this order by your Commander-in-Chief, let him resign here and now."

"Mr. President, I cannot condone the killing of American citizens."

"I'm surprised, Colonel, you have been my trusted Marine Corps Aide for more than two years. Even before I was President."

"I'm sorry, Mr. President, but I don't like the path your administration is taking. If we continue to follow this path I feel our country is doomed. Just look how many states have left our union, and now this national uprising. I will submit my resignation from the Marine Corps tomorrow, Mr. President."

"That's too bad, Brian, you could have had a great future in the Marine Corps. You could have made General," the President added.

The President asked the M.P's guarding the War Room door to escort the Colonel from the War Room.

"Anyone else?" the Commander-in-Chief asked the group.

"Yes, sir, there is. I'm General Sherwood, Mr. President, and I agree with Colonel Peterson. I cannot stay in your service under these circumstances. I will resign my commission as of tomorrow, Mr. President."

"I accept your resignation with regret, General, but I must ask you to leave the War Room," the President insisted.

"Good god, is there anyone else?" President Goodwin asked, shaking his head,

No one else in the War Room came forward.

"Gentlemen, I'll be very brief. We have the best military in the world and have recalled thousands of our troops from foreign bases to help suppress this civil unrest. But as of today, we have not stopped this carnage. Our troops are required to stop foreign and domestic forces that threaten our constitution and country. I want this stopped immediately, gentlemen. Do whatever it takes to stop this, no excuses, just get it done." With that, the President got up and headed for the huge War Room door and the short flight back to the Oval Office.

Chapter 10 – Civil Disorder

When the President's helo landed on the West Lawn of the Whitehouse, he could hear and see the massive crowds clamoring at the fence surrounding the Whitehouse. He told one of the pilots, "If that crowd breaks through that fence, they will trash the Whitehouse and burn it to the ground."

As President Goodwin exited the chopper, he was surrounded by a half dozen Secret Service agents. Threats against the President's life were received by the thousands each day since the rioting started. There were so many the Secret Service couldn't investigate them.

The President was escorted all the way to the Oval Office. He entered his office and sat at his desk while thinking, "My god, when will this end? If this doesn't stop shortly, we won't have a country, I'm afraid."

A large group estimated at over three thousand well-armed individuals had been gathering in Merryville, Louisiana over the past four days. They had pick-up trucks with mounted weapons and over one hundred ATVs, mountain bikes and dune buggies.

General Montgomery was notified by Mexican General Rōjas that this mob is growing daily. Rōjas believed that they would cross into Texas at Bon Wier by route #190 within the next day or so. The General moved some Texas and Mexican troops to Bon Wier, which is directly across the border from Merryville, Louisiana. "If they cross the Texas border I will attack," he informed General Montgomery.

"I agree, General," he told his Four Star Mexican friend. "You do whatever it takes to stop these rioters from entering our country. 'Shoot to kill' is the order of the day to prevent this mob from entering Texas."

Major General Montgomery quickly called President Williamson and alerted her to the possibility of a conflict around Bon Wier, Texas. Michael asked Sara to call President Goodwin in Washington and alert him of the coming conflict at the border with Louisiana.

President Williamson agreed and put in a call to Washington.

Chief-of-Staff Mott answered the phone and told Sara that President Goodwin was not available and he didn't know when he could return her call.

 **rickshaw**

President Williamson was pissed, she told the C.O.S., 'If that mob in Louisiana crosses into Texas, they will be attacked and killed. There will be no quarter given," she added.

Sara told that wimp Robert Mott that she didn't care if President Goodwin returned her call or not. Without another word she slammed the phone down in anger. "That son-of-a-bitch is probably sitting right there beside the phone," she said out loud. "But of course he has that powder-puff Mott do his dirty work for him."

Sara called General Montgomery and ordered him not to allow a single individual to enter Texas territory. "If your fight spills over into Louisiana then so be it."

General Montgomery relayed President Williamson's order to General Rōjas, and alerted the other commanders that no individuals must enter the Texas frontier.

Lt. General Wittingham, Commanding General of all military forces in the Western States of America placed an emergency priority call to President Williamson in Flagstaff.

Chief-of-Staff McCarney (Buck) took the General's call and quickly transferred the call to President Williamson.

"Go ahead, General, Buck said it was a priority call."

"It is, ma'am. I've been informed that Russian nuclear subs have surfaced in two places. One off the coast of Fort Walton, Florida and the second sighted about one hundred and twenty-five miles east of Brownsville, Texas where the gulf is about 868 meters deep. While both sightings are in International Waters, both subs stayed on the surface for more than four hours before our Coast Guard forced them to dive and a fishing boat approached the sub."

"Madam President, this is not a good sign, those Russian bastards are planning something, you can bet on it. I'm sure they were taking readings with the help of their satellites."

"You're right, General, that is not a good sign. Please inform Secretary-of-Defense Marshal and National Security Advisor Jennings in Washington."

"This will add to their problems, big time," Sara told the General. "Are you sure Washington doesn't know about the Russian sub sightings?" the President asked.

Chapter 10 – Civil Disorder

"No, ma'am, they don't. We were called directly by a fishing boat form Matagorda Island and the other by our Coast Guard."

"Thank you, General. Please let me know what the Washington group thinks of the Russian subs surfacing off the coast."

"Will do, Madam President."

Sara hung up the phone and asked Buick whether he had heard the conversation.

"Yes, I did, ma'am."

"Well, what do you think?" Sara asked her Chief-of-Staff.

"I believe this is a prelude to something big. It's certainly not a good sign when they remain surfaced for more than four hours."

General Wittingham called Washington and passed on the info he had received on the Russian subs. To his surprise, they didn't seem too concerned about the sighting. They indicated that President Goodwin had more important problems to deal with. Well, I have passed on the information, you do with it what you want," the General said.

"Washington will regret their lack of interest in this matter," the General thought. "The Russians are getting ready for some type of military action, maybe even a missile launch. With rioting sweeping the country, the timing would be perfect for a Russian strike. Europe and Asia have been weakened by the recall of thousands of American troops to support the ZI (Zone of Interior) military in containing the civilian uprising." The General called President Williamson and relayed his conversation with the Defense Secretary and National Security Advisor.

Sara was also surprised at the indifference of Washington on the Russian sightings.

About five hundred armed civilian and AWOL military personnel started to cross from Merryville, Louisiana into Texas. General Rōjas gave the order to fire. Within thirty minutes, the entire group coming from Merryville were killed to the man. Between the chopper gunships and the General's ground forces, the attacking rioters were eliminated. General Rōjas sent a message to the Mayor of Merryville informing him that all attempts to enter Texas would result in death. "Pass the message

and the word that the Texas border is closed to all persons," General Rōjas added.

General Montgomery's headquarters received a message from General Boyd Smith commanding sector #3 (from Denison to Childress, Texas). The message stated that a build-up of men and assorted equipment was taken place in Thackerville, Oklahoma along highway #35, just two miles from the Texas border. "Our flyovers estimated that some fifteen hundred men are camped just outside the town. Within the hour I sent a message to their camp and explained in plain English and in Spanish that if they attempt to cross the border, they'll be met with deadly force. We will shoot to kill and take no prisoners," the General added.

General Montgomery's answer to Boyd was not to allow any individuals to set foot on Texas soil. "If your defensive action takes your forces into Oklahoma, then so be it. Do whatever it takes, the rioters are not going to carry this civil unrest into our country."

After hearing about these two incidents, President Williamson sent a message to Washington complaining that large groups of rioters were attempting to enter the country. "If you can't control these lawless individuals, then we will. We have already killed over five hundred rioters who tried to cross our borders. The killing will continue as long as they keep trying to cross our border and enter our state of Texas." Sara knows that Washington does not have a handle on this civil unrest and are unable to stop these rioters throughout the country. The next stage of the unrest was all out civil war against Washington and the Goodwin administration.

"We must pray to the almighty," Sara said, "that a civil war does not rear its ugly head and destroy their country and possibly spill over to the Western States of America."

Sara leaned over the desk and pushed the intercom button for her Secretary, Mrs. Bakker.

"Yes, ma'am," Ruth answered.

"Ruth, would you please contact General Wittingham and have him call me when he can. Nothing urgent, Ruth."

"Right away, ma'am."

Major Paulson, Aid-de-Camp to General Wittingham, called President Williamson and said that the General was in the field inspecting the border troops and their equipment, but he would leave a message with his inspection party.

"That will be fine, Major, but this is not an urgent or a priority call, you understand."

"Yes, ma'am, I do."

"Thank you, Major."

Sara hung up the secure phone and leaned back in her soft leather chair and thought, "my hair will be gray, or even white, before my Presidential term is up. There are so many crisEs that they must be numbered," she thought, shaking her head. While Sara was in deep thought, the secure line rang and jolted her back to reality.

General Wittingham said," Madam President, Major Paulson said you called earlier."

"Yes, I did General. I just have one question, do you think our forces are ready for anything along our entire border with Goodwin's America?" Before the General could answer, Sara continued, "if you feel we don't have enough troops along our border, President Lazzara has offered an additional two or three divisions of ground forces."

"At present, ma'am, I do believe we have sufficient forces manning our eastern borders. We can repel all rioters with little trouble, but if the Goodwin military forces attack us with everything at their disposal then all bets are off. We cannot win against the Washington military, Madam President. I feel they would have little reason to wage war against us at this time," the General added.

"Thank you, General, let's hope your assessment is correct. Major Paulson said you were on inspection tour, how is that going?" she asked.

"So far, so good." he answered. "The commanders I have seen have positioned their forces at the most vulnerable spots within their assigned areas. Was there anything else?" the General asked.

"No, Charles, I just wanted your opinion."

"Thank you, Madam President."

Sara replaced the phone in the receiver and wondered if the General was right in guessing that Washington would not wage war against the W.S. of A.

 rickshaw

At 03:30, General Montgomery was informed that a force of some twelve hundred men and women were trying to cross from Merryville, Louisiana into Texas.

The aircraft assigned to General Rōjas was patrolling the border when they spotted the large assembled force moving towards the border. While the attacking force was still inside Louisiana, the Mexican General ordered his mixed force to attack the violators and shoot to kill. "These people must be on drugs," General Rōjas radioed to General Montgomery at their headquarters. "We killed a large group on their last try, and they're going to lose many more today," the General promised.

"Keep those rioters and military scum from entering any part of Texas," General Montgomery told his Mexican partner.

"We're not going to fight on Texas soil, we'll hit them well before they get to the border," General Rōjas answered.

"Do whatever you think is best," Montgomery told his friend.

"Yes, sir, I will."

While the rioters were still in Louisiana, the Mexican General ordered his mixed forces to attack the border busters and shoot to kill. The skirmish only lasted an hour. The ground forces, with the aid of a dozen attack helicopters armed with six barrel Gatling guns, attacked the mob and killed or wounded over eight hundred. The choppers broke the back of the mob who scattered in all directions. The gunships also destroyed all the abandoned vehicles and equipment.

After his forces returned to the Texas side of the border, General Rōjas called headquarters and described the action to General Montgomery. He first indicated that they'd had two deaths and only a dozen wounded.

"Thank you, General, let's hope this will end the foolish attempt to enter Texas or any other state."

General Montgomery called Lt. General Wittingham and relayed the action taken just west of Merryville, Louisiana. The Commanding General said, "The attacks in Texas have been the only ones so far." Both Generals engaged in small talk before saying goodbye.

Chief-of-Staff McCarney rushed into President Williamson's office and said, "Madam President, turn on the T.V. President Goodwin is on T.V. speaking to the American public."

President Goodwin was on T.V. explaining to the American public that with the one hundred thousand military personnel brought back from bases overseas and added to the home based forces, the military and law enforcement are making headway in stopping the madness that has gripped the country. "Rioters and other law breakers are being rounded up, and yes, some are being shot for looting and other capital crimes. This is a dark period in our history and should not have happened," the President said, raising his voice.

"Every man and woman is responsible for taking care of their families and themselves. That means have a job and support you family. It doesn't mean ride the wave of welfare, food stamps, housing allowance and a long list of other state and federal giveaway programs. You individuals who have a large number of children by a large number of men expect the state and federal government to pay for your indiscretion and support your family are in for a rude awakening. Hear me and read my lips the changes in the welfare law and other giveaway programs will stand.

"I'm asking you, Mr. and Mrs. America, go to work, pay your taxes and support your families and live the American dream that has made this country great. My administration will not allow this country to slip into a civil war that would transfer this nation into a third rate county ruled by thousands of lawless mobs.

"Thank you, my fellow Americans."

With that last statement the T.V. director said," Mr. President, that's it."

President Goodwin left the Pentagon with General Wolford and headed for the Oval Office.

In Flagstaff, President Williamson turned off the T.V. and asked, "What did you think of his speech?"

"I don't know," Buck answered. "Either he is correct and they are gaining ground on the rioting and lawlessness, or he is losing the battle big time and desperately trying to appeal to the American people as a last resort. Our reports coming in throughout their country are mixed as well, and their T.V. stations only cover the major cities and not the average small village, town and city. Madam President, our satellites passing over their country at night show large fires in almost every major city and small fires throughout the country. These night time photos are showing red glows that are miles wide in some cases. It may be, ma'am, that President Goodwin is full of beans, and it's far worse than he wants to admit."

"You may be right, Buck, the thousands of phone calls and pictures we have received from frightened citizens indicate just that, I'm afraid," the President admitted. Sara continued, "I'm concerned that a full blown civil war might develop from this rioting and lawless action by millions of his citizens. If a civil war breaks out, we'll be in for a terrible time, Buck. No matter what transpires, we must be ready to defend our country from Goodwin's domestic population and maybe his military and even foreign intervention is possible.

"You know, Buck, I think it's time I talked to the Canadian Prime Minister, I'm sure his government is very concerned with the unpleasant developments in the lower forty-two. Would you please contact the Prime Minister and set up a phone pow wow at his convenience?"

"Yes, ma'am, right away." Buck exited Sara's office at warp speed to call the Canadian head of state. Buck got through to Ottawa, and in less than an hour, Minister Pearson was on the phone with President Williamson.

"Mr. Minister, it's good to hear your voice again. I just wish it was in better times," Sara admitted.

"Yes, Madam President, these are very uneasy and trying times, I'm afraid. Before we start, I would prefer that you call me Parnell, Mr. Minister sounds too stuffy."

"Okay. I'll call you by your first name if you call me by mine."

"That's a deal, Sara."

"Thank you, Parnell."

"Now that's settled," he quickly added. "It's your dime, Sara."

"Parnell, the situation in the lower forty-two and Washington, D.C. is reaching a critical point. You heard Goodwin's speech earlier."

"Yes, I did, and I don't believe a word of it. I believe the situation is getting worse, not better. For example, Detroit is directly across the river from Windsor, Ontario, and we can see the entire city is engulfed in flames. They tell me the fires are visible as far as fifty miles away at night. We have military troops stationed along the border and have closed the tunnel from Detroit. We don't want this lawless mob to enter Canada.

"We will use whatever force necessary to stop them from crossing into Canada. As you know, Detroit, for the past thirty years, has been going down-hill. There are so many murders each day that law enforcement can't even investigate them. Blacks are killing Blacks by the dozen daily and nobody seems to care," the Minister said in a low voice. "Most of the U.S. border with Canada has little population, but cities like Detroit are potentially explosive. My other concern, Sara, is crossing our border by boat. We have over a thousand miles of border on the five Great Lakes that are hardly patrolled. My government has great concern that the civil unrest mob might come to Canada to escape the carnage and unrest or want to continue the lawless acts in Canada."

The Minister continued, "I can guess your reason for calling, Madam President. Sorry, I mean, Sara. You're wondering whether Canada can furnish any troops in case Washington and or the lawless mobs attack your country. Well, the answer is 'yes.' Because I know if Washington attacked Canada, you would send help at first call."

"That is true, Parnell."

"I will confer with our military chiefs and get back to you in a day or so."

"Thank you, Parnell Leslie Pearson," she answered.

"You're welcome, Sara Elizabeth Williamson. Did I get your full name correct?" he asked.

"Yes, you did."

"I'll call you soon," the Canadian Prime Minister said, ending the conversation.

"Well, Buck, if Canadian troops are made available, our position will be much better. If we have Mexican, Canadian and W.S. of A. troops available to defend our country, Washington had better think twice before attacking our country."

Within forty-eight hours the Canadian Prime Minister returned the call to President Williamson. He informed Sara that his government had approved the use of Canadian military to help defend the Western States of America. "We can make available the following units:

"Irish-Canadian Black Watch Division with just less than fifteen thousand men. This is a fully equipped combat division.

"The 32nd Air Wing with six thousand pilots and ground crew. This air wing has a total of fifty-eight aircraft which includes chopper gun-ships, F-22 fighters, Harrier jump jets, tank destroyers and a variety of other aircraft. All planes are up to date and one hundred percent serviceable. No matter where they go, they take along their own repair parts and all fuel necessary to keep them flying. The Canadian military advises we transfer these two units to Vancouver, British Columbia. We will hold them in Canada close to the border with Washington State. If you need these units they'll come across your border and be available for duty anywhere within your country. There is one thing the Canadian military insist upon, Sara."

"What's that?" she answered with caution in her voice.

"The command of both units must be Canadian, Sara. We certainly can have duel commanding officers, but the last word must be made by the Canadian officer."

"Very interesting, sir. I must consult with our military before saying 'yes' to your demand. I'll get back to you shortly," Sara told the Canadian Prime Minister.

President Williamson immediately called the Wagon Wheel and contacted Lt. General Wittingham. She explained the demand by the Canadian military and the possible problems that could arise.

The General surprised the President by quickly saying he had no problem with two commanders sharing command. "We currently have duel command with Mexican and W.S. of A. troops guarding the Texas border. This should not be a serious problem in my estimation, Madam President." General Wittingham continued, "Ma'am, we have had many duel commands over the past one hundred years. I have no problem with the concept and demand," he added.

"Thank you, General, I appreciate your many years of experienced and service," the President told her ranking military leader.

"Buck, please call the Canadian Prime Minister and let me know, when he is available."

"Yes, ma'am."

Chapter 10 – Civil Disorder

Chief-of-Staff McCarney called Ottawa again and was told that the Prime Minister was in a meeting with military leaders and wouldn't be available for some time.

Buck relayed the Ottawa call to President Williamson and said the Canadian Prime Minister would call when he was available.

"That's fine, Buck. I'm sure he is extremely busy."

The President's secure line started blinking, and when Sara answered, Mrs. Bakker said, "General Wittingham is on the line."

"Put him through, Ruth."

"Yes, General," Sara answered.

"Madam President, there is one request I'd like to make."

"Which is?" Sara asked.

"Madam President, if we're to allow the two Canadian outfits to join our forces, I'd like to travel to Vancouver and consult with the Commanders of both units. We should know these Canadian military leaders before they join our forces. I want to know these men and be comfortable with them."

"That's okay with me, General, but I'll have to ask the Prime Minister if his government has any objections to your meeting. I can't imagine why he would object. I'll get back to you, General, after I talk to Minister Pearson."

"Thank you, ma'am."

After four hours of waiting, the Canadian Prime Minister returned Sara's call.

"I'm sorry, Sara, I was in a meeting with our top military officials on the expanding Detroit, Michigan problem. That city has been burning for almost a week. There can hardly be anything left to burn, I would think," the Prime Minister added. "That city has been an eye sore and a major problem for many years," the Canadian leader admitted to President Williamson.

"I understand your concerns, Parnell. After our previous conversation I conferred with my military top dog, and he has no problem with a joint command and the final decision resting with your Canadian commander. General Wittingham reminded me that we have the same duel command currently with our Mexican military guarding the Texas border. The General wants to go to Vancouver and meet with your two top commanders of

both units. He would like to know these men in case their forces are pushed into service."

"Certainly, Sara, I would expect nothing less of General Wittingham. All three Generals should know each other in more than name alone," the Prime Minister insisted. "If it's okay with you, Sara, I'd like to make all the arrangements for Lt. General Wittingham, Major General Thom O'Neill and Major General Tedder O'Connor to meet each other in Vancouver, British Colombia within a week, if that's alright with you, Sara."

"That's great, Parnell, I'm happy you're doing it, sir."

"Good. My staff will contact your General when the meeting is cast in concrete," the Prime Minister advised the President.

"Please keep in contact," Sara asked the Canadian Prime Minister.

"Will do," he answered before hanging up the phone.

"Buck, I want it leaked that a large Canadian force has sided with the Western States of America, and combined with the several Mexican divisions and our troops, that makes a very strong military force for the Western States of America."

President Goodwin received word from Secretary-of-Defense Marshal that Canada has supplied President Williamson with a large number of ground troops and a full air wing to help guard their lengthy border.

"That's all we need, the Mexican government has supplied a couple of divisions to guard the Texas border and now Canada is supplying combat troops and an air wing for President Williamson to use. What else can they pile on us?" President Goodwin asked. "We can't take much more," he admitted to the Secretary-of-Defense. Our cities are burning, rioters are roaming the country and some of our military are refusing to shoot fellow Americans who are looting and torching anything that can burn. Mr. Secretary, if the lawless groups get together and form a fighting force with millions of citizens, then a nationwide civil war is a strong possibility," the President admitted. "As your President, I'm running out of ideas to stop this senseless destruction, if our armed forces can't stop this national madness then I don't know what will," he admitted to the Defense Secretary.

"Mr. President, you could reinstate the welfare laws and other social programs."

"Not on your life," the President quickly answered with anger in his voice. "No way, no matter what transpires," he added.

"You're the Secretary-of-Defense, Jon, get out into the field and get your officers and men to stop this national disgrace. Sitting in your office within the security of the Pentagon is not getting the job done. I would suggest, Mr. Secretary, that you start with our own Washington, D.C. before the mobs burn down the Whitehouse for the second time. First by the British and now maybe second by the American people."

The S.O.D. left the Oval Office at the request of his boss and was heading down the long hall when one of his young aides ran up and handed the Secretary a folded note. After reading the message, he turned around and reentered the Oval Office and handed the President the folded note.

The message said that D.C. Mayor Darrell Johnson had been murdered when he tried to stop a large group of rioters from entering the National Museum. The Black Mayor was popular with the mostly Black population of Washington, but his color didn't stop the mob from killing him and trashing the priceless national treasures.

"See, Mr. Secretary, you're too late," the President said, shaking his head and motioned him to leave the Oval Office.

When the Secretary left the Oval Office, the President flopped into his old brown leather chair and thought, "If we can't stop this wanton destruction in the next few days, I'm afraid we're finished as a republic."

Chapter 11
THREATENING WAR CLOUDS

During the next week, the random looting and burning died down because the rioting mobs ran out of food, transportation and everything else to plunder. Most of the grocery stores, restaurants, drug stores, sporting goods, warehouses and distribution centers had been stripped clean and burned. Even National Guard and Reserve facilities were looted and weapons taken by the rioting mobs. Now, the mobs were quickly running out of things to steal and burn while having trouble finding food and even transportation because of the thousands of cars and trucks that were burned and destroyed during their march on the cities. The lawless groups of rioters started leaving the cities and heading for the outlying towns and villages to acquire food and supplies, but to their surprise they were confronted by well-armed civilians who band together to protect their families and property. They wanted no part or participation in the looting madness of the low class trough feeders. Between the armed civilian property owners, local authorities and federal troops, the rioters throughout the country were dispatched, jailed or killed.

Washington estimated that during the national carnage the death toll reached over twenty-two thousand Americans and that it would cost more than a trillion dollars to rebuild the major cities, roads, bridges, utilities and many state and federal facilities that were destroyed.

President Goodwin gave orders that the Army Corps of Engineers be charged with the overall responsibility of rebuilding America.

The President estimated it would take many years to rebuild the devastation caused by the lawless individuals to prior quality of life in America.

The Washington President called President Williamson and said, "I believe that national rioting and carnage has finally stopped."

Sara told President Goodwin that his news was welcome news. She also asked the President if there was anything the Western States of America could provide or do to aide his administration in the clean-up of his country.

President Goodwin said, "Thank you for your offer to help," but indicated that it was much too early to know where and what help was needed. In closing, he said that someone from his staff, or he himself, would contact her with any request for aide and assistance.

"Please keep in contact," she asked.

"You can bet on it," the President answered.

Sara asked Buck to call for a meeting with her complete staff at the Wagon Wheel War Room the next afternoon at 17:00 hours. "Make sure Generals Wittingham and Montgomery are available to attend. If, for some reason, they are not available, we'll postpone the meeting. Once more thing, Buck, I also want Mexican Commanding General Rōjas to attend the meeting."

"You want a foreign officer to attend your meeting in the secure War Room below the Wagon Wheel?" the Chief-of-Staff asked in a questioning voice.

"Yes, Buck, I want the Mexican General to attend."

"Yes, ma'am, it's your call as President."

"It certainly is," she replied shaking her finger at her Chief-of-Staff.

All requested parties were present for the 17:00 hour meeting at the Wagon Wheel. Mexican General Rōjas was surprised at the request by President Williamson to attend her staff meeting.

Sara asked Major General Montgomery to introduce his Mexican friend and the highest ranking officer in the Mexican Army.

Michael stood up and asked General Rōjas to stand and proceeded to introduce him to Sara's staff. He started the introduction by speaking in Spanish instead of English. The War Room interrupted in laughter, and General Rōjas continued to introduce himself in perfect English. The assembled staff liked the Generals rebound and quick action to a funny situation.

Sara stood up and said, "Now you know why I have asked General Rōjas to attend our meeting, he speaks better English than anyone in this room."

The Mexican General smiled and said, "Thank you, Madam President."

The entire staff stood up and clapped loudly for the remarkable General officer from south of the border.

"Now, for the reason I called this meeting. Yesterday, I received a call from President Goodwin saying that he thought the rioting and destruction was finally over in his country. He feels that between the non-rioting private citizens, local police and the presence of federal troops, the carnage is over at last. He said that over twenty-two thousand Americans were killed during the rioting nationwide, and they estimate that a trillion dollars are needed to rebuild the major cities, utilities and etc.

"I have offered our assistance in any way to President Goodwin and his administration, but he said it was too early to know what is needed and where it's needed. He said he would keep us informed on any requirement needed in the coming weeks and months.

"Now, ladies and gentlemen, though the Washington President has indicated the rioting and destruction is finally over, I don't believe we should relax our guard along the border with his states.

"What is your opinion?" Sara asked the group.

General Wittingham stood up and walked over to the huge physical map of the Western States of America and the adjoining forty-two states. He ran his finger along the entire border and said that he agreed with President Williamson. "We should not relax our guard or withdraw any forces from the border area. It's too early and possibly too dangerous not to wait and see what develops. With the President's permission, I would like to ask our General friend from south of the Rio Grande a military question."

"Certainly, General, ask away," she said.

"General Rōjas, would you consider having your two divisions stay at the Texas border a little longer in case trouble rears its ugly head in the near future?"

General Rōjas stood up and told the group, I personally think my Mexican troops should stay until you, sir, are convinced that this crisis is over and its reoccurrence is small. But remember, sir, I'm only the commander and the final decision must be made by President Lazzara. I will recommend to my President that we stay a little longer, but it's his overall decision."

"Thank you, General, you're a credit to all ranking military officers I have known over my long career."

The entire War Room stood up and clapped loudly.

"Does anyone else have an opinion on this crisis?" Sara asked again.

"Yes, Madam President, I do," the Secretary-of-State, Paula Anderson said in a strong voice.

"Go ahead, Madam Secretary."

"I'm concerned about having thousands of foreign troops in our country helping to guard our lengthy border, and the possibility of having more foreign troops coming from Canada. That would mean almost one hundred thousand foreign ground troops and a full air wing would be in our country. That scares me, Madam President. That represents a large percent of our total forces protecting the border and throughout the whole country. I would feel better if all foreign troops were asked to leave as soon as possible, with our thanks for their service to our nation.

"Madam President, remember 'the rise and fall of the Roman Empire' when three out of every four individuals residing in Rome were not Roman citizens. That was the start of the downfall of a great nation, and we should heed that fact, Madam President."

The War Room was dead quiet before Major General Montgomery stood up and said with a voice full of anger, "You're wrong, Madam Secretary. Mexico is our friend, and President Lazzara and my good friend General Rōjas have offered their assistance in time, money and partnership in protecting our country and theirs from an unstable government in Washington, D.C. And your reference to Canada is unfounded as well. They have been our international friends for almost two hundred years, and we welcome their offered assistance, Madam Secretary. As Secretary-of-State, I can't believe you feel as you do, ma'am. Maybe you should rethink your current position."

"That's enough, thank you, General," the President quickly intervened.

"I apologize, Madam Secretary, this is a democratic body and you have a right to your views, even if they're not our government's current policy and view."

President Williamson gave the General the evil eye but said nothing.

"If there is nothing else, let's keep all our domestic and foreign troops at the ready for the next two weeks and then revisit our military position. Do we all agree?" Sara asked the group. "Anyone who disagrees please raise your hand."

Secretary-of-State Anderson raised her hand in the only 'No' vote.

"General Rōjas, please call President Lazzara and get his decision on extending the duty of your forces a little longer."

"Right away," the Mexican General answered.

President Williamson stood up and said, in a loud voice, "Unless a meteor hits Flagstaff or Washington and the oceans raise five hundred feet, let's hold our positions along our borders until we're sure Goodwin is current in his assessment of the crisis."

The War Room emptied quickly, but President Williamson asked General Rōjas and Montgomery to stay behind. Once the War Room was empty, Sara told the Mexican General, "The Secretary's views are her own and not any part of mine," she assured the General.

"That's okay," the General told the President. "She is entitled to her opinion, like everyone else," he added.

"Thank you, General. You're a very wise man," Sara told her Mexican friend.

Both Generals left Flagstaff and flew directly to their headquarters in Texas.

General Montgomery was in his small office looking at various reports when a knock on the door interrupted his thought. A young Lieutenant opened the door and said, "Sir, you have a visitor."

"Thank you, Lieutenant, send him in."

To the General's surprise, it was Lt. Ortiz (Butch) who was wearing civilian clothes. She was dressed to kill. She wore a low cut yellow silk blouse that could hardly contain the D-cup breasts that strained the buttons to their breaking point. Her black skirt clung to her body like a second skin. With her hair pulled back and sporting a million dollar smile, she was a picture of loveliness.

"My god, Maria, you are beautiful," the American General blurted out. He walked over to her and gave her a long and passionate kiss.

She looked up at the General and said in a low voice, "Michael, I love you."

He kissed her again and gave her a hug while whispering in her ear, "I'm in love with you Maria."

She stepped back and said, "How is this possible that an American General like yourself is in love with a poor girl from Mexico?"

"Maria, I have loved you since the early days with your Spl. Ops Company, but I didn't want to use my position as your Commander to put pressure on you."

"You know I'm old enough to be your father," he told his Mexican beauty.

"I don't care how old you are," she quickly answered. "I just want to spend the rest of my life with you, General. I don't care where we live as long as we're together," she said, looking into his eyes.

"I'm going to leave to visit my parents and three sisters in Mexico. I'll only be on leave a week," she said.

"Where do your parents live?" the General asked.

"They live in a small town just west of Tampico, on the east coast. The town is Ebano with a population of about twelve thousand people," she said with a smile.

"Are you going to tell your parents you're in love with a gringo twice your age?"

"You bet," she answered. "I'll tell them how tall and handsome you are, as well as a very compassionate and caring man and an American Major General, to boot," she said with a big smile. "I'll also tell them I'm madly in love with you, and I want to spend the balance of my days with you, Michael."

"When you get back from your leave, we should sit down and make plans for the future, if that's okay with you, Maria."

"Yes, we should," she said, giving him a big kiss. She stepped back, saluted and left the office.

"Oh my god," he thought, "Maria is the only woman I have ever loved. I hope I can make her happy for the rest of my life. She will go from Lieutenant to a Five Star General in our house," he said with a grin.

Maria arrived in Ebano, Mexico and went straight to her parents' house and knocked on the front door. Her mother answered the door and couldn't believe her eyes. She hadn't seen her oldest daughter since she was wounded during the drug wars. Maria asked about her three younger sisters and her mother said they were away in college and doing well. After many kisses and hugs, they left the house and went into town to the only drug store, owned by her father. He was the only pharmacist for miles around. When Maria and her mother entered the drug store, her father was filling a prescription, and when he looked up and saw Maria, his eyes were filled with tears. He came around the counter, picked up Maria and started twirling around and around. When they stopped, he hugged her as only a proud father can.

"Father, I have something to tell you and mother. I want to get married," she blurted out.

Her father looked at her mother and said, "You want to get married?"

"Yes, I do, father."

"Who is this lucky man?" her father asked.

"His name is Michael Montgomery, father, and he is an American."

"A gringo?" he answered.

"Yes, a gringo," she said. "He is a Major General in the W.S. of A. Army, and he is a perfect gentleman, father. I just know you and mother will love him."

"That name, Montgomery, sounds very familiar," her father said, rubbing his chin.

"It should father, he was our Commanding officer. Michael and General Rōjas were in command of our Spl. Ops Company in Querétaro."

"Do you love him, Maria?" her father asked.

"Yes, I do, father."

He gave her a big hug and said, "If you truly love this American then you have your mother's and my approval to marry."

Maria was so happy to hear both her parents say it was okay to marry this Army officer.

"Does he speak Spanish?" her mother asked.

"Perfect, mother. Better than I do," she admitted.

Her father closed the drug store early, and the three headed for home outside Ebano.

Butch returned to Army Headquarters in Texas after spending the week with her parents. She had a glow about her that her fellow soldiers couldn't help notice, her close friends

asked her what's up, but she wouldn't divulge anything about her personal life. Two days after she returned, General Montgomery asked to see her.

She related her week with her parents and said that they wanted to meet him whenever it was convenient for him. Michael agreed that they should fly to Tampico and drive to Ebano to meet her parents as soon as possible.

Maria mentioned that her enlistment was up in less than ninety days, and she probably should resign her commission at that time.

Michael said, "In the American Army, an officer can resign at any time, but it usually takes a couple of months to process his or her request to end their military service. I don't know the rules in your Mexican Army," Michael admitted. "You should ask General Rōjas, he certainly would know the regs. I would like you by my side as my wife and not a Lieutenant," he said with a smile.

Maria smiled and said, "I love you, General Montgomery, and stood on tip toes and gave him a sloppy kiss on the cheek.

"Now, Lieutenant, I would suggest you get back to work in that Headquarters of yours and do some work." She laughed, kissed him again and quickly left his office to seek out General Rōjas.

During the next two weeks, the national crisis in the Washington forty-two continued to subside. Only a few small incidents were recorded throughout the entire country. The well-equipped military and police seemed to have control of the situation at last.

The devastation and loss of life was far more than earlier estimates. Most of the large cities like Detroit, Los Angeles, Miami, Columbus, Indianapolis and New Orleans were gutted and square mile after mile needed to be demolished and eventually rebuilt. Very little, if anything, could be salvaged. Other cities like Washington, D.C. had many priceless national treasures stolen or destroyed. Washington's estimate of one trillion in damages was going to be low, they now admitted.

President Williamson was at her desk when Chief-of-Staff McCarney came in and said Washington had just revised the figures of the rioting and devastation. Buck told the President that the new estimate is well over a trillion dollars.

"Buck, call the Vice President and ask him to arrange a meeting at the Wagon Wheel as soon as possible." The Vice President called all parties, and within twenty-four hours all parties were in the War Room many stories below the massive military facility called the Wagon Wheel.

President Williamson entered the bomb proof War Room and sat in her usual spot at the head of the massive table. Nobody sat down before their head of state was seated.

"Thank you, ladies and gentlemen, for your quick response, I know some of you came a considerable distance for these meetings, but I felt that since the crisis within the forty-two has apparently eased, we should discuss our next move, or moves, with regard to our military buildup along our lengthy border and other problems of the day."

"General Wittingham, you're first, sir. You're the ranking military officer, and we want your professional opinion on this matter."

"Thank you, Madam President. In my opinion, the various info we have received from their capitol and other areas of their country is credible, ma'am. My staff and others believe the nationwide rioting is over. We also have been told by Washington that the various leaders of the rioting have been arrested or killed, and thousands of persons who participated in the wanton destruction have also been imprisoned.

"Now for your question about our border. I feel it would be a safe bet to remove our military from the border and restore normal border operations. I feel we could let General Rōjas and his two infantry divisions return to Mexico with our undying gratitude for his service to our country. General Rōjas, his staff and division commanders were top notch career officers who worked well with my staff and various commanders like Major General Montgomery. At the same time, Madam President, we should thank the Canadian Prime Minister and his government for offering their services in our defense, if needed.

"Thank you, General, that was very eloquently stated, and you're right, we owe a great deal to President Lazzara, General Rōjas and the Mexican government. And we won't forget the Canadian Prime Minister Parnell Leslie Pearson."

President Williamson pointed and said, "General Montgomery, you and General Rōjas guarded our Texas border.

Do you feel it's time to pull back our military and return to normal border activities?"

"Madam President. For the most part, I agree with General Wittingham, but I would not pull back all our forces from the border. Most of the border, maybe, but not the Texas border. I would keep a few companies at key locations and continue the daily sorties for at least another month," General Montgomery advised the Commander-in-Chief and War Room attendees. "One last thing, ma'am. I wish Lt. General Wadsworth had been well enough to command our forces and defend the Texas border during this crisis. I was told earlier today that the General is doing extremely well after a triple by-pass. I know we're all praying for his speedy and complete recovery and return to his military duties."

Every man and woman in the War Room stood up and clapped for the recovery of General Wadsworth, and President Williamson lead the spontaneous reverence for one of their respected General officers.

"Thank you, General Montgomery, for your comments and insight."

"Anybody else?" the President asked.

"Yes, Madam President, I have a comment," the Secretary-of-State said, standing up. "I feel it's past the time for our Mexican friends to return home. We didn't need their services during the crisis, and we don't need them now. I vote we send them home as soon as possible," the Secretary added as she slowly sat back down.

President Williamson jumped up and shouted, "You're out of order, Madam Secretary. Your negative attitude towards our Mexican friends is unwarranted," Sara said in a very loud voice. "Do me a favor, Madam Secretary, keep your big mouth shut for the rest of this meeting or I'll have you removed," the President threatened. "I'm beginning to wonder just how did you get to be my Secretary-of-State with that narrow mindedness of yours. But since I'm the President of the Western States of America, I can correct that mistake here and now. Sergeant-at-Arms, would you please escort Paula Catherine Anderson from the War Room and the Wagon Wheel."

Paula was escorted from the War Room without saying another word.

Chapter 11 – Threatening War Clouds

Sara stood up and said, "I'm truly sorry, ladies and gentlemen, for my behavior in front of this body of professionals. I should have dismissed the Secretary in my office and not in front of this body. I must have missed Supervision #101 in college, but I do apologize for my anger and I will try to hold my outbursts to a small roar."

Sara continued, "I tend to agree with General Wittingham that we can allow the Mexican troops to leave our border and return to Mexico."

"General Montgomery, how long will it take for the thirty thousand soldiers to pack up and leave for Mexico?"

"Ma'am, I would guess it should take about two weeks or a little less. Remember they brought their own artillery, vehicles, weapons, ammo and a dozen choppers with Gatling Guns and other various supplies. They were self-contained, Madam President, General Rōjas insisted they bring all their own gear. He wanted to use this border crisis to test the overall readiness of his troops, equipment and transportation. He also insisted that all his officers from Captain and above speak English. He wanted nothing lost in translation between his Mexican officers and our commanders."

"I think they should be back across the Mexican border in ten days," General Montgomery added.

"Thank you, General, I'll contact President Lazzara and let him know his Mexican troops can leave shortly and return to their bases in Mexico. You can tell General Rōjas that he'll be hearing from his President in a day or so. But before Rōjas departs for Mexico, the two of you should determine where to place your small companies along the Texas border." Sara continued, "After the return of the Mexican troops is complete, we must talk about your border security job. You'll be starting your agency from scratch and setting up state security offices and hiring thousands of new border agents. Our borders with Washington's forty-two, Mexico, Canada and the very long west coast stretches more than fifteen thousand miles, as we can figure. The exact mileage is unknown," the President admitted.

"Your job in keeping our country Safe will be monumental in this government and will require a cabinet post as National Security Director."

The War Room group again stood up and cheered for the newest cabinet member, Major General Michael Montgomery.

"In the next few weeks, I'll have meetings on your first year budget, Michael, and it will be sizeable, I assure you," the President promised.

"Thank you, Madam President, I will do my very best to insure that our thousands of miles of border are secure and protective of foreign intervention by undesirable individuals."

"Now, another subject. We must put the final touches on our government," Sara told the group. "I have been dragging my feet, I admit, but we must finally have a constitution in place and start making national decisions with our whole elected members and not just me as your President. All eight states have had their elections and are waiting to send their elected reps to Flagstaff.

"I will call a full congressional meeting shortly so we can start the democratic process to become a full-fledged government and nation. Our First Congress will meet in the newly completed Freedom Building across the boulevard from the Military Wagon Wheel. This huge building is a beautiful example of ancient Greek architecture, with its huge marble columns and massive stone walls. That building should stand for a thousand years, if man leaves it alone.

"Thank you, ladies and gentlemen, this meeting addressed some very important issues of the day. Please keep your subordinates informed on all issues, no government secrets of any kind. I want this Western States of America government to be completely transparent in all its dealings and transactions. Our government is for our people and not self-serving against our people.

"Have a safe trip returning home and make this country proud of your government service."

It only took nine and a half days for the thirty thousand Mexican troops commanded by General Rōjas to pack up their equipment and assorted gear to move south on route #35 to the Texas-Mexican border. Before crossing the border, the Williamson military officiated by Major Generals H.G. Miles and Russell Winslow presented every Mexican soldier with a specially designed medal and ribbon to be worn on their Class "A" uniforms. The ceremony was held just outside Laredo, Texas and lasted a full hour. After presenting the medals to the Mexican troops, their Commander General Rōjas was presented with a bronze plaque in honor of his service to our country.

The two divisions of Mexican infantry took three full days to move their personnel and equipment across the bridge and Rio Grande separating the two Laredo's and two countries.

It was somewhat orderly, but still a military cluster-fuck in getting the massive amount of men and equipment across the small bridge in just three days. But even with the bridge bottle neck, they got the crossing done in seventy-two hours. Before crossing into Mexico, many soldiers said they would miss the Texas supplied chow. They ate three squares a day and had additional rations if needed. Almost to the man, they enjoyed their Texas assignment, the chow and the weather being a lot cooler than their bases five hundred miles south of the Rio Grande.

Before General Rōjas' Headquarters started moving south with his troops, Lt. Maria Ortiz (Butch) had asked the General about the regs pertaining to the resignation of a Mexican officer. He told Maria that whether an officer or enlisted member, they must stay in uniform until their enlistment is officially up.

Maria had called Michael and explained what General Rōjas had said about the possibility of early separation from the Mexican military before she had to leave to assist in the move to Mexico. She told Michael she would call him when they got settled in Querétaro, Mexico. Maria reminded him that she had less than ninety days to serve before they could be together for life. He told his future wife, "Just do your job and we'll be together in a matter of months."

Before the Mexican General left for home, he and General Montgomery selected four sites along the Texas border where a small contingency of federal troops would be stationed for an undetermined length of time. These four sites had a total of less than a thousand men and women.

A month after the Washington crisis died down, President Williamson decided to have the first meeting of Congress to be held in Flagstaff.

The eight states of the Western States of America would be represented by the following elected state officials:

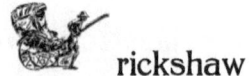 rickshaw

	Senators	Congressmen
California	2	12
Arizona	2	4
New Mexico	2	4
Texas	2	10
Oregon	2	4
Washington	2	4
Alaska	2	8
Hawaii	2	5
	16	51

16 Senators
51 Congressmen
1 Vice President
68 Voting Persons

The elected state officials were summoned to the Freedom Building in Flagstaff for the First Congressional meeting and assembly by Vice President Richardson. When the roll call was finished, all elected officials from the eight states and the Vice President were present and accounted for.

When Vice President Richardson pounded the gavel, the First Congress of the Western States of America was officially open.

The Vice President, still standing shouted, "Ladies and gentlemen, the President of the Western States of America." Everyone in the Freedom Hall stood up clapped and whistled for a full two minutes before Sara held up her arms and motioned for them to please be seated. When the noise died down to a dull roar, Sara said, "Thank you for that warm welcome to our brand new Freedom Hall and the First Congressional meeting of our fledging country."

Sara started by saying, "We don't have appointed committees yet to delve into our many problems, so for now we'll have to vote on issues with the full Congress. As you're very comfortable in your color coded leather chairs, you can see the console in front of you that has an electric voting machine with, I believe, five buttons. There is also a large screen that will display the issue in English, Spanish and French.

"Now our first order of business is our new Border Security Agency. We must provide a first year budget for this new and necessary federal agency that will help manage and protect our fifteen thousand miles of border. We actually think the border mileage is closer to twenty thousand miles. Our country is surrounded by the Pacific Ocean, Mexico, Canada, the Gulf and seven states of the so called Washington union.

"This Border Security Agency (BSA) will be headed up by Major General Michael Montgomery. His new title will be Border Security Director and it will be a cabinet post with only one boss, and that's me. The first year and the next two years budgets will be huge because the General must start this agency from scratch. While setting up eight state agencies to hire thousands of border agents, guards and related jobs. Between checking passports, visas, cars, trucks, planes, boats and ships, this agency will certainly have their hands full. Besides all that, they must keep the undesirables out as well.

"Now, for the changes in border policy. Once the agency is up and running, there will be profiling of Muslims coming from Iran, Iraq, Saudi Arabia, Canada, Mexico and a dozen other countries. That also includes Muslims coming from the forty-two states as well," the President added. "If you're a Muslim and a male, you should be prepared to be searched and questioned as well as have your paperwork checked and double checked. Israel has profiled for the past ten years without a terrorist incident, and we will do the same.

"Last week, I checked with our Supreme Court and they voted four to two in favor of profiling certain religions and groups, to be determined by the Border Security Agency, the office of the Vice President and the Secretary-of-State. Now, I realize we currently don't have a Secretary-of-State. Secretary Anderson was dismissed, and I have not appointed her successor because Congress should elect her replacement, not me. But in the meantime, if I feel we need a S.O.S. before Congress can elect someone to hold that important office, I'll appoint a Secretary on a temporary basis.

"I'm sure your reps have a lot to discuss, so I'll say goodbye. Our First Congress, I'm so proud of all of you and our country as well." President Williamson waved and left the podium for her waiting car and the short drive to the capitol building and her office. Before she entered her car, she could still hear the loud clapping and cheers coming from the Freedom Hall. Sara smiled as she entered the limo.

General Montgomery was in his office seven floors below ground at the Wagon Wheel when a call came in telling the General he had a visitor at the main gate. He started to ask who it was when the phone went dead. He tried calling the main gate, but the line was busy. He put on his coat and headed for the express elevator that made it top side at warp speed. He went to the main gate and inside the guard shack was Maria. He picked her up, kissed her on the mouth and said, "Where did you come from?"

She said, "General Rōjas let me go a couple of days early because he wanted to get rid of me," she said with a big smile.

"You look stunning, Maria, you're more beautiful than ever," he said, hugging her again.

"Where can we go?" she asked Michael.

"Do you have a pass?" he asked his future wife.

"Yes, sir, she does, I made out a temporary visitors pass before you got here, sir."

"Thank you, Sergeant."

"You're welcome, sir."

"Are you hungry, Maria?" he asked.

"I'm starved," she answered. "I could eat a house, as you Americans say."

"Okay. Let's head for the main cafeteria on the ground floor and get a bite to eat."

"Lead the way," the ex-Lieutenant said, holding the General's arm in a tight grip.

"I assume your military service in the Mexican Army is now over?" he asked.

"That is correct. As of yesterday, I'm a lowly civilian," she added with a smile.

After they placed their order for lunch, they sat down waiting for their number to be called, when Maria said, "Do you know what that friend of yours, General Rōjas, did?"

"What did the General do?" he asked.

"That skunk tried to get me to re-enlist for another six years by offering to promote me to Captain on the day I re-enlisted," she said, shaking her head.

"I would have done the same thing, my dear, you're a great combat soldier and one fearless in battle, as I have seen many times in Mexico. That Captaincy Rōjas offered is nothing compared to your rank once we're married. I may be a Major General with Two Stars, but you'll be a Five Star General in our home," he said, looking into those big brown eyes filling with crocodile tears.

"I love you, Michael, with all my heart," she whispered as they finally called their chow number.

General Montgomery and Maria flew by commercial airlines to Tampico, Mexico, rented a car and drove the thirty-two miles to Ebano to meet and visit Maria's parents and her three sisters who were home from school and college.

Maria and Michael went straight to her parent's house outside Ebano. Both parents were waiting on the front porch when they arrived. As soon as they got out of the rented car, they were hugged and kissed by her mother and three sisters. Maria's father shook the General's hand for a full minute then gave him a bear hug. After that warm welcome, everybody went inside, sat at the kitchen table drinking a local brew of some kind.

Maria's father asked Michael if he was a real American General.

Michael answered, "Yes, a real Two Star Major General. When I worked for your President Lazzara, I was only a Colonel," he said with a smile.

"Our Maria told us you were her Commanding Officer during the drug cartel raids. When she was wounded she came home to recover and told us about her brave Commanding Officer from America and Mexican General Rōjas."

After a typical Mexican lunch, the whole group went into town to see her Dad's drug store. After the store tour and a spin around the town, they headed back to her parent's home for a day of relaxing and getting to know one another. Maria and the General spent the better part of two days visiting her parents and sisters. Before leaving, Maria's father asked only one favor of them and that was when they decided to marry,they have the wedding there in Ebano.

The General looked at Maria and she said 'yes' with her eyes.

Michael said, "Mr. Ortiz, if that's your wish then that is what we'll do."

Both parents hugged each other and said, "Fantissimo."

After the long Mexican goodbyes, they drove back to Tampico and the long bumpy flight back to Flagstaff. When they arrived in Flagstaff, the General made arrangements for Maria to stay at the local Ritz-Carlton until they could find suitable housing.

General Montgomery called the President's office in the capitol building and asked Chief-of-Staff McCarney to schedule a meeting with President Williamson.

Within an hour, Buck called back and informed the General that the President would see him tomorrow afternoon at 15:00 hours.

Mrs. Bakker ushered the General into the President's office, and he was quickly pointed to a large brown leather chair by the President.

"Good to see you again, Michael," she said, shaking his hand before he could rise.

"Thank you, ma'am."

"I won't take up much of your time, but I have a little problem, or I should say a large problem with my job as Director of Border Security."

"Continue, General."

"Madam President, I'm going to be married in the near future to a wonderful Mexican national and that presents a real security problem."

"You're right, General, that is a real first class problem," the President admitted. "A real problem," she added.

"As you know, General, anyone with a secret or greater clearance cannot have a spouse that isn't an American citizen. In your job as Director of Border Security, your clearance must be above 'top secret' and most likely 'for your eyes only,'" the President told the General, shaking her head. "We have very few options or choices," she grudgingly admitted.

"Number #1. You'll have to resign your position as Director of Border Security.

Number #2. We'll have to pass a special law for you only to change the requirements for your security clearance on the job."

"Madam President, there is a third option, which is to not get married. But that is not an option as far as I'm concerned."

"When do you intend to tie the knot?" Sara asked.

"Very soon, Madam President, very soon."

"Let me look into this matter and see what we can do, General. I'll get back to you in a day or so."

"Thank you, Ma'am. I didn't want to plunge our country into the pit of despair, but I wanted this personal issue solved one way or the other before the issue leaks to the public."

The President smiled and said, "The pit of despair, General."

Both burst out laughing.

The Chief-of-Staff informed the President, "In the past few days, thousands of individuals, and even whole families have been flocking to our border crossings trying to leave the Washington forty-two and enter our W.S. of A."

"Our borders are open," the President said, "but we must be very restrictive on who we give visas to and allowed entry. The Western States of America is not going to be a safe haven to all comers and be turned into a welfare state where half the population contributes absolutely nothing but feeds at the government trough. We say enough of that welfare and giveaway programs with the Washington union."

The President continued, "Ours is a new country where people can work, be happy and raise their families. I must stress the word 'work.' All citizens will work. If you're disabled and can't work, that's one thing, but all able bodied people will work or starve. We did not create this new nation to let the bottom feeders reap the spoils from the hardworking public and allow them to reside in subsidized housing, drink beer, watch T.V. and collect a monthly check from the state of government. Some states in the Washington union have paid as high as forty thousand dollars a year to their welfare recipients to do absolutely nothing but crank out additional dependents.

"Our Flagstaff government and our eight states will not support a population that doesn't work. We have thousands of jobs for skilled, unskilled and disabled workers. Many companies hire workers that are mentally slow, missing limbs, obese or have other mental, physical or health problems. The bottom line is most people can find work if they want to," the President concluded.

Sara said, "Sure, now that I need a Secretary-of-State we don't have one."

"Why do we need one right this minute?" Buck asked.

"Sit down, Buck, and I'll tell you why." Sara explained the problem that General Montgomery had presented to her and that he deserved an answer in a day or so. She told her Chief-of-Staff the few options and said that she didn't want to change the regs to accommodate a single person.

"Rather than change the regulations pertaining to top security and above, why not give Maria citizenship under specific reasons and special circumstances."

"Yes, Buck, that's a great idea."

"Please call the Chief Justice and have her call me at her convenience," the President asked.

"Right away, ma'am."

The Chief Justice of the W.S. of A. Supreme Court returned the call and said, "Madam President, Chief-of-Staff McCarney called and said that you have a unique problem."

"Yes, I do, Chief Justice.

"The phone line is secure, so I can explain my problem over the phone. The President told the complete story and when she finished, the Chief Justice said, "That is a problem, but give me a day and I'll look into it, Madam President."

"Thank you," Sara told her long-time friend and college roommate. "If there is a way around this, I'm sure she'll find it," Sara thought.

Within twenty hours the Head Associate in the Office of the Chief Justice called President Williamson and explained how the problem could be solved. She also apologized for the Chief Justice not calling due to her elderly mother being rushed to the hospital early that morning, but she knew that the president was looking for an answer as soon as possible.

"Madam President, Mexican National Maria Ortiz can become a citizen of the Western States of America under Section #12 of 'Special Authorization to Citizenship' after being recommended by the sitting President of the Western States of America. That President must submit the special request with all pertinent information to the Chief Justice of the Supreme Court, who by law must rule within thirty days. You have the following options, ma'am:

#1. A citizenship without a W.S. of A. passport.
#2. A temporary citizenship for a specific period.
#3. A citizenship for abandoned children.
#4. A citizenship for spouses married to military or government officials and personnel in high secure and secret positions.

"I'm assuming, Madam President, that option #4 is the appropriate one?" the Chief Clerk asked.

"Yes, you're correct," the President answered.

"Okay, Madam President, I'll forward all the necessary forms and paperwork to your office later this afternoon. If you or your staff have any questions after receiving the requirements, please call me, Chief Clerk Alexandra Malenkov, if the Chief Justice is not available."

"Thank you, Alexandra, you have been very helpful. If you're talking to the Chief Justice, please tell her we're praying for her mother to get well."

"Yes, I will, ma'am."

The necessary paperwork from the Justice Department was delivered by special messenger to the President's office.

President Williamson briefly read through the two dozen pages of instructions and scanned the many forms required to obtain this special citizenship. Sara called in Chief-of-Staff McCarney and assistant to the President, Beverly Wolcott, to start gathering the necessary info required by the Justice Department. She also instructed them to contact General Montgomery and Maria when necessary to get the ball rolling. "Be sure to get the General's permission to speak with Maria before you contact her. On the other hand, maybe it would be better for all parties if you talked to both of them together while acquiring the necessary information. I'm sure Maria would feel better if the General was present," the President added.

"Yes, ma'am, we'll hop right on it," Buck assured the Commander-in-Chief.

Secretary-of-Defense Waterman called Mrs. Bakker and asked to speak to the President with a priority message.

Ruth informed the President that Defense Secretary Waterman was on the secure phone and must talk with her immediately.

"Then put him through, Ruth."

"Good afternoon, Mr. Secretary, what's up sir?"

"Madam President, I have just received word from my sources in Washington that Russian submarines have surfaced and were spotted just ten miles off the coast of New York City and just thirty miles off Port Eads, Louisiana taking latitude and longitude readings as well as sonar depth readings. When the Coast Guard planes circled the subs, they continued to stay surfaced taking readings. When surface ships were dispatched to the area, they submerged and disappeared.

"The Washington military are up in arms over this violation of sovereignty by surfacing within the twelve mile limit. The sub could see the New York City skyline from their deck. President Goodwin sent an urgent message to Russian President Alexander Petrovich advising him to recall his war ship from our coastal waters. He also told the Russian leader that if a Russian war ship is caught within the twelve mile limit, it will be attacked."

As the Defense Secretary was informing the President of the Russian problem, Mrs. Bakker entered the office and said that a Navy Aide to the Secretary was in her office with an important message.

"Send him in, Ruth."

Naval Aide Lt. Commander Marian Loomis entered the President's office, saluted and said, "Mr. Secretary, a message from General Wittingham." She handed the folded message to the Secretary and waited for him to read same. After he read the note, he folded the paper and handed it to President Williamson. Sara read the note and said, "Commander, do you know the contents of the note?"

Commander Loomis said, "Yes, ma'am, I do."

"Thank you, Commander, please wait outside for further instructions."

"Yes, ma'am."

Sara went around her desk and sat down slowly. "You better have a seat, Mr. Secretary, while I gather my thoughts. I want to read the messaged out loud," she said. She unfolded the paper and started.

"Mr. Secretary, I have just learned from sources in Western Europe that troops by the tens of thousands are having exercises near the borders of Romania, Azerbaijan, Georgia, Ukraine, Moldavia, Belarus, Latvia, Estonia, Lithuania and Armenia. The very reliable source said this is no exercise, but a planned buildup of some sixty-four divisions, or approximately one million men. This does not include four fighter wings and six bomber groups. Along with all this, the Russian government has alerted another million reserve personnel for possible service. They believe that Russian President Alexander Petrovich has ordered the takeover of Europe by military action. That's all of Europe. Petrovich has threatened for years and now has the military might and equipment to do it. His tank force alone is more than twenty thousand medium and heavy tanks. They're afraid Petrovich is ready to strike a fatal blow to Europe for the third time in just one hundred years.

I await your reply and instructions, Mr. Secretary.

Lt. Gen. Charles Wittingham
Commanding General
Western States of America"

Chapter 12
WORLDS IN CHAOS

After Sara re-read the message, she asked the Secretary, "Is this an iron clad fact, and has this been confirmed by a variety of sources?"

"The note doesn't say, ma'am, but I'll contact General Wittingham right away."

"Hang on," Sara said as she pressed the button on the intercom. "Ruth, please contact General Wittingham as quickly as possible."

"Yes, ma'am."

Within a few minutes, the red light on the intercom started blinking. Sara pushed the button and said, "General, Secretary Waterman and I have just read your message and we're wondering, has this been confirmed by other sources?"

"Yes, ma'am. Our satellites along with Canadian sky birds have detected large groups of men and equipment poised along their entire border with every eastern country. Along with this, we have noted the various countries have called to arms their entire military forces in response to this Russian build up and threat. I might add, Madam President, that all the military combined of these countries, plus France, Germany, Spain, Italy and others cannot stop the Red Tide that would sweep over all of Europe in about five weeks or less.

"Since the Second World War, Europe has rebounded and built beautiful modern cities only to the threatened by the Russian appetite for land, wealth and slaves. The beautiful cities of Europe will be surrounded by the Iron Curtain that will transform their beautiful cities to dull drab and cold war torn cities with no hope for the future.

"One more thing ma'am. If World War III breaks out in Europe we, I mean the Western States of America and the Washington forty-two, will be powerless to either help Europe or stop the Russian bear from raising the hammer and sickle in every country in Europe. Remember, the use of atomic weapons is not an option in Europe, because the Russian government does not want to destroy the very land they want to plow in the future.

Old fashioned tank, artillery, air power and a million or more ground forces will be the order of the day.

"One more thing, Madam President, the advancing Russian armies will use the same tactics as the German Army did before entering Paris. They'll give the cities an ultimatum, either surrender or we'll raze your city to the ground.

"Unless attacked by Russia or China, we might have to set this war out," General Wittingham admitted.

"Thank you, General, for your observation and comments. Either the Secretary or I will contact you shortly with instructions."

"Yes, ma'am, my headquarters and I will be waiting."

Sara turned off the entire intercom and said, "Mr. Secretary, what the hell do we do now?" She continued:

- What if Russia does attack all of Europe?
- What if Russia attacks Europe and Washington?
- What is Russia attacks Europe, Washington and Flagstaff?
- What if Russia and China join forces to conqueror the world?

"If Russia and China join forces, then the Western States of America and the Washington Forty-two will be speaking a foreign language," the Defense Secretary said in earnest.

"I agree," Sara admitted."

"I better send the Commanders back to the Wagon Wheel."

"Certainly, Mr. Secretary."

When the Defense Secretary left the office and closed the door, Sara realized she was alone with all these domestic and foreign problems and mounting crisis. In the end, she alone must make the decisions that will protect or destroy her country.

Chief-of-Staff McCarney and assistant to the President Beverly Wolcott filled out the necessary forms while interviewing both General Montgomery and his future wife, Maria Ortiz. Once all the signatures were gathered and witnessed by a federal judge, the entire package was delivered to the President's office for Sara to review and write a letter of Special Request addressed to the Chief Justice of the Supreme Court. Once the President wrote the letter and delivered all required and necessary documents to the Supreme Court, the thirty day clock would start.

The Chief Justice had told President Williamson that she would look into the matter as quickly as she could, but now with her mother being rushed to the hospital the decision could be delayed a bit.

The next day, after the Justice Department received the documents from the President, Chief Clerk Malenkov called the Chief Justice and informed her that all necessary documents, paperwork and signatures had been received and dated.

The Supreme Court Justice instructed her Chief Clerk to review all the documents and give a yes or no decision to the President's request. She informed her Head Clerk that she would approve whatever decision she came to on the matter. While this is unprecedented, it is still very legal under the circumstances.

After spending two full days reviewing the Special Authorization to Citizenship Law and other laws pertaining to citizenship, Chief Clerk Alexandra Malenkov came to a decision. Alex called the Chief Justice and told her that in her opinion, the Mexican National, Maria Ortiz, should not be given a special citizenship.

"That's your decision Alex, and you know by law you're not required to explain the reasons for denial to citizenship."

"Yes, I understand that, Madam Justice. Do you want me to inform the President?"

"No, Alex, I will call President Williamson myself. She will be devastated with the ruling, but that's why we have laws and rules."

"Thank you, Alexandra, for your time and effort researching this difficult problem in government."

The Chief Justice called her friend and President. She informed Sara the ruling was 'no' for granting Special Citizenship to Maria Ortiz. When President Williamson heard the ruling, she became boiling mad and could hardly talk. She asked, "What was the voting?"

"There was no voting, Madam President, the decision was made by my Chief Clerk Alexander Malenkov under my authorization."

With that admission, President Williamson slammed the phone down and threw the phone and receiver across the room.

The sound was so loud that Mrs. Bakker came running to see what had happened. Sara motioned for Ruth to leave her alone. Ruth understood and closed the door behind her.

Secretary Waterman returned and said, "What was that noise all about?"

"I dropped the whole phone," Sara answered.

"Well, Madam President, I assume you're going to call an emergency meeting on the Russian crisis."

"Yes, I believe we should. The situation isn't going to get any better."

"Mr. Secretary, will you arrange for a full meeting of the staff for tomorrow morning at 11:00 hours?"

"Yes, ma'am, I'll get right on it."

Sara called the Wagon Wheel operator and asked for General Montgomery. Michael answered the phone on the first ring and said, "Madam President, have you received any word yet from the Supreme Court?"

"Yes, General, I have, and their ruling was not in our favor, I'm afraid."

"What do you mean?" the General asked in a loud voice.

"The request for Special Citizenship was rejected by the Chief Justice of our Supreme Court. The ruling is final, I'm told."

"Well, that cuts it, Madam President. I now must choose between my job as Director of Border Security and marrying Maria Ortiz, who is the only woman I have ever loved in my entire life. This really stinks, I have dedicated most of my life to the military and protection of the United States, before and after its breakup. I guess Special Consideration for the good of the nation isn't in the cards for Maria and me. I will give you my answer in a day or so," he told this Commander-in-Chief. "But first, I must break the bad news to Maria. She will be crushed by the awful news, she was looking forward to becoming a citizen of the Western States of America and having a happy military life together. I don't know what she'll do now, she loves me very much, but my government not allowing her to become a citizen might change everything.

"For the first time in my long military career, I'm not proud of my government, I know I'm bitter, ma'am, but I can't help feeling that way." Without saying goodbye to the President, the Two Star General slowly replaced the phone and ended the conversation that may end his long military service. But the final decision would be his alone, or would it?

Maria was in the hotel taking a shower when Michel called and told her that the Supreme Court had said no her application for Special Citizenship. When Michael finished, there was silence for a long time, and he said, "Maria, are you still there?" He could hear crying before she replaced the phone in the receiver and ended the one way conversation. The General left the Wagon Wheel and drove through heavy traffic the entire twenty miles to the hotel to find Maria had already left for the airport and booked a flight to Tampico, Mexico. When Michael arrived at the airport and found a parking spot, the flight to Mexico had just left Flagstaff.

He was devastated, for the first time in his life he didn't know what to do. Should he fly to Tampico and salvage his relationship or let her spend time with her parents and call her later when she has cooled somewhat. He went with the last option, let her cool down and see what happens

In the mean time, he must decide whether to stick with the Border Security job or become a civilian and marry her, if she still wanted him. If he decided to leave the service, his pension as a Two Star General would be enough to last him two life times, and besides, his family was very wealthy, so funds would never be a problem. If he married Maria, they could live high on the hog for the rest of their lives in W.S. of A. or Mexico. "I really don't care where, as long as we're together, Northern California or Mexico," he thought.

After two days, Michael called Maria's parents' home in Ebano to find that she had left the previous day by plane to Army Headquarters in Querétaro. She had told her mother she wanted to talk to General Rōjas about something, but didn't elaborate, her mother said. Michael thanked Maria's mother and placed a call to Army Headquarters in Querétaro. In perfect Spanish, he asked to speak to General Rōjas.

After s short wait, the Mexican General was on the phone with his American friend. Before Michael could say anything, General Rōjas said, "I assume you're looking for Maria."

"You are correct, sir."

"Well, General, she is here asking to be reinstated in the Mexican Army as a Captain. So far I have refused, waiting for your call, General."

"You're very perceptive, my Mexican friend."

"Yes, I guess I am," the Commanding General answered."Would you like to speak to Maria?"

"Yes, please."

The General handed the phone to Maria and she said, "Michael, I'm so mad at your country. I love you, but your country doesn't want me. But every day for years, hundreds of Mexican nationals crossed the border and eventually received benefits from Washington. But they don't want me for some unknown reason. That's not fair, Michael."

"I agree, Maria, but let's not have this set back ruin our lives for the future. I love you, Butch, and I want to spend the balance of my life with you."

"I want some time to think, Michael."

"Okay, Maria, take as long as you need, but please keep in touch."

"I will, Michael."

Maria hung up, and Michael put the phone down slowly and thought, "What can I do now?" He called President Williamson and explained the call to Maria and indicated he might have to resign his commission and return to civilian life.

Sara told Michael not to be hasty in his decision to leave military service. "Things have a way to balance out," she said. "Hang in there, General. I'll get back to you in a day or so," she promised.

"Thank you, ma'am."

Sara said, "Enough is enough," she called Chief Justice of the Supreme Court and told her the decision passed by her Chief Clerk is not fair or just and will be superseded by a Presidential Order. "As President, I will override the ruling and have the Justice Department issue a citizenship to Maria. Not a special citizenship, but a standard citizenship with a normal passport. Maria will be eligible for dual citizenship with Mexico and the Western States of America.

"As the powers invested in me as President, I have the authority to change any Supreme Court decision. Normally it takes a two-thirds decision of Congress to override any high court decision, but under the circumstances I am overriding your court decision. Your court will be notified by messenger that I have reversed your ruling on this matter.

"You may think so, Madam Justice, but your high court is not the final word on all matters in this country. While most of your opinions and rulings are correct and just, your judges and clerks are still subject to personal reasons and prejudice feelings of the day. A full court decision should be the norm, not the exception, Madam Justice. A full vote should be required, not a quick look and decision by a non-justice then approved by yourself as Chief Justice. You should take a closer look at your high court and make appropriate changes necessary to insure fair and just rulings," the President advised. Sara hung up without allowing the Chief Justice to answer the overruling.

President Williamson immediately called General Montgomery and told him her one sided conversation with the Chief Justice and her decision to override the high court ruling in Maria's case.

General Montgomery said, "Thank you, Madam President, you are the real Commander-if-Chief of this nation."

"I will continue to use my powers as President when injustice is uncovered. You may call Maria and tell her of my decision and ruling. Her citizenship and passport will be issued by the Justice Department here in Flagstaff. She will be notified when to appear and take the oath of citizenship. After the ceremony, she will be given her passport and citizenship papers."

Within minutes, Michael was on the phone to Querétaro and talking to Maria. She was so happy that President Williamson had overruled the high court in favor of her. "General Rōjas just said I can hop a military flight from Headquarters to San Antonio tomorrow around 10:00 am."

"Very good, Maria, I'll make reservations for your flight from San Antonio to Flagstaff. Tell the General, 'thank you, for everything.'"

"I will, Michael, I love you and I'll see ya tomorrow sometime."

After the many days of fighting the issue, he felt as though a huge weight had been lifted from his shoulders. "Maybe there is some hope remaining in our society," he thought.

Defense Secretary Waterman received an urgent call from the Goodwin administration. Defense Chief Marshal wanted to discuss the Russian crisis with his counterpart in the Williamson government.

Secretary Marshal asked, "If the Russians attack Washington, will the Western States of America join Washington in the fight against the Russian machine?"

"Mr. Secretary, I have not discussed the topic with my President yet, but I can't imagine sitting idle while your forty-two states are being attacked by nuclear weapons. If Russia attacks your country, they'll certainly use nuclear tipped weapons to destroy your country and bring your administration to its knees. When they send missiles to your cities, any military installations in our country will be drawn into the fight by association. If we combine our forces, we might have a slim chance. If we hesitate and wait and allow the Reds to strike first, the war is lost in the first few hours. If we launch our nuclear arsenal, we must strike Russia proper hitting the largest cities and military installations at the same time. That would mean a total of two hundred and fifty two nuclear devices would be fired at Russia proper. Flight times would range for twenty-one minutes to one hour and thirty-seven minutes to impact."

Secretary Waterman continued, "We should, as soon as possible, alert the Canadian Prime Minister and the President of Mexico. If we're attacked, all four of our countries will be in harm's way with the possibility of returning to the Stone Age in a matter of hours."

President Williamson told Mrs. Bakker that she wanted to be alone and undisturbed for the rest of the day.

Ruth asked the President if she was okay.

"Yes, I am Ruth, and thank you for asking. I just want to gather my thoughts on our problems and the looming crisis."

Ruth said, "Please wait a minute." She rushed from the office, but returned quickly with a pot of Nal'Chik Russian tea from the Kabardinho-Balkariya region in southern Russia and a plate full of her famous sugar cookies. "This will help you solve these many domestic and foreign problems," Ruth said, placing the tray on the President's large desk.

"You're so thoughtful, Ruth, these assorted goodies will certainly help me think straight."

Ruth said, "I'll make sure you're not disturbed for the balance of the day, ma'am," as she closed the office door quietly.

Sara dispensed a large amount of her favorite Russian tea into an extra-large cup and sat back in her leather chair to think about the problems confronting her country and the entire world.

- Russia seems to be preparing to invade Europe.
- Russian submarines surfacing off the New York and Louisiana coast.
- Russia has called up a million reserve personnel to add to the million plus already positioned at their lengthy border with Europe. Even with these numbers, Russia has an additional ten million men and women that could quickly join the march through Europe.
- China has been spending fifty percent of its national budget on defense. This includes hundreds of new surface ships and submarines and three new bomber groups with its new Ningbo long range and high flying tactical bomber.

China has ten million men and women in uniform with another ninety million in reserve. These numbers are staggering and worrisome to military leaders in Europe and the West.

- Not only is Europe going to burn again for the third time in one hundred years, the continent of Africa along with the Middle East is close to all-out war that will cost some nine hundred million lives.
- Rioting in the Washington forty-two states has caused thousands of unnecessary deaths and over a trillion dollars in public and private damage.
- Mexico is finally winning the long standing drug war because of President Pedro Lazzara. Mexico is starting to boom with the help of the W.S. of A.
- Europe is having a giant shadow cast over all its countries and it resembles an Iron Curtain again. Only God's intervening could stop this madness I'm afraid.
- The Western States of America with its four original states plus four additional states is flourishing at last. And for the first time has a woman President. Me.

- If World War III erupts throughout the world, its estimated that some five hundred and seventy-five multi-tipped missiles will fly back and forth and when exploded will produce enough energy as almost thirty million tons of T.N.T.

This madness will cause billions of deaths while destroying every major city and poisoning the air and water for a hundred years or more. The debris caused by the thousands of nuclear explodes will circle the globe for a decade of more. The dark middle ages will return again. A nuclear winter is possible for any survivors.

Life as we know it will end in less than a single day, and the Northern Hemisphere will be void of human and animal life. It will take Mother Earth centuries to recover from the damage caused by the irresponsible human kind.

- The whole world is in a slow burn mode which can ignite instantly into a full blown fire storm. Nations are not content with what they have and are willing to start World War III to gain more.

Sara slowly drifted into deep sleep while pondering the many problems facing her country and the world.

"The End"

"California, Arizona, New Mexico & Texas secede from the Obama Union"

Illegal aliens, high unemployment, Obama Care, Federal mandates, foreign policy failures, massive tax increases, trillions in debt, scrapping the Constitution, scrapping the Second Amendment, cherry-picking laws for political gain, government increasing giveaways to the millions of bottom feeders and non-working Americans and aliens, along with the continuous lies by the Obama government to the American public.

What's next? Anarchy – Armageddon or Civil War?

rickshaw

Alternate Ending# I.

President Lazzara and five members of his civilian staff headed for Benito Juarez International Airport to board his Lear Jet for the short flight to Army Headquarters at Querétaro City and a meeting with the Army brass.

Once airborne, they leveled off at twenty-three thousand feet, and immediately the two pilots knew something was terribly wrong. The fuel gage read a full 1800 lbs. of fuel at takeoff now read only 285 lbs. At less than 300 lbs. the two engines will start to sputter and in less than a minute, stop.

Captain Herrera said, "Mr. President, we are out of fuel. We will fall like a brick shortly."

"Can we glide and land?" President Lazzara quickly asked.

"No, sir, we will crash nose first at four hundred miles per hour, and there is nothing we can do but ride it down, I'm afraid."

"Good god, there is no end to the cartel violence and destruction in our country. May the next President of Mexico do a better job of wiping our country clean of this scourge of mankind and their poison. I hope my family will und_____."

At that moment, the President's plane hit the ground and a fire ball lit up the sky for miles. News of the crash and the death of President Lazzara and his staff reached Army Headquarters within the hour. General Rōjas and his staff were devastated at the news of their President's death at the hands of an unknown drug cartel.

President Williamson was awakened by Ruth Bakker, "Sorry, ma'am, but I have some terrible news. We just received word that Mexican President Pedro Lazzara and his civilian staff were all killed in a terrible plane crash in Mexico about two hours ago. General Rōjas said it was murder at the hands of an unknown drug cartel."

Six months later another critical situation was unfolding in Mexico.

China was asked by the newly elected Socialist President of Mexico to provide a strong Chinese military force to guard their two thousand mile border with the Western States of America.

 rickshaw

The Republic of China provided fifty thousand ground troops and two new diesel-electronic submarines to patrol the waters off the west coast from California to Washington State. Each Chinese sub carried sixteen nuclear tipped missiles and twelve torpedoes that could find their targets with deadly accuracy up to twenty-two miles. Once the torpedoes are locked on their target, it's almost impossible to shake loose these Chinese devils.

"The End"

Alternate Ending# II.

After the two year term of President Williamson was up, a nationwide primary was held to elect the candidates to run for the Presidency. The elected President would fill a full term of four years only. Each President could only serve one four year term, according to the new constitution.

The three months of campaigning was climaxed by the selection of a popular illegal alien from Nuevo Laredo, Mexico who represented the Social Progressive Party and wanted to become President of the new Northwest States of Mexico.

The W.S. of A. constitution plainly states that the elected President must be a natural born citizen of the Western States of America or a citizen of the Washington forty-two.

Vice President Richardson, who was running for President said, "No illegal alien could run for or be elected to the office of the President." But to no avail, the illegal alien supported by the fifteen to twenty million illegal aliens who were allowed to vote and a couple million Mexican-Americans made it possible to capture the electoral votes by a slim margin and the popular vote by a wide margin.

The W.S. of A. Supreme Court voted five to four to change the constitution to allow a non-citizen to become President.

This was just the beginning of the end of the Republic.

"The End"

Richard N. Shaw

Richard N. Shaw writes from years of traveling throughout the world and observing the various countries and their governments.

He is a Civil War and WWII buff and has over one hundred books on the two wars.

Richard's first book was "The Next President of the United States" and his current and second book is "A Crack in the Union". His future books have the following titles.

- December 7th 2016
- The Last Breath of Freedom
- The Final Chapter
- Nazi-America
- The Downfall of a Great Nation
- World Domination (China & Russia)
- Mexican Brief
- Hibernation

Mr. Shaw is a Republican Conservative and believes in less government and stronger states rights where state citizens and their representatives make their laws without being constantly overruled by Federal liberal judges and their socialist ideals (unconstitutional ruling).

He also believes in less taxes and the freedom for companies and individuals to start a new business without government interference with massive regulations and taxes that discourage entrepreneurship.

With more than sixty-two current conflicts, genocide, wars and global terrorism the world outlook for the remainder of the 21st century is bleak at best. One slip by a nuclear nation and WWIII will become a reality and billions will perish.